MIDDLESBROUGH
WITHDRAWN
LIBRARIES AND INFORMATION

CUT AND RUN

CUT AND RUN

Nigel Jepson

Book Guild Publishing
Sussex, England

AB		MO	
MA		MR	
MB		MT	
MC		MW	
MD	5/06		
ME			
MG			
MH			
MM			
MN			

First published in Great Britain in 2006 by
The Book Guild Ltd
25 High Street
Lewes, East Sussex
BN7 2LU

Copyright © Nigel Jepson 2006

The right of Nigel Jepson to be identified as the author of this work has been asserted by him in accordance with the Copyright, Designs and Patents Act 1988.

All rights reserved. No part of this publication may be reproduced, transmitted, or stored in a retrieval system, in any form, or by any means, without permission in writing from the publishers, nor be otherwise circulated in any form of binding or cover other than that in which it is published and without a similar condition being imposed on the subsequent purchaser.

All characters in this publication are fictitious and any resemblance to real people, alive or dead, is purely coincidental.

Typesetting in Baskerville by
SetSystems Ltd, Saffron Walden, Essex

Printed in Great Britain by
CPI Bath

A catalogue record for this book is
available from the British Library

ISBN 1 84624 008 5

Chapter 1

Hanging around the squalid-looking entrance to an inner-city apartment block was making Simon feel distinctly uneasy. He had arrived five minutes before the agreed time but now it was fifteen minutes after and there was still no sign of the person from the property agency. Regretting not taking a mobile number, he anxiously kept on looking up and down the street, if only to give a signal to passers-by he wasn't loitering there. The occasional person went in and out of the block and, mindful of the cold morning air, held the door open for him. Each time, he had politely declined. The experience was beginning to exasperate him. He tried hard to ignore the piles of rubbish-bags tipped all over the pavement. The thought flitted through his mind to abandon the whole idea. Perhaps it was an omen telling him he should stay put at Willow Cottage after all. To stop himself getting any more agitated, he reluctantly decided to give it another quarter-hour till 10.30. The fact was he didn't have anything else to do with his time. That had been the story of his holiday to date, so why let it get to him? Besides, there were plenty of other agencies he could contact.

As if tuned in to Simon's thinking, a diffident-looking young man appeared round the corner thirty seconds before the deadline, brightly announcing: 'Hello, I'm Joe. Sorry if I've kept you waiting!'

Inclined to challenge the word 'if', Simon wasn't given opportunity.

'Only, had a bit of a rough night . . . By the way, I take it you are er . . . Simon Russell?'

Nodding curtly, he felt inclined to make some abrasive comment but, for whatever reason, bit his tongue. After all, it was still the Christmas holidays and people were bound to have their minds on other things than work.

'Be as quick as I can,' the young man promised, fishing out a bundle of keys from his pocket. Not wishing to appear awkward, Simon followed him in, bracing himself for the inevitable sales patter. Whisked up in the lift, they were inside the flat in no time at all.

'Well, what do you think?' said Joe with a slight gasp in his voice, as if not a little awe-struck himself.

Pressed for an immediate reaction, Simon stuttered uneasily. It wasn't as if he had ever seen inside a city apartment block before. He had not a single point of comparison. Although he didn't want to admit it, his first impression of spaciousness was favourable. He instinctively felt he could be comfortable living there. Besides, he wasn't even having to pay rent. The consultancy firm was doing that on his behalf.

Rather than talk about the flat itself, the young man seemed much happier extolling the virtue of its central location: 'All night-life within two minutes!' No more than two or three years out of school, he was obviously more accustomed to selling flats to like-minded young blades than a late-middle-age stick-in-the-mud such as himself.

Simon made straight for the windows on both sides and checked the views. Neither angle was exactly spectacular: one straight across to a multi-storey car park and the other directly down a narrow thoroughfare leading to a pedestrian precinct and another block of high-rise buildings. The bleak anonymity of the view matched his present state of mind completely.

'Of course, these are only the basic furnishings. You'll want to add your own, I imagine . . .'

He heard the young man's voice trying to turn his attention back to the interior of the flat. With the words 'your own', a sudden panic seized him which he did his best to hide. A troubling voice started up inside his head. 'What on earth am I doing here, tearing up my roots?' But another cried out just as quickly: 'What roots?' Almost in the same moment, he became composed again, not needing to remind himself why all this was necessary. The young man went on outlining various points about the flat but Simon was having difficulty concentrating. All the time he kept returning to the imponderable matters that wouldn't go away.

'Why Leeds?' The question turned itself over in his mind. What on earth was he doing here in the first place? He tried reassuring himself it wasn't exactly the other end of the world. The basic point was that it was somewhere different. That was all that mattered to him at the moment. He desperately needed to put the past behind him as quickly as possible.

Distracted by his thoughts, Simon tried with difficulty to switch back again.

'It seems fine, just what I'm looking for . . .' Mechanically uttered, the words hardly seemed convincing, not even to the young man who was so keen to sell him the flat. Simon realised his thoughts could be translated to mean he'd settle for anywhere at this moment in time. The whole business was so bizarre he didn't have the faintest idea what he might be looking for in a living-place.

'Here's the kitchen,' the young man stated in a tone that assumed one kitchen was much like any other. 'Microwave over here . . .' he added, seeming to take it for granted that convenience cooking would be the order of the day.

'Other amenities . . .' he said, pulling doors open to reveal devices such as a washing machine. 'Handy for yourself . . . and anyone else . . .' He paused in case his sentence should be finished for him. But Simon had no wish to spice up the conversation by giving clues about his personal circumstances. The young man took note and changed tack again.

'Living room . . . comfortable, you can see . . .' It was noticeable he had lapsed into a careless sing-song voice that appeared to accord with his client's obvious desire to keep it simple. All Simon remembered was that he seemed to go on about everything being IKEA.

'Bedroom . . . king-size double bed . . . wardrobe . . . What do you think?'

'It's all fine,' Simon blurted out, oblivious as to whether he sounded discriminating or not. In truth, all he wanted by now was to be left alone to ponder his new environment. Fate seemed to have it in store for him. He supposed he could have turned it down if he had wanted to, but why put himself to extra trouble?

'What do you think then?' The opening inquiry had resurrected itself as the question intended to clinch the deal.

'Yes it's fine, er, fine . . .' Why did he have to make it sound as if the words were prised from his lips? He tried again and this time managed to impress with his alacrity: 'Yes, it's fine!'

'So you'll take it?'

'Yes, for an eight-month lease,' Simon replied, at last showing some awareness of the basic details of the transaction.

'Eight months it is . . . If you'd like to sign here, here and here,' the young man directed, thrusting a complex-looking document in front of Simon and a pen for him to sign in the said three spaces. With the signatures obtained, a self-satisfied expression came over the face of the young man, making Simon feel something of a sad walkover. Within a moment, he had promptly turned on his heels and departed.

Disconcerted by the sudden silence, Simon snatched up the bunch of keys lying in front of him and tried to recall which key opened which lock. But he hadn't been listening to anything. He had stood aside and allowed everything to take place, in a blur. With more time on his hands, he couldn't help looking at things in a more exacting light. The kitchen was certainly adequate, he reckoned. Pulling drawers open, he wondered how he could have forgotten to inquire about basic things like cutlery. Finding all the drawers and cupboards empty, his instinctive reaction was that he could bring stuff over from Willow Cottage. But wouldn't that defeat the whole purpose of the exercise? The last thing he wanted was anything with the power to remind him of his former existence. Irrespective of extra cost, that must be the main consideration.

He liked the fact it was open-plan, with the kitchen and the L-shaped living room connected. The accumulated space looked bigger and less closed-in. What if everything was IKEA? In his mind's eye, that was a place where young couples made pilgrimages, queuing for ages at check-out points. Here he was, and he didn't even have to assemble any of it. Not that he would have been capable. He liked the fact that everything was ready-made. Again, it suited his mood exactly. He'd never really looked closely at the effect of window-space before but he thought he liked the openness. He noticed the light as it filtered through, imparting a gleam on the wooden floor tiles. For a moment, he stationed himself by the glass dining-table. Thinking of light again, he reassured himself it would comfortably double as a work-desk. The notion occurred to him that he would have felt too self-conscious checking all this out in front of the young man. The more he began to start taking proper stock, the greater the number of things he noticed. Although there were electrical sockets everywhere, the living-room looked sparse without items he took for granted, such as television, CD player and telephone. Undoubtedly, there were all kinds of new decisions he was going to have to make. He began to realise it was yet another part of the process of reappraising his life.

It hadn't quite dawned on him before, but he was going to have to fend for himself in more respects than one. He had safely got beyond the stage now of secretly hoping that Leonie might miraculously turn up again as if it had all been a simple, temporary misunderstanding. He had decided on his own that he needed to live somewhere else, even though he could so easily have stayed on in the same house. Over the past few weeks, he had come to accept he was going to have to take much fuller responsibility for his life. For a man of his age, it seemed a bitter pill to swallow.

Safe within a setting he could call his own, he was in a stronger state of mind to reflect on the impact of Leonie's leaving him. He couldn't deny it had felt horrendous having to cope with a pain that had taken so long to subside. Nor had it helped his peace of mind belatedly to discover a note she'd left which simply announced, almost as a throwaway line, that she was about to set off on a round-the-world trip. Not that it gave him any details as to an itinerary. He hadn't a clue where she was now. It wasn't even like Shirley Valentine and he could track her down to a Greek island if he so wished. Despite her denial, he still agonised over the possibility she'd left him for someone else. Perhaps she had wanted to spare him the extra anguish. He tortured himself imagining a cosy little scene, two love-birds enjoying cocktails somewhere like The Raffles Hotel. In any case, she was spoilt for choice now. He sneaked glances at world weather charts, unable to fight back an instinct to read of a deadly tornado, hoping she was caught up in it. But, knowing her, she was bound to have worked everything out properly. It was winter here and she'd have gone somewhere idyllic in the southern hemisphere and everything would be paradise . . .

Despite the odd self-indulgent hope, the telephone-line had remained stubbornly dead. In a strange sense, it seemed to help that he had no real friends to have to break the news to. Hadn't she always mocked him for being a 'Billy-No-Mates'? Besides, it would have made him desperately awkward broaching the subject with anyone else. Although he knew none of it had any bearing on his capacity as a headteacher, he felt somehow tarnished in that direction too. Whatever anyone else might think, he could no longer be happy with anything he had been doing before. In a professional sense, he had felt it incumbent on him to inform his deputy, Richard Preece, but mainly on the grounds that he wouldn't have liked the younger man to hold an advantage from having heard the news from another source. News spread like wildfire within and across school communities.

However, the discomfort he felt about having to give an account of this personal misfortune to others couldn't begin to compare with the pain of trying to explain it to himself. He still couldn't properly reconcile himself to the fact she had deserted him with no apparent warning-signs. The most galling thing was that, for the life of him, he just hadn't seen it coming.

He had surprised himself by imparting his rather dubious news to his PA, Caroline. She had only joined at the start of the last term. Her arrival had in fact been a breath of fresh air to him at the time, particularly bearing in mind the awkward manner of her predecessor, Mrs Ellison. He hadn't felt any particular onus to confide in Caroline but had noticed that, if on any occasion something might have gone wrong for him at school, her response had been most sympathetic. While Richard had reacted with brusque acceptance on a 'need-to-know' basis, Caroline had managed to sound genuinely concerned for him. Perhaps it was different for men and he was being too harsh on Richard.

Dramatically, he had decided he didn't want to go on working at the same school. Before mentioning it to anyone, he had scoured the adverts for somewhere else but nothing had grabbed his attention. Besides, there was generally too long a wait before being able to take up any new appointment. Recalling some casual mention made by a head from another school about doing work for a management consultancy, he had impulsively keyed into a few websites and found himself pondering a whole host of acting headship posts across the length and breadth of the country. It didn't take long to appreciate they were all so-called failing schools without a captain at the helm, and therefore not the most popular or attractive of options, but then was that so important? The idea of vacancies waiting to be filled, even if only temporary, seemed strange but curiously inviting in his present circumstances.

The mood he was in at the moment, it felt as if he was applying to join the Foreign Legion. Still, he had enough sense not to sign his life away completely. Exercising some degree of caution, he found himself agreeing to a provisional two-term stint. He could only assume the agency had carried out all their vetting behind the scenes. Due to start in January, he was becoming more nervous by the day, and it began to dawn on him he hadn't actually clapped eyes on the school on a working day yet. Yes, he had visited the place but it had been the last day of term, on a staff development day, with no students around to give it a proper taste of reality. Though he had felt moved at some point to say his motive in going there was 'to make a difference', he couldn't really picture yet what that 'difference' may be. He had spoken to the assembled staff and got the impression they were just grateful to have an experienced head filling the gap. The salary had pleasantly surprised him, with temporary accommodation thrown in, but then the stakes tended to be higher in relation to schools in so-called challenging circumstances. He hadn't allowed himself to dwell too much on the broader issues as to why the school was in such a mess, thinking he would have time enough for that when he started. At least it had stopped him feeling quite so sorry for himself.

Fortunately, the Chair of Governors, Ted Bingham, was perfectly prepared to accept the situation without giving it the slightest second thought. To Simon's surprise, not a flicker of doubt was expressed over Richard Preece taking over as Acting Head in his absence. Quoting the budget situation, the Chair of Governors had in fact taken the liberty of pointing out that the school would benefit significantly in terms of making a financial saving over the period in question. From being worried whether he would be allowed to go, Simon had ended up being concerned by just how dispensable he suddenly appeared to be.

For Richard's part, he managed to sound a lot more responsive upon hearing this particular piece of news compared to that of Simon's marriage break-up. Of course, it had a more direct impact. Being asked to take over the running of the school for two terms was no light undertaking. But knowing how ambitious Richard was, Simon could tell from the way his face lit up how much he would relish the task. Nor would the extra money in the monthly pay packet harm the situation of a man with a wife and two young sons.

Sitting quietly at the table, still intent on absorbing his thoughts, Simon's attention was momentarily distracted by what sounded like someone shouting from the street below.

Moving to one of the windows, he satisfied himself it wasn't coming from this direction. But the noise – now sounding like two people having a row – was still plainly audible and he reckoned it must be coming from somewhere inside the building. Even though he couldn't make out any of the words clearly, the shouting was loud. As he moved round the flat, the trail led him back to the small sealed-off entrance-area and his front door. Opening it with a mixture of curiosity and trepidation, he caught sight of an agitated-looking woman beating her fists on the door of a neighbouring flat, shouting at the top of her voice: 'Tom! Open up! It's me . . . Suzanne! Look, you won't get rid of me that easy, you bastard!'

Perhaps, with the advantage of hindsight, he should have retreated behind the door again if he had had any regard for his safety and well-being. However, he couldn't help being curious about what was going on. It didn't take rocket science to work out there must be someone the other side of the door, presumably by the name of Tom, otherwise she wouldn't be shouting so forcefully. He did stop to think for a moment what he had let himself in for and what kind of people must live in these flats. But the woman, perhaps in her early thirties, seemed anything but a hopeless case. Stylishly dressed, she looked far from unattractive. It was difficult to tell for sure, because she was crying and make-up was streaming down her face. Feeling a pronounced sympathy with anyone suffering from distraught emotions, he thought twice but managed to find it within himself to offer some kind of comfort.

'Now, now, things can't be all that bad, can they?'

Perhaps if he had left it as a statement rather than a question, a better outcome might have been achieved. No sooner had the sentence escaped his mouth than he realised he was repeating a phrase his mother had used to soothe him whenever, as a boy, something had happened to make him unhappy. But somehow he realised straightaway his words of comfort were failing to have the desired effect. They caused her to stop shouting, but the woman's eyes suddenly narrowed and she stared at him as if he was the main architect of her troubles. Thwarted in one direction, the temptation of taking out her pent-up wrath on a new victim seemed irresistible.

'And who do you think you're staring at . . . you dirty snoop!'

Stung to the quick by the wild injustice of this remark, he didn't know whether to refute her accusation outright or simply ignore it. Did he step boldly out onto the corridor or hastily retreat back into his lair? In the event, the woman let out a final expletive and stormed off down the corridor, not bothering to wait for the lift. Listening to the angry click-clack of her heels on the staircase, he waited until he heard the slam of an outside door before feeling able to breathe easily again.

At this same moment, the door of the adjacent flat quietly slipped open as though in similar response to an 'all-clear' being sounded.

'I'm truly sorry you had to suffer that indignity . . . having to encounter one of my rare dissatisfied customers!' he heard a voice pipe up with a faintly transatlantic twang. As he hesitated, unsure what to say in response, the man's face came more prominently into view, a lived-in face of someone probably ten years or so younger than himself.

Becoming even more nervous at what he was submitting himself to, Simon said spontaneously: 'If you don't mind my asking, is it some sort of clinic you run?'

The man let out an enormous horse-laugh. 'No, but the life of a serial philanderer can be tough at times!'

All Simon could do was stare back open-mouthed as the other man declared: 'If you don't mind me saying so, pal, I'd say you've got a helluva lot of living to catch up on!'

Chapter 2

Tom Judd sprang awake. Daylight was pouring in through the windows. He found sleep difficult at the best of times, and it added to the problem that the curtains were so flimsy and threadbare. He had been meaning to change them for some time now but had never quite got round to it. Cursing out loud, he sat up in bed and checked the clock. It was only 7.45.

Every morning, the same wretched thought slammed into his consciousness first thing. What was he doing holed up in this godforsaken place when he could still be living like a king in New York? Then, for about the hundredth morning running, the cruel reality dawned on him that he was lucky to be alive at all.

The idea occurred to go back to sleep, a fair enough proposition on a Saturday morning, but his head was in too much of a spin. He decided to get up and make breakfast. If it had been New York, he would have mooched out to any one of several diners open in the neighbourhood. Here, nowhere opened until the sacred hour of nine and you were still mighty lucky then to find anywhere serving a decent meal. On the point of switching the radio on, he thought he heard a sound at the door.

Startled, he wondered who it could be at this hour. Slipping on his dressing-gown, he crept to the door but couldn't hear anything the other side. Still feeling disorientated, he began to think he must be imagining things. Then, unmistakably, he heard another knock.

Panicked, he nervously inquired: 'Who is it?'

'It's me, Suzanne!' And after a further slight pause, in sugary tones, 'Well, let me in, silly!'

He cursed himself for the rashness that prompted him to betray his presence. Otherwise, he could have maintained he was asleep and just hadn't heard. But it was much too late to play dumb now. Words of welcome didn't exactly trip off the tongue. In New York, he had entertained sophisticated women. Now, he was reduced to slumming it with Suzy.

'I take it you're on your own?' A daft thing to say, but how could he tell? She might be looking for somewhere conveniently central to extend a Friday night spree with a gang of fellow-bingers.

'Of course I am!' The emphatic nature of the retort suggested there was a fair chance she was in control of her faculties.

With an air of resignation, he reluctantly unlocked the door but barred entry until fully satisfied she was alone. Then, because past experience demanded it, he carefully took stock. But the truth was he couldn't fault her on outward appearance. She was dressed in an expensively tailored designer suit. It wasn't difficult to spot when she was suffering. The tell-tale signs would be obvious: chipped fingernails, haggard eyes or ruined make-up ... but today she passed every test, looking immaculately well-presented. Wishing he could say the same for himself, he detected a rueful smile around her lips as she noticed him still in his dressing-gown.

'To what do I owe the dubious pleasure?' he said, as though acting out a role in a Noël Coward play. The situation seemed so surreal, perhaps he ought to have greeted her with a burst of *Poor Little Rich Girl*. At a loss to know how to respond, she had the flurried manner of an actress forgetting her lines. Despite himself, he couldn't deny she was appealing in a superficial kind of way. Her face was pretty, framed by her shoulder-length chestnut hair. And he always had been a sucker for a slim waistline. Indeed, the whole impression was quite intoxicating, and it wasn't 8 o'clock yet. He was still wondering what he had done to deserve the visit.

'I had the air hostess dream, you know the one when I'm arriving back in the country in the early morning hours and terribly keen to see you again.'

He took another look at her and decided she wasn't wearing a British Airways uniform. Not unless they had commissioned Gucci.

'Where have you flown in from this time?'

'I thought you liked that game!' Her lips were pouting playfully.

Intent on bringing the conversation down to earth again, he pressed: 'Why didn't you ring first?'

She stared blankly for a moment before protesting: 'But you were expecting me!'

He glanced back at her, puzzled.

'In my dream, you were expecting me.' She gave him a mock-amorous glance.

'Have you been home yet?' he inquired, pouring cold water on her flights of fancy.

'Do I look as if I've spent the night on the tiles?' she replied, more sharply.

'No, but nor do you look as if you've come in on Flight 309!'

She laughed and sought to appease him: 'After the last time, I was frightened what you might say.'

'I'm not surprised. By the way, I don't want you going anywhere near that new chap next door. He might get the wrong idea altogether. He actually asked me if I ran some sort of clinic.'

'What did you tell him?'

'Never you mind!'

Losing interest in this line of conversation, she asked impulsively: 'Do you mind if I use the loo?'

'No, of course not,' he acquiesced. Something about the manner in which she bustled past him made him feel uneasy again.

It was as well to expect the unexpected as far as Suzanne was concerned. His mind recapitulated the various ways she could get up to mischief in the bathroom. On second thoughts, it gave him an opportunity to take necessary precautions elsewhere in the flat. Extracting his unopened bottle of single malt from the drinks cabinet, he stowed it away behind a huge box of dishwasher powder in the cupboard under the kitchen sink. Likewise, he secreted three bottles of white wine from the fridge. Given the slightest encouragement, sober as she seemed at the moment, she was capable of drinking the place dry inside the hour.

Upon emerging, she announced: 'By the way, you really mustn't tell me if you have any coke in the flat.'

'I haven't touched it in fourteen weeks!' It was the unkindest of reminders.

'I do admire your determination and self-control, Tom. I wish I could do it.'

He felt a pang of sympathy. It seemed to be getting progressively harder for him to remember, as time went on, that they had first met as part of a circle, from all types of background, confiding in each other that their lives were ruined through addiction. She had introduced herself as an air hostess then. Although she had since admitted it wasn't true, he still wasn't sure what she did for a living. She wouldn't tell him. He guessed it was something like interior design because on odd occasions she made remarks about room décor that sounded professional.

'I wish I could do it,' he heard her reiterate, this time making it sound more like a forlorn hope. He found his sympathy rapidly waning. How many times had he patiently listened and talked with her without it making the slightest difference? Today, he didn't feel like rising to the bait.

'You know how much I like talking over my problems with you,' she continued. Fighting to keep his face as expressionless as he could, he cottoned on to the familiar, ingratiating way in which her voice became honeyed and inviting. Images involuntarily sprang into his mind of the occasion which had ended up with her smashing his stereo with a hammer from the DIY box. At times like this, he desperately needed to exercise his will-power to keep uppermost in mind her uncanny potential to do him harm, physically and emotionally.

'You can make a cup of tea if you like and bring it through.' Her voice was now oozing with suggestiveness. His eye was taken by the innocent-seeming hitch she was giving to her skirt. He didn't need confirmation where she was meaning him to go with the cups of tea; but just in case he hadn't twigged, she tilted her head meaningfully in the direction of the bedroom. He seemed to have lost the power of speech suddenly.

'Don't forget it's been a long flight and I want my own needs serviced now!' He tried to look as if he was ignoring her but he could sense his pulse quickening. His eyes followed her as she sidled off.

A few minutes later, nursing a cup of tea in each hand, he made his way from the kitchen. He called for her to open the door.

'Just a moment!' came the hurried-sounding response.

After a further ten seconds or so, the door eased open.

He had half-anticipated catching her lying in some provocative pose. He certainly hadn't expected to find her still fully clothed.

'Don't you want it then?' he asked, speaking plainly.

'No, I'm terribly sorry I forgot I said I'd meet a friend in York at ten. If I don't get off now, I'm going to be late!' She gave him a peck on the cheek and, taking advantage of the fact he had both hands full, left him standing there. The next thing he heard was the sound of the outside door closing behind her. Conflicting emotions of relief and disappointment overtook him, although he couldn't say which felt stronger. In the end, the sheer unpredictability of it all left him feeling utterly drained.

He had found himself slipping back into bed and falling asleep with surprising ease for a further hour or so. Waking again, he decided to get dressed. Catching sight of his trousers lying across the back of a chair, he instantly had a premonition and stretched across to check the contents of his back pocket. It came back to him that he had withdrawn £200 from a cash-point the night before. Detecting a slight bulge where something lay wedged against the lining, he felt a crashing sense of relief. When he pulled out the contents, however, there was no sign of any banknotes, only a folded sheet of white paper. Unravelling it, he read, plastered in red lipstick:

THANKS
DARLING
IOU XX

Seeing the cups of cold tea, abandoned by the side of the bed, he felt like kicking them hard against the wall but somehow he managed to control himself. Instead, he wanted to pour out all his venom on Suzanne. But it was futile. He didn't even know where she lived. He loathed himself. It was his own fault for allowing himself to be robbed blind. Recalling where he had stowed away the alcohol, he took the three bottles of wine into the bathroom, uncorked each in turn and watched himself in the mirror as he emptied the contents straight down the plug-hole. On the verge of following suit with the bottle of single malt, at the last moment he couldn't quite bring himself to waste it so badly.

For a short while, the wild thought entered his head to see if his new neighbour across the way might care to join him for a dram. He checked his watch and realised it was an insane idea. But pouring himself a tumbler to settle his nerves, the familiar taste felt heavenly. The sensation was much too divine to limit to a single unit.

An hour later, he had consumed the entire bottle. After that, despite the morning light pouring through the wide open curtains, he slept like an angel for a solid twelve hours.

Chapter 3

Simon's life had been turned upside down but in some ways the full scale of it still hadn't sunk in properly. Starting at this new school in only a few days' time, he had leafed through some materials about Bentwood School sent him by the Local Education Authority. He could see one or two obvious things that needed addressing from the most recent Inspection Report. However, the last thing he wanted was to get himself alarmed out of all proportion. As far as adjusting to the flat was concerned, he wasn't too much bothered for the time being, so long as he managed to survive from one day to the next.

The aspect of his new life that had really fired his senses up was the immediacy of living slap-bang in the city centre. In his present state of shell shock, he reckoned it must be having a therapeutic effect because he had already developed certain pleasurable little rituals over the holiday. One of the undoubted perks of his location was that it only took him two minutes to reach a Waterstone's bookshop. If he ever saw Joe again, he would make sure he understood it wasn't proximity to night-life that was the flat's main asset.

Today was the third day running he had followed a routine of strolling out in the cool morning air to read his newspaper in a café before doing some gentle browsing in the bookshop. He had broken new ground on this occasion by getting into conversation with the chirpy *Big Issue* salesman who seemed to be a fixture by the front door. On previous days he had felt slightly threatened by the man's habitual touting for custom and shuffled past with averted gaze. But today he had felt an emphatic impulse not only to invest in a copy but also to exchange a few pleasant words into the bargain. Perhaps it would have amounted to no more than standard civility in other people's eyes but, for himself, it was an adventurous, almost headstrong undertaking. When he thought about it more, he couldn't really explain his change of heart. He had somehow caught himself responding instinctively to an everyday situation, instead of with his normal show of reticence. He was taken aback by the sheer spontaneity of his reaction. It was as if he was acting involuntarily and completely out of character.

These little signs were in some ways worrying to him. For hadn't he made it a condition of his existence not to take risks? From an early age, Simon's outlook had been based on playing it safe. If he hadn't become a teacher, he probably would have ended up as a bank cashier or a tax officer. He liked to work things out methodically and had sought to apply this principle to life. He had never lived beyond a 20-mile radius of where he was born. Whenever he read stories in the papers about people giving up their job and taking on something different, he generally wished them well, even if another side of him couldn't deny secretly hoping it would end in grief. There were few types of people he had ever found it in him to despise, but sixties-style hippies came desperately close.

Against any sort of setback he had encountered over the years, Simon's natural reaction had been to take it squarely on the chin. His temperament, which seemed purpose-built to absorb pressure, was handed down from his parents. The Russell creed, bred in him from the earliest age, rendered it obligatory to take the rough with the smooth without as much as a quibble. In recent times, he had had plenty of cause to reflect on the merits or otherwise of this philosophy. Patience no longer seemed such a virtue. Up to a few weeks ago, he might have argued it was better just to take things in one's stride. It had been a boast of his that no misfortune, however great or small, had ever succeeded in upsetting his inner calm.

Certainly, it could be argued that he hadn't fared so badly in life through observing this distinctive stance. Both his parents, now unfortunately passed away, had loved him enormously and been proud of his achievements. In pursuing his vocation as a teacher, his slow but composed approach had eventually commended itself to those in influential positions. Career-wise, he had overtaken others whose initial enthusiasm ended up exposed as shallow keenness to please. Never likely to act rashly, he placed great store by listening to the wise counsel of his elders. As part of a large group of young teachers who had started at the school at the same time, he could have found himself attracted into relationships with any one of several interested young women. Marrying Leonie, Head of Science and five years older, he had looked up to her as being much more experienced in life's ways. Feeling honoured to be picked out, he was quite content for her to make the running in their relationship. He probably couldn't have coped with taking the initiative in such matters. As he didn't fully understand the nature of his emotions towards her, it certainly could not be levelled against him that he had been swayed by impulsive or passionate instincts.

Leonie had often joked about mothering him. Prone to feeling insecure, he had craved reassurance more often than she would have liked. As a single child, having to cope with the death of his parents in his early twenties seemed to render him much more mature in outlook. Those who might otherwise have said he wasn't ready to take on the commitment of marriage had seemed only too pleased at the time for him to have this void in his life filled. The same people who had almost written him off as a callow probationer, with little capacity to improve, found themselves rapidly revising their opinion. Although he never admitted it to anyone, not even Leonie, he felt quietly proud of how he had managed to turn this corner in his life. How ironic to recall now that his marriage to Leonie had once seemed a heaven-sent present for coming to terms with adversity.

Nor did he have any younger family members to draw comfort from. Having loved his own parents so much, he dearly hoped to be the father of children, but this was another misfortune he had had to endure. There was no reason not to trust Leonie when she had said she wanted children too. With some couples, he wryly noted, starting a family appeared to happen either almost casually or else as a natural priority. Whenever there had been a conversation about children, it was invariably closed down quickly or became negative. It had played on his mind when Leonie said to him, almost wistfully: "You'll still love me if we don't have children, won't you?" He hadn't known how to handle such a hypothetical-sounding proposition. Of course, he would go on loving her. That went without saying but, although he didn't actually venture it, he felt like adding that he never wanted it to be an either-or situation. Ultimately, as always, he had been prepared to accept the hand dealt out by fate. It was like the weather in summer. Grand hopes might be entertained, but the best face had to be put on it if sunshine failed to materialise.

Spending his working days with children had become double-edged for a period of time. In one sense, consolation was to be found in knowing he was helping to shape a whole host of young people's lives for the better. In another, however, it served as a daily reminder of the missing dimension in his life. Never giving voice to his disappointment, instead he concentrated his energies on the here and now, burying himself ever more intensely in work in an effort to compensate for the severe blow to his desire for fatherhood. When colleagues at work showed signs of flagging towards the end of a term, it was Simon whose commitment went the extra mile.

Having ample time now to reflect back on things, he realised what a driving-force Leonie had been in his life. It was she, of course, who had suggested he should respond to an advert she had seen for Head of Maths in a nearby school in Manchester. From the first time he had met the Head-teacher of the school, Philip Cunliffe, Simon really wanted the job and was delighted to be appointed. Philip Cunliffe, by then a man in his early fifties, had acted as mentor throughout the middle stage of Simon's career. Philip's wife had died from cancer. They too had been childless and it wasn't difficult, even for Simon, to work out why the older man adopted an almost fatherly interest in him. Perhaps he had just been fortunate to surface at a stage of Philip's career when he needed someone to whom he could pass on his accumulated wisdom. Certainly, Simon had proved a willing disciple. By the time Philip was ready to retire, following a short illness which did not seem particularly significant at the time, Simon was well established in the role of Deputy Head and, at forty-two years old, the obvious choice in succession to Philip. Within only two years of retiring, no doubt worn out by the attritional cares of headship, Philip had died prematurely. For Simon, the blow of losing his mentor felt as bitter a loss as that of his parents. His means of coming to terms with the tragedy was by doing everything he could to make sure the school retained the same ethos.

But somewhere along the way, his relationship with Leonie had borne the brunt. As Simon devoted more and more time to building the school's reputation, he had sensed he and Leonie were growing apart in many ways. He still felt confident, though, that the gap was not so pronounced that other people would notice. For all her own loss of ambition, never seeking to be promoted above head of department, she seemed proud on the face of it that he had achieved the status of a headteacher and was committed to making a success of the job. More so because they hadn't had children, their longstanding relationship mattered immensely to him. So long as they stayed living together, he didn't mind how often she went away on trips or holidays with people from school. It was a solid relationship, he believed, based on mutual interest. He was more than prepared to accept that his duties as a headteacher often meant that he was a less than attentive partner himself. Although communication was not always strong between them, things still seemed tacitly understood on both sides.

All this sense of confidence on his part had made it even more difficult for him to be prepared for the moment when Leonie told him she was leaving him. The impact it had had on him still sent him reeling. After all, there had been no trace of build-up to her unambiguous-sounding statement of intent. What on earth was she doing? He couldn't begin to comprehend. He had started quizzing her as though he were addressing an eighteen-year-old student leaving school after A-levels. When she used the word 'leave', perhaps she was conveying her intention to take a gap year and then come back? No, she was telling him it was for good. But why? She couldn't answer that question. She had started saying something trite about still feeling unfulfilled. He felt a shock-force explode in his head like the walls of a dam ripping wide open: 'Christ, woman, you're sixty; what do you think you're doing? It doesn't even start to make sense!'

He had physically pinched himself to make sure he wasn't dreaming it. No, he was sitting four-square in his familiar armchair in the living-room of Willow Cottage, the house they had lived in together for thirty years. And, unquestionably yes, for the first time he was unable to control his emotions and prevent himself from losing his temper.

'Who is it?' he bellowed, catapulting himself out of the false comfort of the armchair and seizing her roughly by the shoulders. The sanctity of a room that had known only peace and tranquillity before suddenly seemed violated beyond redemption.

As she silently stood there, withstanding the grip of his hands and refusing his demands with a quiet shake of the head, he had felt a crazy impulse to force it out of her. She continued to hold her ground motionlessly, her eyes burning with the same steady resolve, and he experienced a wilder craving to knock her head against the mantelpiece and dash her brains out with one blow.

Instead, as though possessed, his hands feverishly clutched hold of the nearest object to hand, a vase of flowers, and hurled it into the fireplace.

'I don't suppose we could talk about this!' he shrieked hysterically, with jagged fragments of pot ricocheting all over the pristine floor.

'You've never shown much willingness to talk before,' she said, breathlessly, with little suggestion of compromise. To the contrary, he detected a faint edge of recrimination in her tone.

'Even if it's true, that's not the point!' he spluttered indignantly. 'Can't we sit down and talk matters over now?' It mortified him to think his voice sounded almost pleading.

'It's too late!' she answered summarily. He didn't take kindly to the fact she seemed to want to be in total command of the situation.

'Get out, then, leave me!' Barking out orders, however pathetic, seemed at least to give him a spurious sense of being in charge for a moment.

'I will!' she said in a level tone, stepping over the debris with quiet disdain and leaving him behind in the room.

Feeling impotent to stop her, he ventured as far as the door and took hold of it, slamming the block of wood time and time again with ever greater force in a frenzied effort to separate it from its hinges.

Then, belatedly pulling himself together, he had nervously carried out an inspection of the whole house on tiptoe, somehow still hoping to find her tucked away in some unsuspecting nook or cranny. But, after an exhaustive search, he had to accept she was gone. Not only that, but he realised many of her possessions were already gone. The rest of the evening and much of the following day, he spent alone in the house in blind despair, crying his eyes out.

Chapter 4

He was waiting to have his hair cut. The immutable law for Simon was to start back at school looking spick and span.

A couple of years ago, Leonie had finally forced him to abandon his longstanding loyalty to the ancient brotherhood of male barbers. Before realising what was happening, he had been sidetracked into a place he was later to discover was called a salon, and bundled unceremoniously into a chair. Leonie had said afterwards, if she had taken a picture of him sitting there looking so threatened, it would have borne the caption: 'Wanted in 42 States, Criminal Dies in Electric Chair'. To add to his discomfiture, a female materialised brandishing a pair of clippers. Trapped beyond recall, sneaking only the odd covert glance in the mirror, he had felt too shy to establish eye-contact with the young woman announcing herself as Miranda. The abiding memories he had carried away from that first encounter were threefold: her hands had a tactile effect as smooth as butter, she had tried to entice him into conversation about holidays and, lastly, he remembered observing out of the very corner of his eye that she was wearing a sort of studded belt around her slender waist.

Banking on him not doing a Houdini and wriggling free of the cape and rubber collar that bound him, Leonie had felt it safe to go and do some shopping. Returning twenty minutes later to pick him up, when he emerged from under wrappers, she had christened him 'new man.' Utterly opposed to the notion of a 'make-over', he could only recall feeling a strange sensation of soreness of the head as though having undergone minor plastic surgery. Refusing to inspect himself in the mirror in case he let out something unpardonable, he had waited until getting home to express his opinion. Only then had he grasped the full enormity of what had transpired. It felt as if every reference-point he had ever clung to before had been cast 180 degrees adrift. Even then, he had failed for ten seconds to pick up on the one unthinkable difference: she had changed his parting to the other side . . . No wonder it had taken him several hours to stop trembling!

He could afford to smile about the memory two years on. Although he would have been loath to admit it, even now, wild horses couldn't keep him away from his visit every six weeks to the salon. But even so, he couldn't help feeling strangely awkward today. Normally, he felt totally relaxed arriving and being asked to take a seat in the waiting-area. He had never thought he would confess to such excesses but he even liked flicking through the glossy magazines lying temptingly on the table. For the world, he wouldn't have been caught buying one but it was interesting (he stopped short of the word 'titillating') to tap into the various salacious bits of so-called celebrity gossip in those random few minutes. If pressed, he would have justified it by claiming it helped him to keep up to date with what young people tended to talk about, even if it always seemed to follow similar lines – who had been evicted from the latest reality series, or which poor socialite heiress had been dumped by a rock star. But, today, he felt too much on edge to give time of day to the glossies and instead sat there tapping his finger-tips on the arm of the leather-upholstered settee. The thought even occurred to him that if he was endeavouring to make a complete break with his previous existence, coming here would have to go too. Naturally, he would still need to get his hair cut somewhere but he could easily find an alternative place in Leeds.

As if to heighten his sense of unease, it seemed to be taking an eternity today for Miranda to come to greet him as she usually did. More often than not, he would have spotted her on arrival, doing something like putting the finishing touches to the previous client. He could remember once before turning up only to find that she had rung in at the last moment saying she was ill. Even though he was sure all the staff were highly competent, it hadn't felt the same having a substitute. As well as it being very reassuring having the same person every time, he really did look forward to picking up the conversational thread with Miranda.

'Hi, there, Simon!' His spirits lifted to hear the familiar, cheery welcome as her face appeared round the corner. He had the usual warm glow from how pleased she appeared to be to see him again. 'Do you want to come this way?' she said invitingly. 'Sorry I was held up.'

Momentarily, he recollected the scene with the young man from the property agency the previous day but, on this occasion, he would not have thought to object. It was funny that even though she seemed to remember everything about him on a conversational level, she always needed him to remind her which side he had his hair parted. Over six weeks, it seemed somehow to lose itself altogether. He felt like reminding her that she was the one who had changed it. Or had it been Leonie? Despite his misgivings, the surprising thing was that people had generally commented on how much younger the change of parting made him look. The thought entered his head briefly to have it changed back again, through sheer spite, but he decided it was too petty a gesture to make in the scale of things.

With the little ritual of the parting over, Miranda consigned him to a young girl to have his hair washed before returning for the main business. It always amused him to have a coffee brought while his arms and hands were ensnared inside a voluminous smock. He usually waited for her to pause, before taking a sip, but today it was an indication of his mood that it hardly seemed important one way or another. More often than not, conversation might be slow to pick up between them. He appreciated she had lots of clients and it must be hard remembering them all. Although he nursed the hope that he was a bit more special, he never wanted to run the risk of sounding presumptuous. He waited tentatively for her to say something.

Compared with when he first used to come, he was much less embarrassed now about catching her image in the mirror. Today, she seemed a little subdued, almost pensive. Perhaps it was just his own mood making him think that way. Miranda wasn't as ostentatious as some of the younger ones. She didn't wear anything garish and always looked stylish and presentable. Approvingly, he observed what she was wearing: a neat white top, a small crucifix, an elegant pair of black trousers and comfortable-looking pumps. With a sudden pang of guilt that he was studying her too closely, the awful memory came back to him of that woman labelling him as a snoop.

'How was Christmas?' he heard Miranda ask in a gentle matter-of-fact tone.

Perhaps it was the sheer simplicity of the way the question was put that stumped him. For an agonising few seconds, it was as if he had lost his tongue. Then, in a feeble-sounding voice, he was only able to come up with: 'Oh, not bad, you know . . .' In instinctive self-defence, he deflected the question back to her: 'How about you?'

Dismissively, she replied: 'I don't think you really want to hear about my Christmas!' In one sense, it relieved him to hear her sounding a bit disgruntled. Perhaps it shouldn't have surprised him, knowing as he did that she had three young children and a broken marriage. After all, he was the one accustomed to playing the soothing role in their conversations. Not that she went on about her problems gratuitously. It was only on a gradual basis that she had begun to confide in him and it made him feel privileged whenever she happened to disclose anything new.

'I bet yours was nice and quiet!' he heard her prompting him again. It sounded almost as if she was teasing him with a cosy chocolate-box picture. 'Just the two of you?'

A disturbing impulse began racing inside his head. Despite having already made a conscious decision not to burden her with his misfortunes, he now felt a sudden need to disabuse her of any comfortable notion she might have of his marriage. He knew he only had himself to blame for giving her that view. Still, he did not say anything. Instead, he went on watching in the mirror as she engaged distractedly in searching for a piece of equipment from the bottom of a drawer.

'Are you all right, Simon?' The deep note of concern in her voice startled him. She had been about to start blow-drying his hair but stood frozen. For a moment, he couldn't work out why she was asking the question at all. Then his eyes switched from looking at her image to catching sight of himself in the mirror and worst of all the contorted expression of anxiety on his face.

'Yes, why?' he proffered back, lamely. Struggling to inject some composure into his facial expression, the wavering tone of his voice was now the giveaway.

'Well, you don't sound it. There's something wrong, isn't there?' Miranda was looking searchingly at him but it was as if the eye-contact was suddenly much too tenuous through a plate of glass. The next thing he knew she was there standing directly over him. Relatively slight of stature, her presence still felt imposing. He was in a complete quandary to know how to react. He felt an enormous temptation to blurt out everything, but that would have been acting pathetically. Bearing in mind there were lots of people within hearing distance, he could only think of one other line to take.

'Do you mind if we go somewhere and I'll try telling you?'

In the same breath, it occurred to him she would probably have another client straight after.

Hesitating only for a moment, she discreetly went across to the counter and returned to confirm a gap in her schedule. After she had finished doing his hair, she said there was a coffee-bar round the corner where they could talk in confidence.

Five minutes later, sitting the other side of the table from Miranda, it felt a much different one-to-one contact than in the salon. He fought back the unwanted thought how attractive she looked, but although she was ready to listen to him so sympathetically, he still wasn't exactly sure how to express himself. In the end, he simply told her the truth about Leonie and how unexpected it had been. He feared he might break down but somehow he managed to keep his emotions under tight enough control. He felt very grateful that Miranda heard him out in a controlled manner that lent him confidence to articulate his feelings. At the end, though, she said in a slightly unnerving tone of voice: 'I hope it's made you feel better by talking about it.' Pausing for a moment, she added: 'You don't have any regrets having told me, do you?'

At first, he had been unsure how to respond and found himself asking awkwardly: 'Do you mean – do I think I can trust you?'

She tossed her head. 'I hope you feel you can!'

He thought about it hard before finding himself saying out of the blue: 'Well, I've never kept my eyes open before when anyone has cut my eyebrows!'

She stared critically into his face for a moment and then burst into laughter.

It took him aback because he had caused her to smile once or twice before but it was the first time he could remember making her laugh. Her face looked so open and relaxed that any remaining tension seemed completely dispelled.

'Tell me, where did you have your hair done before me?'

'A long succession of silent men!'

It felt even better hearing her laugh a second time. 'You're not suggesting I talk too much, are you?' A sudden thought seemed to make her more serious again. 'I remember when I first mentioned about my ex-husband...' She paused for a moment as if needing to check that he remembered too.

'Yes, I felt sorry for you. By the way, you explained things very maturely, much better than I did just now.'

'I'd had time to get over it. It isn't the same for you.'

'But I should be able to cope better.'

'You will,' she said, as if keen to change the subject back to something lighter. 'Look, tell me seriously who chopped your eyebrows before.'

'How far do you want to go back?' He caught her looking unsure. 'I can go back to the late sixties when my father took me to the barber's...'

'That is going back a long way!' she said with a wry smile.

'All I can say is, at that time it ranked alongside going to the dentist, but at least the dentist said things like "Now this isn't going to hurt!" He was lying, of course, but the barber ... the barber never said a word!'

For a second, she glanced uncertainly back at him as if wondering how the conversation had taken this unexpected departure. Out of interest, she followed up: 'Did he ever ask you how you wanted your hair doing?'

It pleased her to see him looking in a better mood.

'No, short, back and sides ruled! If you asked for anything different, you'd be written off as a smart alec. The nicest thing was that the barber had a dog. I think it was called Monty. It sat in the corner with a baleful gaze, watching all the hair-clippings collect on the floor. There was no such thing as booking an appointment. You put your head round the door and took your turn squeezing up on the plastic-covered bench.'

'Sounds like he was in demand. He must have been good at cutting hair,' she offered.

'I'll tell you, I'd never have kept my eyes open when he was cutting my eyebrows. If he missed you then, he was bound to catch your ears.'

She winced in mock pain. 'Poor little boy! Didn't you complain to your dad?'

She noticed with pleasant surprise how he didn't mind her gentle mockery.

'Oh, he would never have complained himself.'

'And there was no talking at all?' She changed the subject back again.

'Well, occasionally, football or cars.'

'Never subjects we get on to then?' she inquired with a twinkle in her eye. 'I could run to *Footballers' Wives*, or you could interest me in a nice convertible!'

He broke off for a moment, seemingly distracted: 'You know I'm not sure whether it was the barber that was called Monty or the dog.'

She looked at him bemused for a second or two before answering: 'It had to be the dog.'

'How do you know?'

'The man sounds as if he would have been too old.'

'I don't get it.'

'The dog was probably named after General Montgomery. I wasn't born until the seventies but that much I would guess.'

He looked back at her, genuinely impressed.

'I'm not just a pretty face, you know. There may be more

bimbo hairdressers around these days but credit some of us with brains! Which reminds me, I'm afraid,' she said, pausing to look at her watch, 'my next customer will be waiting for me.'

As she got up from her chair, the words carelessly slipped out of his mouth: 'Can I see you again?'

'Yes, in six weeks' time.' Her tone didn't sound too brusque, more mindful of the usual time-gap between his visits. He didn't feel crushed. 'In the meantime, take care and I'll look forward to hearing about how well you're doing.'

As she left, he felt a sudden instinct to call after her: 'What if I need to see you in the meantime?' But he didn't, because it might have sounded presumptuous. In any case, he guessed she would just have said, 'You won't, you'll be fine!' which is what he knew he should be telling himself in the first place. Wasn't he a big boy now? He shouldn't need anyone to hold his hand.

Chapter 5

Tom Judd would have gone back to New York at the drop of a hat. The chance to go and work there had been miraculously presented to him in the 1990s, only to be cruelly snatched away from him a decade later. America was his father's place of birth, if not his own. It had always exerted a powerful influence over him. The first time he had travelled there, as a boy in the early 1970s, he had crossed the Atlantic with his father in a grand luxury liner. As they reached New York in the early hours of the morning, the eerie silhouette of the Manhattan skyline had captivated his senses.

Born in England, Tom had been sent away to a public school. His father had been keen to give him the best chance of acquiring a sound education and a strong sense of responsibility. In both respects, Judd Junior had sadly disappointed. Rebellious of nature, Tom's only saving graces were the talents he developed in essay-writing and long-distance running. Indeed, these qualities had stood him in good stead for his chosen career in journalism. But, expelled from two different institutions, once for drug-taking and the second time for joy-riding in his housemaster's new Jaguar down the M1, it was fair to say that Tom had failed to live up to his father's expectations. Other potential education-providers were less than impressed by mere promises of endowments from a feckless man whose other main quest in life seemed to be short-lived relationships with English women from landed families. Tom's father had drunk himself to death a long time ago and gone to the grave without ever revealing the identity of Tom's mother.

From his early twenties onwards, Tom had striven to make his mark in journalism. He was never content to be based too long in one place, and his thirst for adventure had taken him to most of the world's leading trouble-spots. Serving stints in Nicaragua, Beirut and Afghanistan, his lengthiest spell was in Northern Ireland reporting on the violence in the eighties. In the eye of every storm, he seemed intent on playing Russian roulette with his life. Women, alcohol and drugs were the indulgences that kept him going. Encountering danger and upheaval round each corner, everything seemed short-lived and disposable. Trust was the rarest of commodities. In exceptional circumstances, when the possibility arose, fate had a remarkable habit of mocking honourable intentions. This was no more true than in the case of a friendship he had formed with a Royal Ulster Constabulary policeman by the name of Mark Leslie.

Tom kept few mementoes from his past, but a photograph of the two of them standing together in running gear was one of his most prized possessions. He only had to look at the photo and it had the power to evoke the drama of that episode in his life. He had first interviewed Mark after a bout of mob violence on the Ormeau Road. A few days later, he had happened to encounter him drinking with some other colleagues in a Belfast pub. Respecting the off-duty rights of others, Tom had been surprised when Mark chose to come across and talk to him. They had got into conversation about many things other than the immediate perils of life in Ulster. He remembered Mark mentioning he was planning to run a half-marathon for charity. At first he had thought he was trying to collect sponsorship money. It only dawned on him after a while that he was trying to get him to run. Contrary as the notion was to Tom's profligate lifestyle, it had struck a chord and reminded him of how keen he had been on running when he was at school. He had been so impressed by Mark's enthusiasm to help the cause of promoting good relations between Protestants and Catholics that he had ended up joining a group of runners who used to go to the coast at weekends for training runs across the sands. It was returning home to Belfast by car one evening on a country lane with Mark, just a mile before they reached the safety of the motorway, that they had been stopped and Mark had been shot dead by IRA gunmen. The only consoling outcome was the huge groundswell of support for the cause he had espoused. Tom could still remember the well of emotion he felt finishing the crossing-line of the event that symbolised everything his friend had stood for.

Partly from horror at what had happened, Tom's interest had rapidly turned away from reporting from the front line to the safer territory of analysing politics. However, here too he had made it his business to stalk danger. In 1992, all his various appetites and cravings in life had seemed blissfully satisfied in the form of an invitation to go and work for an international magazine based in New York. The icing on the cake was that the lucrative contract included tenancy of a palatial apartment overlooking Central Park. With his star in the ascendancy, he had been in constant demand as a guest on network current affairs programmes. His speciality was in debunking so-called icon figures. Provocative but entertaining, his stock-in-trade was showering contempt on the establishment. Haggard in appearance and famously immoderate in his alcohol intake, he gloried in tormenting opponents with a wicked brand of invective. The fast and furious style of his delivery had studio audiences baying for more. Adapting to a New York life-style had not been without its challenges but he had worked on the principle of exploiting his

Englishness to the full. From the start, he had identified with a distinctively English tradition of involvement in American politics. One seasoned commentator had likened his modus operandi to that of Frost when he had nailed Nixon over Watergate. Judd twanged raw nerve-ends by unearthing controversies relating to past chapters in US foreign policy. Raking up America's Cold War record, he generated heated debate over the role of luminaries such as Kissinger. For a while, it had seemed he could get away with saying anything that entered his head, however profane.

In his forties, with two ill-fated marriages behind him, he had turned his back on any further such commitment. Not that he could survive without women entirely. Or, as he had to concede, a certain type of woman at that point in his life – mature but always well-preserved, usually trapped in a dull marriage, with differing degrees of mental sharpness but invariably leading a spoilt and dissatisfied parasite existence. The saddest thing was that he found the company of such women irresistible, particularly when his powers of discrimination were blunted by recourse to his favourite combination of cocaine and single malt. Alone with Alice or Fiona or Sophie, any pretence of self-sufficiency gave way to a squalid, physical instinct for gratification. Nor, however sorely he might tax his conscience later, could he restrain himself from the next bout of reckless indulgence.

Eventually, he couldn't go on trying to cover his tracks and he was thrown out of his job and apartment on the same day. He had made so many enemies along the way, by the end they were queuing up to stick the knife in. For the last two years he had been walking a tightrope in his fight against dependence on cocaine. Although a confirmed atheist, in his worst moments he had bucked his principles and prayed to die. The memory haunted him of his first wretched experience of the stuff at a country-house party somewhere in Berkshire, when it had given him a gagging sensation as if a bee was stinging up his nostrils. The experiment should have stopped there, but instead it had given way to a lifetime dependence. From using coke as a pretext for winding down after hazardous reporting assignments, he had kept on deluding himself he was master not servant of the habit. Coining in the kind of money he was in New York, although he didn't exactly shout it from the roof gardens, snorting cocaine was just one of the several perks he came to take for granted.

Nothing had really prepared him for the profound shock of losing his fabulous job in America and being dumped back where he started. The effect had devastated him, reducing him to a degraded form of existence on his knees with a craving most days for as much as three grams. On bad days, it was five, and afterwards he cried for the earth to swallow him up. Appalling as it was to reflect on now, it hadn't been until the end of the summer of 2003 that he had been able to accept the fact he was addicted. He had sought help and joined a support group. Until then, despite his bruising sense of desperation, he had managed to convince himself he was still capable of sorting out the problem without the help of others. The thing that had finally clinched it for him was realising he was no longer physically able to put pen to paper without coke as a crutch. Like a drowned rat, he had ended being washed back up on English shores.

Headaches and deep-seated angst were lasting legacies of his obsession but the hope at least had returned that he might somehow be able to go on adding one more day to the last without caving in again. The indignity of constantly having to admit his addiction to the rest of the circle was not something he had felt easy about to begin with, but he couldn't deny it lent him strength. It was only within the last few months that he had begun to believe again in any kind of future.

Approached by one of those right-wing rags he wouldn't have touched with a bargepole before, he had agreed to help as part of a research team undertaking a pseudo-sociological study of dangers to the well-being of youngsters between the ages of fourteen and nineteen. Various locations had been earmarked and he had been landed with Leeds. He accepted the job; it wasn't as if he had been spoilt for choice. Having plied his trade in strife-torn theatres of war, it had seemed pathetically tame by comparison. But the experience was proving unnerving. He was assigned to examine the effects of teenage binge-drinking in city centres, and one of his earliest abiding memories was the riotousness of marauding groups of girls in scanty battle-dress, pissed out of their minds, tearing around on turbo-driven stilettos.

He had soon realised the thanklessness of the task. At least, he was part of a team engaged in tracking down teenagers willing or half-sober enough to hold what passed for interviews. The supposed idea was to 'get inside the mind' of these alcohol-crazed young people. From bitter experience, he knew the teenage mind wasn't a place he wanted to go. At a time when he was frantically trying to salvage his own life, it seemed ridiculous that he should be exposing himself to this demented twilight existence. He knew well enough what a massive test of will-power it was to stay the right side of the precarious dividing-line between order and abandonment.

The other explosive threat to his welfare came in the form of Suzanne, a Molotov cocktail in her own right. Her most recent visitation had not only been menacing but also hugely embarrassing. She was still a user and, even when she was not high, her behaviour was erratic and irresponsible.

Tom had felt contrite enough to go round and apologise to the new occupant in the flat opposite. Thank goodness, he had not succumbed to the idea of inviting him round for a morning malt! It made him cringe, recalling the exhibition he had made of himself on that dreadful occasion when Suzanne had misbehaved with such spectacular effect on the corridor. At least the visit had given him a chance to introduce himself a little more formally and politely. Thankfully, Tom picked up that the man did not want to make too much fuss of the incident. They had even engaged in a little civilised conversation, during the course of which he discovered his neighbour was, of all things, just about to take up a new post as headteacher in a failing inner-city school. To Tom, it sounded almost as insane a proposition as his own job, but he didn't think it his position to say so.

It occurred to him that some of the youngsters he saw out and about at night might well attend Simon's new school as pupils during the daytime. Then, he had found himself asking Simon what on earth had made him take it on. Again, he appreciated the other man could have told him to mind his own business, but he was civil enough to answer the question.

'For different reasons, I suppose, including one or two that are personal. The main thing is that I want to be of benefit to young people. I'm ready for something new and I need to see whether I can make a difference.'

No paragon of virtue, Tom was conditioned to suspect anyone who claimed to do things for altruistic reasons. However, he had found himself convinced by the understated but compelling nature of Simon's response. There was an unmistakable sense of purpose about him, as if he saw his job as more of a mission in life. Experience had given Tom a sharp instinct for being able to see through the bullshit. It was obvious the two of them were complete opposites but he felt an instant respect for Simon. The dignified manner of his expression gave Tom a strong yearning to befriend him if he could. In some ways, Simon reminded him of Mark Leslie. For several reasons, not least the unfavourable first impression he himself had made, he knew it was unlikely they would become friends. But if there was only an outside chance, he would make the most of any further opportunities. Despite all his inadequacies and character flaws, something of the other man's qualities might just rub off on him . . .

Chapter 6

It was Thursday and he had just about survived the first three days. His other school already seemed a lifetime ago. Beforehand, he couldn't have grasped the enormity of the challenge facing him. It felt as though he had walked into a cauldron. Trapped inside, the natural instinct was to seek to escape the heat. Of course, if the fire had been real, he wouldn't have hesitated to call the emergency services. The trouble was, though, he was the one assigned to put out the flames.

He knew the fire-fighting analogy ran the obvious risk of sounding over-dramatic. He wouldn't have wanted to use it to anyone else, but it summed up his own feelings exactly. With both staff and pupils, the tension ran sky high. The hardest thing had been deciding whether to go round dealing with trigger situations or stand back and give things a chance to sort themselves out. The first approach had proved demanding and the second only invited further disaster. To begin with, it wasn't clear whether what was happening was normal or hyped-up. At one point on Tuesday, he had suspected it was being staged for his benefit. By Thursday, the only thing he was one hundred per cent sure of was that nothing could be described as 'normal' at Bentwood High.

At his old school, Simon liked to think he had a bit of presence as Headteacher. Pupils had at least seemed to notice him when he was around the place. On Monday, he had decided to start as he meant to carry on by positioning himself at the front of the hall to set the right tone for Year 11 assembly. Again, there was no reason to believe that any of it was orchestrated but he found himself standing there, totally ignored by bedraggled-looking groups of fifteen-year-olds sauntering in and carrying on aimless conversations. Apart from the flustered Head of Year, who turned up late, apologising that he had been busy counselling a pupil, form tutors were conspicuous by their absence. If Simon had not chosen to try and start proceedings himself, he was quite sure that the rowdy elements would have just gone on talking amongst themselves. The assumption had to be that on most occasions they did. As a few form tutors started trickling in with registers tucked under their arms, it served to confirm Simon's initial impression that assemblies were held for registration purposes and nothing more.

He had planned to talk about new year resolutions. In the event, it had proved an ambitious aim to bring the disparate bunch of pupils into any semblance of order. The Head of Year had optimistically led him to believe he was capable of getting the group of 120 individuals quiet, but hadn't managed it. Simon had felt a duty to step in, and took the opportunity to introduce himself. Most of them were curious enough to give him time of day. However, attention spans proved alarmingly short. For a brief while, he went on gamely trying to command his audience's attention, reminding them it was respectful to listen. His appeal had limited effect. At least he felt he had succeeded in making a point. Providing food for thought afterwards, he had added 'improve discipline in assemblies' to his own list of new year resolutions.

With staff, he picked up different sorts of vibes. Unlike the pupils, the staff by and large seemed good at knowing what was expected of them. They just had immense difficulty in carrying out these expectations on the ground. If it had been a theory test, they would have passed with flying colours. He had got the same message on the staff development day he had attended at the end of the previous term. It was obvious the school had a great number of experienced and knowledgeable teaching staff. Many of them seemed to have served their whole career at Bentwood. However, as he walked round school, it was obvious that very little learning seemed to be taking place in classrooms. As with the atmosphere in the assembly-hall, a sense of purpose was clearly lacking. In practical terms, it illustrated to him why the school had been put in special measures in the first place.

The massive doubt that continued to gnaw away inside him was whether his own particular character and range of skills were right for the demands of this new job. He had never been exposed to a similar situation before. His preferred style in the other post had been to take strategic responsibility for the direction of the school, confident that he could delegate day-to-day running to other members of staff. Although he had been an effective classroom practitioner throughout his career, his management skills had tended to take him away from direct contact with pupils. Here at Bentwood, it dawned on him how vital it was for the Headteacher to be a role model to other staff if the school was to succeed in coping effectively with challenging pupil behaviour. Delivering a professional verdict was one thing; being able to put the situation right in practice was totally different. There was bound to come a point when he wondered if he had done the right thing coming here. He hadn't envisaged the question grabbing him by the throat in his first week.

Other things had had a strangely destabilising effect on him, such as receiving a 'Good Luck' card on the first day from his PA Caroline. Or rather, she wasn't his PA now. He wished he could have brought her with him because his new one, Wendy, reminded him uncomfortably of old Mrs Ellison.

'Don't expect me to make cups of tea for you!' she had taken it upon herself to warn him on his first day. He could tell he wasn't going to be pampered.

Another obvious cause of concern to him was the lack of back-up on the senior management team. Bentwood wasn't such a big school but he still would have expected there to be two deputy heads. With the school now eligible for extra government grants to help it out of special measures, he had already decided to recommend to governors making a second appointment. The existing deputy, Bill Deacon, had served virtually his whole career at Bentwood.

From chance conversations with staff, he found the main issue preoccupying them, apart from finding out more about himself, was the exact nature of the circumstances prompting the departure of his predecessor, a man who had served as head there for the last fifteen years. Because he was still a bit in the dark himself, he couldn't give an answer. At the same time, it must have been clear to anyone that going into special measures had a lot to do with it. Even so, most staff seemed to be in denial. It was much easier to believe the inspectors had 'got it wrong'. The main area of doubt seemed to be whether the old head, Matthew Chalmers, had chosen to go or been pushed. Unofficially, Simon had gathered it was a bit of both. For his part, he was at pains to say the past was no longer relevant. It was taking the school forward that mattered now. He only wished he could feel confident in his heart of hearts that he was the right person to do it!

He noted uneasily that this was probably the first time since Monday that he had stopped for breath during the school day. However, even though these few moments of enforced idleness were self-imposed, they were making him feel extremely uncomfortable. It was compounded by the fact that he was expecting a visit from the Director of

Education at 2.30. Sitting at his desk, he reckoned that creating a relaxed image, or at least not looking scared, was the impression he should be creating. But the slight delay in John Armitage's arrival was making him nervous. He had started involuntarily drumming his fingers on the sides of his armchair, an action which connected in his mind with waiting for Miranda. Heaven help him if he found himself unburdening to John Armitage in the same manner. It might well prove to be the shortest headship on record.

Why, he asked himself, did he feel guilty sitting there? Didn't he deserve a short break? He'd been on his feet all day, not even stopping to take lunch. His eyes roamed restlessly round the room, really absorbing the austere surroundings for the first time. Everything about the first few days had been so hectic, he hadn't had time to set up base properly yet. From the neglected look of the school, he guessed Matthew Chalmers couldn't have been too concerned with appearances. Bits of paint had flecked off the walls and whoever had given the room its last lick of paint hadn't bothered to do behind the radiators.

Reproaching himself again for just sitting there, he idly glanced at his in-tray but decided against tackling anything at this moment. To avoid becoming restless, it occurred to him he might advantageously place himself in the front entrance area instead. Jotting down a swift note in the diary he always kept to hand – 'Do up office' – he rose from his seat purposefully. There was bound to be something quick and useful he could do, such as scoop up an offending piece of litter or two. With the impulse coursing through his veins to go out and check, he had just reached the door when he heard the phone ringing on his desk. His first reaction was to ignore it but realised it would probably only be Wendy telling him his visitor had arrived. Picking up the phone, it was Wendy's voice he heard but with a different message.

'Could you go to Room 56 to sort out a discipline problem?'

Instantly he replied: 'I'm expecting the Director of Education any minute, you know,' half in mild protest, half as stern reminder.

'I'm sorry, I've tried everywhere else,' the voice came back, 'but I can't get an answer. I thought you may need to deal with it. Only the note says a teacher's been punched.'

So much for the litter check, he mused.

As though unnerved by the silence, he heard her voice urging: 'What do you want me to say to the boy?'

Suppressing an instinct to lay it on the line what he wanted her to say to the boy, he bit his lip and settled for a tetchy: 'Tell him I'm on my way.'

If he was lucky, he could manage to sort it out quickly. However inconvenient, he had to admit it did sound serious. There was something about her manner that got to him.

He put the phone down. There was obviously nothing he could do but go and deal with the wretched problem. Forgetting the fact he didn't know where Room 56 was, he was in no mood to betray trepidation. Nothing was to be achieved by being faint-hearted. Blind instinct propelled him in the right direction. As he approached the trouble-spot, the atmosphere of tension was unmistakable. Spotting a bunch of over-excited pupils, mainly boys, hanging around outside a classroom, he found the only consoling aspect was that their demeanour stiffened somewhat upon his arrival. In a no-nonsense frame of mind, he checked it was Room 56 and took a swift look inside. Seeing no sign of a teacher, he promptly questioned the class. 'I think he may have gone off to the smoking room, sir,' an unhelpful voice piped up. He would have followed up harder on this remark, but the first thing was to clear the group off the corridor and shepherd them back into the classroom. He could tell something must be wrong from the shamed looks on one or two faces.

At that moment, Bill the Deputy entered the classroom looking extremely agitated.

'John Crabtree!' he shouted. 'Come with me!' Nonplussed, Simon was prepared to give Bill the benefit of the doubt that he hadn't caught sight of him.

'It wasn't me!' the boy protested.

'Mr Worrall has said so. That's good enough for me.'

'You can ask anyone. It wasn't me!' The accused boy truculently stood his ground.

While this interchange continued, Simon glanced around the room. From looking relatively chastened only a few moments earlier, the class was on the verge of uproar again. With great difficulty, he took matters into his hands to restore a vestige of calm. At the same time, he motioned Bill outside the door where they could discuss the matter from a position of safety.

'I feel I'm being undermined,' he heard Bill snarl. 'It's John Crabtree and he needs dealing with. Now!'

Simon felt like laying it on the line. Instead, aware they were in full view of the class, he adopted a pacifying tone. 'I have no doubt you're right, but do you mind if I bring the boy out myself? It's going to be very awkward if the situation gets any more confrontational with the whole class here.'

Thankfully, Bill didn't seem to have a problem with this, but being able to extract John Crabtree was hardly a foregone conclusion. Returning into the fray, behaving calmly at all costs, he felt the atmosphere was like a football crowd waiting to hear the ref's verdict over a disputed penalty decision. The first thing he did was quieten them down again. Then he sidled up to John Crabtree's desk, quietly asking him to leave the classroom for a word. Prepared for any level of negative response ranging from silent refusal to foul expletives, he purposely avoided putting any sense of threat into his voice. Although thinking about it for a second or two, the recalcitrant-looking pupil reluctantly agreed. A discernible gasp went up amongst the class, as if a miracle was unfolding.

Outside the classroom, with his heart pounding a little less strongly, he was surprised to see a somewhat changed expression on Bill's face. With a nonchalant air, he informed Simon that he had just received a note saying it had been a case of mistaken identity and that Mr Worrall was now pointing the finger at someone called Jake Cooper. 'Oh, by the way, the note also says your visitor is waiting for you in the entrance area. Do you want me to take over this business?'

'I think you better had!' Simon muttered between clenched teeth.

He stole a glance at his watch and saw it was gone 2.50. Returning quickly, he caught sight of a distinguished-looking grey-haired man in a blue suit and red tie impatiently pacing up and down the entrance-area.

'I'm sorry I'm late,' Simon blurted out. 'Have you been offered a coffee?' he added, anxious to placate the Director of Education.

'Don't drink coffee,' John Armitage muttered brusquely. And then with a knowing look: 'I gather you've had your hands rather full!'

Making a mental note to have a word with Wendy on the subject of receiving guests, he felt it incumbent on him to try to play the matter down gamely. After all, the last thing he wanted was the Director of Education forming the view that Bentwood was in a state of chaos. 'Oh! Just routine, nothing really to bother about.'

'Routine, eh? I see . . . I see! Remind me, what time did we agree to meet? Wasn't it 2.30?'

Simon was not to be fooled by the playful-sounding tone of voice. He had fallen into a trap of his own making.

'Would you like to come into my office?' he asked politely, in an effort to shepherd him somewhere less public. However, the same technique that had worked with John Crabtree didn't succeed this time around.

'Sorry, in actual fact, I have to be going. I have to be back at the Town Hall for an important council meeting at 3.15.'

'Only a flying visit, eh?'

The Director looked back at him uncertainly. 'Yes, just to welcome you into the fold. Perhaps we might get a chance another time. By the way, there's a heads' meeting next week. I expect you'll find it useful. Well, very nice to meet you. Leave you to it. Best of luck!'

Frozen to the spot, Simon stood there trying to reconcile himself to the fact that his first meeting with the Director of Education had lasted no more than sixty seconds. The next thing he heard was a glass panel sliding open and the cheerful-sounding voice of Wendy.

'Oh, by the way, I thought you'd want to know Jake Cooper's father has been on the phone. He was asking to speak to you personally. Something about a mobile message from his son. Father says he wants to know what you're going to do about Mr Worrall assaulting him.'

Feeling mildly traumatised by the hapless turn of events, Simon retreated back into the bleak interior of his office and wrote a note in his diary to remind himself to buy a couple of potted plants. There had to be some way he could make a difference.

Chapter 7

Miranda wondered whether she was ever going to have a life she could properly call her own. Approaching thirty, she envied the young girls at the salon who valued their independence enough not to want to settle down too early. As for herself, she had fallen into the trap of her parents' and grandparents' generations of getting married straight out of school, with children on the way a year or two later. Ian had been her playground sweetheart and it had seemed natural at the time to believe in 'happy ever afters'. But, while she was sidelined at home looking after three children, Ian's attention had been attracted elsewhere. Familiarity seemed to have bred more than a touch of contempt and he had deserted her for this woman at work called Joanne. Over the last eighteen months, Miranda had been having to fight tooth and claw for maintenance. Worse than that, he was never too bothered about seeing the children, which made things even worse for them emotionally. At least she had the house, although it was becoming more and more difficult to keep up the mortgage payments. She was grateful for the help she received from her mum, who lived nearby and was willing to look after Jack, who was still not old enough to go to school, on the days she worked part-time at the salon. She had to work, otherwise it would have been impossible to make ends meet.

On Saturdays, she usually dropped the three of them off.

Borrowing her mum's car, she was now on her way to work. Tuesdays were never too busy but Fridays and Saturdays were always hectic. Although the traffic was lighter than on weekdays, she was already a few minutes late. Her eldest, Kerry, had played up, having to be told yet again that she wasn't old enough at nine to spend the day in town with a group of school-friends. Miranda felt guilty because it was her mum who was going to have to cope with the inevitable tantrums. Her mum had always been one for peace at all costs and tended to be soft with the grandchildren, which made things worse when they were back at home. On such days she looked forward to going to work, but not to picking them up again.

As a hairdresser, she was more than used to listening to other people's problems. It came with the territory. Perhaps it did her good being forced to switch off from her own. Not that it was always the same. Although she never let it show, she sometimes got fed up having to hear how wonderful everyone else's life was. The women who were her regulars seemed to fall into definite categories. First, there were the middle-aged prima donnas with an all-year-round tan, natural or fake, who bragged about themselves. Imagining themselves the centre of attention, they spouted at volume so that no-one could help but pick up the names they dropped: cars or designer clothes or C-list celebrities. Usually, it was just a matter of feeding a line and sounding suitably impressed at the right moments. They always had their hair done exactly the same way in a sorry attempt to defy the ageing process. Younger women were a lot more experimental, not only liking the idea of changing style every now and again but also generally grateful for how it turned out. With them, the conversation tended to be fairly relaxed, without too much in the way of airs and pretensions. Because she was of a similar age, she felt a natural affinity and things weren't so stilted.

The most difficult were the occasional customers, of whatever age, who seemed so unhappy with themselves from the moment they arrived that nothing in the world could please them. Putting full responsibility on the stylist to carry out some miraculous transformation in their appearance, they didn't even have the faintest clue what a successful outcome might look like. Not that she didn't welcome a creative challenge, only it usually involved endless sifting through catalogues, constant changes of mind back and forth and then sitting there in a screwed-up state of tension right up to the wire. If they were still unhappy at that point, you didn't know what you were going to do. The Bridget Joneses put it down to experience. It was only the real hardcore that postured and flounced off angrily. If you were lucky, they made the one visit. In the end, the worst they could do was not give a tip.

The client she was with now, by the name of Emma McCready, however, didn't fit any of these particular categories. The way she had walked in, it looked as if she knew she had made a big mistake and was about to make a quick u-turn and never be seen again. Probably in her mid-thirties, her black hair was now mostly greyed. Wearing it shoulder-length didn't do any favours, making her appearance plain and unkempt. She had obviously had to build herself up to come at all. It needed a lot of gentle coaxing to get her to sit down and discuss any way forward. Luckily, the fibre of her hair was quite strong, which suggested it would benefit from cutting and shaping. Emma had been honest, confessing she hadn't bothered much about her hair previously, content to settle for what she called a more natural look. Miranda found herself secretly wondering why Emma was wanting to give herself a complete change of image. But whatever the reason, it wasn't her place to pry. Even so, it seemed glaringly obvious, bearing in mind her pretty face and round blue eyes, that she should have done it years ago.

From the outset, Miranda was confident a simple bob and choirboy fringe would be just the ticket. But if it proved difficult enough to convince Emma on this score, she thought she was going to collapse when Miranda suggested she should have her hair dyed blonde. Yet it made perfect sense. It toned in perfectly with the colour of her eyes and her pale, freckled skin. Miranda understood how Emma might have doubts due to the fact she was naturally brunette. Perhaps it went deeper than that. There seemed something reserved about her nature that suggested she might well hold out against anything artificial or too different. But, as if somehow realising she had nothing to lose, she had ended up agreeing with this idea too. Finally going about her business, Miranda couldn't help but feel amused, wondering how Emma would have reacted to the notion of having a nose job or breast implants. Thank goodness, she only cut people's hair for a living!

Not that her new client needed a complete make-over or anything. Having a trim but shapely figure, she was attractive enough by any standards except perhaps her own. The way she resisted the temptation to look at herself in the mirror seemed positively self-disapproving. Without much to say for herself, Emma had seemed content to remain quiet, although she had unnerved Miranda at one point by suddenly letting out: 'It's not going to look too brash, is it?'

'Everything's going to be fine,' she had sought to assure her client, as if indeed she was a doctor carrying out plastic surgery. 'I think you're going to be pleasantly surprised at the difference.' She noticed how Emma started smiling nervously. Rightly or wrongly, she took it as a positive sign. Visibly, she seemed to become more confident, not afraid to look in the mirror to see what was happening. Establishing occasional eye-contact, it seemed she was beginning to trust in how things would turn out.

'God, I need it to make me look different!' Emma

exclaimed, with downright conviction in her voice. For the first time, Miranda began to think that Emma might not be such a shrinking violet after all. Or perhaps the new look was already helping to make her feel bolder.

'Perhaps we all need a make-over from time to time,' Miranda said, without thinking, kicking herself the moment the words had escaped her.

'We do indeed!' came the unexpectedly cheerful response.

Laughing openly with one another, the relationship instantly seemed to become more relaxed.

'You know, I think I'm just going to go for it,' Emma went on in carefree vein. 'I don't care what people say!'

In place of the tense and hunched demeanour, she appeared to be opening up more every second. Miranda found herself warming to her new client in a way that hadn't seemed conceivable five minutes earlier.

When it came to the moment of suspense, seeing the final outcome, Emma's mouth opened in amazement. 'Oh, is that really me? I don't believe it!' It was touching to see how she reacted like a little girl opening a Christmas present that totally exceeded expectations. To think how scared she had looked coming into the salon, she walked out like a model on the catwalk. Miranda felt a little peeved with herself for not being a bit more inquisitive, particularly about Emma's reasons for wanting to make the change. Probably, though, it was best not to rush things. From suspecting Emma might belong to the category of one-visit-wonders, she felt distinctly hopeful she would join her cohort of regulars. The session had undoubtedly proved the highlight of her day.

However, the sheer intensity of Saturdays always left her feeling dog tired by the time she picked up the kids from her mum. Trying hard not to look too weary and jaded, she was more than aware of the load heaped on her mum in looking after them all day. Not without a certain trepidation, she ventured inside. Crossing her fingers, she always tended to prepare herself for the worst. Then she might just be pleasantly surprised. Relieved to catch the sound of gostering laughter, she found them happily engaged in a game of snap. Even little Jack was watching on curiously from the comfort of his baby bouncer as they played with cute pictures of animals they had drawn on to cards in the morning. Miranda rued she was never so imaginative herself. Doing her best to brush such unhelpful thoughts aside, she realised the least she could do was take them off her mum's hands as quickly as possible and get them back home. In her mind's eye, she already saw herself leaving Kerry and Bart to watch telly whilst putting Jack safely to bed. With such routines firmly in mind, the party was soon ready to leave. Blessing her luck that it wasn't raining, she was turning the corner, within about a hundred metres of home, when Kerry shouted out: 'That's dad's car, isn't it?'

In an instant, it seemed as though Miranda had lost her ability to think straight or be in control of things. Kerry was shrieking with excitement.

'Look, he's standing at the door!' She was waving frenetically. It was hard to tell whether he had noticed or not. Instead of joining in with his sister, Bart looked up uncertainly at his mum as if somehow needing her approval.

In truth, Miranda knew it had reached the stage where she could no longer stomach the sight of Ian. It didn't bear thinking about how they had spent so much of their lives fawning on one another, only for things to go terribly wrong any time he was called upon to show a sense of responsibility.

Then the same thought struck her as it had often done before. How dare he brazenly turn up on the doorstep like this? Recently, he seemed to be making a habit of it. She put it down to his cowardly way of seeking to gain access to the children. With them there, she wasn't so likely to ask awkward questions about maintenance and other issues like that. Well, he could blow that for a game. See if she cared! Her blood was boiling. She'd had enough of his slimy ways . . .

The only trouble was, though, she still didn't quite know how to handle the children's reaction. Meeting up with their dad, whatever the circumstances, was bound to affect them emotionally. That was why she could do little to stop Kerry running on ahead in uncontrollable glee. It was the familiar old situation. She was caught in a cleft stick between doing her best by the children and having this rat of a man to deal with. She composed herself, straining not to let her angry feelings get the better of her. The last thing she wanted was to offset any comfort the children might derive from his occasional visits. At least Bart stayed by her side and didn't desert her. As Kerry dashed joyously into her father's arms, she couldn't help but notice how he stood his ground, looking casual and faintly embarrassed.

Over the last few yards, although needing to concentrate on levering the pushchair over the small step at the gate, she kept her eyes fixed critically on Ian's face. She wanted him to know she was only having truck with him for the children's sake.

'Hello, I'm just in the district so I thought I'd drop by,' he trotted out, as though somehow he was conferring a favour on them all.

Despite the strength of her feelings, she knew she couldn't really refuse to let him in but she was damned if she was going to make him feel welcome. She settled for: 'It would help if you rang to say you were coming.'

Practised in the art of sidestepping barbed comments, he did his usual trick of playing up to Kerry. More often than not, it entailed getting silly with her. This time, heaving her up in his arms, he twirled her round and round to add to her giddiness.

'Will you please put her down before she is sick all over the place?' Miranda urged.

'No mum, it's fun!' Kerry protested half-heartedly. Eventually, he put her down on the pretext his arms were tired.

Opening the door never failed to remind her of the decision to change the locks. It had somehow marked a symbolic end-point. Up to that stage, she would probably have taken him back. But the sickening truth was he was much too happy in this other woman's company. Though he had never given any indication of wanting to return, taking it upon herself to exclude him from the house had made her feel slightly more in charge of the situation.

'Do you mind if I come in?' The words were tossed out in a quiet, unassuming tone and to no-one in particular. The children instinctively looked in their mother's direction for a response. She could tell they would have been gobsmacked if she had put her foot down and said no. It was another classic instance of emotional blackmail. For a moment or two, he stood there shuffling hesitantly from one foot to the other as though not unduly bothered one way or the other. When they went in, he followed suit, slinking in at the rear, presumably taking silence as assent. She already had her hands full looking after Jack and putting him to bed. She was still keeping her anger under control. Desperately trying to put the children's interests first, she knew the other two were starving, so she went into the kitchen and took a packet of fish fingers out of the freezer.

'How long are you staying for, Daddy?' she heard Kerry, back in the lounge, putting sweetly.

'It depends,' he replied in a quietened voice. 'I could take you out to Burger King if you like.'

'Oh yes, that would be great!' came back the spontaneous reply.

'You'd better go and ask your mum first,' he added, as though bending over backwards to be considerate.

The next thing she knew, Kerry was standing beside her in the kitchen.

'Mum, is it all right if Dad takes me out? I don't think Bart's so keen, but I want to.'

Miranda looked her straight in the face. She couldn't find a suitable response.

'Mum, please!'

Still not sure how to reply, she could only accept it wasn't Kerry's fault. She had a right to see her father and the last thing Miranda wanted to do was to lose her temper with her daughter.

'You stay in here a moment, will you, love? I just have something I need to say to your father.' She reassured Kerry by smiling, so she wouldn't think anything was wrong. Then she stepped into the lounge.

Instantly, she took sight of Ian slouching as of old in his favourite armchair. Something snapped and she couldn't stand it a moment longer.

'Listen, I want a word with you . . . outside!' The sense of an ultimatum in her tone took both of them back. Nevertheless, he didn't exactly look in any hurry to abandon his comfortable position.

'Did you hear? I have something to say!' Raising her voice to the level of a command, she fixed her eyes on him without hint of compromise, summoning him to the door. 'Now!'

As he arched his eyebrows, the unmistakable smirk on his face clearly questioned the urgency. At the cost of jumping through one or two more hoops, it seemed like he was going to get his own way as usual.

Eventually, with a weary air, he raised himself. Incensed by his body language, she felt more emboldened than ever to give him a piece of her mind. With the children safely inside, she didn't care which of the neighbours heard. She was intent on giving him both barrels.

'Look, you listen and get this straight!' Taking a deep breath, she knew what she wanted to say. The only thing left was to press the trigger.

'Stop treating us like shit. When you start paying on a regular basis, then you can come and take them out for one of your dirt-cheap meals. And not just Kerry. Got it? Until then, none of us want to see you!'

As he stood there with mouth gaping open, she took the opportunity to dart back inside, slipping the chain behind her.

With her heart pounding, she stood for a few moments behind the door in nervous trepidation. Still fearing the worst, she half-expected Kerry to bolt indignantly out of the kitchen and catch the sound of Ian's coaxing voice desperately trying to wheedle himself back into the fold. Holding her breath with so much effort that it made the veins in her temples throb with pain, she waited for the silence to be broken, but miraculously it seemed to hold. For one heart-stopping moment, a noise started up. It was only Jack stirring in his cot, though. Half a minute later, standing her ground, she heard the sound of a car door slamming followed by the revving up of an engine and the skid of tyres as a vehicle roared off down the road.

Now she was able at last to breathe more easily, tears began to stream down her cheeks. Dreading the retribution still to come from Kerry's reaction, she wiped her eyes clean and built up the courage to go back into the kitchen. Miraculously, she found her daughter calmly attending to a neat row of fish fingers on the grill-plate.

'Don't worry, Mummy, I'd much rather have your fish fingers than anything from Burger King.'

Miranda saw a funny side she wouldn't have dreamt possible a minute or two ago.

'None of us are going to win any prizes for healthy eating, are we?' she let out, with a peal of hysterical laughter.

Kerry's expression didn't alter.

'Don't be silly, you give us plenty of fruit and vegetable all the time.'

There was such an earnest look on her daughter's face that Miranda didn't know how to react. And then, they were suddenly joined by Bart, as if relieved to hear his mother laughing. Hugging each other, the sound of Jack going on crying out for attention only seemed to unite them even closer. However hard she had found it to cope as a wife, she was at pains not to forfeit her role as mother.

Chapter 8

With three weeks under his belt, Simon was starting to feel a bit more established. He had got past the point where every pupil's first question seemed to be 'Are you the new Headteacher?' Of course, he had already introduced himself formally in all the different year-group assemblies. He liked to think he was applying a stronger degree of discipline to the school compared with that first Monday. By stating the point long and hard in staff briefings, he thought he had got the message across about staff setting a good example to pupils at all times.

He admitted it was early days yet, but generally he seemed to be picking up encouraging reactions from staff, particularly those who were keen on setting consistent standards. He was still finding Wendy and Bill difficult at times but did his best not to let it affect him too much. The only problem was that, as PA and Deputy respectively, he depended on them more than any of the other staff. He had endeavoured to explain to them what he expected. Both had listened with the same distant, forbearing air. He reckoned if he had tried to be more specific and given examples, such as what had happened on the day of John Armitage's visit, he would have been banging his head against the proverbial brick wall. He still hadn't made up his mind whether they were being obstructive or just obtuse; perhaps it was a case of being used to doing things their own way. Taking the longer view, it would need much more than two terms to make any appreciable difference in their case.

With regard to the idea of appointing an additional deputy, he took comfort from the fact that the Governing Body had agreed to his proposal. It had not been as straightforward as he would have hoped, though. One of the staff governors, Mike Benson, appeared to question the proposal on the grounds of whether it was strictly necessary. Taking the bit between the teeth, he had argued the case energetically, stopping short of expressing reservations about Bill Deacon's capacity to do the job. In the end, on the basis that the school should be seen to be supporting its new head, the Governing Body had finally acceded. After that, he had wasted no time in working up an advertisement, which had duly appeared in Friday's press. Provisional dates for short-listing and interviews had been agreed and, despite the usual conventions determining starting dates, he nursed the hope that an exception might be made in view of the school's situation.

'I thought you would want to see today's mail.' He heard Wendy's voice in what sounded like cheerful mode. He had learnt, though, from the incident over Mr Worrall and the Cooper boy, that it was a dangerous assumption to make. If pressed, she would probably have described it as gallows humour built up over a long time working at Bentwood.

'It's the top one!' she gasped, with the kind of expression that passers-by adopt when a fire engine screams past.

Trying not to look unduly alarmed, he absorbed the fact that the letter-head had 'Headteacher' and 'Personal and Confidential' plastered all over it. In other circumstances, he might have taken time to stretch a point in this respect, but his eye had already been caught by the letter's opening paragraph announcing an impending visit from a team of Her Majesty's Inspectors.

'I was just thinking – late February doesn't give much time, does it?' Wendy casually interjected.

His mind seemed to stop working for a moment. Then something snapped inside his head like a blood vessel bursting and he shouted at her: 'Stop being so bloody presumptuous!'

She visibly jumped and took a shocked step back. However, he was in full stride now. 'I wouldn't mind you ripping open an envelope addressed to me, marked "Personal and Confidential", but you even have the nerve to tell me what it says inside!'

There, he had blown it good and proper. Here he was, having prided himself on being the soul of calmness throughout his career, ranting now like a complete lunatic. It wasn't possible to say which one of them looked more anguished.

'Matthew Chalmers never spoke to me like that ... not in fifteen years.'

Tempted to take her to task over such an inane response, he decided to ignore it. Showing no reaction, he feigned getting on with paperwork. As she let out a deep-throated moaning sound and fled the room with a wild, indignant look on her face, he glanced up for the briefest of moments. Determined to stick to his guns, not a muscle flickered in his facial expression.

Was there a destructive streak in him, after all? He felt a strange tingle in his body. Comically, he found himself wondering if a mad scientist hadn't somehow taken control of him. Was this the first tentative step on the way to becoming a full-blown Jekyll and Hyde monstrosity? Foreign to his usual altruistic instincts, yet another question started pounding in his head: didn't the whole damned lot of them need a thorough kicking up the backside?

*

During the course of the first few weeks of term, Caroline couldn't readily explain it but she had begun to feel a lot less settled in her job. In many ways, she missed Simon but was putting it down to the uncertainty surrounding the changeover arrangement. From time to time, she had paused to wonder how he would be getting on in his new school. It was probably because he was so busy that he hadn't got in touch. A few times, she had thought about making contact but decided it would be best not to bother him. Her job was to respond to calls rather than initiate them.

As a PA, it was difficult to be seen as an individual in your own right. The worst part of it was feeling joined at the hip to one's boss. Needing to look after someone else's interests in almost every respect, whether male or female, it was vital to ensure that the partnership kept on the right track. Almost exclusively, she had worked for male bosses. Once, when she was very young, she had learnt a valuable lesson after sliding uncomfortably into a relationship with a married man ill at ease with the frustrations of his family life. It didn't need a degree in human psychology to see that stressed executives could become vulnerable in weak moments to the ready temptation of obliging Girl Fridays.

Fortunately, ever since, she had watched herself very carefully. If she hadn't felt secure, she had learnt ways of managing it diplomatically. Now, in her mid-thirties and still unattached, she was conscious more than ever of wanting to preserve the quality of her life intact. As long as she could satisfy her penchant for smart clothes and regular holidays abroad with friends, she was more than happy. She would have loved to be able to afford a classic sports car but for the time being she was content with her Tigra.

When presenting herself for the post at Ashdown, her first impression of Simon Russell was of a polite and considerate person with a pleasantly understated sense of humour.

She instantly sensed he was a reliable type she would feel happy with. She had also liked the idea of moving into the school setting, where there was a greater degree of free time in the year compared to commerce. When Simon had confided in her about his marriage, she had felt enormous sympathy. She was surprised by him wanting to share it with her. It had come as a shock because there had been no indication anything was wrong in the first place. She prided herself on being able to pick up on the smallest clue if someone close to her was going through a personal crisis. In this instance, she hadn't detected a thing. Perhaps, looking back on it now, that was the whole nature of the trauma for Simon himself. It had been a bolt out of the blue for him too.

Then, equally suddenly, he had announced he was moving to another school. Although she appreciated her own sensitivities were the least important consideration, she couldn't help feeling a slight sense of dissatisfaction in terms of the effect it had on her own situation. Just as she had been beginning to feel comfortable in her work, Simon was up and gone and there was a new relationship to build up all over again. And then in some ways, the fact that Simon hadn't gone for good made everything even more double-edged and complex to adjust to. As things stood, it appeared he would be returning at the start of the next school year in September. To be fair to Richard, he had taken it upon himself to try and allay her concerns as best he could. He had referred to the following two terms as a holding operation. Even the Chair of Governors, Ted Bingham, had taken the trouble to show his appreciation. He had pointed out to her that, with the swap-over of Heads, her role was vital in terms of providing the necessary element of continuity. Thinking more along these lines, she had determined the best outcome would be if things continued to work smoothly and no-one noticed any difference at the end of the two-term period.

She knew from experience, of course, it was never plain sailing changing bosses. Richard Preece was noted for having a determined, some would say hard-edged, streak to his character. From what Caroline knew of him, she could hardly see his general outlook softening when he took on the acting headship. If anything, she was ready for his style to become even more uncompromising. With Simon, there had always been an endearing hesitancy which made her feel he actually liked sounding her out on things. He had never put any onus on her but conveyed the flattering impression he valued her opinion. She thought it attractive in men to have a more vulnerable side to their character.

By contrast, from the very outset, Richard had never seemed in a moment's doubt about anything. Taking up the reins of office, the term 'holding operation' appeared to vanish from his vocabulary. He started with a firmness of intent that seemed instantly to rule out any possibility of Simon ever returning. Once or twice, she had found herself wondering how Simon might have dealt with a given situation, but any such speculation appeared redundant in the light of Richard's innate determination to steam ahead with his own programme of action.

Since Simon's departure, little or no contact seemed to have taken place between the two of them. Granted authority as Acting Headteacher, Richard was evidently intent on living up to the role. After all, the prevalent thinking was that Simon would be up to his neck in sorting things out at this other school. In these circumstances, it was to be taken for granted he wouldn't want anyone worrying him over trivial matters relating to Ashdown.

Nevertheless, taking all this into account, she had found herself agonising over whether she ought to try and keep him fully informed about what was happening. Otherwise, he would wonder later why he hadn't been told. She wanted to avoid misunderstandings which might threaten their working relationship when it resumed. Whenever she thought like this, the question of loyalty arose somewhere at the back of her mind. Accepting she was Richard's PA for the time being, her conscience kept warning her that she owed it to Simon to do her best to protect his interests over the longer term.

On one or two occasions, she had subtly tried to persuade Richard to contact Simon, but his response was always defensive, as if by doing so he would be admitting weakness. Once or twice, she had been on the point of contacting Simon herself but for whatever reason she had held back at the last moment. Nothing ever seemed quite pressing enough on a single-item basis. At the same time, she didn't want him thinking she was in the business of making empty social calls. This was why she had confined herself to sending him a 'Good Luck' card. Certainly, she couldn't deny having felt genuinely concerned for him at the end of the previous term. But the more she gave it thought, absorbing himself in new challenges was probably the best way of taking his mind off other problems in his life. In this sense, she had clung on to the philosophy of 'no news is good news' as a sign he was coping.

It came as a complete shock to her system when Simon arrived unheralded at Ashdown at 5 o'clock that same evening. The first she knew was catching the sound of a knock on her door and thinking it must be one of the school caretakers checking something or other. She knew it couldn't be Richard because he had already set off to an LEA meeting.

Opening her door, she was startled by an angry question thrown her way: 'Where the hell has Philip Cunliffe's picture gone?'

The situation seemed extraordinary, as if she was being harangued by someone she didn't know from Adam.

'The picture?' she repeated, too panicked to think straight.

'Yes, someone's taken the picture down in the entrance area,' he cried out. The relentless, hostile stare in his eyes was foreign to her memory of him. She kept looking as if she must still have got the wrong person. Was it the new school doing this to him?

'Please, come and sit down,' she said, having finally managed to satisfy herself it was indeed Simon and not some insane impostor.

'What else has changed?' he persisted in a resentful tone.

'Shall I make you a cup of coffee?' she offered, keen to assuage his anger. 'What are you doing here?' It seemed a perfectly natural question to ask but she realised it might sound a bit direct, particularly in his present mood.

Luckily, he didn't seem offended. His slowness to reply was because he couldn't think of an answer that made sense. Hadn't he only popped by just on the off-chance after a long, hard day at Bentwood? He didn't think for one moment she would want to hear about the maddening encounters he had had today, particularly the one with Wendy, his so-called PA.

'I was early for an appointment at the estate agent's, so I thought I'd just drop in on the way.' It was the partial truth but he didn't feel like giving any more detailed account of himself. Besides, there were other more immediate concerns to give voice to.

'Even the trophy cabinets aren't where I left them!' he exclaimed with feeling.

She was struck by a pang of guilt. It had crossed her mind at the time he might not take too kindly to the changes. Although of course it wasn't her decision, she recognised she hadn't done anything to try and prevent the re-vamping of the entrance-area. As his PA, she suddenly felt culpable. Handing him a cup of coffee seemed a hollow, worthless gesture, as if it was all she was good for. Shy of making eye-contact for fear she might incur further wrath, she felt as though she had forfeited his trust.

Then, with a totally unexpected brightness to his voice, she was amazed to hear him say almost repentantly, 'It's my fault for not keeping in touch. Anyway, I'm sure none of it is important in the long run.'

Emboldened to look up at him, she now wondered whether he was saying it purely out of kindness. The expression on his face was transformed, almost saintlike in composure. Again, she didn't seem to recognise the person she thought she knew so well.

'I was only thinking how much upheaval I've created myself at Bentwood, and here am I, getting into a lather about one or two piffling changes to the entrance-area!'

To hear him talking in such a philosophical vein felt an enormous relief. It was as if a massive pressure had been lifted off her shoulders. It helped her get over the feeling she was directly accountable for everything.

'If you ask me,' he continued, 'it's not before time that picture of Philip Cunliffe came down. You can have too much of tradition. It holds places back. New situations demand new approaches.'

Was she really hearing him say this? She had to pinch herself. Suddenly, his attention was taken by the time. 'Look, I have to go. As I said, I have to be at the estate agent's.'

'Are things going well . . . generally?' she nervously asked, almost as an afterthought. It would have been remiss of her not to inquire after his general welfare.

'Yes . . .' he said thoughtfully, but again feeling reluctant to expand. Reverting to a more businesslike tone, he added: 'Tell Richard I'll give him a ring at some point in the near future. I'm glad we got the chance to have a chat. Take care!'

She watched carefully as he departed. Fortunately, he retraced his steps back to the entrance-area. For one moment, she had thought he might go to his room. She wasn't at all sure how he would have reacted to the fact Richard had had it redecorated in the claret and blue colours of his favourite local football team.

Chapter 9

Gasping for breath, Tom Judd felt an initial burst of relief. At least it hadn't been the wretched nightmare in which he was manically arranging lines and lines of white powder. Allowing a few moments to recover, he wasn't sure whether relief was the right word for it. In the dream he had just woken from, he was running with Mark Leslie along the deserted Magilligan Sands in a gale-force wind that was blowing them backwards. For some reason, he had let out a shriek but it was lost in the deafening roar blasting across the beach like sustained artillery-fire. They were running towards the familiar turning-point at Mussenden Temple, five miles distant. Out to sea, choppy waves were heaving up and down. Everything in view looked raw and threatening. He sensed the need to protect Mark. After reaching the foot of the cliffs, they turned back. The wind was directly behind them now. They were running fast but Mark was bowling along at an incredible speed. Tom cried out for him to stop but his voice didn't carry. He was racing further and further away. Clouds were scudding by and Tom couldn't make anything out. There was a last roar and then suddenly everything was still. His eyes frantically scanned the huge expanse of sand but his friend was nowhere to be seen . . .

Reminding himself it was almost twenty years ago, he started to wonder why his subconscious was haunting him with the memory. It still racked him with guilt how he had scoffed at Mark for varying the route home each time. Considering the number of deaths he had reported himself, it had been the height of irresponsibility. Contrary to his dream, Mark hadn't gone missing out there on the beach. An hour after they had finished the practice run, it was IRA weaponry that had roared unforgivingly. Mark was singled out, while he himself had managed to crawl free of the car wreckage when the guns had fallen silent and the assassins had departed. The tragedy might have taken place two decades ago, but time had completely failed in terms of its proverbial healing power. The pungent smell of burning oil as the car caught fire seemed as vivid to him now as it did on that wretched summer day in Ulster. As if to expunge the lingering taste from his mouth, he hauled himself out of bed and strode to the bathroom. Brushing his teeth, he distractedly studied a chart he kept on the wall beside the basin.

Using it to switch his mind away from the memory of Mark Leslie, he took consolation in the fact that he had crossed off fourteen weeks. Despite his continuing propensity for the odd malt, he had proudly stayed clean from coke for a total of ninety-eight days. 'One day at a time!' was the message he had had rammed into his head by Rob, his sponsor, whose job it was to shepherd him through the arduous twelve steps, supporting him in ways only another recovering cokehead was able to do. The long-haul Cocaine Help programme was geared to twenty months. Staring at the chart put things in perspective; he could see where he was and how much further he still had to go. 'One day at a time, one step at a time!' he knew he had to keep telling himself. The analogy was often made to mounting an unending staircase. You could never afford to speculate too far ahead. It was vital just to concentrate on putting one foot in front of the other. Otherwise, you could fall back down again to the bottom in the blink of an eye.

After his last encounter with Suzanne (he sincerely hoped it would be the last), he had spent the whole of the next day repeating over and over the Serenity Prayer that always ended the CH meetings: 'God, grant me the serenity to accept the things I cannot change; courage to change the things I can; and wisdom to know the difference.'

He didn't need to look at the copy of the prayer on the wall. He knew it by heart. Realising that carrying out the message was the most difficult part, he further recognised it was about defining boundaries and sticking to them. It meant doing everything necessary to prevent relapsing. That was what had persuaded him to cut himself off from so many of his previous friends. In particular he couldn't afford to hang around those who, through no harmful intention of their own, were able to go on enjoying their lives to the full, and sleep it off whilst not getting addicted. It was revealing how many of his former friends fitted into this category. But for him, there was no halfway house. Everything was black or white. The stakes had suddenly become so high that he had to take courage into his hands and cut himself off. At times, he felt so isolated both in mind and body that his instinct was to seize on anyone's company so long as it didn't remind him of his addiction or past troubles.

He couldn't deny that clinging on to the prayer's message had helped him to rationalise and make sense of his life. His previous failure to do so had further exposed him to the obsession. For increasingly over the past fourteen weeks, his biggest realisation was that he actually became an addict the very first time he snorted. He had come to see that the problem had never been the coke itself. It was more an outward symptom of a mysterious pain that had started up some time in his childhood and resurfaced with a bang after America. Equally, he understood that saying no to coke wasn't going to 'cure' him as such. Recovery from addiction was an essential part of the programme, but the harder truth, more unpalatable in many ways, was that his life needed complete overhauling. You couldn't hope to make progress on this front just by sitting tight and ticking numbers off on a chart.

There were many different ways he had tried to fill the vacuum so that he wouldn't have time on his hands to sit there dwelling on his misfortunes. For example, simple as it sounded, taking physical exercise was helping greatly. He had enrolled at a gym and was endeavouring to keep to the weekly schedule devised for him by one of the assistants there. For someone who had spent the whole of his life rebelling against any form of regimentation, he appeared to be succumbing to it as gently as a lamb at the moment. He seemed positively to crave the comfort to be gained from following robotic routines. An hour's input made up of a mindless twenty minutes on the treadmill, a further twenty on the bike on a so-called hill climb and a final twenty grappling with dumb-bells not only gave him a curious satisfaction from completing the challenge but also an enhanced sense of physical well-being. Heretically, at the start, he had even likened the sensation to the early stages of a high from coke but quickly dismissed it as a far from helpful comparison to be making in the circumstances. Driven by his memories of Mark, he had worked up a vision somewhere at the back of his mind of entering for a half-marathon again, or if he allowed his demons literally to run away with him, why not the full course? If he worked out a training programme and managed to keep to it, surely it was within his capabilities?

Another positive benefit from taking physical exercise was the boost it had given his self-esteem. Feeling the instinct to reward himself after a session, he had built up a pattern of other innocent pastimes in a further attempt to promote a mood of contentment. The gym was just a short walk away from his flat. On the way back, he would treat himself to a large mug of decaff cappuccino at the local Starbucks and take time doing his cryptic *Guardian* crossword. You couldn't be a journalist without liking to play with words. Previously, such activities would have seemed rather trivial but, following on from his physical exertions, it made him feel much more at ease with himself.

Work permitting, he would try to get there as often as he could during the week. But his job was a huge bugbear in this respect. Its very nature threatened his capacity to make any real progress in overcoming problems. Insultingly, it seemed as if he had only been given the assignment because he was considered some kind of expert in the field of human depravity. Although teenage bingeing was sometimes described as a new phenomenon, there was nothing really new about it at all. The project, dressed up as a research study by an ambitious editor, concentrated on big city centres infected at night by swarms of teenagers exhibiting animalistic behaviour around clubs. One part of his job had been to interview spokesmen for the local magistrates, who had caved in to the powerful brewery lobby by granting new licences in their hundreds. Now the government was even talking about twenty-four-hour licences. He knew he should have turned down the work but he was desperate for the money.

Emma McCready had never supposed it would be easy breaking up with Ralph. At certain times, particularly over the last two or three years of their relationship, she had found it utterly impossible to know what to do for the best. Throughout the whole of that troubled period, her mind had veered wildly between the two extreme mindsets. One was praying he would decide to leave Maggie for good. The other was cursing the day she had set eyes on him in the first place. The added complication was that she felt sure he would have left his wife if she had chosen to press the matter. He had so often asked her if that was what she wanted him to do. Nor was there any real issue of guilt over children. Both his sons were in their twenties and settled in jobs away from home. However, although she could see it was her own happiness at stake, the idea of pushing him into making a choice seemed repugnant. It was only when she hadn't seen him for a few days that the dreadful thought occurred to her that she was deceiving herself. But whatever voices she heard in her head, she never felt compelled to put things to the test.

She was sympathetic enough to realise how damaging the effect of losing her husband might be on Maggie. The bouts of depression which had, according to Ralph, taken hold in recent times would undoubtedly have ended up destroying her. In one sense, it had been a continuing source of relief to Emma that Maggie had never found out about their relationship. As for herself, although she felt she knew Maggie well enough from Ralph's descriptions, she had never actually laid eyes on her. Nevertheless, without mentioning it to him, Emma had often debated with herself whether to force the situation by making contact. In the end, she had resisted that option as well. No doubt, looking back now, it had been the constant agonising over the whys and wherefores that had scuppered the relationship. Absurdly, the question of Maggie's vulnerability had completely taken over as the key issue in the range of considerations, ethical or otherwise.

The passion that had first driven them into each other's arms had subsided long before any final decision needed taking. Ardent memories of the heightened excitement of first carnal acts, intensified by the sensation of stolen fruit, had become tamely diluted along the way. It was as if someone above had ordained that the purity of the juice was too strong for their own good. Ultimately, no scenario seemed to present itself that offered grounds for optimism about the future. In many ways, it had made her feel as depressed as the woman she was deceiving.

Although she didn't think of it as an act of kindness at the time, with the advantage of hindsight, she could see now that Ralph had looked to put her out of her misery. At first, however, she had seen it as an almighty nerve. He, who never seemed able to make his mind up about anything, must have had to steel himself to break the news. She wouldn't have minded but, as a young woman, it was troubling having to accept that she had wasted her precious twenties on an older man who had brought her nothing but anxiety and premature grey hair. It might well have been the only alternative left in a relationship that was going nowhere, but it just didn't seem fair that he should be the one to decide the outcome. Despite all the misery and despair she had suffered, the sad reality was it mattered more to her than it did to him. She had firmly believed he was the one who stood to get hurt when, all the time, it was herself. Even in her most vulnerable moments, she had taken it for granted he needed her rather than the other way around.

Surely, he couldn't have failed to see she was the trapped one in the relationship. Hadn't they both always understood, even if tacitly, that their lives were inextricably linked? Irrespective of him being married, it counted for very little in truth. Couldn't he have accepted that, however unhappily things tended to drag on, life was always full of imponderables which might or might not be resolved today, tomorrow or the next day? In the last resort, however dissatisfied she might have felt over a period of time, she had hated the moment arriving when a line was drawn under their relationship and it was pronounced over. The reason why she was incapable of summoning up the energy to be angry was probably because, in the end, she had to concede it was the only acceptable outcome. If it meant having to change her whole outlook on life, it was something she would just have to adapt to. Transforming the way she presented herself to the world was one way of putting the experience behind her.

It had always been in her character to be determined in everything she did. From childhood, she had been fiercely independent and keen to do her best. Although her parents were originally from a poor part of Ireland, she had been born in the relative affluence of Manchester. Patrick, her younger brother, had been born physically disabled and destined to be in a wheelchair all his life. As a result, Emma had grown up much more appreciative of the fact she was sound of limb herself. In her early teens, she had developed the irrational fear that her body might somehow fall to pieces if she didn't exercise vigorously. It felt as if she was compensating for Patrick's incapacity to take part in sport. At school, her favourite subject was PE, and winning a place in the athletic team meant everything to her. Small and hardly weighing anything, she was led by her natural stamina to specialise in cross-country running. She had studied A-levels and won a place at Loughborough University, where she trained to be a PE teacher. Eventually, she had become Head of Department.

As other people collected stamps or antiques as a hobby, Emma stored up marathon events. In recent times, she had become more ambitious in her choice of venues. Over the years, she had taken part in most of the main UK events, including London. She had also run in Europe, but the previous November she had extended her horizons to New York. Running for charity seemed to justify all the effort she put into her training. Although Patrick was in his late twenties now, she had never let herself forget how disadvantaged he had been in his boyhood. This was why she had come to enlist as a member of a team raising funds for the disabled.

She had anticipated that New York would be exciting but it had blown her senses. The sheer vibrancy of the city, its electric charge, together with the massive scale of the skyscrapers, had rocked her emotions. On Ellis Island, staring across at the Statue of Liberty, she had felt at one with the millions of others before her who had breathed in the heady atmosphere and found themselves hopelessly intoxicated. The initial reservations she had harboured about brash American extravagance and hollow materialism had been transformed along the way into unswerving admiration. Up to the morning of the race itself, the physical activity seemed for once to pale into insignificance beside the overwhelming attractiveness of the setting. Then, caught up in the thrill of the event as never before, she had felt carried along on a cushion of air across the five islands to the final stretch through Central Park. The cheering crowds of spectators round the course seemed to propel the runners forward at breakneck speed. She had beaten her personal best by a couple of minutes or so.

Landing back in Manchester, she felt as though the experience had given her a reinvigorated belief in the possibility of achieving greater things. For example, she had always nursed the ambition of becoming a deputy head but wasn't sure if she had the confidence to branch out beyond her subject-area. Part of her felt quite comfortable conforming to the stereotype picture of the PE teacher donning a tracksuit all the time. But since adopting a different, more adventurous outlook to life, she had not only gone on the right training courses but surprised people by occasionally wearing a smart suit. It was amazing the effect it seemed to have. She was used to thinking of herself as rather plain and ordinary but it rapidly dawned on her that a deputy headship was not beyond her powers so long as she was willing to look and act the part. Of course, she knew she was kidding herself if she thought it was all down to power-dressing, but it was amazing how everyone seemed to react as if she had suddenly converted herself into management material overnight.

Determined to show she could succeed, she was ready to put her inhibitions behind her and make a statement about how she wanted to present herself to the world. Even so, she never imagined she would resort to such a radical change as dyeing her hair. The possible adverse reaction of others had left her feeling very nervous. She had suspected people might accuse her of being false and pretentious. But it had only taken a single glance in the mirror at the salon to convince herself the change had been long overdue. In fact, it made her cringe thinking what she must have looked like before. As if her main objective was to remain anonymous, she had been content to stick to the same old-fashioned image. Despite her trepidation, the visit to the salon had been an undoubted success. It had certainly made heads turn in the staff room! Then, she had found a letter waiting for her at home saying she had been called for interview. It was the first deputy job she had applied for. On impulse, she had splashed out on a new red outfit and a gorgeous little pair of black shoes. It had all worn rather a big hole in her credit account. What the heck!

Claret and blue were the colours on Richard Preece's mind: regrettably those of his football team that had just been thrashed 4–1 at home. He and his two sons were trooping out of the stadium in the company of thousands of other disconsolate fans. It hadn't been an altogether happy season so far and the team was languishing an uncomfortable point or two above the relegation-zone.

Apart from his wife and family, Richard's other consuming passions in life were football and school. He couldn't help feeling Ashdown was in an almost identical predicament to his beloved football team. Both had known former glory days. Since being a pupil there himself, the fortunes of school and team had always seemed synonymous. Stretching back twenty years, he had stood shoulder to shoulder on the terrace with his mates, chanting the side on to championship success. But then a decline had set in. For a football team, the downward slide could be unerringly measured in terms of defeats and subsequent relegation.

Trudging back to the car, as the car park took time to clear, it was their familiar ritual to tune in to *Sports Report* on the radio and catch the classified results and match reports. However, despite the boys' lively interest, Richard found himself unable to concentrate, dwelling instead on his team's plight. Even worse, he started comparing the situation with school. As far as the football went, he wasn't arrogant enough to think he could do a better job as manager. He was pretty sure, though, he was capable of lifting the fortunes of Ashdown so long as he was given enough time to tackle it. That wasn't to say he didn't respect Simon Russell. He had many qualities and had served a goodly stint. But for all faithful servants, there was a time when the energy started waning. He could only imagine how he would feel when he reached his mid-fifties. Probably, by that stage, it would be tempting to join the advisory service or consider early retirement.

To be honest, he found it totally incomprehensible why Simon had taken it upon himself, at his age, to carry out missionary work in such a tough school as Bentwood. He could only think his wife's desertion had separated him from his senses. As always with Simon, it was difficult to know for sure what was going on under the surface. At first, Richard had just taken it at face value when he had announced he was going. On a personal basis, it had suited him well enough. After all, he was on the point of applying for a headship. Doing two terms would give valuable experience for the future. He had always assumed he would have to apply externally.

Now, five weeks in, he knew it might sound smug but he felt utterly confident in his ability to do the job to the highest standard. Even in this short space of time, he had demonstrated what could be achieved with a more active, hands-on approach to management. The trouble with Simon, and Philip Cunliffe before him, was that they took things almost for granted and then wondered why things went wrong. By contrast, his own greatest strength was the ability to grasp the realities of a situation and make the most of it. The categorical imperative facing any modern-day headteacher, or football manager for that matter, was to embrace the climate of change with a positive attitude. As far as the future of Ashdown was concerned, nothing whatsoever was to be gained by looking back to the past. Call it symbolic, but that was why the picture of Philip Cunliffe had had to go. Deep down, he wasn't sure whether he could stomach going back to being a deputy again. But until Simon made his future intentions clear, he was stuck in no-man's-land. It went completely against the grain to go on acting as a stand-in. It wasn't anything to do with being disloyal to Ashdown, simply that he had to sort out his own future. This was what had prompted him a week ago to send for details of a headship post in another school. In normal circumstances, he would have consulted Simon first, but instead he had taken it upon himself to broach the matter with the Chair of Governors.

'Dad, are we staying here for ever?' The frustrated tone of the plea gave an added edge of irony to the thoughts he had been having. His attention switched automatically back to the radio. All the main match reports seemed to have finished. Looking out across the park, he could see it was virtually empty. They would normally have been halfway home by now. It wasn't like him to be slow off the mark. Concentrating on the road ahead, he decided there was nothing for it but to fill in the application form as soon as possible.

Chapter 10

Tom Judd was wedged in the middle of a horde of unruly young teenage girls, queuing to gain entrance to an Underage Club at 5 o'clock on a Saturday afternoon. Events were conspiring against him even more cruelly than usual. His fellow-reporter Tanya hadn't shown up and nor had the photographer. He was also supposed to be interviewing a local police inspector but he was nowhere to be seen either. None of this made him feel one jot better, abandoned as he was in the midst of a sea of mini-skirts, skimpy tops and precocious footwear. In the manner of an anthropologist studying the habits of an esoteric indigenous population, he couldn't help but be disturbed by the sheer volume of body-piercings, ranging from eyebrows to bare bellies protruding under midriff tops. Flesh was being paraded as if it were going out of fashion, not to mention it was a bitterly cold day in January.

In a few more moments, his senses were further assaulted by the arrival of a sinister-looking detachment of Goths, kitted out in long black leather coats and vertiginous platform boots but even more distinctive for their pan-stick make-up. They oozed a kind of tribal disdain for anyone not similarly attired. Eventually, he felt prompted to make a hasty, ill-considered retreat down a flight of steps towards the back of the establishment for a breath of fresh air. Thinking he had escaped the worst, he narrowly managed to avoid putting his foot in a puddle of vomit before encountering a group of youths knocking back cans of alcopop.

At this point, he would have given anything to be able to turn his back on the whole sordid business. Casting one last despairing glance around in hope of finding another adult, he picked up sight of a middle-aged man walking along the street in his direction. Although still twenty paces or so away, there seemed something vaguely familiar about him. But Tom couldn't be sure. Then, as he stood there trying to work it out, a voice from the crowd had shouted out coarsely: 'Hey Sir, fancy a beer?'

He noted how, understandably, the figure ignored the offer and tried to continue on his way. It was Tom's own fault that, recognising his fellow tenant, a greeting somehow escaped his lips.

'Hi there, Simon!'

Doubly mortified, Simon Russell's face bore the hounded look of a stag cornered on all sides.

'What's going on here?' he let out awkwardly, as if happening upon a bit of barging in a school dinner queue.

Then, a girl with spiky, purple-dyed hair, followed up: 'Fancy a snog, Sir?'

As a howl of derision went up amongst the baying pack, Tom felt a compelling instinct to rescue his friend from any worsening predicament.

For his own part, Simon was completely mystified by the turn of events. One moment, he had been strolling in leisurely fashion back to his flat from a visit to Habitat in search of light fittings. The next, he had obviously been spotted on the street by one or two Bentwood pupils. As if this wasn't enough, he had then found himself bundled into a seedy-looking club ostensibly for self-protection.

Simon remembered Tom saying he worked with young people but without going into much detail. He had the impression at the time he must be a social worker or something similar. He wasn't sure now. Before he could elicit any further information, they had already sidestepped two bemused-looking bouncers and collided with a police officer.

'Inspector Pearson,' a squat, overweight figure in uniform announced himself.

'Oh, I didn't think you'd be inside,' Tom blurted out.

'Yes, it looked much safer,' the Inspector tried to joke before turning more serious. 'If you've got questions to ask, you'd better make it quick.'

As Tom took out a note-pad and launched into his interview, Simon set about excusing himself. But the Inspector went on talking very earnestly, rapidly switching his agitated gaze from one to the other and back again. For the time being, it was hard to escape.

'I don't mind telling you, this is a policing nightmare. We're effectively baby-sitting rather than crime-fighting. If they're coming to the disco, that's OK. Otherwise we tell them to go home. But they don't. Many of them, the worst ones, just want to hang about getting drunk even at this time of day and cause nuisance.'

Looking around, Simon found himself becoming more nervous again. The bouncers were now beginning to let youngsters in. Another encounter with some motley crew from Bentwood looked very much on the cards. But it still remained difficult to extricate himself because Inspector Pearson was lecturing them ever more intensely. His innate respect for officers of the law would have made it seem like an act of civil disobedience to ignore what was being said to him.

Meanwhile, Tom kept feeding more and more questions. 'But you can have them for under-age drinking, surely?'

Something seemed to make Inspector Pearson uncomfortable for a moment. 'You *are* both reporters, aren't you?'

The pair of them exchanged quizzical glances. Waiting in vain for Simon to say something, Tom took it upon himself to introduce his associate with an inescapable tone of pride.

'No, my friend is a headteacher.'

The Inspector looked at Simon with renewed interest. 'Oh, you'll know what I'm talking about then. It's the same young people. You'd be interested to see them in a different context, I expect?'

Although he still couldn't quite work out how he had become embroiled in all this, it was getting more awkward to back out of by the minute. It felt as if there was an onus on him to demonstrate solidarity with this other arm of public services.

'So you're on for a walk round the patch tonight?' Inspector Pearson inquired with the force of a rhetorical question. Disconcertingly, he was still addressing both of them. Simon was painfully aware of getting drawn into something that had nothing to do with him. Seemingly in league, they were both staring in his direction for an answer.

'It would be merely in an observer capacity?' he pathetically sought to establish.

'Oh, yes, we won't have you in the front line! Nine o'clock by the Black Prince then? And let's see what the evening brings. If it's like the last few weeks, I don't think you'll be disappointed!'

Most of the teenage crowd had squeezed inside by now. For a short while, they stood together watching the melee in front of them. To Tom's relief, the photographer had finally turned up and at once started taking shots of youngsters cavorting around the dance area. When he started training his camera on a couple fumbling in a dark corner, Simon felt it was definitely time for him to leave.

'Say, I kind of feel responsible for you getting mixed up in all of this,' he heard Tom's voice drawl in that transatlantic twang he seemed to revert to on certain occasions. What was there he could say in response? He certainly hadn't chosen to get involved.

'No, you shouldn't feel bad about it,' he replied tolerantly, but determined he wasn't going to turn up for the 9 o'clock encounter.

'Look, I'm going to be here probably no more than another half-hour. Why don't we meet up at Brown's for dinner? That would be civilised. Don't worry, I'll pick up the tab,' Tom gallantly offered.

Flinching, Simon protested: 'Er . . . I'm not sure.'

But Tom wouldn't budge. 'It's the very least I can do. We can have a relaxed meal and then go straight from there. What say we meet in the entrance at seven?'

'Um . . . er . . . fine,' he heard himself weakly acceding.

Outside, the fresh air seemed to make his brain start working again. Reproaching himself, he had cause to wonder why he was so assertive at school and yet such a complete doormat anywhere else.

That evening, Simon and Tom met up as planned to share dinner together. They talked a lot about living in Leeds and spare-time activities. Although it wasn't such an easy topic for Simon, because he didn't have many, he listened willingly enough to Tom going on about his fitness centre. It even made him feel he perhaps ought to take up something similar himself. They had a pleasant enough meal.

Dutifully, they then complied with the arrangement to meet up with Inspector Pearson and his henchmen in the city-centre. They stayed in the vicinity for about an hour or so. The Inspector seemed keen to give an account of what had happened so far on the patch, a business precinct studded with neon-lit drinking halls. The list of incidents to date seemed imposing. Two drunks had been picked up with stab wounds. An ambulance had had to be called for a woman stoned out of her mind. Two men had been forcibly ejected from a pub. A complaint had been made by a man insisting he had been assaulted by a doorman, but the CCTV camera hadn't apparently shown anything conclusive. Reports had been received of an unprovoked attack and a victim had been found on a kerb, nursing a bleeding head wound that needed several stitches.

'And that's what we call a quiet night!' said the Inspector rather predictably. It was obvious he was out to impress them with the scale of the task.

The pair of them stayed on a while as messages were frantically relayed back and forth on walkie-talkies. Eventually, they bowed out gracefully instead of staying on for what Inspector Pearson called 'red meat' time.

Tom, feeling able to wind down at the end of his reporting stint, suggested they find a place to go and have a quiet drink. It was an odd sensation to Simon, being out and about. In another sense, it felt strangely empowering. Despite himself, he was almost happy to be roaming town in someone else's company. He was more than willing to leave it to Tom to decide where to go. Besides, he wouldn't have known where to start. They went to one pub and came out after two or three drinks. He had half-pints and Tom had double Scotches. Tom insisted they go to another pub with what he called 'a better atmosphere'. Despite staying there a while, Tom started to get a little restless again, as if he was looking for yet more excitement. Simon suggested they went home but, with a beseeching look, Tom talked him into stopping off for one last drink in another pub.

When they got through the door, Simon's apprehensions were immediately raised by the spectacle of semi-naked women dancing erotically on a stage. Wanting to hide his face, Simon didn't plan on staying a moment longer and turned on his heels.

'It's only fun!' Tom shouted out over the boom of the music. As if to prove his point, he glanced nonchalantly in Simon's direction before wandering over to take a first-hand look for himself. Rooted to the spot, Simon watched in disbelief. Tom suddenly appeared to recognise someone and became extremely incensed. At first, Simon suspected his anger was directed towards a person in the crowd. But the next moment he saw Tom gesticulating wildly at one of the women on stage and screaming at the top of his voice: 'Give me back my money, you tart!'

Scrambling to lever himself on to the stage, he found it was higher up than he had thought. From a distance, he looked suspended in mid-air. It didn't stop him continuing to hurl abuse. Finally, one of the women moved forward with an almost pitying expression on her face. Simon thought she was about to assist him. The last thing he heard Tom shouting was: 'No, Suzanne! No, Suzanne! Please, no!'

The mention of the name vividly reminded Simon of his encounter outside Tom's apartment. He felt a sudden frisson of anticipation. As the woman moved nearer, the expression on her face changed from sympathetic to taunting. With an effortless backlift of a thigh boot, she delivered a single blow to Tom's groin that sent him crashing to the ground four or five feet below. As soon as his body hit the floor, he was surrounded by a posse of attendants who hauled him unceremoniously to his feet and frogmarched him off the premises. Confined to the role of onlooker, the only consolation Simon could think of was that Inspector Pearson hadn't been on hand to witness the scene.

The whole unfortunate evening ended with Simon taking Tom back to the apartment block and putting him to bed. Although Tom was still in pain, at least all the anger had been knocked out of him. Puzzlingly, he kept on mumbling the same words time and again: 'God, grant me the serenity . . .' He was evidently struggling to finish his sentence, but Simon didn't know whether to put it down to physical suffering or plain memory lapse.

It was only when Simon was going to the bathroom to fetch a glass of water that he happened to see a prayer on the wall that started with these words. He was also intrigued to spot a chart by the side of it with dates and ticks all over it. Unable to make sense of the chart, he made a mental note to ask Tom about it in the morning. He could only think it must have something to do with some possible fitness regime.

Returning to the bedroom, he discovered Tom lying face down on the bed asleep and snoring with his mouth wide open. Simon prodded him on to his side. As he went on looking at Tom, albeit not a pleasant sight, he was surprised that he managed to put feelings of revulsion to one side. Not so long ago, his response to the situation would have been one of mild contempt. He still couldn't say he approved of Tom's behaviour but, despite himself, he felt a lot more compassionate than he might have expected. Hoping it didn't boil down to just weakness on his part, he defended himself on the grounds it wasn't right to dissociate himself from Tom at this point. For one thing, it would have been far too easy. He couldn't exactly explain why, but he felt determined to assist in whatever way he could. In essence, it had become a duty of care.

He had looked after countless thousands of adolescents before but it was the first time he had taken such responsibility for a grown-up. But taking another glance at Tom lying there helplessly, he decided he definitely looked much more like a child than an adult.

Chapter 11

Sitting on her own in a cramped office, Emma McCready was trying her best to keep calm. In less than ten minutes' time she was due to be called for her final interview. Other types of dreadful experiences rumbled through her mind, but not even the dentist's chair came anywhere near. At least it was possible to anticipate the exact nature of the physical pain from having a tooth drilled. This was proving such a stressful up-and-down experience, she couldn't possibly guess how it might end.

From the evidence so far, she couldn't have done too badly. The proof was that she had been shortlisted through to the final stage. The cut-off point had come after lunchtime when three of the original five candidates were told they were still in business. It was the impression she was making on Simon Russell that she was most worried about. She wasn't sure what to make of him. Or, more to the point, what he was making of her. One moment, he seemed calm and almost laid back, trying to put everyone at ease with amusing little asides. The next, he came across as intensely analytical and wound up. She found it impossible to know how to react. In the end, she had thought it better just to be true to her own personality. She hoped he would be able to tell she was committed to her work. At certain points, she had said things which had amused the more extrovert-looking panel-members, although the most she had been able to extract from Simon was a cautious smile.

With all the waiting around, it was difficult to keep things in perspective. Was there any significance in being called first? At least, it would be over and done with quicker. Anxiously, she glanced around the cramped little room and began to fear she had misheard the instructions. Perhaps Simon Russell wasn't coming to take her to the room and she should be going there on her own. She began to panic, wondering if it was not too late to withdraw. But, however tempting, she knew she had to be bold because there was no going back.

Mulling things over in her mind, she felt it had been right to admit to the panel she had been in two minds about applying for the post in the first place. Otherwise, it might have seemed she just sailed into things without thinking. On the positive side, the advert and details had been attractively presented. To her mind, it looked like a school that was going places. She further welcomed the fact that the Head had been up-front in his letter to candidates about the toughness of the challenge. And yes, perhaps on the downside, she knew enough about its current position to be aware he was telling the truth. The fact that he hadn't been there long himself was an added recommendation. For one thing, it meant he couldn't be to blame for Bentwood being put into special measures in the first place.

She knew enough about schools to know you could never tell what the atmosphere was like until you saw it first-hand. In the event, she had not witnessed anything unduly worrying. She and the other candidates had been given an informal tour by representatives of the Student Council. Although some classes looked a little unsettled, by and large things were under control. At one point, she had spotted Simon Russell in action, marshalling pupils down a long corridor in a friendly but purposeful manner. She had been impressed that he was there on the spot, visible to everyone.

'Emma! I'm sorry to keep you waiting!' It sounded startling to hear his voice again, as if it was the last thing she had been expecting.

'I ought to tell you that one of the other candidates has just dropped out . . . er, withdrawn,' he elected to mention, rather irritably. His manner seemed a little agitated and she felt an instinct to soothe him. But wasn't it her own nerves she should be bothered about?

'Not that it affects your own position, I hasten to add!'

She wasn't sure how to construe this. Could his words be taken to mean she had no stronger chance now, even though the field was down to two? She told herself to stop putting irrational interpretations on things. He seemed to be motioning her out of the room and she rose to her feet. Then he seemed to be pondering something and remained rooted to the spot, as if puzzled and unsure what he was doing. For a ludicrous-seeming moment, it occurred to her she might even need to remind him about the prospective interview, in case he had forgotten.

'It's just that . . .' he started hesitantly. She strained to pick up the end of the sentence but it didn't seem to be forthcoming. They stood there for several uncomfortable moments staring blankly at one another. The tension was only broken when he smiled unexpectedly and said in a bright tone of voice: 'Tell me, *you* don't think it's such a terrible place, do you?'

'Of course, I don't!' she responded. She didn't like to tell him she had been thinking of withdrawing herself, even if it had been down to nerves.

'Oh, that's good then!'

The huge smile that irradiated his face banished any remaining trace of nerves she may have had. As she left the room in Simon's company, the interview seemed to have become altogether less menacing in prospect.

At the end of his duty, Bill Deacon returned to his office. Slumping down in his chair, he was relieved lunchtime had passed off uneventfully. As with maiden flights of aeroplanes, 'uneventful' was the best verdict you could have. On certain days, particularly when it was chucking it down and the cherubs had to be inside, proper supervision was impossible. He had never had much success trying to persuade other staff to volunteer. In his view, the culture in schools wasn't a patch on the spirit and camaraderie he recalled from his days in the RAF. It wasn't as if he didn't understand where teaching staff were coming from. Given the wear and tear of being at the chalk face all day, he acknowledged the benefit of taking time out at lunchtime to recharge the batteries. Simon Russell had come up with a scheme involving payment of staff. Not unexpectedly, it only seemed to entice one or two who were attracted by the extra pocket-money.

On the point of pouring himself a coffee from his flask, he caught sight of a note on his desk. Examining it more closely, he recognised Wendy's slanted handwriting. The note read: '*Just to let you know. 3 down – 2 to go!*'

His immediate reaction was that he didn't need busybody Wendy telling him what was going on around the place. He had his own ways of finding out, thank you very much. He already knew that one of the three shortlisted candidates for the afternoon had offended Simon Russell by dropping out at the end of lunchtime. Apart from the fact she liked to spread gossip, he didn't know why she was getting so excited. Probably she was jumping on the bandwagon of staff disapproval towards the whole idea of the appointment in the first place. Or, perhaps, as the latest paid-up member of the club to have had a bollocking from the new head, she was gratified to see this project of his taking a bit of a nosedive.

Personally speaking, this wasn't a day he had been much looking forward to. He understood what some staff meant when they said the money could be better spent appointing two classroom teachers instead of creating another management post. Probably, there wouldn't have been so much complaining if the appointment had been internal, but the Head in his wisdom had rejected all six inside candidates without qualm at the shortlisting stage. Bill knew that the likes of Mike Benson had complained from the outset that the post wasn't really necessary. Now that someone was being sought from outside, it seemed even more of a snub to those who had dedicated long years of service to the school. Apart from that, there was the extra cost.

All in all, he had thought it appropriate to keep himself out of the way during the last day or so. According to a reliable source, some of the senior staff were doing their best, subtly or otherwise, to put candidates off. Simon Russell would no doubt have been livid if he had caught wind of it, but again Bill didn't feel it was in his own best interests to get too closely involved. A part of him remained sceptical anyway about whether candidates would allow themselves to be influenced one way or another by what people might tell them on the grapevine. If they had their heads screwed on, they made their own minds up. Never mind all the behind-scenes skulduggery, everything seemed to be going off as per programme as far as he could tell.

If he had been asked his opinion (which, incidentally, he hadn't, especially not by Simon Russell), he would probably have agreed with the need for a second deputy head appointment. After all, wasn't he the one who had argued, until he was blue in the face, that he was overloaded as single Deputy having to do the job of two people all the time? For this reason, he had never been able to concentrate on any one thing for long enough. It was bound to affect his performance and probably helped to explain why, in the long run, he had not been shortlisted when they were casting around for a successor to Matthew Chalmers. Or perhaps it was taken for granted that those who were there when the school went into special measures were tarred with the brush of failure. Although he hadn't made much fuss at the time, he thought it pretty insulting that one of those management consultancy firms had been authorised to pull in a fly-by-night outsider. In his view, such an approach couldn't help but add to the existing state of instability. What the school desperately needed was a permanent successor in place. He accepted it stood in Simon Russell's favour that he was an existing head with several years' experience behind him. But then, if you were brought in from the cold, it was inevitably going to take much longer to get up to speed. The main trouble with the new head, Bill felt, was that he seemed trigger-happy implementing change. Of course, there were bound to be things that needed tweaking but it didn't seem fair to condemn existing arrangements out of hand.

Suspiciously, the main criterion for the new deputy head appointment seemed to boil down to willingness to roar into action at the speed of light. Except for sharing a cup of coffee with candidates in a general get-together the day before, Bill had not seen all that much of them, let alone either of the candidates taking part in the final session this afternoon. Of course he had made it his business to know which of the five it was ultimately down to. Of the two, he felt more pleasantly disposed towards the man, who seemed a decent, hard-working type. He had to admit, though, he didn't care much for the woman candidate. She had even taken the liberty of quizzing him about his management style. As if it was any business of hers! When he had sought to deflect the question a bit, he couldn't help but catch her withering glance.

The morning session had not exactly gone to plan for Simon. He may have felt more reassured by what he had just heard from Emma McCready but he still knew a tough afternoon lay ahead. Though the six-strong panel had condescended in the end to take another look at certain candidates, he felt it had needed all his powers of persuasion; they had seemed hell-bent on undermining the credentials of each successive candidate.

There was no way he could relay any of this sub-plot to Emma. Of the two remaining candidates, she was his preferred choice by a street. With the afternoon session looming, he appreciated that everything was still in the melting-pot. The other remaining candidate, Brian Roebuck, had half-impressed him with an air of steadiness. But the job was going to need more than that. It would need considerable drive and energy. Much more than any other candidate, Emma lived up to the mental picture he had in mind of what it would take to carry out the role effectively. Everything he had seen so far pointed inescapably to the fact that she was the right person for the job. The challenge for him personally was to ensure he succeeded in convincing the rest of the panel.

As he held the door open and quietly ushered Emma into the room, a dignified hush fell over the room.

'May I take this opportunity to welcome you to the afternoon session,' the Chair of Governors stated in an exaggeratedly formal manner. 'I'm glad you haven't dropped out yet!'

Despite the snigger this remark prompted around the table, Simon made sure he kept his face straight. At this stage, he was not prepared to humour misplaced attempts at jollity. As he had hoped and anticipated, nothing seemed to daunt or faze Emma. She glided over this first hurdle smoothly by smiling and taking it in good spirit. From the start, Simon noted approvingly a mental alertness to match the air of vivacity. Not only did she have solid theoretical answers but she made sure they related directly to the school. It was obvious that she had given a lot of thought to the management style that would be most appropriate to Bentwood. He felt particularly pleased when she nailed a tricky-sounding question on factors affecting pupil behaviour. It required her to illustrate the range of strategies she would put into practice. Tellingly, she made a point about the need to ensure that rewards and incentives were given as high a profile as punishments and sanctions. At the end of the long sequence of questions, Simon felt confident she had given an excellent account of herself. In addition to her sense of commitment, which shone through with burning intensity, she also demonstrated a basic humility that was appealing.

'At the end of the interview, do I take it you remain a firm candidate?' He heard the Chair of Governors ask the obligatory question at the end of a forty-five-minute interview. As she responded in the affirmative and rose to go, she half-turned at the door and must have picked up the look of approval on his face.

However hard he tried to recall afterwards, nothing much stayed in his mind after that moment. He remembered Mike Benson making a cryptic remark along the lines of 'Do we have to go to the trouble of seeing the next candidate?' He could still vaguely conjure up a picture of Brian Roebuck's interview but he hadn't really been listening. The high point had come and gone with Emma and everything else after that seemed hollow formality.

Mercifully, not a single member of the panel seemed in doubt as to who was the right person for the job. In the time it took to bat an eyelid, the unanimous decision was taken to appoint Emma. Nothing else seemed left to be said, then, in the nick of time, it dawned on Simon that the panel hadn't yet ascertained when she would be free to take up the post. From his point of view, now that the date of the HMI visit was decided, it was obviously a case of the sooner the better. As well as following up on this matter, Simon was delegated with the pleasant task of breaking the news of the panel's decision.

Expecting to find both candidates still on site, he was relieved to learn from Wendy that Brian had asked if he could be notified at home. Directly, he went to the room where Emma was waiting. Popping his head round the door, he didn't want to prolong the agony and informed her of the panel's decision.

'Did I really get chosen? I don't believe it,' she responded in a dignified, restrained manner. But then, after a second or two more, she let out a spontaneous cry. 'You don't know how thrilled that makes me!'

He could tell how much it meant to her and he felt himself wanting to share her mood of excitement, as he put the crunch question about when she was able to take up post.

'I'm not sure,' she replied ingenuously. 'Isn't it the start of the summer term?'

'Only I er . . . the Governors were hoping it could be sooner.'

'Do you want me to ask?'

He hadn't known how she would react but the natural look of determination on her face confirmed his strongest hopes.

'Yes, if you would.' He knew he couldn't afford to build

his hopes too high. The decision would depend on the Head and Governors of her present school. 'Don't forget to say how desperate we are to have you!'

Two days later, still in the dark as to what was happening, he had left a message for her to ring back. Finally receiving a call, he held his breath. There was a short pause on the other end of the line before she let slip in a mischievous-sounding tone of voice: 'At first, they wouldn't hear of it. But I told them how absolutely desperate you were and they must have believed me. I'm able to start after half-term.'

Chapter 12

It still seemed unnerving seeing the bold 'For Sale' sign outside Willow Cottage. Simon had finally authorised estate agents to put it on the market but the decision hadn't come lightly. It had taken him so long because he had been busy at Bentwood. Even so, he hadn't felt like committing himself too quickly. Lack of contact with Leonie didn't help. Nor did it do much for his peace of mind being left to speculate which exotic point she might have reached on her global itinerary. His own life journey was punishing enough at the moment.

For six weeks since Christmas, he had barely been able to bring himself to go back to the house. Unoccupied, it was vulnerable, but at times he wouldn't have minded if it had been broken into. The way he felt, it would have vindicated the negative, almost destructive, feelings he harboured. But, as with the challenge of his job, he recognised practical matters had to be dealt with sooner or later. Unless he took control, it seemed his whole life would go on in limbo. Although he had managed to cope in a lot of other ways, Willow Cottage stood as a tangible reminder of the misery that had been inflicted upon him. As with his relationship with Leonie, he had been in the mindset of believing the house represented security and continuity in his life. While the edifice of marriage had already crumbled, Willow Cottage, even though still standing, mocked all his former hopes and aspirations. In the early stages of his torment, the wild thought had crossed his mind of hiring a demolition company to raze it to the ground. He had dreamt it was struck down in a thunderstorm. Needless to say, neither of these things had happened and it stayed intact as a monument to his woes and misfortunes. The worst he had actually done was to give a severe clipping to the branches of the four weeping willows that gave the house its name. Knowing the branches would never re-grow, it seemed a symbolic way of exacting revenge.

Bearing in mind he was only due to serve two terms at Bentwood before returning to Ashdown, his flat in Leeds would never amount to anything more than a stopgap arrangement. At least if he sold this heap of stones in the meantime, he would have time to look for somewhere else. The very last thing he wanted, though, was to have to return to the house he had shared with Leonie all those years. He had to make a complete break. If Leonie ever got in touch again, he would be more than prepared to share the proceeds from the sale. But she obviously wasn't giving it any thought at the moment. Clearly, he would have to shoulder the responsibility on his own. Since she had always been the one to deal with life's practicalities, there was an added irony to the situation.

In the event, the transaction was thankfully proving a good deal less awkward than feared. From the moment he had contacted the estate agents, they had spared no time in getting on with the job. He hadn't really been in any mood to shop around but had settled for a firm enjoying the heaviest slice of the local paper's advertising section. His main reservation had been about the individual assigned to selling his house. He couldn't have tolerated anyone as flash and arrogant as the young blade Joe who had hauled him round the flat. Luckily, he had been given an experienced-looking type called Alan who had impressed Simon from the start with the seriousness of his manner. If the various rates for all the different elements seemed a little steep, at least there was some consolation from knowing he was dealing with a reputable and long-established firm. The process was smoothly under way. As well as the boards going up, a brochure had been drawn up within the week. The pictures couldn't help but leave him with mixed feelings. Inescapably, they conjured up in his mind an image of Leonie and her ecstatic reaction when they had come across this pretty stone cottage for the first time. He might not be able to find it within himself to admire the place so intensely now but these fresh snapshots brought back a wealth of memories. Nor, however, could he look at these same photographs without suspecting the thickset walls had been hiding something from him all those years. House and marriage had been inextricably linked in his mind with the notion of permanence. The sad truth, though, was that while the stone cottage remained as beautifully unspoilt-looking on the outside as it had been on the day they moved in, his marriage lay in ruins. While it transpired the property had apparently soared in value in the intervening years, his marriage amounted to nothing.

At least, he had resigned himself to putting sentiment on one side and treating the sale of the house purely in the light of a business undertaking. Taking a practical view, it was handy that the half-term holiday week loomed because it meant he could be on hand to show any interested parties around. After that, he would be quite happy to leave the job to Alan. He had no idea how long the process was going to take but the prospect looked reasonably encouraging at this early stage in proceedings. The most immediate task was to try and make sure the cottage, badly neglected over the last few weeks, looked the part for when visitors came. Most of the jobs that needed doing, such as tidying up the small garden round the back and giving the inside of the property a thorough cleaning, he had left to contractors. He was conscious, though, he had a bit of work to do himself in sorting out what he was going to take with him and what he would leave. Knowing he had nowhere else big enough to store things, his preferred option was to throw all fixtures and fittings into the deal. Until recently, a lot of items in the house would have held immeasurable sentimental value, but that too had changed.

On the Friday he broke up for half-term, he motored back over the Pennines to spend a few days at his old house. Leaving through the school-gates, he felt an immense, added sense of relief from knowing he had a week's break ahead of him. Of course there was also the obligatory paperwork to do at some point. The inspection in late February occupied his mind considerably and he still needed to complete a progress report for HMI within the next two weeks. But at least he had time off without having to contend with the usual day-to-day hassle. Similarly, he took comfort while negotiating the traffic from knowing he would have a whole week's grace from that too. Emerging on to the motorway, he began thinking back over his first six weeks at Bentwood. Despite all the problems he had faced, the half-term seemed in retrospect to have flown by. On reflection, it certainly felt as though he had made the right decision, radical as it had seemed at the time, to uproot and take on a new challenge. He suspected he would only have wallowed in self-pity if he had remained at Ashdown.

Cruising the forty miles or so, he began to feel almost carefree. It was only when he arrived within about five miles of Willow Cottage that he began to feel more tense, as if entering foreign territory. Although he had made more frequent visits of late, they had been short and always involved meeting up with Alan. Coming nearer, it struck him this was the first time in weeks he had visited on his own. Much as he tried telling himself he was only there to carry out routine tasks, he could not deny feeling nervous. It somehow seemed as if the house had already been taken off his hands and, by going in on his own, he was committing an act of trespass.

Passing through the nearby village, he found himself checking to see if everything was still as he remembered. He examined the facia above the newspaper shop to check it was in the same hands. Studying the faces of passers-by, he felt perturbed if he was unable to recognise them by sight. He knew it was ridiculous, except that everything seemed to be taking on a strange, dreamlike quality. Making the final turn down the long winding lane that eventually led to the house, he knew from experience how murky and ill-lit it always was. Watching closely as the headlights picked up the stark, overhanging branches of trees, he felt hemmed in on all sides as if the car was squeezing itself forward inside a narrow tube. As he reached some rising ground, he noticed white patches of frozen snow. Mindful of braking gradually, he carefully negotiated two slight bends in the road. His senses seemed in a heightened sense of alertness. In the past, he wouldn't have given it a second thought. Even the usually welcoming sight of the row of terraced cottages, a hundred yards from his journey's end, seemed to stand out in menacing half-shadow. Anxious to witness friendly evidence of human life, he only spotted the occasional light at a window. Otherwise, everything seemed dark and prohibiting.

As he eased his car into the driveway, the building had a derelict look with the fast, fading light vainly pressing against the window-panes. Fighting an irrational impulse to reverse straight out again, he supposed he could have gone out for a meal somewhere instead. But, although he could feel a certain contraction in his stomach, it wasn't down to hunger. Finally switching the engine off, he remained motionless in the driver's seat, feeling distinctly hesitant about surrendering the cocooned warmth of the car for the frosty emptiness awaiting him inside. He darted another nervous glance up at the house. From his crouched position below, it seemed to tower over him as though he was the one under surveillance.

Trying to distract himself, he recalled how Leonie had always kept an outside light on, connected to a time switch, which came on at night to make it safer to reach the back door. He made a mental note to replace the spent bulb. Whatever else, the outside light had made everything a lot more welcoming than was the case tonight. He tried telling himself it was only the difference between daytime and night-time that accounted for his mood of apprehension. The best thing was to put himself back into the frame of mind he was in when the photographer came and the place was bathed in sunlight. In any case, it was only because he was out of the routine of coming back here in the dark. It had never held fears for him before. No doubt once he got inside, he would instantly forget it was such a cheerless night outside.

Getting out of the car, he felt a sharpness in the air which made him gasp. He couldn't see things very clearly and just managed to avoid bumping into a wheelie-bin. Remembering how slippery the paving-stones could be, he cautiously manoeuvred the ten or so paces that led to the back door. As he turned the key in the lock, he felt like an estate agent visiting a house for the first time, unsure what he would find. At first, the door resisted his pressure. It felt, for a disconcerting moment, as though someone must be standing at the other side and pushing against him. He was slow to realise it was an accumulated stack of mail that had wedged itself under the door. Again his stomach tightened as he flicked on the porch light, half-expecting someone or something to leap out at him. Cursorily, he glanced at the pile of letters, most of which was junk mail. Taking a deep breath, he took the plunge and dashed round the place switching on lights and radiators and closing curtains behind him.

Letting out a sigh of relief to find no sign of the house having been disturbed, he initially began to feel more relaxed. The memory returned to him how many times over the years they had discussed the merits of having a burglar-alarm fitted. In the end, it was only because they were both rather technologically inept that they hadn't. Now he might have only a few more weeks to tough it out before it became someone else's decision. In the meantime, he was just thankful the house was intact and free from intruders. It was yet another thing that was under reasonable control and on the verge of being resolved. In an easier state of mind altogether, he went upstairs and changed out of his suit into something more casual from his overnight case. On a practical level, the most immediate question facing him was where he was going to lay his hands on a square meal. The tightness in his stomach had disappeared and he was feeling hungry. Because there was nothing in the fridge, he would have to make a visit to the local chippy if he wasn't to go starving. He put his coat on again to go back outside.

On the point of opening the door, he caught sight once more of the batch of post scattered across the mat. Bending down to scoop the bundle out of the way, his original impression was confirmed that most of the mail was worthless. However, in amongst the garish-coloured flyers was one which stood out: a white envelope with his name inscribed in a neat hand which looked familiar. It came to him very quickly that it was Leonie's handwriting. Instantly, the same tension that had gripped his stomach earlier spread across his whole body. His mind seemed to have seized up in numbness. For a short while, he couldn't bring himself to react at all, let alone do the obvious thing and open it. Then a faintly contemptuous thought flashed through his mind that it might have been more appropriate for her to have sent a postcard. It would no doubt have equally well served the purpose of providing him with a reminder that she still existed somewhere on the earth's surface. Urging himself on no account to allow it to disturb his equilibrium too much, he opened the letter and read the contents.

Dear Simon,

I am truly sorry I have left it so long without making contact. I'm also aware I have a lot of explaining to do. If I'm honest with myself, I'm not quite sure where to start. The more I tried to think things through logically, the more difficult it seemed to become. In the end, you could be forgiven for thinking I just gave up.

I didn't really ever intend going round the world and I apologise for telling you a lie. My only defence is that it meant I could escape without being accountable. Trust me, I needed to. The one incontestable fact in all this – which I could never face up to telling you about – is that I had a great shock a month or so before Christmas after going to the doctor. A tiny growth had developed in my breast. As I said, I couldn't bring myself to tell you. Looking back now, I suppose it had a lot to do with how I had been feeling about our relationship and the lack of communication. I didn't see what good it would do either of us. At first, I didn't want to alarm you unnecessarily because the tests might have shown the growth was benign. But, just my luck, they were positive and I still didn't know what to do. The fortunate thing was that I had someone close at hand who has proved very supportive in a number of ways over the years. Although I have only known him a short time, David has been wonderful. Please don't think, though, I abandoned you for him. I'm afraid it was more a case of him taking pity on me. I can assure you he is as good a friend as a woman could have, but I emphasise the word 'friend'.

I want you to know I took the decision wholly myself to go, but he arranged for me to travel down south to stay somewhere close to the treatment centre. Yes, I am undergoing an intense course of medical treatment which is not in the least pleasant and is having the strange physical side-effects that I was warned about. However, I am told it is the only hope of making a recovery. I do not think you would appreciate me going into too much detail.

I realise it must seem almost gratuitous to be informing you of all this now, but the truth is I don't think I could have coped if I had told you any sooner. By the way, the last thing I want to do is to make you feel sorry for me. I know I'm going to have to remain as tough as I can, both physically and mentally. I have to be prepared to go on doing what I think is right in the circumstances and I want you to know I still stand by the decision I made at Christmas. I accept there are many things which we may need to sort out, such as the house, but I hope, God willing, a time may come when we can do so in a reasonably amicable way.

I fully understand how reading this letter may puzzle you or leave you feeling hurt and angry. That has never been part of my intention and I only hope that you can see it the same way. Nor do I want you to worry about me because I am very lucky in the way I am being looked after. The doctors and nurses are very caring and I respect their judgement. Sometimes I think that, if I should pull through, it will be more down to other people's help than my own fortitude.

At the risk of sounding patronising, I hope all is going well for you at work. You remain in my thoughts and I wish you the very best for the future.

Leonie

He checked back to see whether there was any evidence of an address but she had obviously chosen not to share it with him. The only clue, which he hadn't thought of looking for before, was a smudged postmark on the envelope which, on closer examination, indicated 'Oxford'.

Putting the letter down, he felt as though he had just read an obituary, not for one person but for two. He would never know the agony she had already been through and the potentially worse suffering that lay ahead. He couldn't help but take it as indictment, even though he realised it was crass for him to be so self-indulgent in thinking his own feelings counted for anything.

In a reckless state of mind, he spent the night turning everything upside down to see if she had left the faintest clue of her exact whereabouts but, stubbornly, Willow Cottage yielded no secrets. In the end, it felt irrationally as if he was being made to pay for the wanton act of chopping down the branches of the weeping willow trees outside.

Chapter 13

Until recently, Saturday had always been Miranda's favourite day of the week. The problem wasn't the frantic workload at the salon, more a run of unannounced visits home from her ex-husband. She was kidding herself if she thought she had succeeded in laying down the law. The very next Saturday, he had turned up again at the same time, only much the worse for drink. Luckily, she was already back in the house, having collected the children from her mum's. Without the strength of the four walls to protect her, she wasn't sure how she would have coped. It was terrible that the children had to hear his drunken abuse. At one point, she had seriously considered calling the police. In the end, he had flounced off in a temper. The only consolation was that at least the children had been able to see their father in his true colours.

Of course, Ian still hadn't paid a penny's maintenance. She had now come to the decision there was no possible alternative course of action but to pursue the matter through the courts. It was clear she would never succeed in appealing to any sense of reason he might have. She hated the idea of all the administrative hassle but she had to do it to protect her own and the children's future. With her mother willing to continue looking after Jack until he was old enough to go to school, she was also considering going back to work full-time. Besides, the way she was feeling at the moment, the salon was the only escape-route she had from all the worries of her domestic life. At least she was able to switch off and detach herself for a while from the bitter thoughts that beset her. Simple routines at work, which she would have discounted as mundane before, became positively therapeutic in the effect they had on her capacity to withstand other pressures.

Although Saturday seemed to have come round again rather too quickly, she steadied herself not to let the threat of another visit preoccupy her mind throughout the day. But if the same were to happen again, she really would call the police.

In a way, she was proud she hadn't let her problems affect her attitude at work. Arriving of a morning, she made the effort to be as fully prepared as possible. It wasn't as if she had ever been sloppy but it gave her real satisfaction making sure everything was just right. It gave her a chance to impose some order at a time when her personal life seemed so messy and chaotic.

Scanning today's schedule, she was curious to see the name of Simon Russell in a slot in the early afternoon. His last visit stayed vividly in her memory, when an innocent Christmas inquiry had led him to divulge the painful secret of his marriage breakdown. The way in which he had disburdened himself had touched her so deeply that she felt more worried for him than embarrassed. She had always thought of him as calm and unruffled and it had startled her to see him behaving in such an agitated manner. Agreeing out of sympathy to go to the café and listen to what he had to say had thankfully not proved too taxing. Apart from having to take a good bit of leg-pulling back at work, along the lines of dating men old enough to be her father, she didn't regret the way she had acted.

Knowing he was a headteacher gave it an added twist. But she had reasoned that personal misfortunes affected everyone the same. She recalled how his spirits seemed to pick up after a while and she had seen a side to his character she would scarcely have thought credible. It probably had more to do with the stereotype picture of a headteacher she carried in her head from schoolgirl days. Vulnerability was hardly what she would have expected.

But then it was amazing, the next moment, how animated he had become in reliving where he used to have his hair cut as a lad. The comical side of it had resurfaced in her mind on more than one occasion during the last six weeks, and left her smiling inside. Even so, she wondered whether he would come back. For one thing, he was moving off to live somewhere else. For another, she feared some kind of pride factor might kick in. Either way, it felt quietly satisfying to see that he had booked in again. It made her feel trusted, as if confirming her ability to be of help to others in their moment of need.

As the time of the 2 o'clock appointment approached, she began to feel butterflies in her stomach. She told herself to treat him like any other client. It would be reasonable enough to ask him how he was finding his new school. She certainly had no intention of appearing to pry into his private life. It would be up to him to volunteer and then she would react accordingly. There seemed no alternative but to take things as they came. Despite trying to keep her mind fully occupied on applying the finishing touches to her present client, she found herself becoming increasingly distracted by the thought of his imminent arrival. She glanced at the clock on the wall; it showed 1.59. The next time she looked, it said 2.02. Then, a moment later, Tessa at the desk had shouted out: 'Don't rush, your next appointment has just rung up to cancel.'

'Mr Russell?' Miranda confirmed, fighting a stab of disappointment.

'That's the one!'

'Any particular reason?' she asked, trying to make her tone sound casual.

'Just apologised and rang off.'

Miranda felt strangely deflated. She knew how important it was for him to have his hair cut before going back to school. He'd probably had second thoughts and decided to go somewhere else. It wasn't the end of the world or anything. She just would have liked to know how he was getting on, that was all.

'You mean your wife's got breast cancer and she didn't tell you?'

Simon felt himself squirming under Tom's critical gaze. Why on earth had he shared this personal revelation with him in the first place?

'And who's this guy who's set it all up? Has he got a name?'

Unable to take much more of this ruthless cross-examination, he could tell how Tom must have got up the noses of American politicians.

'Look, she's left me. You could say it's none of my business.'

'"None of my business!" Listen, how can you say that?' He continued on the offensive. 'How do you know what state she's in, physically or psychologically? If nothing else, don't you think you've got some sort of moral duty to find out?'

The trouble was, Simon knew the case was unanswerable. He had gone on searching for clues but drawn a blank. He still had nothing to go on beyond the postmark.

Thinking aloud, he put it back to Tom indignantly: 'What am I supposed to do? Call every clinic within a forty-mile radius of Oxford? They're not exactly likely to hand over confidential details about patients, are they? Then what?'

Tom's recriminating stare relented a little. 'Well, at least you're beginning to sound a bit more passionate!'

Feeling unappeased, Simon had an impulse to retaliate. Before he could, Tom had got up, saying in an exasperated tone of voice that he was going to the kitchen to make some coffee. Left sitting on his own in the lounge, Simon seethed at the injustice. At least he had listened sympathetically when Tom had told him about his coke problem and everything else that came in its wake. For a moment, he wanted to turn the tables and go for the jugular. Toying with hurtful phrases to throw back, instead he came to the conclusion it was futile and beneath him. What purpose would it serve? It would have only been another pointless way of diverting his mind from the other things that were gnawing away inside him. He couldn't deny his mind was in turmoil again. Beguilingly, only a week ago, at the start of his holiday, things had at least seemed to be falling into place. But the shock about Leonie meant he was unable to think straight again.

Three sets of couples had come to view Willow Cottage and it had left him feeling even more confused. Sometimes they had asked fiddly little questions about council tax or gas and electricity charges. Realising he should have known the answers, he accepted he must have sounded irritatingly vague at times. Then there were the intrusive types, like the Morgans on the Tuesday, who'd kept pushing him hard on his reasons for leaving. They didn't sound the least bit interested in buying; they were probably casing properties for a hobby. It made his blood boil to think how much time he had wasted trying to answer their fatuous questions. By the end of the third visit, even though the Naylors were a lot more agreeable, he realised he was in danger of becoming paranoid wondering when the dreaded question would come up. In the end, he had decided on the Thursday to return to Leeds and assign the business to Alan from now on.

He had made his hair appointment thinking he was still going to be over there for the weekend. He'd been looking forward to the experience and hadn't ruled out making a special trip. But things had worked out differently. That was how he came to be sitting here in Tom's flat. He had already spent the best part of the day in his company. It was ironic, bearing in mind he had vowed earlier not to have anything more to do with him after the fiasco of a fortnight ago. Insult added to injury, he was now having to put up with Tom haranguing him over the steps he should have been taking with regard to Leonie. Tom had held him to a half-hearted agreement they had made to meet up for a session at his health club. On and off during the day, in addition to indulging in light forms of exercise, his unlikely new friend had inflicted upon Simon a battery of self-revelations that had left his head in a spin.

Though they were on their own for the most part, the steam room and jacuzzi were unconventional settings for anyone bent on confessing to substance addiction. However, Simon couldn't deny it proved absorbing to listen to, even if he had had difficulty at times keeping up with all the various twists and turns in a career that seemed as fraught with peril as his own had been dull and conventional. If they had been sitting across a table, it might not have felt quite so engaging, but the relaxing environment had eased any apprehensions he might have had about hearing the other man's chequered history. He supposed he could have found ways of detaching himself. The simple fact was, though, he hadn't. In the end, wisely or otherwise, he had felt an obligation to reveal a bit more about himself than he might normally have done. This was how he had come to broach the subject of his divorce and moving to Leeds. It had seemed just a matter of mentioning it swiftly and transfer-ring on to another topic. He didn't know whether it was due to Tom's prompting or a surprising inclination on his own part to elaborate, but he had ended up going much deeper under the surface than he had originally intended. Nevertheless, he had still held back at that point from referring to the letter from Leonie. He was thinking he needed more time to digest its impact. Then a pressure had built up inside his head, like the tightening of a screw, and it felt as though he was screaming for relief from the pain. Tom's reaction had shocked him with the force of its directness. In the end, he was left regretting he hadn't kept the appointment with Miranda. No doubt, he could have engineered the chance to share the burden of his worries with her instead. How misguided it now seemed to have rung up and cancelled. He couldn't go back on things, though. But, to avoid turning up at school on Monday looking scruffy, he would need to find somewhere else quickly to escape that ignominy.

When Tom returned, balancing two cups of coffee and some biscuits on a tray, Simon attempted to ask casually: 'You don't happen to know a decent hairdresser's round here, do you?'

'What's wrong with the one you go to now?'

Simon stared back at him uncertainly but Tom continued: 'Correct me if I'm wrong, but I seem to remember you saying this morning you thought the world of her?'

Had he made reference to Miranda this morning amongst everything else? He really was slipping. He supposed he must have done. 'I rang up and cancelled,' he announced in a matter-of-fact tone.

'Why?'

Simon didn't feel like mincing words. 'Because I didn't think I could face seeing her again. Not after the last visit.'

'So you're blocking that out of your life as well?'

Again, although he could tell he was meaning to be provocative, Tom's directness was too difficult to withstand.

'Anyway, isn't one hairdresser much like another at the end of the day?' Simon ventured, not even sure he was convincing himself.

'Didn't you say you felt very grateful to her the last time?' Tom was fixing him with the same critical stare as earlier. 'Did you tell her yourself you weren't coming?'

Tom was getting into full stride now and Simon began to wince under the pressure of interrogation.

'I bet you made up some pathetic goddam excuse!'

'I left a message.' Simon briskly sought to extenuate himself.

'Coward!'

There was a moment's silence but he sensed he wasn't going to be let off the hook. 'If you ask me, though, it's still not too late,' Tom persisted.

'They won't be able to fix a new appointment. Not at such short notice. Besides, I'd look stupid!'

With a withering glance, Tom rested his case.

At two minutes to six, Miranda was tidying things away at the end of a long day. She hadn't noticed the van draw up outside the salon or the woman who came in with the bouquet of flowers. The first she knew was when she heard Tessa call her name out in a very excited tone.

'Aren't they gorgeous?' Tessa exclaimed.

'They are, aren't they?' Miranda had to agree, studying the beautiful arrangement of matching colours and textures.

'Look at the label! I haven't read it, honestly!' But she was unable to stop herself giggling, so Miranda didn't quite believe her.

'It's from Simon Russell!' she murmured appreciatively, with a mild tone of disbelief in her voice.

'What does it say? What does it say?' Tessa persisted. 'Read it out!'

'It says: "*To the best hairdresser in the world! Sorry for the cancellation. Will arrange another time. Best wishes, Simon.*"'

'Oh, isn't that sweet? Looks like you've found yourself a real sugar daddy there!'

Miranda smiled. It did seem a nice thing for him to have done. Totally out of the blue. She couldn't remember the last time she had had such a pleasant surprise.

Chapter 14

Returning to school, Simon had been intent on getting back into routine with a vengeance. By far the most pressing matter on his mind was the Inspectors' visit, which was now only three weeks away. With the house and other matters, he hadn't spent nearly so much time on school work as he should have done. In addition to the heavy amount of administration, there were so many day-to-day aspects of school life needing to be addressed that he never quite knew where to start. He still hadn't been there long enough to be able to take anything for granted. That was why he had come back determined to set a personal example by being highly visible around the place. Also, he was more than aware it was Emma's first day. He didn't want her to have to undergo the same baptism by fire as he had.

However, from the start of the day onwards, things had not exactly gone to plan. After staff briefing, Wendy passed on to him an urgent message to ring Richard Preece at Ashdown. Back in his office, he dialled the direct number that he was still used to thinking of as his own. Listening to the sound of the phone ringing at the other end, he did his best to avoid drawing a mental picture of Richard occupying his desk. A few seconds later, he heard a short greeting uttered in a familiar, nasal tone of voice. Exchanging the briefest of civilities, Simon swiftly detected Richard was in no mood to prevaricate.

'Sorry to trouble you. It's not been easy to make the decision but I'm applying for a headship at another school.' Allowing time for the message to sink in, he paused before continuing: 'I thought I had a duty to let you know.'

For a moment or two, Simon couldn't credit what Richard was telling him. More than that, he felt slightly affronted by the manner in which the message was being delivered. It sounded coldly impersonal, as if he was telling someone he had never met before. Perhaps it was his imagination playing tricks with him. Other than that, the most charitable assumption to make was that he had been out of contact with Richard for so long, he had forgotten how he could sound. But it was undeniable his voice carried an abrupt and pre-emptive edge.

'So you've given it thought . . .?' He found himself back-tracking in a vain attempt to give himself a little more time to weigh up the implications. But whichever way he read it, the news was a bombshell. 'Where is the process actually at, then . . . at the moment?'

'I've been called for interview next week.'

Simon felt like saying it was ridiculous but managed to restrain himself in time. Other reservations flashed through his mind. He still couldn't help wondering what Richard was playing at. He failed to understand the motives behind a decision that, on the face of it, seemed arbitrary and smacked of naked ambition. But then the relationship between them had never been anything other than formal. The nature and tone of the announcement caused him to realise he had never really known what went on inside Richard's head.

'That's quick!' The words escaped his lips as a token reply at best.

'Yes, although I applied two weeks ago,' he sounded keen to confirm. There was a tangible sense of relief in his voice as if he felt the awkward part of the conversation was safely behind him now. However, it left Simon with an overwhelming urge to put him back on his mettle.

'For God's sake, why didn't you tell me earlier?'

Although he could clearly see it was symptomatic of a general communication breakdown between them, Simon felt angry inside. For that, he supposed he had to bear the brunt of the responsibility himself. But the pressure to get to the bottom of things felt so intense that, if he didn't grasp the nettle now, he might forever stay outside the loop. This rush of different thoughts seemed to configurate inside his head, pressing him to pursue an answer to his basic concern more energetically.

'Why didn't you tell me?' Surprising even himself with the confrontational bite he put into repeating the question, he was not prepared to accept the situation as it stood.

Straining to pitch his voice at as level a tone as possible, Richard replied: 'I think it was because I wanted to see if I'd get shortlisted. In fact, I didn't find out until the Friday we broke up.'

Listening intently, Simon detected a defensiveness in his voice as if confirming the suspicion that he had somehow acted behind his back. Even so, there was little he could do about it now. From another angle, he supposed it could have been worse. Richard could have left it until after the interview to tell him anything.

As he proceeded to relay details of the interview arrangements, Simon felt his patience snapping. Reacting fiercely, he broke in: 'It would certainly put the cat among the pigeons if you got the job, wouldn't it? The Governors would have no choice but to summon me back to Ashdown!'

There, he had laid his cards on the table, openly revealing what was really causing him most concern. A tense silence ensued as both of them seemed to need more time to ponder the matter.

'Do you think so?' Richard finally came out with, as if taken aback at the idea. Seeing a catch in everything now, Simon saw Richard's reaction as disingenuous. It was as though his game-plan throughout had been to steer him down a pre-determined route. Although by far the more experienced of the two, he couldn't help feeling he was being put to the test by the younger man.

'Well, what else could they do?' Simon blurted out, despite realising Richard was more than capable of seeing it himself.

Then, as if volunteering a confession, he was surprised to hear Richard admit: 'I suppose the main difficulty I have is the uncertainty over not knowing what you intend doing longer-term . . .' Other considerations apart, his voice suddenly sounded a lot more sincere.

Simon realised he might have reacted too hastily in condemning Richard's motives out of hand, for in truth it was a valid point he was making. Who was he to doubt the motives of others when he had upped sticks so quickly himself at Christmas? If anything, he was guilty of taking it for granted that Richard would be content carrying on as Acting Head for however long he was away. Even though it was only seven weeks so far, he could guess how unsettling it might prove, particularly to someone who felt ready to become a headteacher in his own right. However, for a variety of reasons, Simon preferred to switch the focus back to Richard, not least because this was where the conversation had started.

'Do you really want this post you're applying for?' It could be construed as a daft question but he trusted Richard would see what he was driving at.

Fearing he might slow-time him again, Simon was relieved to pick up a quick response in the same sincere tone of voice.

'I'm not really sure. But as I've always told you, I'm prepared to make a move from Ashdown to fulfil my ambition to become a head.'

Beginning to feel warmer towards Richard by the moment, it didn't stop Simon maintaining a more direct approach.

'If you don't mind my saying so, it's still a funny way of going about things!'

'I don't understand. What do you mean?' It seemed strange and somehow touching to catch a tone of uncertainty creeping into Richard's voice.

He decided to cut to the quick. 'I suppose I'm saying we need to have a frank discussion about where we stand on things.'

'I would very much appreciate the chance.'

Keen to see eye-to-eye, they had ended by agreeing to meet at Ashdown the following evening to continue the conversation.

Glancing at the clock, Simon realised he had been on the phone for quite a time. It was ironic to recall he had come back from the half-term holiday determined to get to grips with day-to-day practicalities at Bentwood.

Up to the present time, he realised he had been in the habit of trying to take things as they came. Now it looked likely, in these new circumstances, that he might have a crucially important decision facing him within the next week or so. If it boiled down to a choice, was he willing to find himself called back to Ashdown, or should he look to commit his longer-term future to Bentwood?

Emma was finding it a culture shock working alongside Bill Deacon. Simon had said that sharing an office with him would be only a short-term arrangement. She was already finding it a bit of a strain. She had thought that the full-length pictures of Spitfire and Lancaster bombers on the office walls reflected his interests as a history teacher but quickly picked up it had more to do with his lifelong affinity to the RAF. When the bell went for the start of Period 2 and he got up quickly from his chair to go and teach, she almost expected him to call out 'Chocks away!' It made her chuckle inwardly but she hadn't suspected characters like Bill Deacon still existed in schools. From the way he had offered his services on that first morning, she hadn't been sure what he had in mind. She didn't get the impression he quite approved of her. Something told her that if he had had anything to do with the selection process himself, she would have been way down his list. On the day of the interview, when candidates had been meeting staff informally, she vaguely seemed to remember having a brief chat with him. She couldn't think what had possessed her to bang on about management styles but he had looked so singularly unimpressed she had dropped the subject like a brick and moved on. She recalled his look of disdain as though she were a trainee pilot baling out on a reconnaissance mission.

Despite this, she couldn't deny feeling great pride and optimism joining Bentwood as Deputy Head. For one thing, she felt fortunate to be able to count on Simon Russell's support. She derived a strong measure of reassurance from their both being new to the school. When she had come for interview, she had been impressed with Simon's own ability to adapt so well to a new environment. She wanted to be able to demonstrate she had it in her to do the same.

It was only 10 o'clock on her first morning but it was already clear Bentwood would prove a tough nut to crack in all kinds of different ways. The main thing was that none of it daunted her and she was determined to pick things up as she went along. In one or two discussions with Simon, when she had visited at the end of the previous half-term, he had run through what were high priority issues. The main, immediate target was to negotiate the HMI visit. She hadn't quite fully appreciated at interview that the next inspection was only three weeks away. It certainly concentrated the mind. No wonder, she had teased Simon, he had been keen to prise her away from her old school at the earliest opportunity.

However, she was at pains to put all previous experience firmly behind her. The butterflies in her stomach may have been worse than on the day of her interview but she just felt thrilled to be given the chance of a fresh start.

Tom Judd was not sure whether he was still up to being flown out to troubled war zones but he couldn't deny being flattered by the offer. In some ways, it could be seen as a sign he was no longer labelled 'beyond the pale'. The fact that he could smile about it now was another healthy sign pointing to his rehabilitation in more senses than one. The main trouble was that it was Iraq. Perhaps he was deluding himself and they were wanting to finish him off properly once and for all. No war zone was ever a bed of roses but, witlessly dangerous as the idea sounded, he hadn't yet ruled it completely out of the question. His contact, a veteran broadcaster for many years in the BBC World Service, had pulled no punches in describing the assignment. He certainly wouldn't be staying in a five-star hotel! It was left that he had a few days to think about it, with the right of first refusal. No doubt, though, there were other lunatics in the frame.

In more considered moments, he would have written himself off as frankly past it. But he couldn't deny there was still a burning need somewhere inside to vindicate himself and show people at large he wasn't a back number. However, there was more than one way in which he could do this. He had to work out whether this sort of assignment was the right move for him at this particular stage of his career. All he knew for sure was he owed it to himself to weigh up the various angles and come to a reasoned decision. Just as it would have been simple to jump at the opportunity, he didn't think it was fair to dismiss it out of hand. At the very least, it had provided him with a means of evaluating his current position against options open to him.

For one thing, he was totally fed up with this sociological study he was involved in at the moment. Prestigious as it may sound, hyped up as a research-based study of the attitudes of young people, he still found himself the one in the team allocated all the thankless tasks in less salubrious settings. He had joked with Simon that, if he had been a teacher, he would have been given all the bottom sets with the delinquent troublemakers. Of course, he had made it his life's work going where the bullets were flying but he had never visualised working with feckless teenagers puking their guts out all over the place. He certainly couldn't stomach it much longer himself.

But if this was the aspect of his life that was intensely dissatisfying at the present time, he could think of one or two things that inordinately pleased him on the other side of the balance sheet. First of all, there was his general lifestyle. He no longer saw himself as the addicted manic depressive of a couple of years or so ago. It was in his own best interest to be positive about himself and then there was a stronger chance of winning the respect of others. The main trouble, he recognised, was the risk of dropping back into the coke habit. But he was still managing step-by-step to build up his relentless tally of consecutive days drug-free. If he could only cure himself of his occasional but devastating penchant for single malt, he would be even happier. To his credit, he had succeeded in maintaining a fitness regime that was having a reinforcing effect on mind and body. Did he really want to sacrifice these hard-fought gains by subjecting himself to the deprivations of war-torn Iraq? Apart from a lack of five-star hotels, he didn't suppose there would be much in the way of multigym facilities!

Unquestionably, just as his own life had moved on for better or worse, he needed to remind himself he had lost touch with the insider world of foreign affairs. To try turning the tide now was a flawed idea that was only likely to rebound on him with an even stronger backlash. In the end, did he really want to put everything at risk, having fought so long and hard to put his life back on a straight track again?

Satisfied that he had thrashed out the issues, he felt like rewarding himself with a single malt. Glancing at his watch, he noticed it was still only 4.30. Exercising restraint, he decided to change into his sports kit and go for a run. If there was any reckless energy that needed burning off, it was better he did so on the streets of Leeds than the highways and byways of Baghdad. And if he wasn't intending going back into foreign affairs, why not just settle for a mad, tempestuous love affair instead? A frightening vision of Suzanne exploded into his consciousness. No, his reformed self should be looking to enter into a serious relationship if at all possible.

Leaving his flat and setting off down the road, he tried to rid his mind of this string of disconnected thoughts. He should discipline himself just to concentrate on putting one foot in front of the other whilst keeping a firm eye out for all potential hazards in his path. His priority had to be to safeguard his future rather than placing it in further jeopardy.

Chapter 15

As if he didn't have enough on his mind, Simon heard from Alan that the Naylors had put in a firm bid at the asking price for Willow Cottage. The news somehow put yesterday's conversation with Richard into even sharper perspective. Everything in his life seemed up in the air at the moment. Before Leonie's letter, he had thought he knew where he stood on the house sale. Despite the fact Alan was evidently just waiting for a call back from him accepting the offer, Simon suddenly wasn't so sure. Complications were appearing to become endless.

Telling Wendy he had urgent business to attend to, he felt guilty leaving school mid-afternoon. It was cutting things fine: he had arranged to get to the salon for Miranda's last appointment slot at 4.45. Then it was a case of meeting up with Richard at Ashdown to discuss the headship situation. He put the call to Alan on hold for the time being. He didn't want to feel he was being rushed into making an irrevocable decision on the house when everything seemed so fluid again. To complicate matters even further, he had taken a call from Caroline saying that the Chair of Governors had also requested a meeting later on in the evening if possible. Feeling it was bound to be connected to the earlier conversation, he could tell the urgency of it from Caroline's tone. Apparently, she had been prevailed upon to stay to arrange refreshments. The Chair of Governors was working late in his office and had asked to meet at 7.30. Caroline couldn't say whether he had in mind a further meeting after that, perhaps bringing Richard into the picture again. In the circumstances, he was keeping an open mind where to stay overnight. He was prepared to stay at Willow Cottage if need be, but his preferred option was returning to Leeds.

Apart from having to struggle across the M62 to make his first appointment on time, he wondered how on earth he was going to explain sending Miranda the flowers on the Saturday. In the cold light of day, the gesture seemed hopelessly over the top. Although he cursed Tom for playing on his susceptibilities, he only had himself to blame for his predicament. Now, trying hard to concentrate on his driving at the same time, his thoughts oscillated unnervingly. Perhaps he could just act in denial and attempt to distance himself from the wretched flowers as if he had never sent them in the first place. Alternatively, he could simply apologise as if it were a silly mistake. Or, failing all else, he supposed he still had the same option as before of ringing in at the last moment and cancelling. But even he could see not going was unthinkable. Wasn't life constantly telling him it was better to take positive action rather than bury his head in the sand? The nearer the car took him to the salon, the more tense he began to feel.

Surprised at the speed of his journey, he managed to find a parking spot fairly easily. It was not yet quarter past four and he decided to have a coffee to use up time. It couldn't help but strike him as anomalous idly sitting there nursing a cup in his hands when he could have been tackling a pile of work at school. What was he doing here anyway? Why couldn't he just have arranged to have his hair cut somewhere in Leeds? Time, which normally flew past, now seemed to be hanging over him like a pall. If it were an angry parent he was about to see or an assembly he was

134

going to take, he wouldn't have felt so apprehensive. In the time remaining to him, he struggled to retain his composure and keep awkward inner feelings under control.

His game plan had held up well until the moment he entered the salon. Feeling highly self-conscious, the last thing he wanted was to feel the centre of attention. Normally, he felt relatively comfortable and at ease. But today it seemed everyone's eyes had flickered his way the instant he arrived. Although he tried not to pick out Miranda too quickly, she seemed to be the only one who didn't take any notice of him. About to panic, he told himself to get a grip. If he was going to read terrible significance into every nuance of a reaction or lack of it, he might as well turn on his heel and walk out now. He steeled himself. It wasn't as if he had committed a crime or anything.

He signed in at the desk and was asked to take a seat as usual. Resisting the temptation to engage in eye-contact, he felt his pulse starting to throb again. He couldn't help thinking the receptionist was having a quiet inward laugh at his expense. Everyone in the salon was probably in on the joke about the romantic old fool who wore his heart on his sleeve. Meanwhile, out of the corner of his eye he seemed to think Miranda must be purposely ignoring him. Perhaps he had been written off her schedule. Likely as not, he was about to be informed he was having his hair cut by another stylist with whom it was less likely he might form an emotional attachment. Could they really do that? Distractedly, he lifted his head from *Now* magazine and cast covert glances around to try and work out who he might be assigned to instead. He thought it funny he hadn't been offered the usual cup of coffee. Perhaps it was part of a general conspiracy to make him feel unwanted. They were intending to forget about him. Eventually, he would twig and put everyone out of their misery by walking out and never coming back again.

Then, with his antennae razor sharp, he was aware that Miranda had finally noticed him. A beaming smile shot across her face like a ray of sunshine breaking through grey skies. He watched in amazement as she stopped what she was doing to run over to him, the warmth of her body language would have been transparent to anyone. He could never in his most optimistic dreams have hoped for such an enthusiastic greeting. His spirits soared as, raising herself up on tiptoes, she planted a kiss on his cheek. His senses felt overwhelmed and at last all his pent-up trepidation had been blown away. Not that he didn't recognise a play-acting element. Despite demonstrating such ardour, he could tell she wasn't in danger of getting carried away. The expression on her face remained gently amused to the point of implying it was his turn to show some warmth of feeling back. But all he could do was stare back at her with a lopsided grin on his face.

'Your flowers were absolutely lovely . . . such a wonderful idea! You didn't need to . . .' There had been a slight pause between each of the statements but he still couldn't think of anything to say in return. He felt so spellbound that she had to motion him over to where he was having his hair washed. It was as well the young girl started off by dowsing his head with a jet of cold water before adjusting it to the right temperature.

When Miranda started cutting his hair, it confirmed to him why it was impossible to think of going anywhere else. The experience always felt heavenly. The touch of her hands felt soothing and immediate. Yet the physical image of her, framed in the mirror, conveyed a picture-book quality that was strangely illusory. His senses always seemed utterly confused. If she spoke, he felt a natural inclination to turn round to face her. He knew it would have annoyed her if he had. For it was vital to remember, whatever else, it could never amount to anything more than a service or a business transaction. After all, she had a job to do. While she was carrying it out, he respected the fact she had to concentrate on what she was doing. Indeed, he loved the earnest way in which she looked so absorbed. However brief it was, usually only about twenty minutes, it always seemed an enchanted spell of time.

'How are things going at your new school?' she asked with a genuine-sounding interest in her voice.

'Oh, getting there!' he answered with an ironic inflection to his tone that made her smile. 'The next hurdle is the inspection coming up. Apart from worrying myself silly over that . . .'

'I told you it would be fine! Do you remember?' As he caught her reflection in the mirror, she seemed to be standing over him like a benevolent guardian angel.

'You did! I'm not sure if I believed you at the time.' Again, she smiled down on him.

'It was a difficult time for you,' she added, in a neutral, unemotional tone. He appreciated she was leaving it to him to tell her as much or as little as he wanted to. After his dramatic outburst the last time, he thought he owed it to her to give a lucid account of himself. But he didn't want to sound too intense. He wanted to convey to her that he was capable of laughing at himself a bit. It seemed to help if he expressed himself in a natural way that showed some degree of human awareness. For underneath all the apparent confidence on the surface, her own life had not been without its fragile moments. Even guardian angels had crosses to bear.

It was at this point that he first became aware of a man standing just inside the salon entrance. At first, as the man exchanged a terse word or two with the receptionist, Simon had the impression he was an employee, perhaps someone on the security side. As the man continued to stand his ground, Simon detected a general air of concern amongst staff. It stemmed more from his manner than his appearance. He was a man of about thirty, well-dressed in a smart coat, but had an impatient air as if dissatisfied or ready to pick a quarrel. Conscious that he was the last remaining client, Simon jumped to the conclusion he might be hanging around for one of the staff. Trying not to let his concern show, he was more than happy to continue chatting to Miranda. He put in a gentle reminder in case she forgot his eyebrows, wondering whether she would pick up on their conversation on the topic from Christmas. But she didn't seem to be listening to him at all. In fact, he began to sense she was more affected than anyone by the disconcerting presence of the man, who had now taken to pacing up and down the area in a manner that seemed ever more openly hostile.

Miranda's unease was growing to the point that it appeared she could no longer concentrate on the simplest of things. Simon had hoped she might feel confident enough to share the nature of her fears but she seemed to have lost all track. Simon couldn't deny feeling highly perturbed, especially on Miranda's account, by the man's threatening presence.

'Who is it?' he tried to get her to tell him.

'Er . . .' It was obvious she knew but she was so transfixed, she seemed incapable of speaking.

'I think I know,' he said, feeling he had no choice but to take matters into his own hands. 'If you don't mind, I'll go over and have a word.'

He had no idea what he was going to say. All he knew was that he trusted in his ability to sort things out. Besides, he couldn't tolerate seeing Miranda looking so desperately unhappy.

*

Ian reckoned he had at last seen the light. He couldn't look at Joanne now without realising what a big mistake he had made. At first, his attraction to her had been overwhelming. Being with her had been such a pleasurable escape from the pressures of domestic life. He had known Miranda from childhood. The truth was that he had found it very difficult to cope when it wasn't just the two of them any longer. With young children to look after, their whole relationship had changed for the worse. He had suddenly felt tied down. Joanne had represented a spark of adventure returning into his life. She had a faintly taunting way of addressing people in the office. Whereas other staff might have resented it, he found himself drawn. Some of her little mannerisms etched themselves in his mind, such as the habit she had of tossing her hair or the way her brow puckered so appealingly whenever she asked him for help with something. Her physical attractiveness was accentuated by a style of dressing that was expensive, chic and made the absolute most of her slim figure. Instead of giving her a wide berth, he had been blown out of the water.

In all senses, his affair with Joanne had proved a chastening experience. Although it was hard for him to accept, it didn't take long to realise he was little more than a pawn in her game. The object seemed to be to see how quickly she could wipe him off the board. Heedlessly, he had sacrificed himself. As soon as she had succeeded in snatching him away from his wife and children, the coveted prize lost all its value for her. Rapidly, she tired of having him at her beck and call. Instead she despised him for succumbing so easily to her entrapment. Desperate to re-stoke her ardour, he had gone overboard arranging holiday breaks to exotic locations. But no matter how many gifts he showered on her, the pleasure she derived only ever seemed short-lived and gratuitous.

With everything spiralling out of control, he desperately wished he could turn the clock back. In a crazy bid to subsidise an extravagant life-style, he didn't have a penny to put aside for child maintenance. It wasn't that he had ever made a conscious decision not to, it was just that one way and another he spent all his money on Joanne. He lived like an addict whose cure was always just round the corner. If and when he saw the children, he spent whatever he was carrying in his back pocket. For periods of time, it had been preferable not seeing them because it didn't affect his conscience so badly. But occasionally he missed them so much he found himself wandering round to the house on the off-chance. He knew if he had said in advance he was coming, Miranda would have refused to play ball.

The last thing he wanted was to pose a physical threat to Miranda. He could see all too well how poorly he had treated her and the children. He wanted to tell her he regretted coming round those two Saturdays. The problem was he didn't know how to go about it. The last time they had talked over the phone, she had become indignant. That was why he had decided to come and speak to her at the end of work. Knowing that she had threatened to call the police the last time he went to the house, he felt very tense. He had asked at reception to make sure it was her last client and then he hoped he would get a chance to talk with her. But somehow his uneasiness had conveyed itself. Or it might have been that she was just shocked to see him in that context. Either way, he longed to have a chance to reassure her before she jumped to the wrong conclusion. Granted it was long overdue, he also yearned to tell her he had left Joanne for good. He was here to let Miranda know there was no need to take anything through the courts. Not before time, he had come to his senses and was more than prepared to pay on a monthly basis. He was keen to persuade her it was something the two of them needed to discuss here and now. He might well be deluding himself but he still hadn't given up hope she might see, from the contriteness of his manner, that he was worth taking back again for their own sakes and the children's. But first, they had to go off somewhere quiet and thrash things out together like two grown-up people.

In truth, he was uncertain how Miranda might react. The last thing he had expected was for her male client, an old-looking bloke, to take it into his head to intervene. Basically, he had been minding his own business standing at the front of the salon. The next thing he knew there was this jerk buttonholing him and even making it sound as if he was acting on Miranda's behalf. He kept on saying he was advising him to leave the premises. To be honest, he felt like clocking him one but thankfully he drew back. Despite the man looking completely ridiculous, puffed up in one of those black smocks, the tone of his voice somehow managed to project an air of authority that left him slightly unsure who or what he was taking on.

As the other man stood his ground, making it clear he would have no hesitation sending for security guards, Ian tried ignoring him and shouted across to Miranda: 'Are you going to speak to me or not?' Seeing that she looked distinctly unwilling, he gave up on his plan and simply walked out of the salon.

Although Simon had managed to contact Caroline on his mobile to say he was going to be late, the encounter with Miranda's husband was still preoccupying him. He hoped his manner wouldn't give too much away on the exterior. Inside, he was churned up. Even to himself, he found it difficult to explain the protective instincts he felt towards Miranda. In the circumstances, he was bound to have been concerned, but it had gone far beyond that. His anxiety on her behalf had felt so intense that he wanted to stay by her side as long as possible to make absolutely sure she was safe and well. Even though he knew it would make him late for his meeting at school, he had found it impossible to wrench himself away. After Ian had stormed off, he had felt a duty to stay a while. Miranda suspected her ex-husband might be lying in wait, so he had offered to accompany her back to her car. It had seemed a natural thing to do and he was pleased when she looked so grateful. Although he knew he didn't live close enough to be of much further use, he offered his telephone number. He felt even more reason to be happy when she gave him hers. He was keen not to want to appear to be interfering but he asked her to ring him if he could be of any help. Watching her drive off, although he knew the threat of her husband was no laughing matter, Simon couldn't help feeling strangely elated the way things had turned out.

When he finally reached Ashdown, he tried to pull himself together and concentrate on matters in hand. He had decided there was no possible point in reproaching Richard for having applied for the other headship post. Nor was any useful purpose to be served by implying that Richard was using it as a lever to force him to make his own intentions more clear. However, it had concentrated the mind and he had already taken the precaution of contacting John Armitage to check his position in relation to his short-term post at Bentwood. Satisfied that the LEA and Governors would be happy to extend the length of contract beyond the current two terms, at least he knew where he stood in that respect.

The conversation with Richard passed off amicably enough. He seemed at pains to reassure Simon he had not intended to steal a march. Simon fully accepted this and gave similar assurances back that he appreciated how unsettling it must be not quite knowing where he stood long-term. The main thing that irritated Simon was the habit Richard had of tilting back in his chair as if he was in charge. Simon wouldn't have wanted him to defer in any way – after all, it was a chance for them to exchange views openly – so perhaps it was being back in his own room and feeling awkward about seeing someone else occupying his desk. The particular way Richard had chosen to redecorate his walls in such garish colours must also have had something to do with it. Eventually, it seemed more like a sparring match. Despite honours being even, it definitely felt as if he were playing away from home.

Simon couldn't help feeling a more serious contest lay ahead with the Chair of Governors. Just as it had occurred to him in recent times that he didn't really know what made Richard tick, he began to feel an even stronger sense of uncertainty over the Chair of Governors, Ted Bingham. Normally, he prided himself on his instinct for reading other people's minds, but it was now beginning to seem almost impossible. He had only been away from Ashdown for three months and already he was feeling completely disorientated. Even Caroline seemed to have a more strained, almost detached manner towards him. He began to think that people must have only treated him in a particular way before because he was the headteacher in post. Now he was elsewhere, it was as if he had never really belonged. Perhaps the simple truth was that his loan transfer to Bentwood meant forfeiting all pretensions to be the leading player on the park at Ashdown.

His working relationship with Ted Bingham had always been for the most part sound and untroubled. As Chair of Governors, he tended to keep his distance from school, trusting the Head to sort things out on a day-to-day basis. Apart from that, he already had enough on his plate in his other roles as businessman and local councillor. Usually frank and cheerful, he looked distinctly sheepish on this occasion. If anything, he seemed like an actor who had learnt his lines thoroughly but was nervous delivering them on the night. Simon suspected some sort of collusion between Ted and Richard. It was as if the stage was now being left to the Chair of Governors. The entry of Caroline, with a tray of sandwiches and other refreshments, only served to heighten the sense of drama. Usually Ted would have tucked in with hearty appetite but tonight he seemed markedly reticent, as though he wouldn't feel relaxed until he had carried out his part. Waiting nervously for Caroline to leave the room, as soon as they were left on their own, Ted opened with characteristic bluntness.

'No reflection on you, Simon, but I have to say the unanimous view of the Governing Body is that we should be very sorry to see Richard Preece go.'

'I agree,' Simon spontaneously replied.

'So what are we going to do about it?' Ted's eyes had a tendency to bulge when he was pressing a point and, at this moment, he was staring at Simon with the tenacity of a bulldog.

'Well, don't think I haven't given it thought.' Simon had learnt over the years it was best not to beat around the bush with Ted.

'You have?' The Chair of Governors responded enthusiastically but still like a dog after a bone. 'Well?'

'The way I see it is that Richard might get the job he's applying for ... or else he might not,' he offered in a measured tone of voice. Wasn't it his duty to point out that nothing was ever a foregone conclusion?

'Indeed ...' Simon enjoyed watching Ted's facial muscles become a bit more taut. As if irritated, he started scratching his chin. 'But ...'

'Of course, he must have a very good chance.'

'So?'

Simon felt it was the right time to cut to the quick. 'Well, one answer could be that I resign and then he can apply for my post here at Ashdown.'

'Would you be willing to do that?'

'Most certainly. I think it would be in the best interests of all concerned.'

It was obvious to Simon that Ted had been prepared for a much harder tussle. His eyes seemed to twinkle with pleasure at what he had just heard.

'Look, I don't want to rush you,' he offered with an expansive gesture of his arms.

'I've decided!' Simon said with an uncompromising air of finality.

'No hard feelings?'

'None whatsoever.' Nor was it a case of dissembling. Simon knew he felt better for putting the decision behind him.

Then, as if to pre-empt any awkward silence at that point, Ted inquired: 'Things going all right at Bentwood?'

'Yes, we've got an inspection coming up in three weeks' time.'

Feeling an evident sense of relief at having steered the conversation away from Ashdown, Ted at last felt at liberty to do proper justice to the refreshments. Within a matter of minutes, they had finished and were ready to go.

Exchanging pleasantries after leaving the office, Simon caught sight of Caroline sitting at her desk in the adjacent room. Glancing up from her work, her face couldn't disguise a look of surprise as if she hadn't been expecting the meeting to be over so soon. He had a sneaking suspicion Richard might still have been on site but there was no sign of him.

As the men talked on in the entrance-area, Caroline had gone back into the office to clear away. Then together, the three of them left the building and wandered out to the car park. Walking at a gentle pace, it instinctively struck Simon that Ted and Caroline were perfectly in step and at ease in one another's company while he seemed very much the odd one out.

On his journey back to Leeds, he told himself he must have been reading too much into the situation. But it caused him to wonder just what he had and hadn't known when he was at Ashdown. It didn't bear thinking about. He had enough difficulty sorting his own situation. However, he was utterly convinced he had made the right decision to resign. Besides, whatever else, he definitely needed to concentrate his full energies on Bentwood.

He felt in a mood to be decisive on all fronts. When he got home, he contacted Alan and agreed to the Naylors' offer on Willow Cottage. Feeling that these various matters were now safely settled, he then found himself fumbling in his wallet for a piece of paper that had Miranda's mobile number on it. Whichever view he took, this was the most welcome thing that had happened to him today.

Chapter 16

Bill Deacon didn't mind admitting he had found the weeks running up to the inspection the most stressful he could remember. It was difficult enough at Bentwood at the best of times. Day-to-day, the simple truth was it was a knackering school to work in. The vast majority of the pupils were from poor backgrounds and there was virtually no support from parents. The whole neighbourhood had been in decline for years. You didn't have to be a genius to realise these kids were bound to have negative attitudes. They certainly didn't respect teachers; if they respected anyone, it was the drug-pushers in their fast cars. The occasional lad might make it as a pro footballer, or a pouting fifth-form madam might score as a page three model. Very few had aspirations to go on to further education. The one certain thing was that pupils at Bentwood were all graduates of the school of hard knocks. All this explained why the place was no picnic to work in.

Having said all this, he had done his best by the school, whatever anyone else might say. It had stung him to overhear Simon Russell describing him to an HMI Inspector as 'jaded and out of touch'. He regarded the statement as patently unfair. Since giving up his job in the services, he had dedicated himself to Bentwood. Others had deserted ship in the meantime but he had stuck to his guns throughout. Looking back on thirty years, it had never been comfortable but he had successfully seen through several generations of pupils. So many times over the years, he had been the anchor-man in times of crisis. What made Simon Russell's comments even more hurtful was that they were totally uncalled for. As new head, he had made a point of preaching they were all in it together. Whatever personal reservations he might have from time to time, Bill always believed in the fundamental importance of team spirit. Nor did anyone need to point out to him how vital a good inspection would be for the future of the school. Of all people, he understood the seriousness of the situation. There was much more at stake for him than Simon Russell if the inspection team chose to do something drastic like close the place. As relative newcomers to Bentwood, Simon Russell and Emma McCready were never likely to be held accountable. Inspectors made scapegoats of old lags like him. It didn't take a fortune-teller to predict who would be first in the firing-line.

Looking back on the term, he could see now he had fooled himself if he thought Simon Russell was going to take kindly to him. There was always a sharp, cutting edge to his dissection of what was wrong at Bentwood. It was crystal clear where he allocated blame for the existing state of affairs. Bill had lost count of the number of times Simon had criticised arrangements that he was personally responsible for. He was so much in the habit of extolling the comparative virtues of his old school that he wondered why on earth he had left it in the first place. He obviously felt he was slumming it coming downmarket to a dive like Bentwood. Things had become even more unbearable when Emma McCready arrived because it meant having to put up with the two of them forever saying things needed turning upside down. After a while, it felt like one constant 'looping the loop'.

Even now the inspection was over, it was galling to hear

the two of them going on about how well the school had come out of it. They wanted everyone to think it was because of the changes they had introduced. Personally, he felt betrayed. He knew he wasn't in line for any praise. In fact, he was more than ready to take his fair share of the blame. But the truth was that he had been cast in the role of the sacrificial lamb. 'Jaded and out of touch' were words he resented badly enough in the first place. But to hear those unjustified condemnations relayed to inspectors was unforgivable. He had already checked with his union but, whilst they sympathised, it seemed there was little he could do about it in any formal sense. The only redeeming aspect was that at least no-one seemed to be doubting his basic competence. With his track-record, he didn't care who it was – Inspectors or Simon Russell – they would have a hell of a job to make any trumped-up charge like that stick. If they were wanting him to go, they were damned well going to have to make it worth his while.

The moment the inspection was over and the team had packed their bags and left, Emma couldn't resist making a beeline for Simon's office. The signs on the first day had been good but now the second was over, she felt desperate to know the final verdict. She knew he would get in touch but she couldn't wait. The Inspectors must have been in his room for more than an hour. Checking with Wendy that he was on his own, she knocked gently. Not wishing to seem presumptuous, she arched her head round the door with an optimistic expression on her face.

'Well . . .?'

For a moment, he stared vacantly back at her. 'Not too bad at all.' He seemed to enjoy keeping the suspense going. 'Pretty good, I'd say.' By his standards, it sounded positively triumphant.

'That's marvellous!' she let out in a sudden whoop of delight. Then, on a practical note, she told him that most of the staff had stayed on in the hope of hearing the outcome.

Not thinking twice, he appreciated the need to go along to the staff room to share the news with everyone.

Although he was feeling jubilant inside, he tried to measure his statements as carefully as he could. From the moment he walked into the staff room, he picked up the expectant air. The look on people's faces said everything and he felt the need to do proper justice to the occasion.

He started out by saying the Inspectors had seen sufficient evidence to show that good progress had been made since the last report a term ago. He went on to itemise all the various areas where it was said improvements had been made. As he spoke, he sought to build up a sense of achievement. When he had finished, there was a slight, uncertain pause amongst staff. Facial expressions, which had been tense to start with, suddenly seemed to become more relaxed. It was as if they had been waiting for a sword to drop on their heads and it hadn't happened. It was no exaggeration to say that everyone looked happy and almost liberated. A large spontaneous cheer went up.

As Emma saw the contented look on Simon's face, she felt particularly pleased for him because she knew how hard he had worked to try and turn things round in a short space of time. She herself had only been there three weeks and, for her, it had just been a case of fitting in as best she could. But she had really come to appreciate, as if she didn't know it before, how tough the job of the Head was in terms of carrying ultimate responsibility. She had seen how tense he had become during the course of the last three weeks. Although he had remained unfailingly polite to her personally, she had observed first-hand the range of different techniques he had used to drive and motivate staff. While everyone else seemed to accept it as necessary, poor Bill was the only one who took exception.

Despite the convivial staff meeting, she heard that Bill had confronted Simon. The upshot was that Bill had threatened to resign. She had to admire Simon for the fact that he didn't seem in the least fazed by the outburst. If anything, he sounded almost pleased. After all, it didn't need a mindreader to see Bill wasn't Simon's ideal choice as a deputy. It confirmed what she had sensed all along that she was the only one he trusted and confided in. This was further underlined when Simon impulsively announced they ought to go and have a celebratory drink somewhere together. He said it would allow him to share with her in more detail the feedback from the Inspectors.

Without a second thought, she agreed to the idea. After staying a reasonable while with the rest of the staff, she followed Simon in the general direction of Leeds. Since it was the same way she normally took home, it didn't make much difference to the length of her journey. She couldn't help thinking again what a nice gesture it was on Simon's part. It made her feel appreciated. She was so used to seeing a frown on his face that it seemed wonderful, even if almost a travesty of his normal appearance, for him to be looking so happy and relaxed.

He had told her before about his flat in Leeds. Living the other side of the Pennines, she didn't know the city very well. She was only used to travelling round the ring road. After they had sorted out the parking, he suggested they go and relax at a wine bar. But, since it was still only 4.30, the one or two they came across weren't open yet. Instead, they dropped into a Starbucks. It didn't seem a bad idea because Emma had to drive home later. Simon queued while she went to sit at a table.

She happened to notice a man sitting at an adjacent table,

wearing a tracksuit, seemingly absorbed in a crossword puzzle. When Simon arrived with two mugs of coffee, this person chanced to look up and exclaim: 'What are you doing skiving off work, Russell!'

Emma felt so nonplussed she had to play it back in her mind to check she'd heard right. She did her best to ignore how flustered Simon looked for a second or two.

'At least I do actually work!' she heard him counter. It came as a relief that he seemed to know the man quite well. Simon's demeanour became composed again, as if it would take more than the odd, provocative remark to knock him off his stride.

'Aren't you going to introduce me?' the man in the tracksuit asked.

For a moment, Simon stared back at him blankly. Not for the first time, Emma noticed it was the more straightforward questions that seemed to stump him. As if to compound the general air of confusion, the muffled tones of a ringing mobile started up in the near vicinity. It took a few seconds for Simon to realise the noise was going off inside his jacket pocket. Eventually fishing it out, he clutched the instrument to his ear. Both onlookers watched as he struggled to engage in conversation.

'Hello ... hello!' he repeated in vain. At one point, he seemed to be appealing to Emma for help. She had noticed he wasn't very confident with technology. 'Er ... I'm just having to go outside a minute.' She wasn't quite sure whether he was saying it for her benefit or the poor person's on the other end of the line. Mumbling apologies and whisking himself off as fast as his legs could carry him, he suddenly shot out of the café area. The next vision they caught was of an importunate-looking figure pacing up and down the other side of the door.

The two onlookers could not help but feel a certain bond developing between them from observing this spectacle. The intensity of Simon's manner seemed to indicate it was a most important call. Before long, he had disappeared completely from view. At the very least, Emma thought, it must have been the Director of Education. Without the benefit of the sideshow entertainment, an awkward silence fell between the two of them. She thought for a moment he might even bury his head back into his crossword.

'Who did you say you were?' she found herself asking to try and pre-empt this happening. Then it occurred to her she had put the question rather abruptly, so she apologised.

'That's all right. I'm Tom. I'm a friend of Simon's,' he said, wondering whether Simon would have seen it in the same light.

'I'm Emma. I'm Deputy Head at Simon's school,' she responded. She didn't want to make it sound as if her identity revolved around Simon but at least it provided a necessary link.

'Dare I ask how it went?' Tom ventured.

The question seemed to catch her unawares. As she looked back at him dubiously, he feared for a moment he'd put his foot in it again.

'Do you mean the inspection?' she grasped. 'Oh, it's gone brilliantly, thank you.'

Her face, from looking rather tired, seemed now to radiate intense pleasure. He couldn't help but feel caught in the dazzle. After a somewhat slow start, he found himself thinking he was warming to her.

'That's why we've come here to celebrate,' she added.

'Here? Celebrate?' His intonation made it clear her last statement had had an amusing effect on him.

'I think we're moving on to a wine bar later,' she felt the need to explain. Why was she sounding like an eighteen-year-old? She found herself racking her brain to remember whether she'd ever heard Simon mention Tom's name before. Somehow, he didn't look like the kind of friend

Simon would have. He seemed worldly in a discerning sort of way and she guessed he had quite a sophisticated sense of humour. Not that she was meaning to be harsh on Simon.

She felt confident in his company and asked him, since he was wearing a tracksuit: 'Do you play sport then?'

'Yes, I like going to the gym and I'm keen on running. Though I must say it's hard going out every day. Especially without having any end goal in sight.'

The sincerity of his tone emboldened her. 'Really? I felt the same until I started running marathons.' As soon as the words had escaped her lips, she felt there was a risk of sounding superior or, even worse, boasting.

She was pleased to hear him continue: 'That's what I tell myself I should be doing. I don't think I could manage it on my own, though.'

'Sure, there'd be thousands of others running with you!' She reacted instantly, hoping she wasn't sounding too much like an over-enthusiastic PE teacher. She thought she wouldn't confess to that role yet. It wasn't necessary. Anyway, they might never meet again. Glancing in his direction again, she surprised herself by thinking it would be a pity if they didn't. She detected a sensitivity about him that was engaging.

And then, as if the spell was suddenly broken, Tom appeared to see something happening in another part of the room and murmured, as if for his own benefit: 'What on earth is he doing now?'

At first, she wasn't sure who or what he could be talking about. Allowing her eyes to follow the line of his gaze, she still couldn't make anything out.

'Simon, I swear he just came back in and went out again! Perhaps my eyes were deceiving me. Anyway, why should I care what that wild man gets up to?'

Turning round and seeing nothing herself, she was of course prepared to take his word for it. The thing that puzzled her more deeply was finding she wasn't too bothered about how quickly Simon returned. Against all possible expectations, she was enjoying this conversation with Tom more than she cared to admit. She couldn't quite work it out. She had an instinct she was going to end up flirting with him or fighting for his soul. She couldn't tell which. On second thoughts, it might end up being both!

Miranda didn't reckon for a moment that Simon thought she would actually remember the date of the inspection, let alone take the trouble to find out how it had gone. After all, she was only his hairdresser and it had nothing to do with her. But try telling that to her in her present mood! Because she had grasped it meant so much to him, she couldn't help but feel concerned to know the outcome. Although she hadn't any real idea what it entailed, she still felt worried on his account and wanted to know he was all right. Having his telephone number was proving too severe a temptation.

How many times today had she taken the mobile out of her bag, thought better and put it away again? Anyway, he'd be too busy to take a call. It was one thing he trusted her enough to give her his number, without her spoiling matters by badgering him unnecessarily. Plagued by conflicting voices inside her head, she surrendered to her gut instinct. She finally took the plunge and rang. What was there to lose? At worst, all he could do was put the phone down on her. He would never do that, though. If there wasn't any answer, she felt confident enough about leaving a message. That would probably be the best compromise. Or she could text him. But, once her mind was committed, she knew she wouldn't be happy until she had heard his voice and spoken with him directly.

Dialling the numbers with studied care, momentarily she resigned herself to picking up the engaged signal. No, she could hear the phone ringing at the other end. Was she ready for this? Steeling herself to sound confident, she anxiously counted down the seconds before the inevitable message service kicked in.

'Hello . . . hello!'

It shocked her to hear a real voice. Only it didn't seem like his at all. Feeling a stab of relief, she wondered if perhaps she had got a wrong number.

'Er . . . I'm just having to go outside a minute.' The voice was definitely Simon's.

She swallowed hard. 'Hello, it's Miranda.'

Realising she had no right to expect him to recognise her voice, she still hoped he might have remembered her name. There seemed an almighty long pause for some reason before she heard her name being muttered faintly: 'Miranda?'

Adding to her anxiety, he appeared unable to communicate. For a moment, she felt like cutting her losses and hanging up.

'Miranda, is that you?' To her delight, his voice began to pick up and sound more enthusiastic. 'Why, it's good to hear from you. How are you?'

'I hope you don't mind me ringing?'

'No, not at all!' She couldn't deny he sounded pleased to speak to her.

'I know it's probably been a very busy day for you . . .'

'The inspection . . . er, yes . . .' His tone didn't betray any particular strain.

'Has it gone OK then?' Might he be thinking she had an almighty nerve ringing to ask him? Steadying herself, she decided to press on irrespective.

'It's gone very well. Thank you very much for thinking about me and taking the trouble to ring.'

His voice sounded grateful and almost emotional. She

didn't know what to say. He hadn't needed to add that last bit. There was a short pause before he spoke again.

'Look, what are you doing later?'

It was the last thing she had been anticipating. Suddenly, she couldn't think straight at all.

'I'm not sure . . .'

'I would love nothing more than to invite you out . . . tonight!'

What could she say? Had she heard right? Where had this come from?

'Pardon?' was the only utterance that managed to escape her lips.

'Or some other night, perhaps, if tonight is not possible?'

'No, I'd love to.' Hesitating, she needed to check whether he meant join him on his own or as part of a celebration party.

'I could book a table for two and come and pick you up at eight.'

The question was answered for her.

'That would be lovely, Simon.'

Within a moment or two, the conversation had finished. It was decided. She couldn't remember the last time she had acted so impulsively. But on a practical note, what on earth was she going to do with the children? Determined nothing would get in her way, a quick phone call to her mum did the trick. It still didn't give her long, though. For another thing, what was she going to wear? She must be crazy!

Tom couldn't help but spot the irrepressible grin on Simon's face when he reappeared. His suspicion was that not even a successful inspection would make him look like that. Suddenly, however, Simon was declaring some urgent engagement had sprung up and he was having to leave straight away. Tom had always reckoned he was the impulsive one of the two but he had to hand it to Simon on this occasion.

Tom immediately had a concern for Emma. It hadn't seemed to occur to his friend that, having dragged her out here, he owed any explanation for what was a complete and utter change of plan. Thankfully, she had not seemed unduly put out, despite Simon departing in conspicuous haste.

Granted the bizarre circumstances, Tom's own evening continued spectacularly well. By the end of it, he and Emma had shared life-stories. What was more, he had stayed on orange juice. Oh! and she had talked him into running a 10-kilometre event with her some time in March. There was life in the old dog yet!

Chapter 17

Leonie didn't really want to write another letter to Simon but David prevailed upon her. It was a necessary stage, he argued, in the process of facing up to the fact that both their lives had changed irrevocably over a short space of time. In the throes of her operation and treatment, the last thing she needed was any extra uncertainty over how others were going to react. If nothing else, she felt cancer had helped her to concentrate on priorities in life. In mind, if not body, she felt positive enough to believe in the future. The purpose of the first letter had been to inform him of her condition but she now felt an increasing need to describe how it had affected her emotionally. In view of what had transpired at Christmas, she accepted she owed him as much. She even felt secure enough in her restored sense of well-being to put her address on the top of the letter.

It was a considerable challenge to get her tone right. On the one hand, she didn't want to come across as unfeeling but, on the other, she hated the idea of sounding mawkish. In practice, she had found it hard striking a balance between the two extremes. But having undertaken the task, she was determined to get it right. With several drafts behind her, she finally managed to produce a version which she was willing to run by David. She supposed she could have passed it over for him to read by himself but it would have felt like forfeiting responsibility. So she made him a cup of tea, settled him down in the chair opposite and read it out to him from start to finish. He said he felt like a captive audience but she knew he was joking. Gently reminding him he was the one who had said it was necessary, she gave him a mock-indignant look over the top of her reading-glasses before beginning.

Dear Simon,

I hope my recent letter didn't shock you too much. I really felt I needed to write and put you in the picture. I hope you don't mind me writing again. Forgive me if it makes painful reading!

At first, when I was diagnosed, I was afraid to cry for fear of reacting too emotionally. It took a lot to accept I was a cancer victim and needed help. The experience has been like a roller coaster. Cancer is weird because, until things get really bad, I know it sounds stupid but you feel perfectly well. The chemotherapy did make me feel awful. It's difficult to explain but everything has gone on happening so fast. David has been marvellous but I also saw a psychiatrist for counselling and was on anti-depressants. I've done my best to work through it and I have been on what they call complementary therapies. I've also taken my mind off things by doing voluntary work. So whatever else, I've tried to keep busy!

Now, three months on, I'm glad to say I feel a new person. I'm even proud of my mastectomy scar. I take it as a sign of what I've become. They say that fear is worse than the disease itself, and that seems true in my case. I think I'm a happier and better person now. It's been like a wake-up call. Only I have the time to do something about it. I've been told I should have no further problems. Even if it does come back, the way I feel is that I've dealt with it once and I'll be able to deal with it again. I've found a new strength I didn't know I had.

I go to the gym and swim every day. It helps enormously, physically and emotionally. Imagine it, I've even started running.

David and I go out every day (very slowly!) and he's even entered us for a half-marathon in June, which we're doing for a breast cancer charity.

Another reason why I'm, writing, I'll be honest, is because I'd really appreciate it if I could visit Willow Cottage again. Apart from collecting one or two things which have sentimental value, I wonder if you might be willing to discuss matters of a more practical nature. I could make it on either the weekend of 6/7 or 13/14 March if convenient. Please get in touch and let me know if there's any possibility.

Best wishes.

Leonie

Looking up from her writing-pad, she asked: 'Well, what do you think?'

'I think it's just right,' David replied, without a moment's hesitation.

She smiled. She hadn't intended changing anything but it felt very reassuring to have his approval all the same.

When Simon came to read the letter, he felt an enormous sense of relief. Although Leonie was clearly very different to the person he once knew, he appreciated how much the experience must have affected her outlook. It pleased him considerably that she had provided her address and telephone number. The worst part before was having no idea of her whereabouts. It had made her seem like a lost person. He could only feel admiration for the recovery she had made, even if strangely guilty that he had played little part in it himself. Feeling genuinely happy at the prospect of seeing her again, it made perfect sense for her to come and collect any items she wanted from Willow Cottage. He wasn't so sure how he was going to break the news about agreeing to the sale of the property. With the handover to the Naylors arranged for the end of the month, it was no bad thing she was able to make it over in early March.

For some strange reason, Simon's mind ran to Miranda. The thought of her momentarily made him feel guilty. But then didn't Leonie have David to comfort her? It was hard telling himself but it wasn't as if he owed Leonie anything in that direction. Why shouldn't he feel happy all round? Not only was he to be reunited with Leonie in a way that had previously seemed unimaginable but, compounding it all, his evening with Miranda had revitalised his self-belief. His impetuousness in inviting her out to dinner seemed to have come from nowhere – he had certainly not planned it in advance – and yet everything had gone so brilliantly from the moment he had picked her up from home, he could hardly believe his good luck. However much he racked his brain to come up with a possible downside to the evening, he couldn't think of one. It had been a perfect success and they had seemed to enjoy one another's company to a degree that he would have thought impossible. He had been electrified by her presence. Indeed, the memory of that occasion had preoccupied his thoughts since in a way that seemed perfectly to match the changing tide in his fortunes. Hearing again from Leonie further stimulated his optimism regarding the future.

Simon's immediate impulse, having read the letter, was to share it with someone. A lot of the content was of a highly personal nature but it didn't seem as if he would be breaking any particular confidence. Nor was there anything in it that didn't reflect great credit on Leonie for the way she had handled the massive challenges facing her. He certainly didn't think she would have minded. Despite all the ordeals she had suffered, a positive tone shone through. As well, he detected a strong feeling of pride in managing to prevail against all the odds. When he showed it to Tom, he did so not unmindful of his reaction to the first letter. He remembered Tom giving him a bit of stick. At the time, he had felt little other reaction than sorrow and a sense of powerlessness to do anything to help. This time, he knew he would be able to demonstrate initiative on his own part. Although he was showing the letter to Tom, he knew he wasn't looking for any second opinion about Leonie's visit. It wasn't stated in the letter but he supposed David would be accompanying her. He had often wondered what kind of person David might be. He supposed he might have felt jealous but somehow he didn't. The other surprising thing was that it wasn't really important to him who David was, so long as he seemed able to offer Leonie the support she needed. In that sense, Simon was very grateful. He harboured no resentment whatsoever. If it needed any firmer invitation, he would be more than willing to give it.

'That woman is so strong!' was how Tom had expressed himself after reading the letter.

Of course, Simon never knew for sure how Tom would react to anything. Somehow, he had suspected it might be a re-run of the first time all over again.

'I've just had a fantastic idea!' Tom suddenly declared, with a look of satisfaction on his face akin to having made a ground-breaking, scientific discovery.

'Is it something I'm going to want to hear, do you think?' Simon responded warily. 'If you decide it is, perhaps you might like to share it.'

Thinking a moment before speaking, Tom still appeared in no doubt: 'Look, Emma has persuaded me to run in a ten-k event – I'm pretty sure it's the fourteenth of March – and that is one of the dates Leonie has suggested. She and David are training for a half-marathon in June. Why don't the four of us – five, if you join in – all run in this event and do it for breast cancer? Obvious, isn't it? QED!'

Simon didn't like to give a response too quickly. To be

honest, his first reaction was that the whole notion seemed preposterous. During the course of the day, though, he began to think he might have been looking at the situation too negatively. In fact, the more he gave the idea thought, the more attractive it began to sound. But he made it clear he wasn't about to rush into anything and would sleep on it.

By the next day, despite himself, he had grown excited about ringing Leonie to see what she thought. After the months of separation, it seemed amazing to be able to dial a few numbers and be back in touch with her. The strange part of it was that he didn't feel at all nervous at the prospect of hearing her voice. It just seemed perfectly natural. Knowing what he wanted to say also helped to make it more straightforward. He was pleased that, in the course of their brief conversation, they seemed much more at ease with one another than before. The exchange was relatively short. The main thing was establishing contact again and feeling able to sort things out. The idea of the 10K run, which he put forward very tentatively in case she thought he was out of his mind, in fact delighted her. She surprised him by agreeing to it straight away. Asking him whether he was taking part himself, he rather spoilt the good impression by showing hesitation.

As soon as he had put the phone down, the uncomfortable thought occurred to him that, if he didn't do something fairly quickly, he would be the only one not in shape for the event. Despite it being the eleventh hour, he decided there was nothing for it but to join Tom on his training runs.

Chapter 18

Tom Judd jolted awake in bed. Bleary-eyed, he peered in the general direction of the alarm clock on the bedside table. It was still only 3.15 in the morning. Two particular anxieties beset him, the first that it was the day of the 10K run and the second that he had poured a bottle of malt whisky down his throat the night before. As he lay there sweating profusely, it slowly dawned on him with a massive sense of relief that the crazy drinking bout had only taken place in his mind as part of a series of dreadful nightmares he had suffered during the night.

Involuntarily, a host of selected other haunting images flashed through his mind. First and foremost was a revisitation of the dire dream that he hadn't had for months of arranging lines of coke with a razor-blade and ending up choking in mounds of white powder. He had somehow tricked himself into thinking, as his recovery went on remorselessly from day to day, that he was exempt both in body and mind. But the truth was that his wretched past habit still had the power to issue mocking reminders from time to time. Yet again, he had also re-lived the scene on Magilligan Sands where the wind was roaring and the mists had enveloped his running partner, Mark Leslie. Hoping it wasn't an omen for today, he wondered if a time would ever come when he was free of these morbid recollections. The thought occurred to him optimistically that in the course of today's run, he might at last succeed in laying one or both of these ghosts to rest for good.

Emma was the best thing to happen to him in ages. Now fully awake, his thoughts started to concentrate upon her. From that first improbable meeting in the coffee-shop, their relationship had gone from strength to strength. He knew he had to keep things in perspective. It was only a matter of two or three weeks but he really had come to believe that she was heaven-sent to help him surmount all his remaining challenges in life. He admired her so much that, never mind a 10K, he would have been willing to run to the ends of the earth for her. When she told him she had done the New York marathon the previous November, he had started trying to persuade her that they should jointly enter for next year's event. After his trials and tribulations of three years ago, he had sworn he would never go back there. But, in the circumstances, he couldn't think of a more rewarding way of returning to his former stamping-ground. As for today's event, he respected Emma for the fact she was so noble-minded. It hadn't taken her a second to agree to run for breast cancer instead of her brother's charity. She had put Tom to shame over the amount of money she had pledged from children at her school. As if all these considerations weren't enough, she was sensationally good-looking into the bargain. How lucky could one guy be, dating a dedicated deputy headteacher who happened to be a blonde bombshell into the bargain!

Tom only hoped he wasn't kidding himself in believing he was in shape to do justice to today's event. He and Emma had done a fair bit of training together in recent times. But he had got the distinct impression, although she was much too nice to admit it, she adjusted her pace to his rather than the other way around. He laughed at himself for thinking that, if the worst came to the worst, he could always run alongside Simon's ex-wife and her partner. Then, conjuring up one last awkward image in his mind, he visualised the pair of them picking up the pace and outkicking him in the last stretch. Anyway, who was he to say they wouldn't be fit enough to leave him standing? On this note, he found himself glancing at the clock again. It was still only 3-something. Despite his troubled sleep pattern, he took the risk of nodding off again in the hope of catching a few hours' innocent slumber.

Simon had also woken up that morning in an anxious state with the day ahead threatening to be a test of character on several fronts. Apart from meeting Leonie again, he still had niggling doubts as to whether he had taken the right decision to enter the run in the first place. Common sense still said he would have been safer spectating. His preparations were woefully inadequate and he realised he would have to take it very gently if he were to make the distance. Although it was a situation he could have conveniently blamed on Tom, in fact he took responsibility himself. He also knew his feelings towards Miranda had very much shaped his thinking.

Despite the thrilling memory of being together and sharing dinner with Miranda on the day of the school inspection, his hopes of the relationship going any further appeared ruined. All the pleasant feelings associated with that occasion had been snatched away from him after another sudden, unexpected telephone call from Miranda a few days ago. She had rung informing him, in a tone that sounded matter-of-fact and strangely unemotional, that she was now reunited with Ian. It had come as a bombshell to him. In other circumstances, he would have been delighted to hear of a couple having a second go at marriage, especially where there were children to consider. Miranda herself didn't seem keen to enlarge on things and he had been too nonplussed to comment. He couldn't deny he found the sudden change of heart unfathomable and had no better idea what her real feelings were on the matter. The news had stunned him. He hadn't thought it his place to question her motives. To his mortification, she had thanked him for all he had done and even gone as far as to say the whole family was grateful. He got the distinct impression she was talking to him more as a father-figure. Again, he didn't know what he could say in response. He didn't want to reveal any sense of hurt. He had ended up filling the uncomfortable silence by mentioning the run instead.

It was then that she had expressed the wish to support the event and bring the family along. Whatever he was feeling inside, he hadn't had the heart to pour cold water on the offer. It seemed there was little alternative but to grit his teeth and put a positive face on things. Actively taking part in the event at least meant he could take his mind off the unpalatable prospect of witnessing her standing in the crowd with Ian at her side.

As soon as she saw the 'SOLD' notice on Willow Cottage, Leonie felt as though another part of her life had been reconciled. Simon had asked if she and David wanted to stay there overnight on the Saturday but she had declined his kind offer. In some ways, it would have been handy but she had already made arrangements to stay with one of her old teacher-friends from school. Besides, she would probably have found it difficult coping with all the associations bound up in living there for thirty years. Going to collect a few of her belongings in the afternoon had meant making a quick raid and getting away as soon as she could. In her present mood, the last thing she wanted was to dwell on the past.

Simon's invitation to take part in the run was totally

unexpected but rather sweet. She appreciated that the idea had come from a friend of his called Tom, someone she had never heard of before. Simon was always such a loner, it seemed uncharacteristic hearing him refer to 'a friend' and she wondered whether, improbably, he might have become a little more sociable in his outlook. Deep down, it had also taken her by surprise to learn from him that he had left Ashdown for a challenging inner city school. If she had succeeded in carving out a new life for herself, she had to hand it to Simon that he too had not taken things lying down in the last three months. Perhaps the most radical thing he had done was putting Willow Cottage up for sale. She had pictured him living there for ever. Always thinking of him as dyed in the wool and against change, she was absolutely flabbergasted at what he had done. At least, they had had no difficulty in agreeing to share the proceeds from the house sale. She was quite happy going on living with David near Oxford and the money would come in useful.

Of course, she had often thought of the emotional toll it might have on Simon, leaving him so dramatically. If there hadn't been so much to worry about herself at the time, she might have felt a lot more guilty. Visiting Willow Cottage reminded her of his distraught reaction at the time. But again, she could tell from the brief conversations they had on the phone that he sounded far from scarred by the experience now. She liked to think he too might have grown from all that had happened. As she and David made their last-minute preparations before setting off for the run that morning, the whimsical notion came into her head that Simon had never liked baring his legs if he could possibly avoid it. The speculation entered her head as to whether the new Simon would be bold enough to shed tracksuit bottoms...

*

The morning got off to the worst possible start for Miranda. She had warned Ian they would have to get up reasonably early if they were going to make it for the start. But, when the time came, he just decided to go on lying there in bed moaning and cursing. She didn't mind being left to get the children ready on her own. After all, she was used to it. She would have appreciated some help but what she found impossible to stomach was when he finally deigned to come downstairs, he pitched into her violently. It reminded her painfully of his behaviour when he had first struck up with Joanne. She certainly wasn't going to have it dished out to her again. At that time, she had taken all his destructive criticism to heart and even felt guilty and inadequate. She had no intention of putting up with any more abuse. At the back of her mind, the most galling thought was that she had forced herself to make the phone-call to Simon, knowing deep down in her heart how fond she was of him.

Standing up for herself, she had told Ian outright that she didn't want to see him still in the house when she returned. Determined to support Simon's event, she set off as planned, with the children in tow. All the way there, she silently berated herself for having taken Ian back in the first place. There was no other conclusion to draw but that she had acted out of some totally misguided idea she was doing her best by the children. Now she plainly saw that nothing could be further from the truth. Worse than this, she suspected she might have hurt Simon's feelings badly. She had an overwhelming urge to put the record straight.

At that moment, standing there in the cold morning light, she had enough to do trying to make sure the children behaved properly, let alone concentrating on the large group of runners now slowly making their way towards the starting-line. Suddenly, through the wall of spectators, she thought she caught a glimpse of Simon. For a moment, he seemed to be looking in her direction. She had an impulse to shout out to him. As if by intuition, he spotted her but then averted his gaze, almost as if ignoring her. She didn't know what to think but within another second or two later, he glanced in her direction again. Making it seem even more special, Simon actually sauntered over to where she was standing with the children.

'Are you on your own then?' he started, adding hesitantly: 'Er . . . with the children, I mean?'

'It very much looks like it!' she replied emphatically.

'I hope I'll see you at the end,' was all he had time to say further. Watching him run back to his position, she felt a strange thrill to think she was responsible for his hair looking so neat and tidy. From nowhere, the thought also occurred to her that his legs were fairly stunning too.

Emma and Tom finished ahead of the others. He thought he had been doing quite well until they reached the last few hundred metres. Urging him to keep up, she started sprinting flat out. He thought she was trying to give him a heart attack. However, he astounded himself by just about managing to keep up.

Crossing the finishing-line, he felt like collapsing but, gasping loudly, succeeded in staying upright on his feet. He still had enough energy to call out to her: 'Next stop New York, OK?' Taking a plastic cup of water, they stood at the finish amidst the banks of spectators cheering all the runners home.

About ten minutes later, Leonie and David crossed the line, looking as if they had been out for nothing more challenging than a country stroll. Tom, by now fully recovered, started joking about whether they needed to call a taxicab to pick Simon up and give him a lift to the finish. Emma warned him to watch himself if he wanted to keep her as his running partner.

WATCHING SPORT WITHOUT TV

NORTHERN SPORTING VENUES THROUGH THE EYES OF A MAN WITHOUT A SATELLITE DISH.

STEVEN CHAYTOR

"Watching Sport Without TV" has been published by Kipper publications

© Steven Chaytor

First published 2006
All right reserved

A Catalogue record for this book is available at the British Library

ISBN 0-9554419-0-0
ISBN 978-0-9554419-0-5

Print and design by Print Works (NY) Ltd
Contact www.printworks-ny.co.uk

All photographs by Steven Chaytor

For further information on Kipper Publications contact
www.kipperpublications.co.uk or if you have any queries or wish to comment
on this or any other Kipper books e-mail kipperpublish@aol.com

This one's for Doug

Contents

1. Introduction — Page 1
2. Riverside Stadium — Page 3
3. Brunton Park — Page 10
4. The Stadium of Light — Page 18
5. St. James' Park — Page 25
6. The Reynolds Arena — Page 32
7. Kingston Park — Page 39
8. Newcastle City Pool — Page 46
9. The Riverside County Cricket Ground — Page 54
10. Trimdon Community College Association — Page 62
11. The Wynyard Club — Page 67
12. Victoria Park — Page 78
13. Sedgefield Racecourse — Page 86
14. Billingham Forum Ice Arena — Page 94
15. Millfield — Page 102
16. David Lloyd Health and Raquets Club — Page 110
17. Gateshead International Stadium — Page 118
18. So What? — Page 126

1. Introduction

Let me be clear from the start. I love sport. I also have a television. However, I do not subscribe to Sky Television. I am not the owner of a dish. My house is not adorned with a black wok. These are essential facts to provide background to the following chapters.

You see, I firmly believe that those people who only see sport through a television screen are actually seeing something slightly unreal. Their judgement is impaired by only seeing the very best of a given sport on their screens. Top class performers become their benchmark. The best becomes the norm. Anything they perceive as being not as good as the best is crap. How else could a serious sports watcher conclude that Tim Henman is a loser, is not world class and has under achieved? How else could a real sports fan conclude that Frank Bruno was a useless donkey who couldn't really box his way out of a wet paper bag? How else could anybody seriously accuse the England football team of being useless, passionless also rans when they regularly achieve quarter final status in major tournaments? So they're not the very best in the world but they're bloody good at what they do. They are so much better than the people who criticise them that they shouldn't be on the same planet.

The TV screen sanitises everything. It reduces everything in scale and effect. It removes the rough edges and, in some cases, the humanity. And now, of course, the arsenal of cameras and commentators that can see things and judge things in a way that is impossible to the naked eye, from ground level or in the frenzy of competition, has convinced dipstick spectators and journalists that perfection is possible. I'm not even convinced it's worth striving for. After all, it's the imperfections in sport as much as the skill and athleticism that make it so exciting.

Viewing sport live adds another dimension - several other dimensions - to the spectacle. You are able to understand the scale of the playing area, the intimidating proximity of the crowd, the effects of the weather. You can hear the sounds from the stands, the voices, the music. The traffic on the nearby road, the pa announcements. You can hear the quips, the jokes, the abuse. You can feel the anger, the joy and the despair. You can smell the grass, the beer, the sweat, the hot dogs. You are part of the spectacle not just a distant, detached observer.

But it's not just being there that adds so much to watching sport it's also getting there. Travelling to a sporting event offers the excitement and anticipation of arrival and build up. It allows you to see the sport in it's proper setting, to experience the town in which it's located. Feeling the pre match atmosphere while walking to a football ground offers a little more to the senses than settling down to watch the adverts with a stubby before Steve Ryder introduces summeriser Sam Allardyce before kick off. Parking up at a golf tournament, walking the course and smelling the grass, seeing the players honing their swings on the practice ground beats waiting in your arm chair for Gary Lineker to do some cheesy introduction. Flicking the TV on to catch a few highlights is fine for what it is. After all, we can't be there at every event. Watching the 'live' action on TV gives a sense of real time to the event. But both are pale imitations of the multi-layered experience that 'being there' offers.

One of my favourite pastimes when out and about is keeping an eye out for look-alikes. The human race can only present so many variations on a theme so there's a good chance you can see some unlikely looking people in some unexpected places. You can't do that sitting on your sofa. Well, I suppose it depends where your sofa is. Or whether you have a house full of celebrity look-alikes. Or whether or not you give a damn about such a trivial and frankly, juvenile pursuit. Nevertheless, the following chapters offer not just a personal view of sport in the raw but sightings of what look like some of our most famous fellow humans in places and doing things they probably wouldn't wish to be made public.

Finally, you'll notice that there are almost three years between the first venue visit and the last. This is not because I only attended sixteen sports events in three years. It owes more to the totally unplanned and arbitrary nature of the writer and complete lack of a pencil and paper at other times. The times and dates are, of course, irrelevant to the exercise

Blimey, I hope that this introduction hasn't sounded like too much like an essay. It's just that when you see sport on TV you might be a little more appreciative. A little less critical. Or at least, a little more informed about your criticism. All I'm trying to say is 'get of your arse and go and watch some proper sport in the flesh'!

2. The Riverside Stadium, Middlesbrough.

Sunday 28th December 2003.
Middlesbrough v Manchester United, Carling Premier League.

It does seem faintly ridiculous to be dressing for a football match as if preparing for an evening at the ambassador's residence. Jacket and tie required. Dinner will be served at 2.00pm. Any special dietary requirements? Drinks will be served throughout. Welcome to the world of corporate hospitality. Welcome to the modern football business.

I am the lucky recipient of a kind invitation to join those lovely people from Radio TFM for the big match against champions, Manchester United. I have only 'boxed' on a couple of occasions but always feel slightly guilty. This is not really how football was meant to be viewed. This is not really how it's supposed to be. However, I wear my guilt lightly and deem it impolite to refuse such benevolence so here I am, suited and booted, scrubbed up and ready for dinner and a footie match. Oh, my Catholic guilt.

As you approach The Riverside Stadium, sited beside the river Tees co-incidentally, there is an immediate sense of before and after that strikes anyone who knew the old Ayresome Park, scene of so many false dawns for The Boro over the past century. Ayresome was the epitome of football in the community, land locked and almost hidden, as it was, behind the general hospital and the back streets of west Middlesbrough. For Ayresome Park read Mannion and Hardwick. The Riverside, by contrast stands out like a lush and vibrant hair on a bald man's head positioned, as it is, on the de-industrialised Middlehaven site, an area in dire need of a transplant. However, one of the great advantages of the new home is the simplicity of finding it. Turn off the A19 and onto the A66 and you're only one more turn away from being more or less there. Entering Middlesbrough by this route takes the car driver straight through the heart of the town at a slightly unnerving half-building height. The road planner decided to drive this particular stretch of tarmac right through the only old buildings in town, successfully cutting off the commercial centre from the old town and the river. Now the town is trying to reclaim the river through the Middlehaven development that is spearheaded by The Riverside Stadium. Who'd have thought Middlesbrough FC would be leading the way?

But there it is. Pretty damned impressive actually. A capacity of 35,049. All covered and all seated. Huge white external framework holding up the roof and two giant red pillars at the main entrance to add a touch of grandeur and sense of arrival. It's right on the river, the old docks a hint of the past, The Tuxedo Princess moored a few yards away as a floating nightclub, a more realistic pointer to the future. Where Teessiders used to toil and sweat, they now come to see their team in action in a twenty first century stadium. Looks like people had better get used to the idea of Middlesbrough being a big football club.

I drive over Harold Shepherdson Way and approach the stadium car park hoping to take further advantage of my hospitality ticket. I wind down the window and lean towards the open space to speak to the attendant on the entrance.

"Excuse me. I have an invitation to one of the boxes. Can I park in here? "

I'm hoping he's impressed.

"No. "

He's not. I'm a little deflated. Not that important then.

"You don't have any advice I suppose? "

The attendant looks at me for a second, clearly making a snap decision on whether to offer advice or abuse. Luckily, perhaps after consideration of his employment prospects, he opts for the former. "Turn around. Go round the mini-roundabout and follow the road round – over there, look. Past the ground there's a place you can park. They'll look after your car. "

I follow the instructions - kindly given - and arrive at a kind of lock-up place. It's pitted with pot holes and puddles but there are a few cars there.

"Do I park in here mate?

"Yeh. Three pounds. "

The bloke looks like he should be working for Phil Mitchell. When he tells me the car will be safe I believe him. When he tells me they never shut I believe him. When he explains they're a twenty-four hour operation I don't doubt a word. I do begin to wonder, however, what their core business is. Probably best not to ask. I park up and wander the few hundred yards to the stadium past the usual stalls – badges, hotdogs – and saunter round to the main entrance to get my bearings. And there they are, Hardwick and Mannion, symbols of the old club and still the two most famous and revered Boro boys, each cast in bronze and placed on a plinth to welcome visitors and remind the world of two of football's genuine greats. Each strikes a pose that encapsulates their abiding images. It's worth taking a moment – and a camera.

But never mind all this tourist stuff, what about my dinner? There is much milling around by fans without ties and jackets as I make my way to the 'executive' entrance where I am greeted at the 'front door' by a regular beauty who is dressed in a very short skirt. She is doing her utmost to welcome the guests with a smile despite the fact that it's freezing. I look again, as you do, and realise it's Victoria Beckham. She really should be wearing something warmer, I advise. She's polite and professional enough to smile back but her lips are so blue conversation is limited to "up the stairs sir. " At least they could have let her wear trousers. I knew this was a posh do but this was ridiculous. Victoria also thinks it's ridiculous. I can tell. She has forsaken Madrid for Middlesbrough for a weekend job designed to get her more 'in touch with' the game and she's decided, quite rightly in my opinion, to get amongst the fans. Well at least some of them, the ones in suits and ties. A girl's got to start somewhere. She's clearly missing David but it's a very valuable learning experience so I leave her to her duties. As I ascend to the mighty corridor of boxes I can just hear the faint Essex tones of "up the stairs sir.... up the stairs madam" trail off into the distance.

The inner sanctum is populated by suits and gowns, the whiff of aftershave and perfume. Many of the chaps are young and sharp and have gelled hair. I am not impressed by gelled hair. Gel has no place on a man's head. Who in God's name wants shiny, spikey hair? What is it with male grooming these days? It's all incredibly civilised though. A person in a uniform is kind enough to direct me to the TFM box, through the restaurant and on the left at the far end. The restaurant is packed. Long tables, short tables, waitress service and good manners. Women who wonder why they are here. You can see it in their faces, you really can. Blokes determined to have there fill 'cos it's on the company. Blokes who wonder why they are here - they don't really like football. Women having a ball 'cos it's a bit of a do. What a strange and wonderful melange. Then there's me taking any opportunity I can to see my team, Manchester United. Oops, better not tell the TFM guests. I'm sure to be a lone voice in a box full of Smoggies.

"Ah, you must be Steve. Glad you could make it. Glass of wine? "

"Don't mind if I do...Thanks. "

I'm greeted warmly and professionally by a TFM commercial manager and introduced to the other guests. There's around a dozen of us. Most of them seem to be from the motor trade and far from being the only Manc, half the box is rooting for United. Of the others, about two are Boro fans, there's a couple of Darlo supporters and one or two whose highlight is almost certainly going to be the lasagne.

It's a small but comfortable box. No table. We eat buffet style on our knees, me trying not to embarrass myself by over filling my plate and everyone looking for some way to deal with a glass and a plate at the same time. Like a little party really. You know the ones, where you think everyone knows each other but it turns out they don't. I'm introduced to a very decent chap who I learn later that week has just been awarded the OBE in the New Years honours list.

"Eh, have you read this? I was at the match with him on Sunday. Never said a word."

Well, of course he wasn't supposed to. So well done him for containing his excitement. Come to think of it though, he looked like a man about to be honoured.

The party pootles along with polite conversation and pudding while the girl comes round with the betting slips and we watch some build up on Sky TV. But I'm most impressed by watching the warm up routine of Roy Carroll, Tim Howard and coach Tony Coton. The Man United goalkeeping trio form a triangle and proceed to hurl and kick balls at one another from no more than ten yards and not once do I see a dropped ball. It's like a circus act. It's as if they're using one of those kid's fluffy balls with velcro gloves. Worth a standing ovation for that alone. I impress other members of the box by knowing who they are and explaining what they're doing.

There is a certain satisfaction and mounting excitement factor as you observe a modern stadium filling up before kick off. It's not unlike watching and waiting as a barman pulls a pint of Guiness. Slow, particular, lip-licking, a growing anticipation of what's to come. A little shamrock drawn into the head. Well, maybe not the shamrock. The decibels gradually but perceptibly rise as kick off approaches and Alistair Griffin, the local boy made good from Fame Academy, treats us to a 'live' version of his self-penned 'Bring it on'. I expect the crowd to take the piss but they don't. They applaud him warmly, perhaps knowing he's a Boro fan and he trots off with his guitar and woolly hat knowing he's played at The Riverside Stadium. This is all an enormous thrill for the woman who thought the lasagne was to be the highlight of her day.

The teams enter the arena to a roof-lifting roar as we don our top coats and hats to step out of the box to our seats and join the real crowd. The Man U fans to our right, in the South Stand, are up on their feet and making a helluva din. This is the cue for half a dozen Boro fans in front of us to start yelling at them.

"Sit down yer Manc bastards! Sit down!. Oi, steward...get the bastards to sit down! "

One bloke will eventually shout so much his head will turn purple, huge veins will form a 3D map of Middlesbrough on his temples and his head will literally explode. His body will, however, remain active in his seat as he continues to wave frantically and gesture angrily at the United fans. A bit like a decapitated cyber man in a Boro scarf.

There's a great atmosphere in the ground with almost thirty-four thousand people warming the late winter afternoon with a lot of hot air. Every challenge on a Boro player is greeted with blood curdling screams of rage and hatred that you might imagine would only be silenced by the public hanging of a United player. The early exchanges are pretty even and the pace is frantic but United kick the wind from the collective sail of the crowd by taking the lead through a Quinton Fortune drive that is deflected in off the hapless Danny Mills.

The bank of United fans are on their feet.

"Ban the bastards from the ground!... Sit Down you Manc Bastards!!!! "

All good, clean fun. The man with no head is forming gestures I've never seen before.

In an incident that is doubtless the consequence of a twitchy referee who has no desire to be lynched, Darren Fletcher is booked for breathing on the neck of Juninho as he's tracking him towards the United area. The crowd goes wild with approval. It's the high spot of the half for Boro fans.

"Yer hot air breathing Manc bastard!! "

Half time arrives and the under performing Boro are spared the wrath of their own fans as a chorus of derision aimed at Man United rings around the stadium. At this stage I'm normally used to forcing my way through rivers of people to the refreshments then having someone piss on my boots in the gents. However, the world of corporate hospitality allows me to slip back into the warmth of the box, take another glass of wine and have a chin wag with someone who wants to sell me a VW. The woman who admired Alistair Griffin and the lasagne so much has retired permanently to the box with one of her mates. They could be sitting at the hairdresser's – probably wish they were. Though she wouldn't have got to see Alistair Griffin at the hairdresser's. Having said that, I don't know where Alistair gets his hair done.

Apart from two other visits to The Riverside, all of my previous Boro outings have been to Ayresome Park with all of it's historic constraints, failed (and perilously sloping) leisure centre and lousy netties. The Riverside, by contrast, has space and air. It's got the reception of a hotel, proper retail operation (formerly known as the club shop), conference, education, training and banquet facilities – a car park for God's sake. The stands have rubbish names mind you. They're imaginatively called north, south, east and - wait for it - west. Still, if you're a boy-scout in the crowd, or even a muslim, it helps to know which direction you're facing. Let no-one be in any doubt, however, that selling the old stadium may have been an emotional decision but it was also the best thing Middlesbrough ever did – apart from signing Bosco Jankovic. The only draw back is that in the Holgate End I wouldn't have had a woman sitting next to me eating lasagne (which was actually very appetising) and talking about Fame Academy. Still, you can't have everything, can you?

Back to the football. The Boro fans have refuelled for the second half and are abusing the United fans with a renewed vigour and passion. Nevertheless, the best they can do is rouse the team to a couple of limp efforts on goal and one or two dodgy tackles greeted with glee and not a little blood lust. They are overcome with a mixture of delight, vengeance and highly vocal mirth when United midfielder, Fletcher is sent off. After having been yellow carded for a first half breathing offence he is given a second yellow and subsequent red for being foolish enough to be in the same half of the pitch as Greening when the Boro man tripped over his own feet. Thus Darren Fletcher became the first footballer in history to be sent off for walking and breathing. Even I thought it was funny.

At the final whistle the jeers of the remaining Boro fans are drowned by the cheering United contingent and the stadium empties like a wash basin with the plug pulled. Modern stadiums have many and wide exits. We boxers are offered another drink. The drivers refuse, offer our thanks and leave – from our own special exit of course. Victoria Beckham is at the door to wave goodbye. I sense sadness in her eyes that her singing career is over and disappointment that she thought football was more interesting than this. She smiles the weakly smile of a hungry stick insect and dreams of lost girl power. I traipse back to the car park, hunched against a freezing December night, past Mannion and Hardwick and offer mental apologies to them for attending a football match dressed for a dance. My car is safe. Phil Mitchell is chewing on some raw meat and swigging petrol from a broken bottle while a small queue of vehicles is attempting to exit the compound into the departing traffic. It takes about an hour but at least I've got Five Live to keep me company and when all's said and done, I've watched a Premiership match for free, had my tea thrown in and been greeted by an ex-Spice Girl. All that and still time to get home for Last of the Summer Wine. It's not a bad life really.

Best thing about the visit:
Darren Fletcher's hilarious sending off and the man with the exploding head.

Worst thing about the visit:
Darren Fletcher's ridiculous sending off and the 'arse' with the exploding head.

Best thing about The Riverside:
The lasagne and the statues to Hardwick and Mannion.

The worst thing about The Riverside:
The name. All right, all right, we know it's a stadium beside a river!

What happened next?
The Tuxedo Princess is towed away and Boro win the one and only major trophy in their long history when they beat Bolton to take the Carling Cup. They are the first big winners in the north east since Sunderland in 1973. This is bad news for Boro fans so they begin to twitter and whinge about their manager, Steve McClaren, not being attacking enough, passionate enough, tall enough, too ginger. Newcastle fans would sacrifice body parts to win something. Boro fans regard it as an insult to their heritage as also rans. I'll never understand. They go on to reach a Uefa Cup Final and MacLaren becomes the England manager. And Boro fans, being how they are, celebrate the passing of the most successful manager in their history. I'm sure they'll be much happier if Gareth Southgate is able to take them back to the days of their former mediocrity. Ah, happy days.

3. Brunton Park, Carlisle.

SATURDAY 17TH OF JANUARY 2004.
CARLISLE UNITED V YEOVIL TOWN, NATIONWIDE LEAGUE THIRD DIVISION.

I love going to Brunton Park. It's what I call a proper football experience. The type that takes you back to the days before corporate hospitality boxes, prawn sandwiches, Sky telly and ticket hotlines. It's a ground where I've heard the crowd taunt players with cries of "Oi, you're not fit to shod horses you" and "that bloody winger should be diggin' up tatties. " I don't wish to deal in stereotypes and pointless nostalgia but this really is the place for a hat and muffler, a pie and a pint and stamping your feet to keep warm on a genuine terrace. I love it.

Carlisle have played here since 1909 when the team transferred from Devonshire Park in the town. It had only been five years earlier, in 1904, when Carlisle United was officially born. On the 17th of May at their AGM in the Temperance Hall, Caldewgate, Shaddongate United members voted, in an animated meeting, to change their name to embrace the city in which they were based. Now, I don't know about you but the thought of a team in the current Football League called Shaddongate United fills me with delight. In fact, I vote that all teams in professional football revert to their original names. Roll on the next Manchester derby between Newton Heath and Ardwick FC. And who can wait for the next Tyne Wear clash between Newcastle East End and Sunderland and District Teachers' FC. Proper football names - and there's something about visiting the current Brunton Park that seems to confirm the DNA link between those emerging professional teams and the modern game. Shaddongate's hairy caveman is not so different from Carlisle United's telesales operator.

Back in the real world, United were fifteen points adrift at the bottom of the Third Division a few weeks ago and seemingly relegated by November but have staged a remarkable revival and are now within dreaming distance of Darlington. Despite the mighty George Reynolds, Darlo are falling faster than Robert Pires in the box. Are George's days numbered? You bet they are.

My personal record as a Carlisle guest supporter since 1986 has been pretty damn good. In fact, I was almost moved to ask the former chairman, Michael – "beam me up Scotty" – Knighton for a free season ticket since my appearance was nearly always a guarantee of three points. I've never actually seen The Cumbrians any higher than the third division (as I will always call it) but I've seen some brilliant, rumbustuous encounters laced with moments of genuine footballing quality. There has, of course, been some abject dross. But what do you expect? This is not

The Bernabeu. And like any supporter of small clubs, I have vivid memories of favourite players who will be totally unknown to most of the civilized world. Brent Hetherington, 'The Flying Postman'. The tubbiest little barrel of a bloke who was like Billy Wizz with the ball at his feet. He was a grown up version of the kid in the play ground who got hold of the ball and just ran and ran and ran, sometimes to devastating effect...often not. Malcolm Poskett, lithe, skilled, seventies hair and a natural finisher. Cool as a cucumber and but for a little of the magic dust that is sprinkled on the greats, a talent of the highest calibre. Nigel Saddington, stout and rock-like in defence. Unflappable, impassive and insufferably, wavy ginger hair. Richard Sendall, head like a brick, nearly always a substitute but a shot like a cannon. John Halpin, tricky-dicky winger. Little Scot with a temper, wings on his boots and the ability to delight and frustrate in equal measure. The type who, when he receives the ball, the crowd noise swells up with a provocative "GOWON, GOWON!! " which flicks a switch in his head and off he goes, no matter what the consequences. Fantastic. But that was then and this is now. There are new crowd favourites and a very significant challenge ahead. In their current predicament I feel it my duty to add my weight to the renaissance and help the team against the parvenus of Yeovil Town.

I drop Jennifer in town for an urgent medical appointment – four hours retail therapy in The Lanes where she would undergo liposuction of the purse, having several pounds removed – before parking up at the Viaduct and walking the mile down a tree-lined Warwick Road to Brunton Park. Sandstone abounds on the approach to the ground as it does in much of Carlisle. Large Edwardian residences, some now B and B, some day-nurseries, but everyone a brickie's delight of substance and some scale. It's a pleasing walk paced out by many of the regulars and leading past the ever-heaving Beehive pub populated by the usual pre-match pinters and a handful of all-day boozers.

I'm offered the chance of riches beyond my wildest dreams.

"Golden Gamble ticket mister?"

I decline, perhaps foolishly. I opt instead for a match programme from the geeky kid with the massive bag.

"How much is that? "

"Two pounds. "

I always ask the price because I can never quite believe it. The answer is always the same and I still can't believe it.

It's at this point, in front of the club shop, that you get to choose the east or west entrance off Warwick Road. Should I head for the west, Main Stand replete with Foxy's Restaurant and the members' bar or perhaps the new East stand with it's shiny blue seats and a close up view of the away fans? Both entrances give access to the tin shed Warwick Road End. The Waterworks End has been unused for years other than for 'big' matches. I fancy sitting down so opt for the shiny blue seats because of the easier access to refreshments.

The ground holds 16,651 when full, the like of which has not been seen since January 6th 2001 when Carlisle, or should I say Richard Prokas, kicked the shit out of Arsenal before going down 0-1 in an FA Cup third round tie. A more regular attendance is around four thousand, all hardened to the annual fight against relegation from the Football League. To the north is the glorious Eden river and the eastern corner of Stoneyholme golf course. The scene is green and the sheep couldn't give a bugger. To the south is Warwick Road. To the east is more greenery and the backs of the terraced houses. To the west is Carlisle Rugby Union Club. One of the great pleasures of an early arrival to the main stand is the facility to loiter in the car park with a cup of Oxo and watch a rugger game through the wire fence until the main attraction kicks off. Two sports for the price of one.

As I approach the turnstyle – 'match day tickets only' – I am faced with a crucial choice. Do I opt for the left queue or the right one? That's one person or two. I go for the two suspecting that the one is a bit slow and once I have squeezed into the gap I am presented with a query I haven't encountered since I was sixteen.

"How old are you?"

"How old?" I am intrigued. "Why do you want to know?"

"It's cheaper if you're a pensioner…Five pounds or ten?"

I don't know whether to laugh or cry. "Are you seriously telling me I might be a pensioner? …LOOK!"

"Oh…no…it's just that we have to ask."

I don't believe her. I offer ten pounds in defiance then enter the ground realising that my vanity has just cost me a fiver. It takes me a few minutes to get over this depressing slight. It must have been the hat.

The new East Stand is neat, tidy, blue. It's hollow concrete concourse has bars and refreshments, television screens and those tall, round stools on a stick so beloved of trendy city drinking joints. Except that these are tacky and covered in blue vinyl. This is seriously impressive though, compared to the 'scratching pen' that was it's recent predecessor and which was more akin to watching a game from knackered old shed, which in effect, it was. I join the modest queue for the refreshments. I say modest – there were four of us and two of those were together. I say refreshments - we have an inspiring choice of the usual assortment of pastry laden cuisine with the speciality scotch pie a firm favourite. After considering the menu, I say menu – I opt for a drink only and pay seventy-five pence for my Oxo.

"Any pepper? "

"No.... I don't think so. But there's some salt down the other end, pet. "

It is a cold, still, clear winter day. Bright and fresh and bloody cold. It is a hat, coat, gloves and scarf day but the East stand has the advantage over the west in that it grabs the last, thinning beams of sunlight as the big fireball dips over the skyline. I choose a seat on the halfway line about ten rows back, taking great care to avoid the banks of seats marked 'reserved' but as I am about to relax into the blue plastic I receive a tap on the shoulder.

"That one's reserved, son. "

"Sorry, " I get up and check the seat, "...but there's no reserved sign. "

"Aye, I know. It's been scraped off. "

"All right if I sit here? " I suggest, shuffling along one.

"Oh aye. None of those is reserved. "

None of them are occupied either. He's taking the piss isn't he? But never mind, he's an old man with a thick top coat, a cossack hat and a nifty line in terrace chat so I'll let it pass. He also later proves to have a surprising insight into the tactics of the game. Old man with top coat, cossack hat and coaching badge perhaps.

We are positioned to the left of the travelling Yeovil fans who are singing west country songs in west country accents as the game gets under way. It's a handy spot, adjacent as it is to an area populated by the Carlisle drums and horn section who enjoy nothing better than a bit of 'friendly banter' with the visitors. They are separated only by a sixty foot length of garden webbing from B and Q. Security is everything at Brunton Park. But I suppose it is designed to keep the birds off so it should be able to cope with a few feisty footy fans. It's a decent game but as play progresses, a scruffy bloke in front of us is getting more and more agitated. He is manically ravaging a Cornish pasty whilst charging to the barrier above the entrance steps to berate the linesman who appears guilty of nothing more than wearing shorts in cold weather and waving a silly flag. The scruffy bloke is Jim Royle. Or is it Ricky Tomlinson? In fact, it's both of them.

"Linesman my arse! "

Flakes of pasty come showering through his beard then he mumbles and chunters his way back to his seat where he starts fidgeting about like he's sitting on the two biggest piles this side of the border.

The Yeovil centre-half is Hugo Rodrigues, at six feet eight inches, the tallest player in professional football. He's a giraffe. The Carlisle player/manager is Paul Simpson, not tall and possible the fattest player in professional football. A flowing move by The Cumbrians precedes a pinpoint cross-field pass by McGill who finds Simpson fifteen yards from goal on the angle. Rodrigues has aided Simpson by spinning around to follow the flight of the ball and falling to the floor, his legs now twisted into a perfect reef knot. The United skipper has only the full-back and keeper to beat. One belly swerve sends the hapless full-back the wrong way while the left foot thumps the ball home. He bounces to the half way line like an ecstatic space hopper. Rodrigues' team-mates untie his legs and pull him to his feet. Carlisle are "Staying up, staying up, staying up" according to the drum and horn section.

The top coat and cossack hat nudges me in the side and points to Jim Royle who has slumped to the concrete terrace under his seat, apparently unconscious.

"Looks like the excitement's got too much for him. "

Top Coat seems incredibly unconcerned as three St. John's ambulance people arrive, drag Jim Royle into the recovery position and administer oxygen. By now it's clear that Jim is having an epileptic fit. Top Coat is phlegmatic but not without compassion.

"He can't be comfortable on that hard concrete. "

The patient, who is now wearing an oxygen mask and is strapped to a portable chair with a couple of small, wobbly wheels, is shaking like a tumble drier as he is eased down the steps by the doughty St. John's crew. Jim Royle is Hannibal Lector.

"He's missing nowt, " says Top Coat by way of consolation. Although it's actually quite a good game and I can see Jim trying to crane his neck while being bumped down the steps.

Half time arrives with a roar from the appreciative Carlisle crowd. Their heroes have performed well against top opposition. A taped announcement is played to comply with some Health and Safety legislation. The voice speaks in a deep, monotone Cumbrian accent, a man who sounds so depressed that the message itself is a danger to the public in that it is sure to induce suicide in anyone remotely near the edge. A more chipper voice then announces the half time scores from around the country prompting at once ironic cheers and then desperate groans. Top Coat has disappeared and then reappeared without my noticing, clutching a Mars bar and a cup of tea. Good teeth for an old geezer.

The half-time entertainment arrives on cue. The excitable PR bloke carries on a little tombola tumbler from which will be pulled the winning Golden Gamble ticket. It's at this stage that we are often invited to stand up and give a mighty Cumbrian welcome to a special guest who will draw the winning ticket. Sometimes it's genuine footballing legend like the time when 'The Preston Plumber', Tom Finney, made a surprise entrance to a rapturous reception. However, it's more often an old United favourite like Rory Delap whose been injured and is visiting the old home town and popped along to the match. Usually, it's one of the current team returning from injury or a promising reserve whom some of us may have heard of. But today – it's the PR man. He hasn't even been able to persuade the ball boy to help him. Never mind. At least he's trying to sound excited.

"Come on…. someone out there must have it. Someone in the main stand? Yes, I think this one should be in the main stand. "

The tension is unbearable. Will the winner show himself? Has he gone to the netty? £300 pounds is not to be sniffed at and nor is it as a figure emerges triumphant from the crowd to a minor ripple of applause from those not tearing up their losing tickets. We are all exhorted to attend the next home and away fixtures then the PR bloke is gone. Brilliant.

The sun has dipped behind the west stand now. This is the main stand with seating on the top tier and standing on the bottom. It houses the directors' box and glass-panelled room for the press plus a small hospitality suite – with no-one in it. Old Trafford it isn't but it's a small club trying to do the things that big clubs do. And why shouldn't it? It's a beautiful but cold sky and I dash off for an Oxo to warm me through as the second half begins – best time to avoid the queue. Top Coat can't understand why they are not using width – too narrow.

The football continues to fizz. It's a genuinely good game with decent technique, a good tempo and a lot of spirit from a side apparently doomed to relegation. This is not a relegation performance and that is confirmed by another 'bring the house down' goal, this time from Craig Farrell.

"Paul Simpson's blue army! Paul Simpson's blue army!"

The drum and horn section are ecstatic.

I swear it feels like a cup final. There is nothing quite like football fans who find optimism in such adversity. As well as they are playing, it would still be nothing short of a miracle if Carlisle were to stay in The League. But football fans believe in miracles: that's the whole point. Top Coat is well pleased with events, nodding sagely and giving the odd, slightly strangled yelp of appreciation when something meets his approval. Personally, I'm so confident of the victory that I leave my seat with a minute of normal time remaining in order to 'beat the crowds' and retrace my tracks to Tescos front door where I am to meet my beloved at five fifteen. I spare a thought for Jim Royle on the walk back up the Warwick Road but something tells me it's probably not unusual and he'll be back at the next home match spitting pasties at the linesman.

Jennifer is framed in the glow of Tescos front door and I can see the silhouette of several bulging bags.

"Ooh…I'm shattered. I've not stopped all afternoon…. and most of it will have to go back. "

I confess that such shopping expeditions are a complete mystery to me.

"So, what was the score then? "

"We won two-nil. It was a cracking game. Carlisle played really well. "

"Oh good. Does that mean they'll stay up then? "

"Ah…well…"

The best part of the visit:
The laconic wit of Top Coat. A man of the darkest humour, compassion and a searing insight into the game we call football.

The worst part of the visit:
No pepper for my oxo. Mind you, there's salt at the end of the counter. Good God.

The best thing about Brunton Park:
If you're bored you can watch the sheep and they've got an end named after the waterworks.

The worst thing about Brunton Park:
Stupid pointy floodlights. I'm sorry, you have to see them to understand.

What happened next?
Despite an heroic effort Carlisle were relegated to The Conference but were cheered all the way by supporters who enjoyed a near miraculous end to the season. They came straight back up at the first attempt beating Stevenage 1-0 in the play-off final at Stoke City's Britannia Stadium. Then they did it again, winning the Football League Division Two. The town and football stadium suffered the worst floods in living memory – a goldfish, now at home in a tank positioned in the club foyer, was found washed up in the goal mouth, a metaphor for Carlisle's recent, 'clinging to life' existence then revival. The waterworks end is back in use. Coca Cola took over sponsorship of the League. Nothing stands still in the modern game. I never saw Jim Royle again but Top Coat is still in the same seat – with the same hat, the same coat and the same Mars Bar at half time. Oh, and Paul Simpson having apparently lost some weight, has been poached by Preston North End. Not that the two things were necessarily connected – unless, that is, that Preston have a thin manager policy. Sorry, I'm rambling.

4. The Stadium of Light, Sunderland.

S̲u̲n̲d̲a̲y̲, 7t̲h̲ M̲a̲r̲c̲h̲ 2004.
S̲u̲n̲d̲e̲r̲l̲a̲n̲d̲ v S̲h̲e̲f̲f̲i̲e̲l̲d̲ U̲n̲i̲t̲e̲d̲, FA C̲u̲p̲ Q̲u̲a̲r̲t̲e̲r̲ F̲i̲n̲a̲l̲.

It's twelve years since Sunderland reached the FA Cup Final and over thirty years since they famously beat Leeds United 1-0 to lift The Cup against all the odds. The 1992 final was a great achievement but the 1973 final was legendary and it's the spirit of '73 that is in the air today. It's not long since Bob Stokoe, the winning manager, died and an appeal fund to raise a statue in his honour has just been launched. Once again Sunderland are in the English second league and once again there is the modern game's dominant force in the other half of the draw. I've got a good feeling in my water.

I've always had a certain attachment to Sunderland. They were, kind of, my second team, Man U being the first. Growing up, nearly all my mates were Sunderland fans and over the years I've tagged along to many a match and apart from when they're playing my team, I've always given them full and vocal support. I'd love to see them rise again. However, here's a question. When they do rise again, what will connect the stars of 1973 with the new aspiring heroes? Not the stadium. Then it was the intense, historic relic lurking in the back streets that was Roker Park. Now it is the modern monument of The Stadium of Light standing proud and slightly boastful above the banks of the Wear. Not the nickname. Then the team was known as the 'Rokerites'. Now they're the 'Black Cats'. Not even the local identity. Then the townsfolk were Wearsiders. Now they're Mackems. If tradition can be wilfully created, then it has been in Sunderland. However, the team still wears red and white stripes and fathers still tell sons who tell their sons about what went before. As ever in life, you can build, buy, sell, invent, remove, replace, relocate, but what remains intact is the unbreakable chain whose links are the people around whom and for whom the football team was created. What connects 1973 to 2004 is the people.

And so, here I am, a Man United fan, a link between 1973 and 2004 and it's my good fortune that Geoff's offered me a lift to the game with his son Simon. I mosey down to their house at the appointed time and Simon is already seated in the car. He looks at me suspiciously for a while then off-loads the all important question.

"Are you a Sheff United fan?"

"No, no, no. Man U actually. But I'm all Sunderland today."

He looks visibly relieved and settles more comfortably into his seat.

"Oh, good, good."

I understand his position perfectly and appreciate the direct approach. Best to get these matters into the open I always think. To further enhance my credentials I make it known that I was actually there at the '73 final and considered myself to be part of SAFC history. However, I have a question for all Sunderland fans and residents. When exactly did you become Mackems? My reason for asking is the clear memory of thousands of Sunderland supporters charging around the Capital singing – "Geordies here, Geordies there, Geordies in Trafalgar Square la, la, la, la, la, la, la, la, la, " and the more robust version "Geordies here, Geordies there, Geordies every-fucking-where. " Now, I venture to suggest that if those words were to issue for a Mackem mouth in the present day he would be squashed into a very small container, taken at the dead of night and dumped onto the Tyne Bridge.

So with the spirit of '73 rekindled by the reminiscing we head north for Sunderland and The Stadium of Light. Built on the site of the old Monkwearmouth Colliery, when opened, this was the largest new stadium construction in Britain since the war and preferred to a redevelopment of the historic Roker Park as the club attempted to lay the foundations for a sustainable effort to join the elite English big city clubs. With a capacity of 48,300 and a fantastic quality to the new stadium, it certainly feels like the home of a major football force. The only problem is that they were relegated from The Premiership last season with the worst performance of any team in the history of the new league. But never mind. There's the whiff of revival in the air under Mick McCarthy. The Black Cats are beginning to purr. Well not exactly purr but perhaps paw nervously at the Kitikat of promotion and prepare to have a shit in the litter tray that is England's second division. Bring on The Blades and – whisper it quietly – another Cup Final.

We head north up the A19, past Peterlee – named after the ex-England medium pacer – Easington, Murton and Seaham. Once hard living pit villages where you were some kind of dilettante ponce if you didn't have a shovel of coal for breakfast, they're now known more for Billy Elliot, Dalton Park and Seaham Hall. That's ballet dancing, posh shopping and being pampered to within an inch of your life in one of the country's leading spa thingies. You know what I mean, strange exotic and soothing aromas, water in all it's most relaxing manifestations and models with long hair and small white towels. Come to think of it, I must find that telephone number. Back in the real world, the Sunderland outskirts soon loom large – the Sunderland Echo building, Nissan and signs for the National Glass centre and The Stadium of Light. It's that easy these days. Sign posts from everywhere to lead you to the stadium – piece of cake. Of course the harder part is finding somewhere to put the motor. There's always the park and ride scheme, free but a long wait after the match. There's the train in from Seaham, no need to take the car to town. Then there's Geoff who 'knows a little spot'. Well, he's from Hendon so if he doesn't know a little spot, who does? We dump the car and head off on a scrubby little path that winds behind a few nasty bushes and corrugated iron fences to reach the main road approaching the ground. You walk about a quarter of a mile with a completely unhindered view of the Stadium of Light sitting high above the river Wear. This is a proper river that ships used to sail on and be launched from. A working river that looks like it retired to grow old gracefully. A riot of red and white ribbons of people converge on the stadium looking like a slowly winding, two dimensional maypole. The overwhelming feeling is of space. There's grass, water, sky. At Roker Park you were lucky to get the sky. As historic and atmospheric as the old place was, the move to this shiny, new home was the best thing Sunderland ever did. The modern way of things demands that whenever a new development occurs, local planners will insist on some kind of artistic content. This fits nicely with the sentimental outpourings that usually accompany the relocation of a football club. So it is no surprise that The Stadium of Light is surrounded by 'creations' linking Sunderland AFC with the mining tradition of the new site. Three great silhouettes of prowling, black cats hang on the outside of the east stand and a giant miner's lamp sits as a proud reminder of the past on a mini roundabout. To complete the artistic theme, some unfathomable modern sculpture spills down the grass embankment to the river. All very nice but I'm looking for the ticket office to collect my pre-ordered ticket. It's a modern brick administration building, known as Black Cat House, quite separate from the stadium and containing a refreshingly swift moving queue. In no more than two minutes I'm ready to stand in a proper queue to get through the turnstile. Geoff and Simon have disappeared to their regular spot and I take my position behind the other patient punters. The stadium oozes quality – proper wooden doors, proper red engineering bricks – you know, a sense of solid and lasting. Many of the bricks are inscribed with the names of fans who paid for the privilege and thereby contributed to the funding of their team's new home. An ingenious scam.

As the queue shuffles forward I notice a police constable rounding Concession Corner from the Metro Radio End and heading towards us. He has a peculiarly effete gait and his head is held in a manner reminiscent of 'a gentleman who wears a little foundation' – slightly tilted sideways and back, looking along the line of his nose. As he gets closer I realise – it's Kenneth Williams. Two likely lads in front of me have seen him before and stage whisper as he passes by.

"Whoops. Here he is. PC Pansy."

"Bet he'd love to arrest someone and get the handcuffs on."

"Bloody hell, look at that walk."

PC Wiliams throws a dismissive glance in their direction as if to say "Common as muck".

I imagine him breaking up a skirmish amongst opposing fans employing those famous nasal tones.

"Stop messin' about you lot."

There's a wolf whistle from the crowd. PC Williams judders to a halt, looks around, throws his head back in defiance, flares his nostrils, tugs lightly at the hem of his jacket and resumes his parade with a haughty defiance.

He trips lightly past us and flicks a speck of dust from his sleeve. Carry on constable.

There's a real sense of excitement building around this encounter. The sun is shining it's late winter, early spring best and there's good humour in the queue. As I shuffle comfortably forward towards the turnstile I am reminded of the stark difference between then and now. Then you would be swept along helplessly by a tide of red and white as you approached the stadium. The back streets of Roker would funnel the river of spectators towards tiny entrances where you would be squeezed through the gap to emerge for air on the inside. It was as if you'd had dived into some underground lake determined to swim under the water to a secret cave and burst into the vastness of the cavern gasping for a reviving breath. The relief at emerging unscathed into the ground was palpable. Nowadays there is comparative ease, no pushing and shoving, no hairy-arsed Mackem pressing up against your back breathing beer and fags into your personal space. No young lads being passed over the heads of the men to avoid being crushed to death. There's orderly queuing, a sense of space and there are more entrances – just more room all round really making the whole process more relaxed and removing the menace. More like going to the pictures these days.

Once inside the Stadium of Light you cannot escape the FA Cup triumph of

1973. If ever a club was defined by one victory, this is it. The names of the great team of '73 are everywhere, every food and drink outlet bearing the name of one of the heroes. Guth's bar is doing brisk business but I decide on cup of tea and a Mars bar from Monty's Magic Diner. Each of the outlets is flanked by a notice board sized biography of the player. This is true homage. When you eventually ascend the entrance to the east stand you emerge into a vast bowl of a stadium that feels as if it has had atmosphere designed into it. This is a noisy football ground. Of course, the atmosphere might also have something to do with the Sunderland faithful, who must be some of the loudest and most prolific singers in the country and I have to say, the songs have moved on a bit since Roker Park in the seventies. Memories of the sheer poetry and dancing melody of that old classic "You're going to get your fucking heads kicked in" make me pine for the present. That particular song was not so much an intimidatory show of force, like the Hakah, for instance, but a statement of intent. Heads were in fact 'kicked in' on a regular basis.

Times have changed though and music plays a major part of the occasion these days. All football teams now feel obliged to enter the field of play with some rock tune blaring out or some quirky little pop tune that has become a 'fans' favourite'. Sunderland signal the imminent arrival of their team with a stirring rendition of the 'Dance of the Knights' from Prokofiev's Romeo and Juliet, which makes the hairs on your neck stand up before segueing into 'Ready to Go' by Republica, which rocks the very foundations of the stadium as the teams run on. My recent visits to Sunderland suggest that this is probably the best time to leave. Sunderland FC, a must for music lovers!

This time, however, it's a rip-roaring cup-tie. Not pretty but plenty of blood and guts. After all, this is Sheffield United they are up against, a team managed by Neil Warnock, a passionate man who is great entertainment but looks like a demented mathematician who reacts to every reverse decision like someone just shoved a hot poker up his arse. It's fair to say that some of his 'passion' rubs off onto his teams. But after fifteen minutes it's the home team that takes the lead through Tommy Smith who is then leapt upon by his delighted captain George McCartney who I'm sure had a walk on part in Waking Ned. But it's the much criticised Stephen Wright who sums up this match for me.

Late in the second half with Sunderland hanging on for victory, he wins a crucial tackle in his own box, beats another man and charges off down the right wing. Surging past another hapless United midfielder, he then slightly over runs the ball which is heading for the Sheffield left back around the half way line just below me. Summoning up every last ounce of energy, determined not to lose possession in open play, he pumps his arms and legs and strains every sinew in his body before lunging into a tackle that takes the ball and the man with a clatter that can surely be heard at the Island Club in Seaham. The crowd errupts in appreciation of this monumental effort with Wright snorting like a bull and steaming like a suet pudding as the United defender drags himself, dazed and confused, from the dewy turf. I'd have paid my twenty-three pounds today for thirty seconds of Prokofiev and ten seconds of Stephen Wright. Memories of a rampaging Dick Malone come flooding back.

As the end of the match approaches, there is that peculiar level of noise and excitement that can only be found in packed football stadiums. The only real cheering is for a ball hoofed high into the stands, thereby wasting more time as the clock runs down or a crunching tackle by a home player, which serves as a conduit for the collective but temporary relief of the fans. But there is a solid background din created by forty thousand people who are simply expressing their nervousness though assorted chuntering, oohing and aahing. If nerves had a sound, this would be it. If nerves had a colour, it would be red and white. If nerves had a smell...well.

At the final whistle there is predictable delight and a roar of appreciation thunders around The Stadium of Light. As the players leave the field there is an enormous roar and the winning team raise their arms and clap hands above their heads in appreciation of their supporters. But the reaction of the fans is mixed with relief at surviving to win with a kind of certainty that it will all go wrong in the semi-final. Sunderland fans are not stupid. They know when their team is not good enough. Let's face it, they've become used to the feeling. Nevertheless, football fans will forgive anything so long as there is commitment. And today they had it in buckets. As the team is roared from the field, exhausted, I wait a while to see the Carling North Stand clear and begin to reveal the famous Sunderland call picked out in white seats amongst the inevitable red - "Ha'way the lads".

Best thing about the visit:
Stephen Wright's rampaging run and the unusual sight of happy Mackems.

Worst thing about the visit:
False hope and a massive queue for a half time drink.

Best thing about The Stadium of Light:
Blistering atmosphere and fantastic music.

Worst thing about The Stadium of Light:
The very name conjures up images of big league success and European glory. Oh, dear. Let's be honest, it's a good name but they pinched the name from Benfica and left themselves wide open to the quite obvious dig from opponents that the under achieving Sunderland were in fact playing in The Stadium of Shite. Perhaps they thought such a name would inspire the team. Hmm.

What happened next?
As predicted, they lose in the Cup semi-final to a Dennis Wise wielding Millwall. Reaching the final would have guaranteed Sunderland European football. But no. They are, however promoted to The Premiership and in 2005/6 demonstrate why most fans wished they had stayed where they were. Like I said, Sunderland fans are not stupid. They know when their team is not good enough. They are relegated yet again in the most abject manner with a record low number of points. It is no exaggeration to say their performance became a standing joke amongst the fans of other clubs. For anyone with any feeling for Sunderland, it's gut wrenching. Now back in football's second tier, the club is run by the Irish 'good cop, bad cop' combination of Niall Quinn and Roy Keane. Never a dull moment eh?

Still, cracking stadium though.

5. St. James' Park, Newcastle.

Thursday 22nd April 2004
Newcastle United v Marseille, UEFA Cup Semi Final

The Magpies haven't won a thing since 1969 when they lifted the Inter Cities Fairs Cup, a distant cousin of the current UEFA Cup. When Bobby Moncur was hoisted high onto team mates' shoulders with the huge silver trophy, it was arguably their finest hour. Now they are two games away from a European final. They are led by Bobby Robson, an old man who is venerated the football world over. Victory will surely lead to the entire city being renamed Bobbycastle.

I decided that I must be part of this famous cup run by attending the big match against Olympique De Marseille. What's more, it was my excuse to visit the stadium for the first time since Gazza was hereabouts. Or was my last visit the Rolling Stones' Urban Jungle tour? Can't remember. Either way there was a loveable genius cum egomaniac with a huge mouth and a drink habit centre stage.

On this occasion I decide to treat my dad and take him to the game and we meet up with brother-in-law Peter, a long suffering season ticket holder, to park at his place and travel into the city by metro from that rapidly expanding suburb that is Kingston Park. It's a warm, early spring evening with a low sun and a hint of tee-shirt in the air. Small groups of Toon fans are picked up by the train as we approach the city where we emerge from the Haymarket station to join a rush of black and white wending it's way through the classic forms of the Newcastle city streets to St. James' Park.

Now, I like Newcastle. It's a great city with history, character, life, vitality. It's where I cut my teeth on live rock concerts in the days when The City Hall was the biggest and most prestigious venue in the north-east. Thin Lzzy, Wishbone Ash, UFO, Yes, Slade, The Jam, Queen, were all beneficiaries of my slightly embarrassed and self-conscious head banging - not enough hair and too keen to listen to the music. But it was a great place to be an apprentice rocker, drinker and confused youth. The city has grown up now. It's become sophisticated. Like me I suppose. Though, whereas my cultural enlightenment has been made manifest in my current disgust for Big Mac and fries, Newcastle's route to refinement has seen it become a capital of culture. The city's great and good have managed to fuse the old with the modern to create one of the 'must visit' cities in Britain, perhaps even Europe.

But it is busy. All those people. I can't stand crowds - unless in a sporting capacity - particularly crowds that seem intent on shopping. When did shopping become a leisure pursuit, eh? When did boys suddenly start to list shopping as a favourite pastime, even a hobby, eh? And the problem with places like Newcastle is that everybody seems to be shopping. And when they get tired of Newcastle centre, they can go to the Gateshead Metro Centre for a change of scenery. I'm sorry, but all this passed me by at some stage of my life. The point being that I tend not to visit the 'toon' so often these days because of the 'shoppists'. However, this game is a 7.45pm kick-off so I have the luxury of visiting the city at an off-peak time. Thank God.

They love their football up here. Cliché, but like most cliches, true. And they're very proud of their heritage. Some would even have us believe that it is more than just a game about which people demonstrate a high degree of passion. Ex-chairman, Sir John Hall tried to sum it up in 1995 – but I'm afraid he went a bit over the top.

"We are like the Basques. We are fighting for a nation, the Geordie nation. Football means so much to us, it's part of our lives. Football is tribalism and we're the Mohicans."

What was he thinking about? The Basques? The Mohicans? And I suppose he's the Geordie Chingachgook. Sir John Hall, knight of the realm and master of the untamed wilderness.

But they're a strange club, Newcastle. They live almost permanently in the 1950s when they had their most recent sustained period of success. Ever since then – Fairs Cup apart – they've been the biggest under achievers in the modern game. Sunderland may not have set the world alight as far as silverware is concerned but in terms of potential unfulfilled they are mere amateurs compared to Newcastle. And they are big. This is a huge club with a huge devoted following, bettered in numbers only by Man U. Their fans have been sitting on the edge of their seats for thirty-five years waiting for the next trophy, which they truly believe they should have, deserve to have, must have. Yet, when you mix with them, as the potential for success gets closer, you can almost feel the tension. It's rather like watching a really famous, seasoned performer stride onto the stage full of confidence – then dry up when he sees the whites of their eyes. Remember Larry Hagman at the Royal Variety performance all those years ago – that's Newcastle. Sunderland, on the other hand, expects nothing but occasionally gets something. An FA Cup triumph in 1973 and a Cup Final appearance in 1992. Their fans are stoic, realistic, accepting. Then there's Middlesbrough fans, who cannot quite believe, let alone accept their new position of north-east top dogs. They have grown so used to being outshone by their local rivals that they cannot handle their current status. They were more comfortable moaning about their lack of achievement. It was a kind of comfort zone. It's almost as if the club has sold out in attempting to climb the slippery football ladder. The Smoggie fans are rather like old labour politicians who were happier in opposition where they could bleat on about everything that was wrong. Gaining power and winning elections is almost seen as a betrayal of everything they stand for. Success just isn't the Middlesbrough way. But Newcastle – I reckon they'd be better off going out on the lash before each of the last dozen games of the season. That way at least they would be relaxed. Get rid of the tension and you never know what might happen. Not a text book approach, I grant you. But let's face it, they've tried everything else.

Today, the team stands two games away from a place in the final of the Uefa Cup. It's their first European semi-final in thirty-five years. So why do I get the distinct impression on walking to the ground, that the fans have already written them off?

"It's good to see Bridges back on the bench. Bit of support for Shearer and Ameobi."

"Who? Bridges? Oh yeh. That forward who doesn't score fucking goals. Great."

"I'm looking forward to seeing Viana tonight. He's due a decent performance."

"He's fucking crap. He gives just gives the ball away. And fucking Robert had better pull his finger out tonight. Lazy French bastard."

"Well at least Woodgate's there to shore up the defence. Class act."

"Oh, he's actually playing a game for us is he. He's a bloody crock. Waste of money."

Expert analysis with just a hint of cynicism and a dash of hopelessness.

You'd think there might be a sense of excitement. But I only sense trepidation and the expectation that it will all go horribly wrong. All right, not everyone is acting like this but a sizeable chunk of the crowd is definitely just waiting for it all to go belly up. For my part, I'm really looking forward to the game. I reckon Sir Bobby is due a bit of luck after a difficult ending to the season. And I'm a big Bobby fan. Top football bloke and now a canny old geezer. Any way, Marseilles have Fabien Barthez in goal and if he plays as eccentrically for them as he did for Man U then the Mags must have a chance. Barthez is a man who appears to have India rubber hands. Everything bounces off them. He's also the goalie who more than any other obviously wishes he was good enough to play out field. But he's not. They rarely are. So I reckon we're in for a night of entertainment from our Gallic friend 'sans cheveux.' What do you mean, he hasn't got a horse?

St. James' Park is a fascinating ground. It's wedged into the city streets where it's been for over a century. In fact, it claims to be the oldest stadium in the north-east, football having been played at that location since 1880, the year Bobby Robson was born. Consequently there is a real sense that it belongs. In fact it almost feels like the city has been built around it. Trouble is, since they started tinkering with it in the 1980's first demolishing and reconstructing the west stand, then the Leazes end then re-constructing the Gallowgate end then sticking an extra cantilevered tier on two sides of the ground it looks like two half stadiums stuck together. The Milburn (west) stand and Sir John Hall (Leazes) end are now gargantuan, double tiered monsters towering over the single tier East stand and Newcastle Brown (Gallowgate) end, which are both perfectly proportioned but dwarfed by their huge cantilevered cousins. I am reliably informed that there are people who simply will not watch a game from the top of the two biggies because it's so high, so steep and so far away from the action. Nose bleed territory. Sherpas required. So that's where they stick the away fans. Clever.

My first ever visit to St. James' Park was on November the 17th 1973. Newcastle were up against a Man United team in rapid and steep decline. But a Man United team in rapid and steep decline is still worth watching and a major attraction. The European Cup winning team had all but disappeared but there was still Stepney in goal, Kidd foraging around up front and..... George Best. Unfortunately, among the first team regulars there was also, Young, Sidebottom, McCalliog, Graham, Griffiths, Anderson and... well, you get the picture. Needless to say, seven games later, Bestie walked out of United for good, dejected, disillusioned and defeated by the mediocrity of a once great team. After a further nineteen games Manchester United were relegated to the English second division. The Mags, on the other hand, while not exactly pulling up trees, were doing all right. They finished fourteenth in the first division and reached the Cup Final. But typical Newcastle. Just when they look like winning something they let the water in. They are hammered 3-0 by Liverpool at Wembley serenaded on BBC One by David Coleman's lovely rhyming commentary, "Keegan two, Highway one. Liverpool three, Newcastle none." Classic.

At least this was an exciting game. Newcastle won 3-2 after being 1-2 down at half time. The pitch was mud with a sprinkling of grass. There were more sideburns on display than a 1973 edition of Top of the Pops. The old, creaking stands are only a memory in monochrome. Compared with today's venue to host Marseilles - well you can't compare them really. The only similarity between then and now was the vintage of the manager. The man in charge in 1973 was the oldest of the old school, Joe Harvey. Macari and Graham scored for Man U. Irish hero Tommy Cassidy got two for Newcastle with George Hope getting the third. George who? I hear you asking. For the record, nineteen year old Haltwistle-born Hope played six games in his St. James' career before being off-loaded to Charlton then York then bye-bye league football after four years. He scored one goal for Newcastle and it happened to be against Manchester United ...and George Best. I don't know what happened to him or where he is now, but I'll bet he's told the story about the day he outscored the Irish genius a few times. By the way, Bestie was fed up and he looked it. I'm sure he already knew he'd be gone by the new year.

But back to this evening's game. We're in the East Stand that backs onto the famous old Edwardianesque terraces that you can see whenever there is an aerial shot of St. James' Park. The big problem is the length of the queues and the arthritic pace they are moving. I'm looking at my watch anxiously, seriously fearing we'll miss the first few minutes of the game. Not so. There is a sudden surge as if the plug has been pulled out and we are sucked into the ground with a full five minutes to spare. A quick glance around the concourse convinces me that I don't wish to wait in another queue for twenty minutes just for a drink so I break the habit of a lifetime and take my seat without slaking my thirst with a bovril.

The stadium is packed. Full. There is not a spare seat in the house. It's an impressive and awesome sight. Over fifty-two thousand fans, some of them even French. They're up in the snow-capped north-west corner with oxygen cylinders for breathing, telescopes for viewing and ropes for abseiling down to the refreshments. At least, we're told they're up on the peak. I can't actually see them though the faint ghostly sound of French filters down to middle earth confirming there is someone up there.

Peter wanders off to his regular spot while we eventually locate our correct seats and find ourselves wedged between half a dozen be-turbaned and bearded Geordie Sikhs dressed in Newcastle shirts to the right and a half dozen be-suited, crew cut Geordie city gents – probably lawyers – to the left. I feel as if we should have brought four more mates along so we could make a set of half a dozen ordinary blokes from County Durham in normal clothes. Never mind. On with the show. We get the obligatory European football anthem then, the entrance of the gladiators, a few forced hand shakes and…a football match.

United start brightly, Ameobi having a couple of decent chances, which fail to make the mark. Lauren Robert is great with the ball at his feet, particularly at set pieces but has his deck chair out when not in possession. Barthez parries a couple of shots that any normal 'keeper would catch and Didier Drogba is kept at bay more than once by Shay Given. The Georgie Sikhs are loving it and having a whale of a time. The Geordie gents, however, are having none of it and are getting a bit narky. Robert is coming in for some 'helpful advise', which I feel confident will escalate to unfettered abuse if things continue as they are. Viana, who I thought was doing okay, is also a man on trial, the crowd just waiting for him to make a mistake so they can rip him to pieces. Old man Robson, dapper in a perfect grey suit and crisp white shirt is directing operations from the technical area with those hand gestures that suggest he is spooning handfuls of bath water out of the tub. That's what managers do these days. Lots of hand gestures. When a man is confined to a small rectangular box marked by a white line, there's not much else he can do.

The second half serves up much the same fare. It's a pretty good game in my opinion, but the Geordie gents have had it with Robert. Any sense of decorum that they might have felt their suits demanded was long forgotten. They leap to their feet with bulging veins, saliva and vitriol issuing from their heads every time the French dilettante shrugs his shoulders following another misplaced pass or failure to track back. Even the Geordie Sikhs are becoming fidgety, fearing the worst. Their protests, however, are confined to sitting quietly, shaking their heads in disbelief. Woodgate clears off the line, Drogba hits the post. Speed misses a sitter and substitute Bridges does well, almost scores – but doesn't. Drogba misses two more great chances and suggests he will be a major threat in the second leg. At the final whistle there is muted applause. It's sounds like everyone has gloves on. This is not a defeat but it's not the result to have 'em dancing in the streets. Retreating to the exit there is a feeling at the pit of the stomach. That feeling that fans get when they know it just got away.

The Geordie Sikhs look as if they'll go home and consider the pros and cons of the match over a cup of tea before watching Newsnight. The Geordie gents look like they're about to kick a couple of walls then go and get pissed.

The metro journey back to Kingston Park is quiet and reflective. Then suddenly, a thought hits me. My trek around northern sporting venues had accidentally turned into a quasi quest to seek out famous faces in unusual places. Victoria

Beckham at The Riverside and Ricky Tomlinson at Brunton Park had started it all but today I had been walking around with my eyes closed. The tension of supporting Newcastle had clearly affected me as well. But then I turn to my left and the scales fall from my eyes. It is James Bolam, Terry Collier. For years now, my dad has been accused of bearing an uncanny resemblance to the Likely Lad. And there he was, cap, zip up jacket, the lot. All we needed now was Bob and Thelma to come along and patronise him and the picture would be complete. I have a momentary thought that my dad could have been riding the Metro all day in an attempt to avoid hearing the result of the match before he watches the highlights 'as live' on TV when he gets home.

"Canny game, Terry" I offer.

"Aye, canny game Bob."

Best thing about the visit:
Seeing a decent European tie that mattered.

Worst thing about the visit:
NO BOVRIL!

Best thing about St. James' Park:
Great views of the game and the ground is in the town centre.

Worst thing about St. James' Park:
Surely it's not finished.

What happened next?
Well obviously, they lost the second leg to a Drogba goal and were knocked out within touching distance of glory. After all, this is Newcastle United we're talking about. Chairman Shepherd sacked Bobby Robson after a slow opening to the next season. Apparently saving the club from the drop and delivering European football and regular top six finishes is not enough. Enter Graeme Souness who proceeds to do much worse despite bringing Michael 'hamstring' Owen to the club. Then he gets sacked. Shearer beats Jackie Milburn's goal scoring record for the club but can't win a trophy and retires. Common denominator in lack of success? Freddie Shepherd.

6. The Reynolds Arena, Darlington.

SATURDAY, 1ST MAY 2004.
DARLINGTON V SWANSEA CITY, NATIONWIDE LEAGUE DIVISION THREE.

Two weeks ago some men with very long ladders and screw drivers arrived at The Reynolds Arena to remove the huge letters on the grey stadium shell that proclaimed the name of the venue and the man who built it. The process of air brushing George Reynolds from the history of Darlington FC was in full swing. Technically, it's not the Reynolds Arena now but there's nothing else to call it at the moment. Love him or loathe him though, it seems a little cruel that the man whose vision created this fine stadium has been dumped so publicly. Mind you, if you ask a hundred people in Darlington whether or not it should have been built in the first place, fifty of them would probably say not. All right, maybe eighty. The conventional world has caught up with George and his unconventional ways and decided that enough is enough. The end is nigh and soon George's monument will bear not his name but that of a sponsor willing to support the ailing club. The Biffa Waste Management Arena. Now that's got a ring to it. I've got an alternative suggestion though. Why not call it the 'Too Large Arena'. Because it is.

But life and football goes on. It's the last home game of the season and I'm looking forward to my first visit to the "Blah, Blah Stadium". Oh listen. Allow me to refer to it as the Reynolds Arena – I've got to call it something. Swansea are the visitors and will be fielding the prolific Lee Trundle and a geezer called Leon Britton. I'm looking forward to seeing a fat oleaginous, warty politician bouncing around at the back but I suspect I'll have to be content instead with the skilful but diminutive midfielder, a 'neat player with good ball control'. Darlington, on the other hand, will be offering two players with an occasion on their hands. Injured goalkeeper, Andy Collett will be finally giving up the ghost and announcing his retirement and defender, Craig Liddle will be making his three hundredth appearance for his beloved Quakers. So, with the sun beating down on a kindly spring afternoon, this should be a pleasant and light-hearted affair to wind up the first season away from Feethams. I drive down to Darlington and onto the new by-pass skirting the east of the town, past the new Morton Park retail ghetto and the new brick train sculpture on towards the new roundabout next to the new stadium. You'll detect a recurring theme here. The last few years have seen endless development on the outskirts of town. Darlington FC has now pitched up on the Neasham Road in a location that couldn't be more different from the old place right in the centre of town, next to the cricket club, Safeways and the old terraces through which many a fan has picked his way to the match over the years. I decide to park at the Tawny Owl pub about a quarter of a mile walk away down the road to Neasham. It's one of those lanes that probably used to be a lovely, relaxing stroll where you could pick brambles under a hazy summer sun with the sound of a corn bunting breaking from the adjacent field and only the odd horse and cart to interrupt the scene. Nowadays you have to dive headlong into the hedge every hundred yards for fear of being run down by some seventy year old widow in a Mercedes or some self-employed electrician in a small red van eating a pie and talking on a mobile phone. Nevertheless, I'm nimble enough to make it in one piece to the roundabout and across into the club car park, which is largely full of pedestrians. Turning and looking back, I realise there can't be many more rural settings for a professional football stadium.

It soon becomes apparent to me that I can't just walk up to the turnstile and pay cash. Instead, I have to queue at the ticket office to buy a ticket which I then hand in as I pass into the ground. A bollocks of a system if you ask me. So I dutifully stand in line with the rest of the non season-ticket holders and begin to shuffle forward impatiently. It's a long queue and I hate queues. Just then I hear a voice shouting out and getting closer. It's the type of voice that is obviously trying to attract attention but I can't quite make it out. As it nears, I also see a hand raised above the queuing heads pushing through each of the lines, then the words become clear.

"Match ticket. Anyone want to buy a match ticket? Discounted. Match ticket for sale. "

It seems a bit steep, touting a ticket at Darlington versus Swansea with a crowd of about three thousand expected. Is he mad?

"Match ticket going cheap. Doesn't anyone want this ticket? " The voice is now incredulous and the ticket is waving furiously.

As he pushes past the adjacent queue, he bumps into me and catches my eye.

"Interested in a cut price ticket, son? "

I make an instant judgement that he's an honest man and ask him how much and what's the catch. I also twig why I think he's an honourable man. It's because he is an honourable man. In fact he's right honourable. The Right Honourable Menzies Campbell MP, Foreign Affairs spokesman for the Liberal Democrats. For those of you not versed in these matters. He's the one they call 'Ming'. Like

Flash Gordon's nemesis, the Emperor Ming and that great rival to WH Smith in my youth, John Menzies, often referred to as 'John Mingies'. Though God alone knows when we started pronouncing E-N-Z, 'ing'. They didn't teach me that at school. I assume it's a Scottish thing, or is that thenz, pronounced thing. Anyway, if it's good enough for Paxman, it's good enough for me.

"Now then Ming. How much do you want for it and why are you selling it?"

"Tenner. It's kosher, don't worry. It's my ticket but I can't stay for the game. It'll cost you twelve to get your own and you'll have to wait in that queue." He motions with his free hand to the crawling line that represents one of my pet hates in life.

"So it's okay then... a proper ticket?"

"Oh, aye, son," he laughs. "I wouldn't pull a fast one. Save two quid and get straight in..... well then?"

"All right. Let's have a look..... by the way, what do you reckon to the war in Iraq?"

"Don't get me started an that bloody fiasco. I've had a consistent line on it from the start. Anyhow, what about the ticket?"

It seems fine to me, so I slap a tenner in his hand.

"Good lad. You won't regret it."

As he hands over the goods, he turns his suave, thinning, white thatched head and disappears into the crowd shouting "Go back to your constituencies and prepare for government!"

'They'll never believe it', I think to myself. 'Ming Campbell was my ticket tout.'

I casually wander over to the gate that Ming had suggested I use and begin to study the words on my ticket. The fly old bugger has only sold me his season ticket for the day.

'SEASON Senior Citizen £138'

Has 'Ming the Merciless' stitched me up? Have I fallen for the 'Ming sting'? Am

Steven Chaytor

I to be accused of being an impersonator of pensioners? I get that sinking feeling that I will either be stopped and refused entry for using a non-transferrable ticket or, worse, the person on the gate will take the ticket, actually read it, look at me and wave me in. It's like Brunton Park all over again.

What the hell. I head straight for the gate, flash my ticket and walk in. I could use it again next season for all the attention the bloke gave to it.

For a team of Darlington's status in the game, you have to say that this is a seriously impressive stadium. All right, the chances of them ever filling it are remote in the extreme. They're not even using the other side of the ground, the North Stand, and that's a lot of empty seats. You can't help but feel this is a club over reaching much like a three-year-old jumping up to switch on the lights but falling way short. You can see the delight on her face as she attempts to flick the switch. You even laugh along with her as she flails about in an inevitably ill-fated effort. Reynolds' doomed and hilarious attempt to sign Tino Asprilla was his entertaining but inevitably failed attempt to switch the light on. George's boast about taking the club into the Premiership within ten years sounds even more ridiculous now than it did then. A bit like suggesting Bruce Forsythe will become the next Prime Minister – 'Nice to govern you, to govern you, nice! ' But there's nothing like ambition and a dream. And that certainly was a dream, or more accurately, a fantasy. Rather than have the big light switched on I think Darlington are destined to be illuminated by the little table lamp in the corner.

Once in the stadium, I decide on a coffee for my pre-match drink and am immediately impressed by something I've never seen before at a football ground. There are orderly barriered queues to the refreshments counter and round the bend after you've been served there is a special self-service trolley affair with your sachets of sugar, jiggers of milk and plastic stirring sticks. Like a proper café. It's practically civilised. I also notice there are many and varied pies on sale. I spot a sign high above the counter, which by way of explanation proclaims proudly, 'Taylors the noted pie shop supports Darlington FC'. How quaint. Then I ask myself, 'noted by whom, and where? ' I've never heard of Taylor's pies. Perhaps I am all the poorer and badly fed for it. Maybe I've led a sheltered life. Mind you, when you discover a pie is 'noted', you tend to want to know why, so you are more inclined to buy one to find out what all the fuss is about. 'What a clever ploy', I think to myself. Drawn in by the siren smell of a meat and tatie pie. Then I snap to my senses and realise that I've very nearly succumbed to the old 'noted pie' trick and I ask for a bag of crisps.

Coffee and crisps in hand, I take a leisurely stroll up to my seat in the South

Stand, which also houses the corporate and administrative functions of the club. I'm roughly at the half way line about half way up the terraces. A perfect position from where to watch a football game. It's a strange atmosphere though. Not unpleasant, you understand, just unlike a normal football match. I'm surrounded, largely, by pensioners – not surprising given Ming's dastardly deception – and youngsters with their dads. It's warm. No, it's hot. The sun is now beating down and there's not a breath of wind. The stand opposite is completely empty. The two ends are not exactly bursting at the seams. One or two of the oldies have come prepared with miniature picnics. Then it dawns on me. It's like an athletics meet. Warm, relaxed, sparsely populated. I've never attended a football match that felt like a track and field occasion. I half expect David Hodgson to wander on to put the hurdles out…but he doesn't.

Instead, there is a proper football moment when the home support give a rapturous ovation for Craig Liddle and Andy Collett as they take the field just before play starts. It's fitting acknowledgement of their respective occasions, one celebratory, the other tinged with a little sadness. Then it's on with the big picture. Darlo manager, David Hodgson, wants his team to end the season with a pride restoring victory. Surely, with nothing particularly at stake, both clubs can relax and entertain. Best laid plans and all that. The first half turns out to be entertaining for an entirely different reason. At one stage it resembles a scene from Braveheart. There are bodies everywhere. After eight minutes Craig Liddle, determined to make this a game to remember, goes clattering into the Swans' keeper, Murphy, practically dispatching him from the ground. He lies in a crumpled heap like a shot dog. When he is eventually dragged to his feet by unsympathetic medics, he hobbles around his goal for a minute or two as if he has one good leg and one that has been on the beer for a couple of days. His left side is totally sober and his right side completely pissed. Every time his wobbly leg touches the floor his hands come up to his head and his face contorts like a squeezed sponge. I shouldn't laugh, but I'm afraid it was funny. Eventually, after more funny walks, he leaves the field to be replaced by the substitute goalie, Freestone. Then, after thirteen minutes, Lee Trundle, the much hyped Swansea centre forward, clashes with a Darlington defender – probably Liddle given his mood - and so damages his arm that he has to limp off. God knows why he is limping. But he looks very sorry for himself. Finally, just before half time, Liddle is rudely interrupted by the fat politician who clumsily careers into him, laying out the home team hero. Of course, he gets up and carries on to the end but is the proud owner of a grazed face and black eye. Who'd have though Leon Britton could pack such a punch.

There is no score at half time. But it takes an army of volunteers and groundsmen a full fifteen minute to pick up the limbs and assorted body parts that litter the pitch and to mop up the blood that is making the lovely playing surface look like the floor of a field hospital. No-one wants to play on red grass.

For my part I grab another drink and read the programme. My favourite section is always the one on the day's mascot, or in this case, four mascots. Kate, for instance, enjoys dancing, singing, reading and shopping. Her favourite players are Chris Hughes and Neil Maddison and she wants to own a chocolate shop when she grows up. Chris, on the other hand, likes football, playstation and drama. His favourite players are Darlo skipper, Neil Maddison, David Beckham and Alan Shearer – in that order. He wants to be a footballer when he grows up. My money's on the girl with the chocolate shop. I'm also attracted to a piece on 'Famous Fan', Tim Brooke-Taylor, 'actor, writer and comedian'. 'What's this?' I wonder, a Goodie who's a Quakers fan. Could this be true? Alas no. It's another confounded syndicated article. He's a Derby supporter.

As I'm overcoming my crushing disappointment at the Tim Brooke-Taylor revelation, the second half is upon us. It turns out to be a fractious and ultimately unsatisfactory affair. The home team is scrappy and disorganised and Swansea look a much better side. They take the lead after fifty minutes only for Graham to give Darlington fans false hope with an equaliser after sixty-seven. When Nugent scores the winner for Swansea on seventy-eight minutes it is all too much for one apparently mild mannered bloke in front of me with his small daughter. He leaps to his feet and spits a hail of profane abuse in the general direction of the pitch. His arms flail about and slash the air as the top of his head hinges open to release a jet of steam that would have put the Flying Scotsman to shame. When he is spent he shakes his neck, sits down calmly, turns to his daughter and pulling a packet from his pocket inquires lovingly,

"Want a sweet pet?"

I think I may have been agog at this stage. At the final whistle there is relief as much as anything from the home fans. After a season where the club has gone into administration and almost out of business, their owner has fallen under a dark cloud and flown the nest and at one point players were not even being paid, they have survived intact. They're still in the league and they still have a team. Darlington fans are a little shell-shocked by the whole Reynolds experience but they live to fight another day. See you next season.

Best thing about the visit:
Little stirring sticks for your coffee and getting in on an OAP ticket.

Worst thing about the visit:
Getting in on an OAP ticket and watching Lee Trundle ponce about for twenty minutes before leaving the battlefield, supposedly injured.

Best thing about The Reynolds Arena:
It's just the best stadium in the division, by a mile and it's got a proper pie shop.

Worst thing about The Reynolds Arena:
It's too big for Darlington and it's always changing it's name.

What happened next?
George is spending some time at Her Majesty's Pleasure. Seems his finances weren't quite in order. Ming Campbell has given up being a ticket tout and forced his way to the top job in the Liberal Democrat Party after pulling the 'Ming sting' on Charlie Kennedy – I'm in good company. The stadium had no name, then the Willianson's Motors Stadium then it was The New Stadium and finally the 96.6 TFM Arena. The team continues to try and impose itself on the Nationwide League Two but draws too many games. Hasn't it always. They change owners as often as names but now appear to have settled on a regime, under chairman George Houghton, that is ambitious enough to buy Julian Joachim, a man, whom whilst at Aston Villa, was tipped for the very top. Oh, bloody hell. Not ambition again at Darlington. It'll all end in tears. I wouldn't count George out just yet - and I expect by the time you've read this it will have changed its name again.

7. Kingston Park, Newcastle.

SUNDAY 2ND MAY 2004,
NEWCASTLE FALCONS V LONDON IRISH, ZURICH PREMIERSHIP

As the Old Gits would have it,

"I remember this place when it was all green fields. "

Not any more. The emergence of professional rugby union in the early 90's coincided with a period when an ambitious Gosforth rugby club moved into their new home and changed their name to Newcastle Gosforth. They had sold their North Road ground, a prime piece of real estate in leafy Gosforth, for a healthy £1.7 million, purchasing the Chronicle and Journal sports ground for a measly £55 thousand. The proceeds would build a new base for the now professional club. That new home was at Kingston Park, the burgeoning Newcastle suburb where land was cheap and plentiful and nicely situated just off the A1. Sir John Hall was sprinkling magic dust onto Newcastle United and Gateshead Metro Centre and decided to throw a little in the direction of the rugby world. Pay a few bob to bring in England's brightest star, Rob Andrew and the rest, as they say, is history. With a little nudge from the likes of Sir John (Gawd bless'im) Rugby Union is now beginning to look like a seriously attractive sport with television coverage, spectators, proper facilities and replica shirts.

Not that Gosforth were newcomers to the big game. On the contrary, this was a club, formed appropriately by a bunch of Durham School old boys in 1877, which developed in the 1970's into one of the premier teams in the country, winning the John Player cup in 1976 and 1977. Men such as Jack Rowell, Roger Uttley and Peter Dixon were giants in the game and they were Gosforth men. So the transformation to Newcastle Gosforth and later, the Falcons was really the re-emergence of a once great team. In an echo of New Labour they were 'an old team made fit for the modern age'.

Now, I like rugby but I've never really been into it – if you get the drift. Always too busy doing some other sport. Despite the fact that I enjoyed the little rugger I played whilst at school – basically the opportunity to pick up the ball, run like hell and knock a few people over –and like everyone, I cheer England to my jingoistc rafters every spring, I have rarely watched the game live. Anyway, I've never really been attracted to the rugby club culture – all boys together drinking, farting, singing songs about virgins and rubbing Fiery Jack onto other people's knackers. Don't get me wrong. I like a drink and a fart as much as the next man but there's a time and a place and fiery Jack is for bad backs and I've never been keen on the herd mentality. But I'm rather drawn to this particular match. It's the last home game of the season. The Falcons are going to parade the Powergen Cup, inspirational Hugh Vyvyan looks likely to be playing his last game for the club and there is talk of exciting young winger, Matthew Tait making a debut. It sounds like a decent afternoon out.

I've got a ticket for the North Stand – open to the elements and in the full glare of the afternoon sun – a cracking place to get a sun tan if the game isn't up to scratch. It's a short walk from the sister-in-law's house through the many streets, closes and cul-de-sacs of Kingston Park estate with every road coned off to prevent casual parking. I casually park up at Judith's house and walk smugly past all the other motorists trying to find a legal spot. Kingston Park is one of those huge, edge of town housing developments that has become almost a small town in it's own right. It's got everything it needs to be self-sufficient, shops, pubs, hotels, leisure centre (private of course) and a metro station. It also has that other characteristic of all such developments, kids. Every home seems to have at least two of them. It's almost an entry requirement. Hence the place is crawling with teenagers and pre-pubescents with baseball caps, bikes and attitude. Ideal fodder for the Falcons' youth set up really.

Kingston Park is a proper stadium these days. Just a few short years ago, there was only one stand, the existing east stand which houses the administration, shops, changing and all-important bars. The rest was grass banks and a bit of temporary seating. But professionalism has taken a hold in these parts and the club has grown in stature and ambition. Probably the very reason why people like me have been attracted to Kingston Park. Now we have the main west stand with it's function and corporate facilities, the covered terrace of the John Smiths Stand and my allotted position to the north end. The back of the north stand still may have the feeling of not being quite finished – temporary refreshments and ticket hut, nevertheless, it's a stadium many a football club would envy and - it's full. Not a space going spare. Ten thousand happy campers. This is just what they had hoped professionalism would bring. But the great thing about Kingston Park, as opposed to my more familiar football haunts, is that old luxury of being able to walk around the ground once inside. Since I am twenty minutes early I decide to have a mooch around. The last time I was able to do this at a football match, the sole purpose of doing so, for a certain element of the crowd, was to get to the other end and beat the shit out of the opposing supporters. Well, it kept them off the streets, you know.

Certain things strike you about a rugby crowd. Firstly, most of them seem happy. Happy to be here and happy to be entertained. None of the football crowd cynicism – 'I've been putting up with this rubbish for twenty eight sodding years' - and none of the cricket crowd loneliness –'where is everyone?' One crowd has been drawn into the world of suspicion and doubt that has enveloped their sport and made everyone think that every tackle is a foul, every fall is a dive, every defeat is a catastrophe and every referee is on the take. The other has simply walked away because in a world of instant communication, instant gratification and the two minute concentration span, a game that is supposed to last four days seems about as relevant as the Black and White Minstrel Show. Ok, so cricket is at least trying now - floodlights and twenty twenty cricket are prime examples of attempts to draw on a new audience by, in one case playing at a time people are actually available and the other, changing the game all together - but people who want to watch the action unfold over a series of days tune in the Big Brother house. Now there's a thought. Transvestite umpires, naked batsmen, silly challenges between overs to win extra runs, players being voted out by the crowd, a dour Geordie commentator - 'Day one in the big brother cricket match and already there's tension about ball tampering in the toilet facilities.'

It might work you know.

The second thing you notice about the rugby crowd is the lack of large groups of teenage boys and nutters. There isn't even the slightest hint of aggro, tension or danger. It's all a bit unsettling really. The place is full of rational human beings, hell bent on appreciating the game without feeling they have to indulge in some kind of phoney verbal war with opposition supporters. Most of the violence that infected football in the seventies has disappeared but the mutual loathing of many groups of opposing fans hasn't. Here at Kingston Park there is jollity and good-natured banter. It's a bloody disgrace.

There is still a suggestion of informality about arrangements at the ground. I walk along in front of the east stand, beneath the bar and towards the player's tunnel where a flimsy rope is hanging apologetically across the walkway to prevent spectators walking in front of the players when they run out onto the pitch. It doesn't really stop anything though and people mill around happily without particular reason. The terraces seem to be full of fifty-year old school teachers, twenty-year old northern based southern students and their trendy, beer drinking girl friends. Nothing wrong with this, you understand. I'm sure they are well motivated teachers, well adjusted southerners and well informed girl friends. But there they are, waiting for the action and being entertained by a bloke dressed as a falcon. 'Flock' the falcon to be exact. He's the official mascot of the club and is a kind of Batman with a spooky bird's head. A falcon's head I presume. He does what all such mascots do, you know the sort of thing, exaggerated hand gestures, hands, or in this case, wings cupped to the ears as he attempts to elicit a verbal response from the crowd and plenty of child patting. But his piece de resistance today is inspired by the visiting team and performed, largely, in front of the visiting fans. London Irish – emphasis on the Irish – is the cue to do an impromptu Riverdance. It was good the first time, even funny the second time. But because the crowd had reacted, he wouldn't stop. There should be a law against it. It's a kind of indecency. Indecent exposure of a latex falcon.

I decide to hang around the limp rope, sensing that I will be able to get a good look at the players as they run on. I'm intrigued about how big they really are. But just as I'm relaxing into my position, with kick-off imminent, I feel a presence beside me.

"Can't stand there sir. "

"Sorry...what was that? " I turn and see a security type person dressed all in black with a radio device strapped to his waste and an ear piece that suggests he's in touch with Mission Control.

"Can't stand there sir. Prohibited. "

I look again and clearly see his shaven head beneath a black cap that my dad might have described as being like a 'pea on a mountain'. It's Matt Lucas from Little Britain.

"So. Only security guard in the village eh? "

"Sorry sir? Village sir? " He doesn't look at me at any time. He's busy doing that secret service thing where they scan all the time but never really look at anyone. He's alert you see. Alert to all the possible nasty things that could happen, like me standing in the wrong place.

His radio crackles and I hear a muffled voice saying something instructional.

"Yeh but, no but, yeh. Okay bud. On me way…. move along sir. "

I move one yard to my right and Matt gives me the thumbs up without seeing where I've stopped and as I wonder whether or not a security guard will feature in the next series, he strides off into the crowd to not look at someone else.

I realise I'm laughing out loud to myself – if that's not a contradiction in terms. (The point is, I thought I was laughing to myself but when I heard the laughter, I realised that it wasn't as private as I'd first imagined and I was in fact being very public.) My Little Britain encounter has tickled me but people are beginning to stare. I'm saved from embarrassment when all eyes turn to the players' entrance alerted by the sound of Mark Knopfler twanging 'Going Home', the theme tune from 'Local Hero', over the tannoy and the thunder of booted feet as the two teams emerge from the tunnel and jog onto the pitch. It sounds like a horse race passing the grandstand. I half expect to hear a Peter O'Sullevan commentary. After all, some of them are the size of horses. It's my cue to head back round to the north stand where I'm supposed to be.

I shove my way to the highest, most central point of the stand where the sun is hottest and the view of the Falcons attacking towards us is uninterrupted. It' s a scrappy affair though. Newcastle should have scored from the kick off but lost control of the ball on the Irish twenty-two and nearly conceded themselves. A good move through the middle forces a penalty that Walder slices wide. However, on eighteen minutes the balloon goes up. The home team runs the ball out of defence and Stephenson the full back surges into the Irish half. He delivers a perfect pass to the galloping Tait who skins the Irish defence, cutting inside to score behind the posts, even finding time to kiss the ball and raise it to the crowd before placing it firmly on the turf. With his first touch of the ball in his first competitive match the eighteen-year-old prodigy had scored a try to send a shiver of excitement around the ground. It's one of those electrical moments that, when the cheers eventually subside, they are followed by a buzz of chatter, like a current wizzing through an overhead wire, as rugby lovers purr over the bright new star who will 'surely play for England before long'.

The fifty year old teachers, knowingly and sagely, "Fine prospect, hope he doesn't get brought on too fast. "

The twenty year old northern based southern students, "GO ON my son! Bring on the All Blacks. "

Their beer drinking girl friends, "Ooh, isn't he lovely? "

The first half wears on. The Falcons continue to have some really good phases of play and increase their lead to 12-6 when Britz scores another try. They leave the field to enthusiastic and contented applause at half time. I decide to find the bar and have a pint.

The west stand is most accessible and comfortable and houses a decent bar. I retire to a kind of side room off the main lounge, looking out over the ground and find I have it all to myself. A kind hearted Geordie bar maid finds me a newspaper, pulls me a pint and I spend a very agreeable fifteen minutes supping and reading in splendid isolation with the muted sound of a heaving bar next door. It's still warm and sunny outside and I'm sure that many of the fans have opted to drink al fresco. But I'm much happier indoors when there's a mad, Riverdancing, latex falcon outside.

The second half struggles to achieve any kind of rhythm, bad handling, stray passes and wayward kicking leading to a stop-start game. It is one of those occasions when the surge of crowd noise that greets an exciting passage of play never quite reaches a crescendo before it slumps back down to a groan of disappointment. After a while spectators find it difficult to even start the surge as they know that it will inevitably end in frustration. And so it proves. Falcons score a penalty but then concede a try and conversion before losing to a late, late penalty four minutes into over time. By now I've vacated my position in the North Stand and moved to a position close to where I had my Little Britain experience with a view to getting out of the ground with some ease. It so happens that this is also where a small but happy phalanx of Irish supporters is gathered and by now they're pissed, happy and egging on the damn falcon whose feet are a blur. Michael Flatley has a lot to answer for.

Good rugby is great to watch but poor, scrappy rugby is bloody hard work. It's a bit like watching one of those games from Jeux Sans Frontieres but without the massive heads and the Stuart Hall hysteria. It can be a thing of beauty, smooth, flowing, thrilling and powerful. But it can sometimes look like a bunch of big blokes running into one another for no particular reason. The last twenty minutes of this game tended more to the 'It's a Knockout' end of the spectrum hence my gradual edging towards the south-east corner exit. Actually, with Jeux Sans Frontieres in mind, Rob Andrew should have thrown on Flock the falcon with his massive head. With any luck the bird would have been plucked in the scrum. Sorry to go on about it, but I believe I speak for the silent majority.

A 15-16 defeat is a poor end to a mixed season but the team sweeten the pill by coming back onto the pitch to parade the Powergen Cup before the home fans. I decide to stick around to end on a more positive note. Hugh Vyvyan is given a fitting ovation as he says goodbye to the Newcastle faithful and the glittering silverware gets the biggest cheer of the day. Then it occurs to me what a decent family atmosphere this is. You could bring your granny without fear of profanity. I haven't heard a single swear word all day – that is apart from what I said to myself when that damn falcon wouldn't stop Riverdancing.

Best thing about the visit:
Matthew Tait's career launching try.

Worst thing about the visit:
That bloody falcon.

Best thing about Kingston Park:
I can park the car at Judith and Peter's house. Handy eh?

Worst thing about Kingston Park:
Celebrity security guards. I don't believe they're trained properly.

What happened next?
The Falcons had a poor end to the season followed by a moderate next season and a poor 2005/6. Rob Andrew has been lured by the RFU to become England's Elite Director of Rugby, basically English rugby's head honcho. You could say his career is on the up. Johnny Wilkinson, on the other hand, has hardly played because of a succession of injuries that would have had him put out to stud if he'd been a horse – perhaps an option he might wish to consider if the latest operation doesn't work. In any case, as Jennifer said when he kicked the winning points in the world cup final, "He'll never reach those heights again. He might as well pack in now. " Wise words from 'er indoors.

8. Newcastle City Pool

Sunday 19th June 2004
Newcastle Graded Meet 2004

If you've ever swum with a swimmer or if you've ever swum against a swimmer, then you will know that swimming is both for those who can swim and for those who are also swimmers. You see, being able to swim does not make you a swimmer. A swimmer can swim but someone who can swim is not necessarily a swimmer. And as for the non-swimmer – well they just can't swim at all. Clear enough? You see, I can swim but I wouldn't call myself a swimmer. However, I'm a big fan of competitive swimming, which is for swimmers.

After the athletics – and maybe even equally – swimming defines for me The Olympic Games. It's fast, it's noisy, it's exciting, it's simple. The one who gets there first wins. None of your fancy marking systems or judges. No difficult to understand rules. No artistic impression. No foul play. No reliance on equipment or the weather. Just have a good bowel movement, shave your chest, pull your cap on and swim like Billy-O. Oh, and by the way, if you're going to win something, you'd better put in several years of hard graft before the bowel movement, training twice-a-day doing up to eighty thousand metres-a-week, missing out on a social life and spending and equal amount of time in the shower washing off the chlorine. These swimmers earn their corn I can tell you.

My eldest has decided to take to the water. Not being one for the clash of hockey sticks or the mannered and slightly showy techniques of tennis, but having a degree of sporting inclination and a hint of competitive edge, she found an outlet in the pool. I won't bore you with the details of her journey from reluctant water baby to wannabe swimming star. Suffice to say that we initially had to practically force her into the learner pool with a cattle prod but now she's grown webbed feet and a dorsal fin. The pool is her second home and now, at eleven years old, she's about to enter her first 'proper competition'. It's the Newcastle Graded Meet at The City Pool. Graded Meets are effectively the first rung on the competitive ladder outside the club gala. She'll be swimming against kids at a similar stage of development from clubs from all over the north-east. It'll be her first taste of competing in an environment where she doesn't know everyone. In fact she knows about three of the several hundred competitors who'll be out there doing their thing. It'll be interesting to see if she's intimidated or inspired by the occasion. Whether she rises to the challenge or withers in the white heat of battle...well, you know what I mean.

Despite being a competitor in most sports at some time of my life, I've only actually competed in one swimming race. At junior school I was entered into the breaststroke in the schools gala. I came second due to the fact that I managed to wave my arms and flap my legs about faster than anyone else thereby making it to the other end like a demented frog but without any hint of technical merit. I don't know why I didn't take swimming more seriously at the time. Perhaps it was my total leaning towards football or maybe, like many boys, I was rather put off by the scary swimming teacher who always seemed to make a point of walking through the lads' changing room to get to the poolside. Miss 'Whateverhernamewas' had a fearsome look in her eye (just the one you understand, the other had been ripped out whilst wrestling a crocodile for a bet at Flamingo Land) and a voice that could make a grown man wet his pants. We would all grab frantically at our trunks as she marched through, pulling them up with such haste that it took the skin off our legs. All, that is, apart from one lad who had recently discovered that thing they call an erection, but clearly had no idea what it was for and would waggle it gleefully at Miss 'Whateverhernamewas' like a mini light sabre.

"Put it away boy!! " she yelled attempting to navigate across the wet tiled floor whilst turning her good eye away from little Luke Skywalker.

She wasn't exactly flustered, more affronted. I thought she was going to turn round and stamp on it like a snail. That she didn't was probably more due to the fact that it would have made us late for the lesson. Or maybe it was because the force was with him. Whatever the reason, she became mesmerised by the tiny weapon on more than one occasion and the boy went unpunished. The rest of us hadn't a clue how he managed it but it was an enviable Weapon of Miss Destruction.

So that was where my competitive swimming career started and ended. However, I've recently taken to the water for fitness purposes. Forty lengths of the local pool at lunch time is a useful method of keeping the blood pumping round when you reach forty four and the bones start to creak. I've grown quite enthusiastic about swimming actually. Perhaps a combination of self-righteousness and being slightly encouraged by the efforts of my eldest. Whatever the reason, a degree of addiction appears to have crept in. And the ugly spectre of competition again raised it's head to me the other day. After completing my session in what I thought was pretty decent fashion, some bloke who'd been swimming in the same lane as me passed the time of day as we both returned to the changing room.

"Hey, you were flying there with your breast stroke. "

"Oh, thanks, " I replied feeling quite smug about my efforts. "Mind, you were churning out the lengths yourself ...and doing tumble turns I noticed. I've never been able to get away with them. All that upside down stuff. "

"Oh, yeh. I taught myself those. I do triathlons and I've really had to improve my swimming leg. I'm all right at the running and cycling but the other blokes were hammering me in the pool.... It's a helluva lot easier with trunks you know. "

"What? "

He temporarily stopped towelling himself and pointed at my cossy. "You should get yourself some proper trunks. You won't half notice the difference. "

"What's wrong with these? " I protested limply.

"Beach wear. No good for swimming. I felt daft in these to start with...but nobody's bothered what you wear. Those things'll be holding you back. I couldn't believe the difference when I changed to trunks. "

I looked down and had a sudden pang of competition. "Well, I must admit, there is certainly a bit of drag. I reckon they must put on two seconds a lap. " I quickly snapped to my senses, however. "Mind you, I think the fact that I'm hauling fourteen and a half stone through the water is probably holding me back even more. "

The triathlete looked me up and down and suddenly understood my reality.

"Yeh...maybe. "

So swimming now features large in my household. And today we're off to the Edwardian splendour of the City Pool in Newcastle. When I say today, I mean this morning. It's a lovely summer Saturday morning with the emphasis on morning. We have to be there at 8.00am to register 'the swimmer' and set her off to the warm up session. Leaving the house at a quarter past seven on a Saturday morning is ungodly and unnatural. I am not a morning person. What exactly I am in the morning I'm not sure. But it's not a person. Nevertheless, the child is excited so the father attempts not to be grumpy. It's difficult. Like trying not to cry at funerals or trying not to laugh at Billy Connelly or trying not to fart after broccoli. But we head north in bright morning sunshine and enter Newcastle with as little bother from fellow motorists as I have ever encountered on this journey. It makes the early start more bearable, almost pleasant. We drop the car in a free parking spot I've stumbled upon behind one of the university buildings and follow a couple of other parents with swimmers along Northumberland

Road to the City Pool. It's entrance is next to that of the City Hall, a concert venue I've frequented many a time in my youth to bang my head to some seventies rockers and drink some bog-awful beer from a plastic glass. In fact, the two venues are part of the same complex that was restored and opened as a civic amenity in 1927. And when they built civic amenities in that by-gone era, they were made to last. The great thing about entering the City Pool is the feeling that you're entering a building of substance. This is no modern, metal clad shed with a hoped for life of thirty years. This will be standing in another century with it's pillared and arched entrance leading to some other amenity even if the pool has succumbed to the ravages of time and the fickle finger of fashion. But today it is a swimming pool and it's crawling with swimmers and coaches and parents. Everywhere I turn I bump into a kid with a swimming cap, a long tee shirt, a sports drink bottle and an energy bar - that's a bottle of pop and a bar of chocolate to you and me. I register 'my swimmer', send her in the general direction of her coach and two fellow club members and make for the balcony viewing area to read my paper and wait for the action to commence.

To get to the balcony I ascend huge stone steps (sadly newly 'B&Q'd' with vinyl) that turn on a half landing before reaching the appropriate level and head off to a small lobby area, at which point I am invited to pay fifty pence for a programme and purchase a raffle ticket to win something that someone has donated because they didn't want it in the first place. Well, this is the amateur end of the sport and fund raising is all important. I gather that the women on the door are from the host club judging by their tee-shirts and general familiarity with the pool staff and the girl selling trunks, costumes and goggles just inside the door. I also gather that they are teachers, instructors or coaches of some kind. They both look pretty formidable in their own way. Not to be crossed or contradicted, I would suggest, unless for a bet or for a point of principle worth dying for. I am immediately and shockingly reminded of Miss 'Whateverhernamewas' and a little shiver runs down my spine as I check my zip. Then one of them lets out a hearty and slightly dirty laugh and I am reassured that at least these two have a sense of humour, which Miss 'Whateverhernamewas' certainly didn't. At least, if she did, it was never revealed to ten year old boys. Still, there's something about swimming teachers. I reckon if we ever have to defend these shores against a foreign invader, a battalion of female swimming instructors should be enough to scare off any foe. If not, at least they can offer swimming lessons in a diplomatic mission..... Perhaps Miss 'Whateverhernamewas' is working for the United Nations as I speak.

"A pound entry – well it's a raffle ticket really - and fifty pee for the programme love, " the larger of the weather girls informs me helpfully.

"Ah...a raffle."

"Do you want an extra ticket pet?"

"So, what are the prizes then?"

"Over there on the table. We've done well this time. A nice selection. I've even bought a couple of tickets meself. He, he, he, he, he!" She's clearly tickled by the raffle prizes and treats me to the dirty laugh again.

I take a quick look. "Tell you what, I think I'll just stick with the one if that's all right?"

Once I've run the gauntlet of programmes, raffle tickets, swimming costumes, goggles and assorted volunteers, I'm through into the viewing balcony of The City Pool. It is spectacularly of it's age. It's not modern, it hasn't been updated, it revels in it's vintage with stepped wooden seating at first floor level around three sides of the pool and cast iron railings with wooden hand rails to prevent the spectator from plunging into the water below. We hover about ten feet above the edge of the pool with every sound from below bouncing around under the arched roof like some giant bagatelle. It creates an intimacy with the sporting arena that is quite unlike most other sports. This is not uncommon with swimming venues but is particularly pronounced in this splendid period piece. And to demonstrate the efficacy of the City Pool in producing swimmers of quality, I am surrounded by the flags of many nations adorned with the names of competitors and the major games they have attended, Olympics, World Championships, Commonwealths. Sam Foggo, Sue Rolph, Sarah Whewell and Chris Cook sit proud atop the list of high achievers from the Newcastle Amateur Swimming Club. The flags reach right around the balcony, hanging triumphantly from the walls and speaking most eloquently of the success borne of this water. I know, I know. Brings a lump to your throat doesn't it?

But that was then and this is now. Today is about looking to the future, to the kids who might one day be celebrated with flags around pools. And it's also about observing the faces and the actions of the parents who only have eyes for their own. The first half hour of action is the warm up when the competitors are called to the pool in age groups to get a feel for the water and to loosen up with a few lengths of easy swimming. Coaches crouch by the poolside shouting instructions to their charges, sharpening technique and urging effort. Officials buzz around the pool with sheets of competitors' names, heat numbers and entry times. The woman on the microphone makes a few early announcements to get used to the technology and swimmers bounce around eagerly waiting their turn to get in the water. Meanwhile, above their heads, devoted, even obsessed, parents ready themselves for a long wait before the race, or races, that matter to them. For my part, that's the 100 metres breaststroke and 100 metres backstroke.

It's hot on the balcony, close and sweaty and there's that lovely essence of swimming pool in the air. There's also a fantastic array of parental support on display. Mothers who are clearly there out of a sense of parental duty and wish little Beccie was into cookery rather than this time and petrol consuming pursuit. They don't look sporty, aren't sporty and don't know where she gets it from. Fathers who are equally uninspired by swimming but have been told to do their bit to support little Bobby. They're unshaven, would have killed for a lie in, have a copy of the sports pages with them and are expecting this to be the slowest three or four hours of their lives. Then there are the enthusiasts. Clusters of mothers who do this on a regular basis. They have jeans and tee shirts, gather in groups of three or four and talk, talk, talk, talk...and laugh, laugh, laugh. The mobile phones are in constant action and they're positioned by the barriers ready to deliver some very vocal support. Then there are my favourites, the sporty dads. They're the ones with track suits or shorts, crew cuts and stop watches. They have lists of the personal best times of their swimmers and will accept nothing less than an Olympic qualifying time from a twelve year old. Otherwise, they're out of the will. Then there are the professional parents, the Cold Feeters. They've brought the lap top to catch up on some work when Jasper is not in view and will be sure that every slice of time not spent encouraging and supporting is spent productively. These are seriously organised people who read too many books about parenting.

Leaning on the railings above the pool, with a group of enthusiastic mothers, is Newsnight's Kirsty Wark. She's an ambitious woman, the 'thinking man's crumpet', but she likes a laugh with the girls and she intends to use her media platform to ensure that little Malcolm gets every possible opportunity to reach his potential.

"I was telling Paxman the other day – he was interviewing the Culture Secretary that night – I said to him, 'Jeremy, you've got to pin that woman down on support for up and coming athletes. What's the point of hosting the Olympics if we don't win a sack full of medals? And make sure she promises that not everything is going to London. What about Scotland? ' You know what he said to me? You know what he said? He said 'piss off Kirsty, you're obsessed.'"

"He didn't."

"He did. But you know, he's such a charmer. We just fell about laughing. "

"Eee. I think he's lovely. I think you can see a twinkle in his eye when he interviews those politicians. And I'm sure he likes that Martha Kearney. Ooo he's lovely. "

The first event is upon us and the competitors are called to the start blocks. They troop in from the holding area just like they do in The Olympics. The swimmers are young and inexperienced and there is a very audible knocking of knees at the start. We have 100 metres free style for boys then girls. Seemingly hundreds of heats with every child's time taken and placed in order of speed on the results sheets. These are, in turn, sellotaped to the wall for success-hungry parents to devour. But it is during the race that the enthusiastic parents come into their own. Particularly the regular mothers and the driven fathers.

"COME ON KYLIE!! COME ON HAYLEY!! " The obsessed mothers screech at an ever heightening pitch as the race reaches a conclusion. It begins to resemble a Beatles concert. The mothers are hopping up and down and reaching over the barrier in an effort to will their child through the water using the powers of telekinesis.

"Go Ben. GO. GO. Harder. Come on. You can catch him. CATCH HIM! " The driven dads clutch their stop watches and beat the hand rail when their boys fail to win. "Damn it. Not good enough. Extra training. "

The Cold Feet mothers close their lap tops as the race begins and smile proudly as Jasper touches to finish. Whether he finishes first or last he'll be fulsomely praised for the effort. The driven dads will look at them as if they're mad. "What do you mean 'well done'? He came bloody last. No son of mine..."

The heats follow one after the other with no apparent break, no stop for breath. A continuous stream of competition, of young novice competitors thrashing, gliding, pulling, stretching, kicking their way through the water to reach and touch and record a time they hope will make their coach and parents proud.

My interest is in the 100 metres breaststroke and 100 metres backstroke for girls and the events follow the same pattern as the others. The same frenetic pace of heat after heat and the same mixture of manic mothers and frantic fathers on the balcony. And which type of supporter am I? Well, it turns out I am the quietly proud type. I watch intently and mutter encouragement under my breath fearing that I will look like a driven, sporty dad then I clap and smile with relief that my swimmer has done well and will feel good about herself. Trouble is, she's enjoyed it so much she wants to stay longer to support one of her club mates. It's been good fun and I've been able to finish most of The Observer but my backside's gone numb and enough is enough.

We leave the venue flushed with the excitement of competition. The pool is still heaving. There are more events this afternoon. The obsessed parents will be replaced by others, the weather girls will sell more raffle tickets to people with pound coins, coaches will continue to cajole and inspire and the screams and shrieks of the possessed mothers will continue to echo around the Edwardian roof void like a thousand wild eyed bats.

We wend our way back to the car, loving the fresh air and revelling in the fact we have respite from echoing pool hall and the screaming of the banshees. And what's more, we have a little black plaque for coming in the top six. Proud swimmer sits next to proud dad in the front seat of the car – and I'm absolutely dying for my dinner.

Best thing about the visit:
Watching the two races that I had an interest in - it's genuinely exciting - and observing the obsessed parents.

Worst thing about the visit:
The long gaps between my races and the inadequate coffee.

Best thing about The City Pool:
It's old, it's atmospheric and in many ways it's beautiful.

Worst thing about The City Pool:
It's in Newcastle. I want it in Sedgefield.

What happened next?
My swimmer is now training five days per week thereby depriving me of my golf. But you'll do anything for the kids won't you? Chris Cook became double Commonwealth Gold medallist and British swimming is fast becoming one of our more successful sports – thanks to an Aussie coach. For my part, I'm still swimming at lunch times when I can. The tiathlete has realised there's little use in encouraging me to wear trunks. Can you imagine buying trunks then swimming like you're in beach wear? It's like buying the best golf clubs and hacking round a golf course - embarrassing.

9. Riverside, Chester-le-Street

TUESDAY, 30TH AUGUST 2005
DURHAM COUNTY CRICKET CLUB V DERBYSHIRE, FRIZZELL COUNTY CHAMPIONSHIP

It's hot, it's sunny, there's a gentle southerly breeze and the sky is bright blue and crossed by wisps of white. England have recently taken a 2-1 lead in the Ashes series, the Aussies are rattled. In short it's a perfect English summer's day. A perfect time and a perfect place to watch county cricket.

I've made a last minute decision to visit The Riverside at Chester-le-Street, home for the past ten years to Durham County Cricket Club, the last club to emerge from the minor counties scene. It was in December 1991 that full county status was conferred upon them, making Durham the first new boys since Glamorgan a full seventy years earlier. In the world of cricket this is a seismic shift. Admission to this particular gentleman's club is a precious gift of rare quality and Durham have certainly grasped the opportunity with eager hands. In fact, they have made such a good fist of it that The Riverside is already a test venue, hosting England versus Zimbabwe on the 5th June 2003 and a regular on the international one-day circuit. In short, I'm visiting a proper cricket ground.

Cricket's a funny business though. When you attend a rugby or football game it's an event, hopefully an action-packed, thrill-a-minute occasion. If you're a half hour late or have to leave a half hour early, you've missed most of it. With cricket, it's more of a day out than an event. More like visiting Hamsterly Forest or Seaton Carew beach with the same approach to clothing options, reading material and picnics. Arriving half an hour late and leaving half an hour early is a positive advantage. After all, you've got eight hours to kill. Approaching a football stadium there is usually a rapid flow of humanity with a rising sense of anticipation, a palette of team colours and a crowd. On the other hand, you can amble towards a cricket ground, stopping along the way to complete a small water colour before selling it to another cricket fan who's always on the look out for the work of local artists. He will then take it home, show it proudly to his wife who's at home baking a pie for his tea, dead head a few roses then return to the cricket without missing a single over. Such is the leisurely nature of the occasion that you may even return to your vehicle to collect something you've forgotten – your Werther's Originals for instance. When did you ever go back to collect something you forgot when going to a footie game? Never.

Being a new cricket venue, built on a magnificent fifteen acre green field site, Riverside is also blessed with plenty of parking, which also doubles up to serve the adjacent riverside park and athletics track. It's convenient in the extreme and a mere two-minute stroll to the main gates where two stewards politely usher spectators to the ticket booth at the next gate. They have time to be polite, even engage in a full-blown debate on the merits of the Euro if you so wish. There's plenty of time between customers. The entrance is next to a small window that is the ticket booth. I accidentally walk through the gate and a lad in a fluorescent vest asks if I've paid once then gone back out. I could have said yes but Catholic guilt is a terrible burden – as I may have mentioned before. I double back to the window where I'm told George will issue me with a ticket. George isn't there; he's chatting to the young lad who just directed me to the window. I motion that there's no-one there and George has a bit of a laugh on realising he should be behind the glass. I joke that I can't seem to give my money away. He laughs again, explains that he got carried away chatting, which I'd noticed, and I exchange my tenner for a ticket before heading back through the gate. The lad who's just watched the whole episode smiles as I lift my ticket in a kind of wave of celebration and George comes back out of the booth to finish the conversation. It feels amateurish but it's not. It's just relaxed and gentle and a refreshing change from the miserable, careless, grabbing, 'couldn't give an arse' attitude of so many people doing similar jobs in other organisations. Mind you, I have to admit there is a definite lack of pressure here.

With ticket in hand and through the entrance, I'm now in a half car park, half access road leading to the back of each of the buildings surrounding the cricket field – all beautifully block paved you understand. I'm behind the main pavilion with it's Tower One and Tower Two full of offices, conference and function facilities and Austins bar and bistro, named after a former Durham cricketer. To the left there's Bannatynes Health Club, named after a bloke on The Dragon's Den, where you can improve your cardio-vascular system whilst keeping an eye on the cricket through smoked glass. Although, my hunch is that the clientele are not fans of the leather and willow. Further around to the right, opposite the health club and adjacent to the scoreboard is the new media centre, a must for any self-respecting international venue. I ascend the half dozen broad concrete steps to emerge above the white spectator seating where I see the huge green circular carpet that is the playing surface, laid out before me with a pristine white rope marking the boundary. The magnificence of Lumley Castle, home of the medieval banquet, stands proud above the trees beyond the east aspect of the ground. The familiar and comforting sight of the two teams at play in their whites with two older chaps in long coats and hats, one behind the stumps and one at square leg, is an oddly reassuring vision. Even my lucky wife, Jennifer, regards this as the quintessential English scene and who is a man to doubt the judgement of his wife? Durham are 100 for 3. I watch an over from the steps as the thin cloud parts to reveal a scorching sun before I double back to the club shop for a scorecard.

It's a cracking little shop with more Durham 'stuff' than I imagined possible. It's like a football shop only with older people and manners. I ask for a scorecard at the counter before noticing that I'm being served by Sarah Louise from Coronation Street. She explains that they've sold out and that Peter's gone upstairs to see if they can get some more printed. I then realise the bloke in front has just asked the same question and he's also waiting for Peter. Sarah Louise asks me if I'm after a haircut, only Audrey's off on her lunch and she has a number of appointments booked in, and she's doing Gail's roots so I'll have to hang around a while. I explain that I'm not in the market for a trim; it's just growing back after being shaved off for charity and I go on to express my sorrow at the way Todd treated her. Still, I admire the way she's found a new interest in cricket. Only sixteen. She's got her whole life ahead of her. Another two chaps come in and ask for scorecards. Sarah Louise remains admirably calm whilst having to repeat the story about Peter continuously. I decide to come back later, ask Sarah Louise to pass on my regards to Gail and head back into the ground.

I saunter back past Austins where two women in black (it's slimming you know) are sitting in the sunshine at a continental style café table. They have a cappuccino each and are conducting a bit of business.

"Do you want the facts in detail? I have the full report with me. "

"No, darling. Don't give it me verbatim - Just summarise. Give me the big picture. "

They are clearly oblivious to the fact that they are in a cricket ground.

I return back up the steps to take a place on the terrace. There are clusters of people and odd individuals all over the ground but I guess that I have the pick of ninety percent of the seats – and Durham is one of the better supported counties. Anyway, I like it this way. No hassle, no pushing and shoving. Nobody giving a damn what you're wearing, carrying or reading. No-one bothering what hobby you've brought to fill in the time. There are several knitters frantically clicking away to my left and there's a man pruning a bonsai tree to my right just in front of a chap with a chain saw carving a replica of the Angel of The North from a tree trunk – I may have imagined some of it. The sun was particularly hot.

I plonk my bag down on the gleaming terrace and watch a little cricket whilst leafing through The Guardian. There's a certain aesthetic pleasure to be gained from watching a professional sportsman in action. The rhythm, the timing, the pace, the style, the ease. Cricket, when played at this level, has all of that. Some of the movement is positively balletic and up to the instant when the ball makes contact with or passes the bat, seems almost choreographed. As I'm appreciating these qualities I look over my left shoulder to see and hear two blokes chattering away.

" Aye. The main bedroom in those new houses is massive. "

"Bigger than yours? "

"Oh, man, you can't compare. Bloody massive. You wouldn't believe it if you saw it. "

"Have you seen it? "

"No, actually. Our lass has though. "

Over my right shoulder a young, attractive woman in a short denim dress and a low cut top has her legs crossed, arms extended by her side, head tilted to the sun and eyes closed. I suspect she's not here for the cricket – and then I wonder why she's paid ten pounds to just sun bathe. Or perhaps she works here and is taking a break – but she's far too relaxed. Maybe she's the girl friend of one of the players and has come to watch her 'fella' in action. But surely she'd be in more exclusive surroundings. Or, maybe I'm falling into a sexist, stereotype trap and she's actually an aficionado of the white flannels taking full cognisance of all the nuances of the great summer game. Or maybe not. Then again it's just possible I'm spending an indecent amount of time thinking about the girl in the denim dress so I decide to go back to the shop to see if Peter has re-printed the scorecards. He has. I buy one for sixty pence and throw in a DCCC pencil with a rubber on top for thirty pence – my pen has run out of ink. At a football match I'd have spent around £2.50 on a programme with about as much useful information as my sixty pence purchase, so I'm quite pleased with my retail experience. Satisfied, I decide to take off on a circuit of the ground. Anyway, I spotted an ice cream van on the open, Lumley Castle side of the stadium and suddenly have the urge for a 99.

The simmering heat makes for slow, deliberate progress along the walkway between the open seating and the pavilion balcony, stopping to watch each ball delivered. Moss hurls one down to Muchall, the Durham number four, and the tell tale 'nick' echoes around the ground followed closely by that moment when the slip cordon leaps in unison to acclaim a catch with a combined roar of "ARGHWIEHSEEE!!!!! "

He is out of course. And as he slopes off back to the pavilion to the accompaniment of a 'pitter patter' of applause, there is a tangible sense of 'here we go, this is where they crumble and the promotion push hits the buffers'. It's a 'Tim Henman in the Wimbledon semi-final' moment. It's an 'England in the quarter-final of the football world cup' moment. It's a 'Jimmy White in the final of the World Snooker' moment. It's a 'Liberal party winning another by-election' moment. The feeling is that this is where it all falls apart. The crowd could be wrong of course but Durham are specialists in the art of the false dawn.

I meander onwards under a relaxed player's balcony, down the steps and over a gravel area leading behind the media centre, in order to get to the other side of the ground. Here, the groundsmen are hard at work wheeling barrows of clippings and turf dressing in front of a series of nets in which academy members and school children aspire to emulate their heroes. They are practicing their cricket skills, unaware of the happenings on the field of play. I make my way behind the new south-east stand and scoreboard to the source of my 99. There's no queue and it's good ice-cream – though you have to be quick with an ice-cream on a hot day. Shame, because I don't like to rush such matters. But that's my problem.

At this part of the ground you're effectively on the grass near the river bank, only separated from the field of play by a waste high green, wooden advertising board looking back towards the main pavilion. Families have picnics laid out on the ground and old couples with deck chairs and parasols get as close to the boards as possible - with their flasks and butties – better to see the action. It feels like the riverside park spilled into this area, almost as if you could walk along the river and stumble upon a cricket game, which you might watch for five minutes then walk on. Something to do while walking the dog. This is also where, on international match days, extra plastic tiered seating is erected to bring the ground capacity up to 15,000. They didn't need the seating today. Our proximity to the river is emphasised by the presence, just over the barrier but outside the boundary rope, of a Northumbrian Water sponsored CMS 'Blotter', a giant thinymujig designed to suck up unwanted water and, presumably, remove it from the field of play. There's unerring logic to a water company sponsoring the 'Blotter' and there's no sponsorship opportunity left untapped here. I look around and see the names of other great northern institutions plastered all around the ground. Northern Rock, The Journal, Arriva, Malaysian

Airlines...Malaysian Airlines?

As I continue my circumnavigation of The Riverside, I'm reminded of the humble beginnings of Durham as a first class county, bumming their way around a series of north-east cricket venues, devoid of a permanent home and a regular source of income. It was good to see top class cricket at Durham, Hartlepool, Gateshead, Stockton but it wasn't home and it felt temporary, which of course it was. But this magnificent, modern venue has evolved into something that many, long established counties would give their silly-long-leg for.

One person who has appreciated the new ground since day one and has squeezed every ounce of value from a country membership is my father-in-law, Doug. I know he's here somewhere, so I decide to hunt him down to spend the last couple of hours with him and the Hartlepool and Sacriston crowd. All gentlemen of a certain age with the advantage of being time-rich retirees. One of the great things about being retired is that you've got the time to watch county cricket. One of the great things about a county cricket crowd is that if you're searching for someone, you can literally check every person and because they're all retired, they don't move around much, making the job even easier. Not so much a needle but a telegraph pole in a haystack. And sure enough, I eventually spot him in front of the media centre, as close to being behind the bowler's arm as you can realistically get without having your view of the delivery blocked out by the umpire. It's the perfect spot from which to view the detail of the game and it's populated by the wily old season ticket holders who are actually bothered about whether or not the ball is seaming and swinging.

I settle down to watch an hour of play from this privileged position as Durham struggle towards 200 before tea. I even get the chance to drink from my flask of coffee. You see, I entered into the spirit of the occasion and found that I fitted very easily into the role of a retired gentleman. In fact, I had a glimpse of what I might be like in twenty years time. Slightly more wrinkled and even less fashion conscious than I am now perhaps. But you know what – it's not a bad life and what's more, you can wear any naff hat you wish and no-one will raise an eyebrow. I'm in the perfect place to view the game but it's not the teams that offer the greatest entertainment. Four pickled people from The Peaks inhabiting the top row of the south-east stand near the scoreboard are declaring their allegiance to Derbyshire at every opportunity and having a whale of a time. They have clearly been supping liberally all day and have just reached that stage of merry pisshood where you feel obliged to sing. With a flag of Saint George spread before them, sun scorched faces and lavishly lubricated larynxes, we are treated to a series of football songs with cricket lyrics.

"One Luke Sutton, there's only one Luke Sutton…"

The Derbyshire captain and wicket-keeper has just caught an edged delivery from Ian Hunter, the ex-Durham seamer, to dismiss Mustard. Hunter was like a man off when he played for Durham and didn't even start a championship game in 2003 before being released to minor counties team, Cumberland. Derbyshire picked him up towards the end of 2004, when he would be free to face his old county.

"Why do they always perform after they've left Durham? " bemoans Doug. "I'll bet you he gets a career best against us. It always happens you know…It does. It always happens. "

About half an hour later, Welch has Killeen caught at second slip by Di Venuto to the delight of the Derbyshire barbershop quartet. It's Welsh's fiftieth wicket of the season.

"Fifty for Welchie…Welchie for England…" They clap out the chant above audible laughter from some Durham fans tickled at the very thought of Welchie turning out for the test side.

It's not long before Hunter skittles out Thorp for the last wicket of the innings and as the disconsolate Durham man heads back to the pavilion followed by a triumphant Hunter, the announcer informs the crowd that he has, in fact, taken a career-best five for sixty-three.

"See. I told you. It always happens. Bloody career best. "

"Got any floodlights, you haven't got any floodlights…Got any floodlights, you haven't got any floodlights"

The 'Derby Barmy Army', as they've informed us they wish to be known, belt out another terrace favourite as the teams depart for tea. On this occasion they choose to mock Durham's lack of permanent illumination. Oooh, how hurtful.

There's only one way to respond to such derision, so we head off to the Colin Milburn Lounge, high in the main pavilion, and have a pint of Guiness.

When play resumes, I catch the first few overs of the Derbyshire innings and delight in seeing Di Venuto, the dangerous Tasmanian opener, drag a Plunkett delivery onto his stumps with only eight runs on the board. A good, positive time to make an exit. I pack my bag and bid farewell to Hartlepool and Sacriston before ambling away from the ground back to the car park. It's at this stage that something dawns on me. Usually, after a football match I'm psyched up, high on adrenaline, happy. Or I'm pissed off, angry and spitting feathers. Leaving a cricket match after five hours, I'm relaxed, without stress and almost carefree.

Never mind Prozac, they should prescribe cricket on the NHS.

Best thing about the visit:
Pure relaxation. I'm dozing off just thinking about it.

Worst thing about the visit:
Too hot. I had real worries about a burnt head.

Best thing about Riverside:
If you're bored you can look at the castle... oh, and draught Guiness.

Worst thing about The Riverside:
It's beside the river, so they called it Riverside. Boro did the same thing. No imagination.

What happened next?
Durham had their most successful ever season. Promoted to the first division in the County Championship and Totesport (one day) League. Paul Collingwood and Steve Harmison play in the victorious Ashes team and they are joined by Liam Plunkett for the tour to Pakistan. And who'd have thought it? Cricket became the nation's favourite game – at least for a week.

10. Trimdon Community College

SATURDAY 2ND SEPTEMBER 2005
TCCA v WITTON-LE-WEAR, DARLINGTON AND DISTRICT LEAGUE B DIVISION

One of the truly great sporting venues in the north of England must be Trimdon Community College, home of the TCCA cricket club, members of the Darlington and District Cricket League since 1984. Lords, Eden Gardens, Sydney Cricket Ground, step aside. This is the only place to play cricket. Well, to be precise, it was the only place for me to play cricket. When a bunch of lads enjoying occasional 20 over knock-about matches suddenly get the urge to play properly there's really only one solution. Form your own team, enter a league and give it a try. So, I'm happy to admit that I am somewhat biased in my assessment of this particular centre of cricketing excellence. But it's place in this anthology is wholly merited since, whatever the quality of the sport on view, it is still a place to sit and watch sport with a pint in the hand and without the distraction of adverts and trailers for other programmes.

The old Trimdon Secondary Modern had long since become a primary school and community facility known as the Community College. There were ample playing fields 'round the back' and – if you looked in the right direction – unhindered views of open countryside. Hmm, canny place for a cricket square. Find the 'new estate' in Trimdon Village, take the long and winding Meadow Road until you come to a small off-shoot called Elwick View. At the end of it is our venue.

Having been to the Riverside earlier in the week to see Durham stuttering and stumbling their way towards the second division championship, I have the urge to visit my old stomping ground. Trimdon Village had no history of cricket until the Community College Association started hosting knock-about friendly matches, you know, reach 25 and you have to retire, that type of thing. Thing is, people got the bug and the fancy idea that we might actually be able to form a proper cricket club. Long story short, after a grant from the Sports Council for an artificial wicket, formation of a committee and an inspection from officials of the league, TCCA was welcomed into the Darlington and District League in 1984. A club was born and I was there at the birth, smoking a cigar and wetting the baby's head.

Twenty one years after it's formation, I am on my way around the back of the school to watch my old team play for the first time in, God knows how long. The cloud is high and blunting the direct sunlight but it's a warm, late summer afternoon. Perfect for slipping on your whites, adjusting your box, turning your arm over and planting your front foot down a lively green wicket. The teams are out in the middle, Trimdon are batting and the opposition has set a tight field clearly expecting some catching practise. Three young boys with a golf club sit on the steps of an old prefabricated classroom adjacent to the field while three TCCA batsmen sit outside the entrance to the bar – which is perfectly positioned twenty yards from the boundary – keeping the score book and chatting about nothing in particular. My presence takes the non-playing spectators to four. But I think I'm the only one actually watching. The golf club is something of a distraction. Actually, one of the lads has a quite decent swing but the other two think it's a special devise for hammering worms into the ground. We're facing south, away from the school and the village across open fields where I can hear birdsong above the unharvested crop. There is no traffic noise, no people noise, no working noise. Sitting with my back to the wall, the gentle sun bathes my face. This is not a bad place to be.

A bloke with a beer belly the size of a space hopper is hurling the ball down from the field end and he's generating a bit of fizz off the pitch. Built like that, he has an understandably short run and fast arm action. He's a bit like a tractor with a sling attached. I ask a young lad holding a batting helmet and clearly preparing to enter the fray at any minute, who they are playing. He looks quizzical and turns to his team-mate who is keeping the score book.

"Who are we playing today? "

"Witton-le-Wear you daft get. "

Witton –le-Wear, " he offers to me. Co-incidentally, this is the only other team I've ever turned out for. Fifteen not out for the seconds and the third wicket of a hat trick for the firsts. Mine was not a glittering career.

"Oi, " the boy with the golf club shouts over, "who y' playing against? "

"South Africa. " The daft get and the scorer dissolve into fits of laughter.

I look up from my note book on hearing the clatter of stumps. The tractor with the sling has just slung one down and dislodged a sad looking stump. The batsman trudging disconsolately back to the 'pavilion' is none other than Alan Lee, one of our founder members in 1984 and a man with the longest and most curved run up in the history of Darlington and District League bowling. It's a little like watching a man in a cricket cap running the first bend leg of the hundred metres relay.

"Now then Alan. Immaculately turned out, as ever. The defensive stroke hasn't changed. "

We indulge in some innocent reminiscing about our beginnings as a fun loving team whose twelfth man was the cool box – appropriately stocked of course – as another wicket tumbles with a spooned catch to mid-wicket. Such is the nature of village cricket that this is the signal for Alan's departure to the middle to take over umpiring duties from one of Trimdon's late middle order batsmen who will soon be required to pad up.

I decide to step into the bar for a glass of cool orange when I see an old bloke with a suitably floppy hat sitting on a stool outside the door watching the match. We know each other - I think - and shake hands.

"Not still keeping wicket then? " I ask playfully.

"Not me, " he says. "That's our Tom you mean. I'm the one that played golf with you. "

I realise I'm speaking to Tom's brother Allan, who is remarkably similar to how I remembered my old cricket colleague, a man who was still behind the stumps at the age of one hundred and seven and bore more than a passing resemblance to the great Godfrey Evans.

"Of course, sorry. You two are the pot model of one another. "

"Here's our Tom now...Here, Tom. There's someone to see you. "

I shake hands with Tom and see that he doesn't recognise me. Though he's polite enough to go through the greeting ritual.

"Don't you know who it is Tom? " asks Allan.

"I'm sorry, son. I don't know. "

"I played cricket with you years ago. Me and my little brother. "

Tom looks straight at me. "I've played cricket with every fucker. " He laughs.

"Well I'm one of those fuckers. Steven. And my brother, David. "

The penny drops, the light goes on and we all confirm our identities to each other and have a good chin wag.

Earlier Alan Lee had informed me that he hadn't seen David for years though David had in fact seen Alan's brother on a number of occasions and mistaking him for Alan, had spoken as if addressing his old cricketing mate.

"David's convinced he's in touch with me but I haven't seen him for ages."

I think I'm going to convene a gathering with my brother David, Alan and his brother, Tommy and his brother Allan. The six of us can then take a good look at one another and put the names to the faces.

As I emerge from the bar I hear another clatter of stumps and pass another bamboozled batsman.

"That bugger kept low off a good length" he explained. "Straight under me bat."

"Aye. All right," came the sympathetic reply.

After watching a couple more overs where no wickets fall, I take my empty glass back into the bar and check out some of the old photographs of cricket teams from the past years – and there I am. With all my blonde hair. Aged twenty-five. Fit as a butcher's dog. No wonder Tommy didn't recognise me.

As I replace the glass I realise who has served me. It's ex Libertines singer, Pete Doherty with a double chin. For some reason he tells me he's feeling tired because he dropped £150 on the bandit at the Labour Club last night. I assume that he must have converted some of it to celebratory alcohol, thus causing the tiredness.

"No. I went to bed early actually."

"So how's Kate then?" I ask sympathetically, knowing that he's going through a bit of a bad patch with his super model missus, Kate Moss. He just shrugs his shoulders. I suspect he's working here to escape the crowds and find some degree of normality and peace in the world of village cricket. A bit of a refuge. He's also probably recovering from his disastrous turn with Elton John at Live Eight. At least the only substances he'll find here are of the pork scratchings variety.

I wish him well and hope he is able to resurrect his musical career but he's already miles away, engrossed in the racing on Channel Four.

As I step back outside I hear another death rattle and another batsman follows the well-worn path back to the bar. The Witton team is looking chirpy and confident and such is the quiet surrounding the ground that you can actually hear the backs being slapped. Ah, but they have yet to face the Alan Lee run up.

I'm in comfortable and relaxed surroundings. More people should be here. This is an exceedingly pleasant way to spend an afternoon. However, there is a matter of national urgency to attend to. England are about to kick off against Wales in a World Cup qualifier at The Millennium Stadium, a venue that is infinitely more difficult to find than Trimdon Community College. So I bid farewell to all and wish them well for the rest of the match. At 42 for 5 from twelve overs, they'll need it.

Best thing about the visit:
Seeing old faces – very old in some cases – and Alan Lee's perfect cricket attire.

Worst thing about the visit:
Home team members didn't know who they were playing. Though that could be construed as an advantage. Otherwise, the broken bench where I used to sit.

Best thing about Trimdon Community College:
It's still going after all these years.

Worst thing about Trimdon Community College:
Becoming an unofficial rest home for rock stars in rehab. Also, it's a shame they didn't fix that bench.

What happened next?
Trimdon finish a moderate season and England scrape a dodgy victory against Wales. I get the urge to play cricket again, as I always do. However, I reappraise when I realise that my cricket boots are knackered and reality and common sense return quickly to slap me round the face when I remember that I wasn't actually that good anyway.

11. The Wynyard Club, Billingham

Thursday 22nd to Sunday 25th September 2005
The Seve Trophy, Great Britain and Ireland v Continental Europe

So, Severiano Ballesteros, one of the greatest names in the history of world golf is coming to Teesside. The swash buckling, fist pumping, all-conquering toreador of the tees and fairways is coming to Teesside. The man who is credited with saving the European tour and breathing new life into a sport with a major image problem, is coming to Teesside. You're having a laugh aren't you? Well no. In fact he's bringing some of his pals as well. Jose Maria Olazabal, Colin Montgomerie, Thomas Bjorn and Padraig Harrington, amongst many others, are also coming to Teesside.

A few short years ago this would have been a ridiculous notion. But now, they're coming here to compete in the Seve Trophy. The bi-annual Ryder Cup style competition between mainland Europe and the British Isles is coming to The Wynyard Club. And best of all, it's only five miles from my house. Will I be attending? Do popes crap in the woods? Is the Bear a catholic? Too right. Any self-respecting golf fan in the north-east has got to make the effort.

Watching golf is an interesting experience and quite unlike any other sport. For a start, you don't have to sit there and wait to be entertained. You can choose to meander all over the course to catch snatches of play, ditching the dreary stuff and moving on to find the fireworks. Alternatively, you can follow a group of players hole by hole, practically treading the same ground as them and walking a good four or five miles into the bargain. It's possible to leave the course completely knackered after a hard day's spectating. You can, of course, choose to pick as spot and watch the world and the tournament go by. But what's the point when you've got the right-to-roam over these many acres. And, unlike most sports, you can see the whites of the competitors' eyes. They are often forced to push their way through the crowds to get to the next tee or take a shot from a position so close you can almost reach out and touch them...not that you would of course...I draw the line at touching professional golfers. Nevertheless, theoretically, you could. But there is direct communication between player and spectator in a way that is not possible in other sports. Sometimes it's a little aside, a funny comment, a thank-you in response to applause. Other times it's a glance of admonishment following the click of a camera, a nod of approval or a look of disgust, often right into the eye of the onlooker. It's a strange paradox given the unnatural, almost hermetically sealed world of some golfers. People who hold out a hand and have a club thrust into it. Who hold up a putter and have it taken away. Who are shielded by someone else's umbrella when it rains. Who have someone else count the clubs in their bag. Who are shepherded from green to tee. Who practise, often alone, for hour after hour, to perfect skills that positively benefit from cutting out the influences of the outside world. Strange then, that they should be closer to the individual fans and spectators who follow their progress than in almost any other sport. Strange, but absolutely fascinating.

But back to Wynyard. I'm genuinely excited about the prospect of seeing world class golfers here on Teesside and…sort of proud that for once it's our area under the international spotlight. I'm getting a lift from Jeremy, who, like me is the lucky guest of those lovely people from One North-East, that government quango that likes nothing more than a bit of regeneration and inward investment. What this means is that we get fed and watered throughout the day whilst having access to a rather lavish marquee overlooking the eighteenth green. But a cursory glance at my dress for the day should suggest to anyone interested that I'm here for the golf and apart from the most welcome posh butties, I expect to be out on the course most of the next six hours.

The Wynyard Club is in Wynyard Village, created by John Hall within the greater Wynyard estate, once owned by the apparently penniless Lord Londonderry who allowed things to slip a little. Now, the 'village' has been developed into a cross between Steptford and the set of The Truman Show. It looks just a little too perfect, darling. They've even created a duck pond - with two ducks. Some of the houses would not disgrace the portfolio of an international hotel chain. It is difficult to understand how you could comfortably live in something so big. "I must remember to visit the east wing this week. I'm told it's lovely in the autumn."

As we approach the golf club, several homes have corporate logos and smart gazebos erected in the gardens. They're entertaining while the golf is on. One such temporary business premise has been taken over by a bunch of companies including Bentley who aren't just flying their flags. Guests at the huge, neo-gothic mansion are being flown around in a helicopter to see the Seve Trophy and The Wynyard Club form the air. And what a bloody racket it makes. It's like Apocalypse Now. I can almost hear the strains of 'Ride of The Valkyres' and Seve standing mad-eyed on the eighteenth green shouting, "I love the smell of napalm in the morning."

We park up at the allotted spot and head off for the hospitality tent to be accepted by our hosts and have a cup of tea and a bun for breakfast before making off onto the course for some golf. Problem is, it's starting to rain and the forecast is pretty lousy. So, it's back to the motor for the waterproofs and brolly. British golfers always carry these two items. After properly equipping ourselves for a day's golf viewing in an English autumn, we turn and head towards the first tee. We pass the tented village with it's bars, commercial outlets, vendors of Spanish golf holidays and villas - the tournament has been organised by Amen Corner, a Spanish company owned by The Ballesteros clan – creche and huge TV screen broadcasting live from the course. Then we pass the army that is the TV production company, European Tour Productions, with their racing green liveried convoy of vans, lorries and strange, adapted vehicles for outside broadcasts. There's a satellite broadcasting mast towering above the course that can be seen for miles around. Sky TV is screening every minute of the action and they are here in force. Whoops, there goes Renton Laidlaw. There's a beehive of actvity around the club house as the marshals, clad in their black 'Seve Trophy Official' uniforms are scurrying backwards and forwards, each with their own individual task to perform. There are ball spotters, rope holders, gate guarders, pass checkers, bunker rakers, those whose job it is to ensure the smooth passage of player from green to next tee and my favourites, the ones with the long table tennis bats with 'quiet please' written on them. They are the best ones because they also have a speaking part. "Quiet Please."

And you know what, at a golf tournament, if someone asks you to be quiet, you are. In fact you get so used to whispering that you whisper when you needn't. There really should be a marshal with a sign saying 'talk normally please'. Most of the marshals are volunteers who are also golf fans, which also explains why most of them look like they're too old for the senior's tour. It's a great job for them, though. And they get to keep the gear. Excellent.

When we reach the first tee it's pelting down. Serious rain. However, I'm not deflected from one of my objectives for the day, to see the man who has the most famous voice in golf, Ivor Robson.

For those unfamiliar with Ivor, he's the tall silver haired man in the perennial green jacket, who looks a little like a coach driver, standing with a microphone on the first tee. He is, in fact, the official starter and has been employed as such by the European Golf Tour since 1975 when he first started the Open Championship at Carnoustie. He always does The Open and officiates at most of the major European events. Today he has an umbrella, but nothing else has changed. He has his clipboard with the official start times. He hands out the scorecards to the players and chats amiably to them, a friendly and familiar face whichever far flung corner of the continent they are competing in. And he's meticulous. There is a large dinner plate sized clock on the tee beside him, which he watches tick around to the precise time. Then, microphone lifted to his mouth, his quite lovely, lilting soft Scottish tones declare,

"Ladies and gentlemen…this is match number three. Representing Great Britain and Ireland, Colin Montgomerie and Graeme McDowell and representing Continental Europe, Thomas Bjorn and Henrik Stenson…. On the tee, Colin Montgomerie. "

As he announces the name of the man on the tee, his voice always rises through the words to finish with a high flourish on the final syllable that implores the spectators to applaud…and they always do. It's worth coming just to see Ivor in action.

When all four men have been announced and driven down the avenue of trees lining the first tee, there are further applause as they march onwards, caddies scurrying after them with heavy bags, bare legs and brollies aloft. The waterproof crowd splits at this point with the followers marching onwards on the outside of the ropes marking the fairways onto which they must not tread and those who plan some stationary entertainment sticking by the first tee for the next group in fifteen minutes time. The match referee, also a wearer of the green jacket, follows the players along with the official carrying the match scoreboard on a long stick. He looks a little like a Roman Centurian in a cagoule.

Wynyard is a parkland course, the first nine holes of which are quite heavily wooded and quite frankly, it's a very pleasant walk even if you're not interested in the golf. Around four thousand people are following the four groups on show today. They are tramping around the course with purpose and spirit, determined to enjoy whatever the weather. And there are some doughty folk out there. Plenty of middle aged women with a strong stride and a sturdy pair of boots and the look of an aged PE teacher. Plenty of retired gentlemen with green jumpers, back packs and thermos flasks. Plenty of blokes who've taken a couple of days off work to see their heroes and have shown affinity with the great outdoors by not shaving. A few younger couples who've decided to enjoy something together so why not a nice walk and a bit of sport at the same time. A few old stagers who aren't up for the footwork but have found a nice spot with the deck chair and lunch box and are staying put until the play has passed them by. Young or old, there's a spot on the course for you and to cheer everyone, the sun breaks through and all the waterproofs begin to be shed as sweat replaces wet.

By this time we've carved our way across the course taking in a shot here and there and come to rest at a point forty yards short and right of the fourth green, an ideal position from which to watch the approach of the group including one of Britain's rising stars, Paul Casey. He has pushed his tee shot into a fairway bunker and is obviously not in a good spot. His escape shot is also pushed and appears to be heading our way.

"Fore right! " comes the call.

"Watch out…duck your heads…step back, " warn the voices around me.

I, of course, have lost sight of the ball and decide the best plan is to stand still, turn my back and cover my head.

Suddenly I hear scurrying and stamping as those around me disperse rapidly, followed by a thud like a mortar shell. I turn round to see Casey's ball buried in the ground about a foot from my boots.

"Bloody hell. That was close. "

"Nearly got you up the arse mate. "

"I wonder if he would have got relief? "

"Nope. Got to play it where it lies. "

For some reason it is amusing to imagine Paul Casey taking a wedge to extricate his ball from my backside – without a divot I would hope.

After the sniggering subsides and our star man arrives at his ball, we are all urged to give him room and we get the opportunity to see, from about a yard away, what he can do with an impossible lie in the rough. So what will a pro do in such circumstances? One thing you notice about pro golfers is the strength in their forearms and wrists. Casey is not a tall man, dark-haired, strong framed with serious face. He stalks the ball and quickly weighs up his options. He takes out a sand wedge and addresses the ball as if he were about to splash out of a bunker. We all look at the lie and assume his only shot is to chop the ball out of the ground like hacking a knot out of a plank of wood. But no. The forearms come into play as he opens the face of the club and somehow manages to force the wedge under the ball, floating it up into the air and onto the edge of the green from where it gently rolls up to within two feet of the flag. It's quite brilliant. In an instant the crowd of admiring amateurs around him realises just exactly how different the professional game is to that played by we mere mortals. He taps in for par and we are left wondering how it wasn't six or seven.

As we scuttle off again, crossing over to the seventh tee to see some par three action, the Bentley helicopter thrashes into action and rises above the bank of trees ahead of us. My God it's annoying. In my mind I draw a home made anti aircraft weapon from my shoulder and shoot off the back rotor sending the stricken craft spinning to earth where it plunges into a stagnant pond. The occupants are unhurt but have the indignity of having to wade through the slimy green stench to reach dry land then have to skulk back to their corporate haven jeered by the crowds who have been driven to distraction by the infernal clattering. In reality, we all just glance skyward and give a little shake of the head.

Down at the seventh tee we watch a series of unerring iron shots that fly at the green and offer birdie opportunities to the swaggering exponents. I say swaggering without wishing to insult the players. However, they do have this air of confidence bordering on arrogance that most great sports performers have developed simply because they harbour no doubts about their own ability. But golfers do it while immaculately dressed with some scruffy oik carrying their business round in a bag. Now, I don't wish to demean the role and status of the caddy. It's a noble profession and can be the difference between victory and nearly. But they are dressed down, they do walk several paces behind, they do strain under the weight of a Sherpa-style load and they are at the beck and call of their masters. This all adds to the air of majesty that surrounds the golfer as he strides away, head aloft, arms swinging in military rhythm, a hand raising in occasional acknowledgement of a star struck gallery. Now, if you don't mind, that's what I call swaggering.

After taking in twenty minutes of both ends of the par three seventh we decide to make the most of our hospitality and work out the quickest way back to the eighteenth green behind which is our host's marquee. The hot roast dinner is lovely, made all the tastier by being free and washed down by a glass or two of equally gratis wine. The highlight of lunch, however, is not on the menu. The great man himself enters the marquee and wanders around purposefully before leaning over one of the tables about ten feet away to talk to some of the guests. He's bronzed, trim but significantly shorter than I'd imagined. But what the hell, he's won five major championships, changing the face of golf and playing in a manner beyond most normal professionals. He was George Best, Gareth Edwards, Ian Botham, Boris Becker, Franz Klammer. He was a hero – is a hero. It's people like Seve Ballesteros who keep us coming back time and again to watch sport.

There are large screens in hospitality showing the action on the course courtesy of Sky Television. It's a little surreal viewing something that's happening just outside and you get that slightly disorientating feeling that what you are seeing is in a far away country. In actual fact I could pick a volauvent from my well-stocked table, hurl it out of the window and probably see it sailing across the TV screen onto the course. I didn't but I could have. So, after having our fill, we set off back to the live action. It's so much better watching sport without a telly.

We march back over to the tenth tee and head straight up to the green in order to see the Montgomerie match arriving. The walk takes us up the length of the par five passing the private dwellings that flank the holes on most of the second half of the course. There is one family who have set up a barbie in their back garden and are sipping champagne as the play passes them by. They're entering into the spirit of the occasion in an admirable way. Equally admirable is the bloke who obviously hates golf and is erecting a wooden gazebo in his garden. He's struggling a bit with some decking and seems to hammer that little bit harder and saw that little bit faster as the play approaches. I see him glance up and notice a discernible curl of the lip. There's a speech bubble above his head.

"No Fancy Dan, Pringle-wearing golfing ponce is going to stop my gazebo. I live in this house. This is my garden. I'll do what the bloody hell I like. "

He proceeds to do what the bloody hell he likes but anger is not the most effective tool in gazebo erecting. I know a thing or two about this. Inanimate objects have been the cause of some of my most stressful moments and I generally find that progress is not made until the mental storm has passed. It's much the same with my golf actually. It is only this season, aged forty-five, that I've conquered my demons and learned that a sliced drive does not mean I am condemned to hell fire and damnation. That a stuffed five-iron cannot be rectified by curling up into a little ball on the fairway and beating the living hell out of the turf. That a fluffed bunker shot is not retrieved by hammering my sand-iron into the floor. A kind of serenity has descended on me in my maturity and I've won three competitions this year. People think I must be on drugs. I now react to adversity like a hippy. Like it's part of God's great plan. Like it's character forming. Where I once saw thunder clouds I now see rainbows – all right, slight exaggeration. But the bloke with the gazebo really ought to chill or he won't live to sit in it.

Down at the green there's an expectant crowd waiting for the Montgomerie approach shot. He's about a hundred and twenty yards down the fairway and about to swing through the ball. It's a thing of beauty the Monty swing. Long, slow, smooth, almost sleepy. But the ball fires straight and true to land as if on a bed of feathers, six feet from the pin. He walks up to the green with partner

McDowell and does that thing with his mouth that all golfers do when they mime the word 'thank you' while raising a hand in casual appreciation of the applause. As he waits for the Bjorn-Stenson partnership to chip onto the green, Monty decides to have a little banter with the crowd next to me. He's polite, chatty, even has a stab at a funny. The crowd loves him for it.

"What a nice chap."

"Not at all like his image."

"I thought he was supposed to be surly."

It is McDowell's putt. Relatively simple and sure to win the hole for Great Britain and Ireland. He rolls the ball forward, the spectators hold their collective breath and.... as it shaves the hole...they groan in unison. McDowell's shoulders slump. Montgomerie turns to his caddie about four feet from us and betrays his feelings.

"Shit."

McDowell, feeling the pressure of letting down a team-mate, slinks past Monty and their eyes meet for an instant. If anybody thought for a minute that this tournament meant nothing to these players but a pay cheque, they should have witnessed that fleeting moment. McDowell looked as if his world was about to end. Monty looked as if he wanted to end it for him.

Arriving at the twelfth green, I spot one of the Sky television on-course staff whose job it is to report back through a radio headset the detail of play that eventually emerges through the mouth of the commentator. There appear to be hundreds of these creatures all over the course. Like tame squirrels.

"Europe have a putt of three feet for a half," he whispers into the mic.

"Great Britain and Ireland are considering whether or not to concede."

I'm assuming they are talking to the commentary box but I feel the need to confirm my suspicions. The one I've spotted has attracted me for another reason as well. It's Charles Clarke, the Home Secretary. That gingery blond stubble and jug ears give it away even though he's wearing a cap. I'm astonished he has the time, frankly, given the pressures of dealing with asylum, terrorism and identity cards, not to mention prison over-crowding. But then I remember that old adage about politicians having a hinterland and I conclude that, on balance, it's probably a good thing that a man consumed by the responsibilities of one of the great offices of state, has an outlet, a safety valve. That it happens to be feeding lines for public consumption seems oddly appropriate.

"Excuse me. I'm assuming you're working for TV."

"That's right."

"So you're telling the commentators the detail of the play and what you say is repeated seconds later to the public?"

"Something like that. But it's not seconds. There's a five minute delay on Sky broadcasts. Gives them chance to iron out any mistakes."

"Five minutes? So it's not really live is it?"

"Oh yeh. It's live. Just delayed for five minutes."

"So it's not live then. It's delayed."

"No, no it's live. Just delayed."

"If it's delayed it can't be live can it?"

"Oh yeh. It's live all right. Just delayed for five minutes."

"But if.... delayed eh?"

"Yeh."

I change the subject. "It must be good to see all these great players so close up. They're in a different league aren't they." "Yeh. Different league. But some of them are shite putters." I look at him quizzically. "Oh Aye. Crap some of them," he confirms.

"Do you really think identity cards are going to work?" I fish for some political titbits.

"No chance. Shite idea."

"Oh.... Right..... Well thanks any way. "

"No problem. Enjoy the golf. Vote New Labour. "

We continue to follow the play around to the sixteenth. It's like a mass countryside ramble with four thousand strangers interspersed with a bit of sport. Watching golf is almost an audience participation affair. You feel like you become, if not part of the action, then certainly part of the course. And it's made even more vivid by the fact that you may have, as in my case, played the course yourself. Unlike most other sports it is perfectly common for the average spectator to experience performing on the same turf as the big guns. It magnifies your appreciation of their skill and leaves you in no doubt about the limitations of your own. Not that I ever was in doubt about my limitations. This just served as a gentle reminder.

Monty and McDowell are beaten by Bjorn and Stenson on the sixteenth. A three and two defeat. They shake hands and pat backs as is the code in golf. And generally, it is well-intended, genuine sportsmanship. Probably the result of the fact that golf matches are usually won and lost according to who played better. Other than the pressure of seeing your opponent scoring well, all of the pressure in golf comes from within. No nasty sliding tackles, gouging in the ruck or hitting below the belt in golf. Basically, there is little reason to begrudge someone a victory if they have a better score. It's fine and understandable to be disappointed but you don't take it out on the other feller. And to round it all off, the applause from the crowd is warm and appreciative of all four players. We decide that, since all four matches are now just about finished, we should head back to the hospitality tent for one last cup of tea and a nibble. The evening is drawing on. The rain has left us and there is a hazy sunshine with a gentle, autumn warmth to accompany us on the stroll back down and across the eighteenth to the marquee. Spectators are drifting away to their cars, marshals are returning to their special marshals' tent, the television squirrels are turning off their radios and the ground staff are already working on the course for the next day's play. While all this is happening you can hear the swish of clubs and crack of balls being fired off on the practise range. Players who have competed all day and entertained so royally are out there analysing and honing their swings. Correcting, fidgeting, adjusting, pefecting.

Ah, so that's the secret.

Best thing about the visit:
Seeing Seve in the flesh. Legend and inspiration. Hearing Ivor Robson live and

immaculate. Legend.

Worst thing about the visit:
Seeing Miguel Angel Jimenez in action. Doesn't practice, plays with a huge cigar in his mouth and appears not to give a damn about anything. Yet look how good he is. It's not natural and it's not fair.

Best thing about The Wynyard Club:
It's five minutes from my house so it's dead handy. And the best bacon butties this side of the Mason Dixon line.

Worst thing about The Wynyard Club:
Thousand pound green fees and bloody helicopters.

What happened next?
I got a handy little chrome flask in my hospitality bag and smuggled Emily in the next day to introduce her to golf. She thought it was brilliant and I couldn't get her off the course. Looks like more expense for the future. Monty's career was firmly back on track. Oh, Great Britain and Ireland won the cup.

12. Victoria Park, Hartlepool

SATURDAY 22ND OCTOBER 2005
HARTLEPOOL UNITED V MK DONS, COCA COLA LEAGUE ONE

If I was to report that I was going to watch a football match at the Victoria Ground (I know it's Park but I've always known it as Ground), it would probably come as no surprise to hear that the weather is cold, wet, windy and miserable. I don't know why it should be so but the two images seem to fit together. And you know what, I don't mind a bit. In fact, I find it oddly comforting and familiar. It's just feels right that we should be having proper autumn weather to accompany a bread and butter game from one of the less glamorous professional leagues. There's been football here since Hartlepools (sic) United played their first game at the Victoria Park on the 2nd September 1908 on what had been the local rugby ground. And since 1921 when they entered the League for the first time, life has been petty much a constant struggle for the club, both financially and in terms of staying in the League. But things are as good as they've ever been at the moment. Pools are in the Coca Cola League One, which to people of my vintage, still means the third division. Along with Coca Cola League Two, this will always be referred to by Premier League prima donnas being interviewed on TV as one of the lower leagues to which they hope not to descend. The assumption, I suppose, must be that I'm going to see a crap match played by a bunch of journeymen who can only dream of being interviewed by a faceless Garth Crooks on Match of The Day. Well, we'll see.

I've managed to strike a deal with my conscience (who's at home baking ginger bread men with Emily and Anna) that if I go to the game I should also return a lamp to Au Naturale, one of the outlets at the Jackson's Landing retail park across the railway tracks from the ground. By the way, the lamp just didn't work. Aesthetically, that is. A bit cheap and plastic looking for it's intended spot. We eventually settled on something with a bit of a chrome finish. Anyway, the point is that free parking outside TK Max, Staples and the aforementioned Au Naturale was ideal for me. A five minute walk to the ground and a trouble free exit guaranteed. I can report a surprising number of men returning lamps and the like, all heading of to the other side of the tracks afterwards.

Anyone who didn't know Hartlepool fifteen years ago can only imagine the changes that have taken place on this section of the east coast in recent times. It's been a spectacular renaissance. Gone are the contaminated, industrial wastelands. Gone is the muck and dirt and rubbish and desolation. Now there are shops, retail parks, apartments, hotels, restaurants, the Historic Quay visitor attraction and, most impressive of all, the focal point, a shiny new marina. This is the type of marina with foreign accents and beautiful people stretched out on deck with a glass of something sparkling – on Hartlepool's three summer days that is. And as if to keep pace, Hartlepool United's football stadium has also been transformed from a pretty dodgy venue where away teams would routinely change in portakabins, to a modern, clean, tight and surprisingly atmospheric arena with a capacity of 7,629. This doesn't seem a lot but it's fitting for a club of this size in a town of this size and has the great advantage that with anything around five thousand in the ground, it feels almost full and can generate a terrific buzz of excitement.

I follow all the other blokes with credit notes for Au Naturale around over the railway line and down Clarence Road towards the stadium. We're approaching from the north-east corner where a large, warehouse looking building houses the club offices and shop. I pop into the shop, which doubles as a ticket office, to ask whether or not it is best to get a ticket there first or to pay at the gate. It is the smallest shop in the world but well stocked. The problem is, they have a security bloke in there who looks like he hasn't been fed red meat for a month and manages to fill half of the retail space. I seriously wonder if they ever sell anything while he's in there picking bones from his teeth and scratching his crotch. Luckily, I'm not in the market for a scarf so I turn on my heels and find myself at the ticket counter - without actually having walked another pace. Three members of staff are trying to sort out a problem in a space designed for one when one of them turns to me to offer assistance. She's tall, well groomed, smartly dressed and well upholstered. There's a certain twinkle in her eye and a welcoming smile. My God, it's nurse Gladys Emanuel.

"Can I help you sir?"

"Are you selling programmes?"

"No. They're just outside and round the corner."

"Do I need to buy a ticket here or is it best to pay at the gate? I want to sit down I think."

"Well, if you want to go into the Cyril Knowles stand …. just here…. you need a ticket first. If you want to go round the other side to the Camerons Brewery Stand you can just pay at the turnstiles. You'll have no problem finding a seat."

"Thanks. By the way, that security bloke's a bit grim isn't he?"

"Oh, don't tell me. It's not what his mother would have expected. What that boy needs is an immediate dose of politeness.... Is that all? "

"Yes. Ger, G.. G.. G.. G.. Great. Th, th, thanks very m.. much. "

She looks at me with a question mark, "Hmmm, you're welcome. "

Nurse Gladys turns to the next customer and twinkles a smile.

"Can I help you sir? "

In one bound I am out of the shop. And in a further four I am face to face with the programme seller.

"How much mate? " I inquire.

"That'll be two fifty please, " comes the reply from a cockney student. A Cockney I tell you.

"Two fifty? " I inquire, feigning shock and incredulity, as I always do when someone sells me a programme.

"Costa livin' mite. " Turns out he's a 'chirpy' cockney who looks like he should be selling me a big Mac with fries. Or even an apple from the market in Albert Square. He's clearly lost and thinks he's selling programmes for 'The 'Ammers'.

I agree that he must be right about the cost of living and head off back around the Rink End of the ground (named after the long demolished ice rink) where the away supporters sit. I can hear the first announcement of the away team and the cheers that greet each name. When I say hear the cheers, I mean each individual voice. I discern that there are three away supporters in full appreciative vocal throttle. In fact, there are so few of them I can make out that one is a little nasal and one has a lisp. Once round the north-east corner where the social club, amusingly titled 'The Corner Flag', is situated I find myself at the first couple of gates to the Camerons Brewery Stand. The land around this corner is still a kind of scrubby mess, the type that is very attractive to people riding scrambling bikes illicitly. Consequently, when it rains, as it often does hereabouts, you find yourself either plodging through or dancing around dirty, black, gravelly puddles. The town's renaissance hasn't quite reached this particular acre. At the gate, helpfully labeled, 'Camerons Brewery Stand seats', I am relieved of Eighteen of my precious pounds for the pleasure of sitting down.

Last week I paid thirty pounds to watch Sunderland v Man U in the Premiership and I can't decide whether that was a rip off or this is good value. I decide that it's like restaurants really. You don't mind paying a few bob if you get a decent meal and a good night out but if the vegetables are stodgy, the plates are cold and the portions paltry, then you're not too happy to pay the bill. So I've decided to make my value for money judgements based on the merits of each individual game. Last week it was worth the entrance money just to see Wayne Rooney, the equivalent of a beautifully grilled sea bass.

Sea bass apart, I am a man of simple tastes and I must have my bovril. Especially on a cold day. Behind the CB Stand, the way to the bovril is up two wooden steps in front of a small cabin. Initially, I'm not hopeful but I'm pleasantly surprised. It's a good sized plastic cup with one of those tops with a hole in that you can sip through. It's hot and it's strong. Thumbs up so far. I ascend the steps to the stand, which has yellow, plastic tractor seats fixed to the concrete terraces. Covent Garden it is not. However, although there are no back rests they're fairly forgiving on the rear so I find myself relatively comfortable as I await the entrance of the teams. The Town End terrace is pretty full now, of home fans of course, while the Rink End has now welcomed about forty MK Dons fans, all comfortably seated. What splendid hosts offering the visitors the best seats. My view is of the Cyril Knowles stand with it's row of executive boxes and players' entrance. Beyond it are the masts of HMS Trincomolee moored at the Historic Quay, the retail park viewed through the north east corner and the more traditional sight of cranes to the north reminding me of the industrial backbone of the town. I know the north sea is there too but it's merged with the full and spitting sky to form a mucky grey back cloth. Just over the back of the Town End terrace is the ubiquitous Morrison's supermarket. More reasons to avoid going shopping.

I'm quietly reading my programme to identify which of the opposition I recognize when suddenly there is a cannon blast, followed by another. My God, we're being attacked! Another blast follows before I remember that the country is celebrating whooping the collective derriere of the French nation two hundred years ago at Trafalgar. Now, Hartlepool has history as far as the French are concerned. The townsfolk (understandably) assumed a shipwrecked monkey to be a French spy – so they hung it. Hence the epithet, Monkey Hangers. Well you couldn't be too careful in those Napoleonic Wars. So the Poolies have every right to celebrate Trafalgar and events over at the Quay are obviously going with a bang. Soon, however, the cannon fire finds itself accompanying the great Rolf Harris classic, Two Little Boys (although not by Rolf), which blasts out of the Victoria Ground pa system as a precursor to the arrival of the teams. It's a surreal moment. Cannon fire, Two Little Boys, Nelson, Napoleon and Hartlepool. It brings a lump to your throat.

The MK Dons are a strange outfit. Really, they're Wimbledon but they've moved to Milton Keynes where they play in the National Hockey Stadium. No point calling them Wimbledon when they have no association with that part of London any more. Any way, a bunch of disgruntled supporters have formed AFC Wimbledon in reaction to the sale of their team. Two Wimbledons just wouldn't be right. It's all a far cry from the heady days of The Crazy Gang when they won the FA Cup and took the first division by storm in the eighties and nineties. But they've survived and now they're pitted against the most successful Hartlepool side in recent history.

Like I said though, a strange outfit. A kind of designer team with a made up name, constructed from the pieces of a former club and holed up in a kind of designer new town. When the teams emerge onto the pitch, I suspect even the MK Dons team has been designed, perhaps by Linda Barker. Their strip is a quite fetching black with gold trims and numbers and manager Danny Wilson has clearly been instructed to follow a strict team selection design guide put together by Linda. It seems all the players either have black skin or ginger hair. Even Danny himself has a hint of a tint up top. Beautiful use of colour and contrast. The Hartlepool team, on the other hand, is in blue and white stripes with numbers that are impossible to read. All their players have crew cuts and look like they should be electronically tagged. Contrast this with manager, Martin Scott, who is under orders from his employers to be smart as a carrot at all times. Consequently he always looks like he's about to deliver a best man's speech in front of a bunch of convicts. I'm afraid there's no consistency throughout the team either, no colour co-ordination, no obvious theme. A design nightmare. Crying out for a make over. Still, I set aside my worries about the clear aesthetic mis-match and hope that Pools can raise their game and win at home for the first time this season.

It's a good game. It ebbs and flows but MK have the upper hand. There's skill on show as well. Richie Humphreys and Tommy Butler are particularly eye catching for Pools, turning and weaving, great movement. But it's MK who take the lead after twenty minutes when McLeod is put through and scores past Konstantopoulos (yes, the bloke who owns the launderette in Eastenders) in a one on one. The crowd falls silent apart from a bus load of commuters from Milton Keynes. When so few people cheer in a football stadium, particularly after everyone else has clammed up, it sounds like a distant echo rising from a cave with a time delay. The other four and a half thousand people present just seem to turn round and look at them with contempt, then turn back to the game.

There appears to be a lot of kids in the CB Stand. On balance, probably a good thing. Better in here than outside illicitly scrambling on scrubby land between the football ground and the local leisure centre. And I have to say there is a decided lack of bad language and anger that is often present in football crowds. The problem is that the three kids behind me really get on my nerves.

"Give it here. "

"No. "

"Give us it now. "

"Get lost. "

"Give us it. "

"No. Gerroff. "

"I mean it. "

"Get stuffed"

"Give us it. "

"PISS OFF. NOW! "

I have no idea what it was but I wish he given it to him.

Half time arrives as the rain starts to slant across the town again. MK have had a goal disallowed just before the break so there's relief that the interruption offers a chance to regroup. There's a rush to the bar, the bogs and the bovril and the five a side goals are dragged onto the pitch. It's showtime folks.

Two schools take part in a penalty shoot out to see who goes through to the next round of the competition. It all takes place in front of the CB Stand and each goal or save is greeted with enthusiastic and supportive cheers or mock groans. One team has a girl in it. It goes down to sudden death ... and the girl misses. She puts her head in her hands and is not consoled by her team mates. The teacher gives her a cursory pat on the head and the boys look at each other. It had to be the girl. At the other side of the pitch Tom Harvey is given a presentation in recognition of fifty years service to the Durham FA. He's been a referee and is now vice president of the Association. Making the presentation is the first elected mayor of Hartlepool, Stuart Drummond, who famously campaigned and won dressed as the Hartlepool mascot, H'Angus the Monkey. The new H'Angus has been cavorting up and down in front of the CB stand over reacting to every slice of action in the penalty competition. All this on top of Napoleon and Two Little Boys. There really is only one place to be on a Saturday afternoon.

The second half starts well for the home team as a cross is turned into his own net by Lewington of MK Dons. The goal is greeted by a feverish response from the crowd and a quick celebratory blast of the old Piranhas' hit, Tom Hark, which the home support belts out arms pumping the air in time to the music. One famous line from that song goes, 'you have to laugh or else you'd cry'. Who says football fans don't have a sense of irony. It's great fun, it's very silly, it's brilliant. The game continues at a pace and Hartlepool are pressing for a winner. Mark Tinkler was brought on as a substitute at half time and is running the show. He's thirty-one now, barrel-chested and with a face that says he'll take no shit from anyone. He runs around with his shoulders drawn up in the manner of a Geordie reveller in the Bigg Market in winter who has a packet of tabs shoved up his shirt sleeve. But regardless of appearances, he sprays the ball about with aplomb and the team gain a fluidity that perhaps was only going to come with the addition of an old head. After eighty minutes, the winner eventually arrives when Lee Bullock rises to head home an angled cross into the box. The crowd goes wild, the Piranhas do their thing and there is still just enough time for Tinkler to get sent off along with MK's Wilbraham. It seems Tinkler didn't take any shit as predicted.

Deep into added time, with a general air of happiness around me, I decide to leave. Frankly it's bloody freezing. The wind is getting up, the temperature is getting down and my fingers are white, four of them without feeling. I re-trace my footsteps back round to the Clarence Road, past a solitary police officer who looks bored to death and arrive back at the Au Naturale car park desperate to get into the motor and get the heater on. With the rain beginning to slash across the windscreen, a fading murky light and the familiar march that introduces Sports Report on Five Live filling the car, I apply my restaurant test to today's game. And you know what, it was a damn good feed. More bar and grill than Gordon Ramsay but well worth the money if only for the little added extras like the Battle of Trafalgar and Rolf Harris.

My hands may be cold but my heart is warm. Victoria Ground has been a good place to be.

Best thing about the visit:
Pools won while celebrating the battle of Trafalgar in the town of French monkey spies. Perfect.

Worst thing about the visit:
The security guard in the club shop. A man not designed for or trained in the retail trade.

Best thing about Victoria Park:
Top class oxo and views of ships' masts when all else fails.

Worst thing about Victoria Park:
Ships' masts can be a bit of a distraction but otherwise, it's got to be the intimidating proximity of Morrisons.

What happened next?
False dawn. Pools begin to slide down the table leading to eventual relegation back to Division Two. It takes my fingers a full two hours to warm through and Jennifer forgot to spend the credit note from Au Naturale.

13. Sedgefield Racecourse

TUESDAY 10TH OF JANUARY 2006
THE FIRST JANUARY MEETING

In the late 1960's, Clement Freud, the hang-dog, chef, journalist, politician and gameshow contestant, wrote an article for a national newspaper about his visit to Sedgefield racecource. He clearly had an experience he was neither expecting nor used to.

"The fact that I write this column lying in bed with frostbite in three toes and a severe cold in no way influences my feelings about Sedgefield – though naturally, my current physical condition has everything to do with my attendance at the northern pleasure resort. Sedgefield is how the other half lives. You approach it by a two-and- five penny bus ride from Darlington where they have a notice about leprosy on the station to make you welcome. The racecourse is almost entirely field, with hardly any Sedge. Small children throw snow gleefully at fat adults – or possibly just at me........ Perhaps the most distinguished thing about the meeting was that Cosmoudan, indifferently ridden by a man carrying 16lb more than his allocated weight finished within eight and a half lengths of the winner. Or would that be the least distinguished thing about the winner? At 12.25 Dashing White Sergeant, heavily supported by my money duly won. Until I fell headlong in the mud in front of the bookmakers' stands, I thought perhaps Sedgefield was not such a bad place, after all. But it is......."

Follow that eh?

Well, Leo and myself decided to do just that for the first January meeting of 2006. The forecast was for wind, cold and around 80% chance of precipitation according to www.weather.co.uk. We are both wrapped up like Nanook of The North; boots, topcoat, hat, gloves, scarf, umbrella. Today is every bit as bleak as Clement Freud described. But I like bleak. Bleak is fresh and invigorating. Bleak keeps the crowds down and subsequently there is less crush – or should I say no crush. As we're neighbours living in Sedgefield village, it's no more than fifteen minutes walk from home to the racecourse. But today the weather is such that we are part of a very small and hardy band making the trip on foot. Even the villagers are taking the car today. As we approach the course, half a mile from the edge of Sedgefield, it's pretty clear that this is not going to be one of the best attended meetings. The stands are not exactly groaning under the weight of spectators rather they're shivering in the face of a brisk south-westerly. But what the hell, this is after all, 'The Friendly Racecourse', so we're assured of a warm welcome.

We make an early decision that we're going 'on the course' rather than in the stands. Things have moved on considerably since Clement Freud's trip and there are all the expected modern amenities in the Grandstand enclosure. But we've decided to rough it in the middle – and it's only six quid to get in at this gate.

"Afternoon gentlemen. Cold one today. That'll be six pounds each please. If you fancy going round the other side later just pop back here and pay the difference." The lady on the gate is dressed for the season and is obviously just glad to have some custom.

"Ernie. Can you show these gentlemen where to go." Ernie can't hear her.

"Ernie," she screeches against the wind, "Ernie."

"Save your breath Pat. I can't hear you. I'm going onto the course so you can follow me around." Ernie had clearly guessed the plot.

"Eee – listen to me shouting," laughs Pat, "I sound like a fish wife."

"You haven't got a nice piece of cod, have you?" I enquire as she cackles. "No, but I can do you crabs." She dissolves in fits as we head off with Ernie.

Where else would you be greeted by a sunny smile on a mucky day, a bit of banter and the offer of a sexually transmitted parasitic louse. The 'Friendly Racecourse' clearly has much to offer, even if some of it you wouldn't necessarily want.

We trudge across to the course enclosure where a single low green structure, not unlike a prisoner of war hut – with more windows and a lick of paint – houses two bookies, an outpost of the tote, a small bar, a couple of tellies and ladies and gents loos. It's directly opposite the main stand and on the infield side of the winning post. Struck me as a perfect position frankly. And about fifteen other punters, all of them with the grizzled look of seasoned campaigners, are there for company.

There's been racing here since around 1732 with the first proper, recorded meeting in 1846. It was part of the Sands Hall estate and very much a hunting man's course, the Ralph Lambton Hunt being formed in 1804 and for many years, retaining it's head quarters in Sedgefield's Hardwick Arms. Edwardian times brought a more professional approach but still it was a meeting for hunting men. By the nineteen twenties, after the resumption of racing following the war time abandonment, there were three meetings including the famous and lucrative Boxing Day fixture. That particular post-Christmas diversion survives to this day along with eighteen other meetings. And here we are on an unforgiving January day in 2006, 'on the course' and probably as close to the racing of old as we are going to get. Not for us the splendour of the fancy new pavilion, opened in 1991, with it's corporate facilities. Not for us a position adjacent to the re-furbished parade ring and winners' enclosure. No, we are going to stand out in the cold on the inside of the track. We're going to get close to the action as the horses struggle up the hill to the finish post. It's a two hundred yard run in after the open ditch last following about two and a half miles of hard slog on a tight, undulating track. In a biting and punishing wind like today I suspect we're going to see one or two crawling over the line.

From our vantage point we also have a perfect view of all the other spectators – or is that race goers? We can see that the stands are sparsely populated and one section appears to be hosting a small band of school children whom I suppose are not betting their pocket money but have come to see the 'gee gees'. They are all dressed for a snowball fight and seem to be holding some form of document. I suppose this is a worksheet – you know the sort of thing, colour in the horses – but it could be the race card, in which case we have a gaggle of pre-pubescent punters on our hands. The parade ring is to our right in front of the small stand with the main pavilion directly in font of us with all the bookies, corporates and course officials. Cameras on cherry pickers are positioned to our left to catch the finish and further down the track near 'the last' to catch the final fence or hurdle and monitor the run in. On a day like today it takes a brave camera man to stand atop one of those extended cranes and my guess is that marines trained in arctic survival techniques were probably drafted in.

So, it's five minutes before the first race, The gg.com Novices' Steeple Chase (class 4). Time to select a horse and have a bet. We stand in the hut to select our nags, studying the form and checking the little pieces of advice on the card, which has helpful hints in short pithy phrases.

'facing a tough task on his chasing debut'
'has strong claims in this contest'
'recent form does not inspire much confidence'
'one to note on chasing bow' – what?!
'could go close now dropped in trip' – eh?!

I opt for Longdale, the 3/1 favourite, who I read 'has claims on the pick of his form' – oh, really? Leo reckons he's studied the information but I think he's gone with his heart by backing the Irish, Silver Sedge.

I'm going a fiver 'on the nose' with one of the on course bookies in the hut who it turns out is Minty from Eastenders. I've lost touch with who is running the bookie's in Albert Square these days but my guess is that Minty will be making a play for it soon after learning the trade 'up north' where he supposed no-one would twig. He hands me my receipt – 3/1 and £20 pay out if I win – and wishes me good luck (or at least that's what he says).

I catch his eye and ask, "Not working at the Arches Minty?"

He pauses, realising he's been rumbled then gruffly issues an unconvincing denial. "Arches?.... don't know what you're talking about," then head down, starts tapping at his lap top again. I wink and tap my nose as if to say, 'you're secret's safe with me.'

The first race starts promptly at 1.10 on the other side of the course close to the Sands Hall and just about in sight with the naked eye. I confess to a little buzz of excitement as they make their way down the back straight with my horse at the front. The field gallops off to the south-west into the face of a steady but unrelenting wind. They're clearing the fences in this race, as opposed to the hurdles. I impress Leo by knowing the difference. He is less impressed by my choice of nag as the race progresses and Longdale struggles to keep in touch with the front and Silver Sedge makes steady progress. As the field passes us for the first time we get that sense of raw power and sheer punishing effort as the horses glisten with sweat, which picks out the muscle definition with every stride. And yes, they do thunder past. Yet you don't see any real sense of effort on the faces of the ridden. They seem to portray complete equanimity, complete poise. If I was thirty years younger or a 'gansta rappa', I might even call them 'cool'.

It's possible I may sound rather innocently impressed by observing at close up horses in full flight. This is because I am not a regular race goer and I'm not a 'horsey person'. On the contrary, my only real experience of the noble beast was being thrown off Angela Redfern's mule when I was about ten years old, injuring my back and causing me to use my first ever swear word in front of my mother. Add to that being bitten by a police horse at Roker Park, then perhaps you understand that I'm not exactly a horse whisperer. But we all have a road to Damascus and I feel a conversion coming on. The galloping racehorse is a truly magnificent and uplifting sight. There, I've said it. I think I may like horses.

The race progresses but Longdale doesn't. As they approach the last it is Silver Sedge that is pushing for the front and it begins to romp away up the hill towards the line, seeming to get stronger as the winning post approaches. Longdale hangs on for a 'far from game' third place, which is no bloody good to me. Still one of us has won. Beginners luck strikes again with twenty-seven pounds in Leo's back pocket.

The wind is freshening even more. It's what they call round here a lazy wind. Too lazy to go round so it goes right through you. Luckily the rain has stayed away but the beany hat and gloves are resolutely in place and I'm zipped up to the chin. The course enclosure is lined with advertisements for the benefit of race goers in the stands. BetFred, Gaming Club, Empire Poker. So people on racecourses only want to see adverts for other ways to gamble? Never mind. If the companies are willing to pay the site fee, the course will be happy to take the revenue and after all, in 1986 Sedgefield was the first ever course in Britain to have a sponsored fence so they know a thing or two about commercial gain.

The green hut is populated by about fifteen of we hardy – or is that foolhardy – punters who are all freezing. Some have brought their own flasks. Others, like us, are gagging for a hot cup of something. We have coffee. Leo's paying 'cos he's flush after his success. As I'm warming my hands around the plastic cup I notice a significant number of small people around me. They look like ex-jockeys, care warn, wirey and at home and they obviously like a punt. I suppose if you've been around the business most of your life it's natural. The atmosphere is one of calm, studied attention. When the race isn't on, the tellies are replaying the proceedings or relaying action from Southwell. The punters go about their business with minimal fuss or interaction much like a bunch of boffins in a laboratory conducting trial and error experiments and waiting for the results. In my case it's mainly error.

The 1.40 has a title to die for. 'The John Wade Equine Fibre and Rubber Conditional Jockey's Selling Handcap Hurdle Race (Qualifier) (class 5)' takes about ten minutes to announce and requires the person on the end of the mic to stop for a sip of water half way through. When the laughing stops I choose Samson Des Galas for no other reason than it's owner is called Naughty Diesel. Fantastic. I take an 'each way' bet in acknowledgement of my lack of success in picking winners. Leo goes for Star Trooper. When the action begins I am able to pick out pink and light blue, the colours of my rider, with relative ease at the far side of the course. So much so, I don't need the confirmation of the on course commentator that Samson Des Galas has pulled up. Another good choice.

Darlington FC – don't worry about the name, it's a moving feast

Somebody bent the roof at David Lloyds

Cricket at The Riverside – pass me my pipe

Tomlinson and Ridgeon made big at Gateshead Stadium

Safety behind the net at Billingham Forum Ice Arena

Riverside Stadium – told you it was beside the river

Trampled in the crush at Brunton Park

The City Pool – old but graceful

Millfield – cold but friendly

Sedgefield Racecourse – I told you it was bleak

Fast horse and slow camera at Sedgefield Racecourse

TCCA – it might just look like a field to you but...

Bright and breezy approaching the eighteenth at Wynyard

Victoria Park – small ground, tall ship

Not a Riverdancing falcon in sight at Kingston Park

St. James' Park – Pompidou Centre, eat your heart out

Stadium of Light – on the way to the match

Stadium of Light without the fans

"Useless bloody French nag!"

On the other hand, Star Trooper, having been about a hundred yards off the front runner Munaawesh coming up to the last hurdle apparently flicks a switch causing a rocket engine to explode from it's arse. It literally leaves a scorch mark as it hurtles up the hill to the finish line, beating a stunned Munaawesh at the post. Even those who knew what they were doing are stunned by the performance.

The next two races follow a depressingly familiar pattern for me but a rather interesting one for my racing partner. It was a pattern that was causing a little flutter of excitement in the enclosure. While my next two bets, Weapons Inspector and Pont Neuf fail hopelessly, one pulling up and the other simply slowing down and walking off the course adjacent to the parade ground, Leo backs Bang and Blame and Ile Maurice, both winners. By now he has the glazed look of a boxer who just got up from the canvas at the count of nine. He's not quite sure how far this will go. Already he can't fit his winnings in his pocket. I've called Securicor to have him escorted home safely and Max Clifford to handle his story. Could he possibly win every race on the card? Could I get one horse to finish?

As race five approaches, a tall bloke – or at least he was taller than all the small people – with a top class beany hat and a comb moustache makes friendly conversation asking how we are doing.

"Well I've been a disaster. One walked home, two pulled up and one walked off. Twenty quid and I've only seen one cross the line - crawling. Mind you, he's won every race. He might go through the card."

"Get away. Bloody hell. Won all four? – What have you both backed next?"

"Well Leo's gone with Get Smart and I've gone with Jballingall."

"Jballingall? Shit – that's what I've got. That's me knackered."

"To win or each way?"

"Oh, I always go each way."

"Well I've gone on the nose."

"Ah! A glimmer of hope then."

Race five sets off at 3.10 and I am amused to see my horse staying with the pace and battling for the lead as they approach the last. A little flutter of hope dances in my chest until Cyborsun finds another gear and gallops clear of Jballingall who struggles up the hill to finish second. Leo's horse does nothing and dreams of a clean sweep are – well, swept away. The comb moustache gives a little punch of delight and waves his ticket at me. His conservative approach has reaped rewards with a return for second place.

Following the post race routine, the winning owner and horse are presented with their prize in the winner's enclosure prompting a burst of emotion from the woman on the PA system. The French horse is hailed in the style of Dave Lee Travis.

"Let's give it up for Cybersun!!" implores the course DJ.

God knows what prompted this attempt to whip up a storm of appreciation. But in fading light, biting cold and with every hand in Sedgefield muffled by gloves, I could hear about three people 'giving it up'. Never mind, it is a valiant attempt to raise the temperature and it is soon followed by another, more sentimental announcement. We are informed by the PA, that clerk of the course, Gemma Charrington, is 'going on to greater things at Hereford'.

"Can we all show our appreciation and give it up for Gemma!!"

In all fairness, Gemma is obviously well thought of and I can detect a warm round of applause and even some muted cheering from the grandstand as the regular punter do indeed, 'give it up'. Or at least some of it. However, I am left wondering what greater things there could possibly be in Hereford.

We decide to have a bet on the last race. For me it's a chance for redemption and for Leo it's a chance to get the final few quid to buy that ocean-going yacht he's been coveting since The GG Odds Mare's Only Novices' Hurdle Race gave him his fourth victory at approximately 2.50. I go for broke with a fiver on the 20-1 outsider, Infini. By now, Minty is unashamedly rubbing his hands with delight every time he sees me approach. To be absolutely honest, I have no idea whether mine finished the race or not. He set off but I didn't once hear the on-course commentator mention his name and there were only ten horses out there. My guess is that he reached the other side of the course, sneaked off behind the bushes for a quick smoke then joined the back of the race on the second circuit before trotting off to his horse box without even bothering to cross the line. You can perhaps detect that I had given up all hope by now – with some justification. Even Leo's luck of the Irish had deserted him.

Never mind. Despite the frozen fingers and the financial deficit, it's been great fun. Cheep, easy, relaxed and a chance to see the 'sport of kings' in the raw and without the monarchy. Clement Freud was obviously on the back foot after the leprosy notice at Darlington station. Thoughts of being met by colony of lepers clearly coloured his judgement. But just as you don't have to go to a Premiership ground to see entertaining football, so you don't have to go to Ascot to enjoy good racing.

We make a snap decision to slope off back in to the village for a quick pint in the Nag's Head - where else after the horses? – and as we are leaving the enclosure are bid farewell by Pat and Ernie.

"Are you the last two lads?" Not a question I'm used to being asked on leaving a sporting venue.

"No. I think there's a couple more left in there."

"All right lads. See you again. Hope the weather's better for you next time."

Sedgefield truly is 'The Friendly Racecourse'.

The best part of the visit:
Just enjoying it all out in the fresh air and watching that bloke's face when he realised he'd picked the same horse as me.

The worst part of the visit:
Being a complete chump at picking horses.

The best thing about Sedgefield Racecourse:
It's ten minutes walk from my house and it's six pounds to get on the course.

The worst thing about Sedgefield Racecourse:
They don't sell Oxo or Bovril or soup in the course enclosure. Don't they realise that in conditions such as those on the 10th of January, coffee is okay but it's not the real deal? Oxo warms you through to the bones in a way that coffee simply can't. Sorry to be pedantic about this but it's a fact.

What happened next?
I suppose Gemma went to Hereford. She obviously knows something I don't. I developed a mild interest in horse racing and a greater appreciation of the equine beast. Leo now lives in the Cayman Isles.

14. Billingham Forum Ice Arena

Sunday 29th January 2006
Billingham Bombers v Sheffield Spartans,
English National Hockey League North

I would wager that not too many people have been to see an ice hockey match live – or on TV for that matter. The self proclaimed 'world's fastest game' has the distinct disadvantage of being played on ice, which in this country is usually only found in freezers and tall drinks in trendy bars or in one of the relatively few ice rinks still open in Britain. Since you can't play in a fridge, this leaves ice rinks as the only option and since they are not numbered in the many, the opportunities for spectators are few. However, if you like your sport raw and uncooked, if you tend towards the rock bun rather than the fairy cake, if you are Status Quo rather than Stravinsky, if you prefer to take a sledgehammer to crack a nut, then ice hockey could be the game for you.

It's probably the best part of thirty years since I last saw The Bombers in action. They were formed in 1973 as the phenomenal growth in the popularity of ice hockey in Britain saw new teams formed, leagues established and spectators descending on ice rinks in their thousands. Gradually, more foreign, mainly Canadian and Eastern European players joined the home based teams raising the profile of the game into a highly fashionable sporting entertainment. But sponsors came and went, the structure of the sport seemed permanently in flux and money dried up, particularly for the smaller clubs. Some teams in more affluent areas and bigger cities prospered but the trend was downwards. Television was no longer interested and the provincial outfits in small towns like Billingham struggled for survival and bumped along the bottom. But the sport has now structured itself to accommodate the professionals in the Elite League, the semi-pros in the English Premier Ice Hockey League and the smaller clubs competing in the English National Hockey League. It is hoped that stability will arise from clubs competing at a level their own finances can support. It's been said before but maybe, just maybe, ice hockey is on the way back. It certainly seems to be at Billingham where they're attracting their biggest crowds for years and The Bombers sit proudly at the top of the English National Hockey League.

The town of Billingham is situated just of the A19 in the Borough of Stockton on Tees, which for people on the other end of tele sales lines is 'somewhere near Newcastle'. There are about thirty thousand good citizens of the town once dubbed as the cheapest place in England to buy a house and live in relative comfort. It's one of those new towns developed after the war, usually around an unsuspecting little village, that has become synonymous with concrete and cladding. It was designed as a paragon of modern, convenient living with it's pedestrian shopping precinct, under-pavement heating, district heating system – effectively a very big boiler for the whole town – and in the case of Billingham, the revolutionary, urban utopian architectural and social landmark that was Billingham Forum. Officially opened on the 19th October 1967 by Her Maj, The Queen, it was described by one commentator who had clearly never come across anything quite like it, as 'a super kind of recreational club'. Today, we call it a leisure centre. But it remains unique – if uniquely falling apart – as a public venue comprising sports facilities, ice rink, swimming pools and a 650-seat theatre. It's a venue that simply would not be considered for a town of thirty thousand inhabitants in today's world of facilities planning models that decide such issues on the basis of numerical analysis as opposed to that uncountable quality known as vision. But it remains the one thing, other than ICI and the 'real Billy Elliot', Jamie Bell, for which Billingham is known – and the people of Billingham are proud of it. In fact, it's even a listed building now. So there.

It was the arrival of this urban 'recreational club' that paved the way for The Bombers ice hockey team to be formed. Durham and Whitley Bay were the nearest rinks and they had their clubs, the Wasps and The Warriers. Now Billingham was ready to welcome the ice hockey explosion to Teesside. And despite all the ups and downs and several changes of name they're still here, they're back to being The Bombers and my interest has been re-kindled. Today I'm here to see the team battle it out against Sheffield Spartans. A win will almost certainly ensure that Billingham secure a place in the League play-offs and give them a great opportunity of actually winning the league, which could well come down to a last match decider against Blackburn Hawks.

Entering Billingham Forum is a trip back in time to the sixties. The straight lines, huge glass panels, and courtyard replete with fish pond and giant gold fish (koi carp to those who are interested in such piscine detail) are pure 'summer of love'. I almost expect to bump into Austin Powers or Napoleon Solo and I'm most disappointed that the receptionist doesn't have a beehive hair do. Stick a couple of fountains in with the fish and we'd be on the set of 'The Champions'. But who's complaining. Retro is in. Just as well really.

I make my way around to the ice arena entrance where I'm greeted by a trestle table and a willing volunteer dressed in a warm top coat, hat and gloves. She's cold because it's an ice rink. She's volunteering because this is the amateur end of the sport. This is Northern League football - with skates on - a good standard relying on the loyal support of helpers and enthusiasts. It's a fiver to get in and a couple of quid for the programme. I pass on the Billingham Bombers beanie hat, though I have a quick feel and admire the quality.

"Hmm. Nice hats. "

"Can I interest you in one? "

"Hmm. No. "

As I ascend the steps to the 850-seat balcony overlooking the ice the cold air from the arena wraps around my face like a cold, wet shammy. If I wasn't alert when I went in, I am now and I arrive just in time to see the teams being introduced to the audience. Ice hockey is an American sport. Americans like their sport with a bit of razzamatazz. Razzamataz usually means a lot of music and plenty of crowd whipping announcements. And to try and create that sense of occasion and familiarity with the teams, the players are called forward one at a time to the centre line with appropriate cheers for the crowd favourites. And like any team sport there are heroes and villains. It's a football match with sticks. There are maybe about three hundred spectators, mainly families, plenty of young girls and a couple of 'real fans' with Bombers replica shirts. Oh, yes, the replica shirt has even infiltrated amateur ice sports. Where commercial opportunity is concerned, you can run but you can't hide. I take a seat (funny expression that – have you ever seen anyone actually take a seat? My experience is that they usually leave it where it is, then sit in it) and drink in the scene as the last of the players – about fourteen each by the look of it – glides into position at the centre line. There's a lovely modern art mural on the wall at the car park end. It's dark blue with some silver swishes and swirls denoting the pattern left on the ice by a figure skating move. Nice. Straight ahead is a large picture of kids' skating mascot 'IC The Bear', a giant skating polar bear. Cute. To my right, Blades Diner is doing a brisk trade in those long sausages and hot drinks. Yummy.

The references to ice and cold abound. You might say that the scene is set. And so it is. But then I'm taken somewhat by surprise as we're invited – no, ordered – to stand for the national anthem. And you know what – everyone stands to attention as Her Maj's theme tune is piped over the tanoy. I'm reminded of the good old days when the telly used to go off at around midnight and the soporific late night announcer would bid us goodnight before the drum roll and anthem officially ended the proceedings. I know that many a loyal subject would leap to their feet then as we did now. A strange and slightly unnerving, reflex action that is quite in keeping with the vintage of the building but out of tune with the cynical age in which we live. When we all recover from this spontaneous outburst of love for the monarchy, the referee, clad in the traditional black and white stripes, drops the puck for the face-off and we're straight into the frenzied and physical action that is an ice hockey match. I'm sure the Queen would have loved it. Talking of the Queen, I can report that the first recorded mention of ice hockey being played in Britain was in 1895. The match took place at Buckingham Palace with two future kings in the palace side up against a squad put together by Lord Stanley, son of the Lord who donated the famous Stanley Cup in Canada, which in ice hockey terms has the same resonance as the FA Cup. So perhaps the royal connection isn't quite as contrived as I had originally thought.

At this stage, it's worth mentioning some of the rules of the game because once you get over a few mental hurdles it becomes a very easy sport to watch. Firstly, there are five blokes from each squad on the ice at any one time. You can't actually see them as they're covered in huge padded uniforms and crash helmets with metal grilles, but rest assured they're in there. They exchange players at regular intervals and for no apparent reason but I suspect it's because some of them are good at attacking and others better at defending. Or perhaps it's just to have a rest – it's a damned physical game. Whatever, the fact is that they are on and off like a bunch of weak-bladdered grannies on a brewery trip. But I soon get over that problem by simply ignoring the fact that anyone has swapped and just watch the ones on the ice. The ones off the ice sit in a kind of enclosure either leaning on the barrier waiting to go back on or growling at their opponents whose enclosure is positioned just close enough for verbal abuse to be exchanged and physical confrontation to be tantalisingly out of reach. It all adds to the theatre.

Sometimes they can be sin binned for penalties incurred. Now most of these penalties occur when someone does something dreadful with the hockey stick. The names of the infringements perhaps give a clue to the need for padding. There's high-sticking, hooking, spearing, tripping, butt-ending (ouch!) and the relatively civilized cross-checking and elbowing. Other than that, they can pretty much belt the puck around the ice as they want. They defend, attack, pass, shoot, block and tackle like a football game. They have a goal minder, though he minds a goal that is hardly larger than himself, who is even more padded than his team mates and in order to win, they aim to score goals. That's it really. But the fun part is the legitimate physical contact. Whereas the modern footballer will fall over, writhing in fake agony as soon as an opponent raises an eyebrow, the hockey player is positively encouraged to 'hit' the opposition. Whereas the modern footballer will collapse theatrically to the turf as if taken out from the grassy knoll whenever an opponent brushes past him and dislodges his Alice band, the 'hit' hockey player will simply 'hit' back harder. The thud and clatter of bodies as they smash into the boards surrounding the ice can send tremors around the rink strong enough to dislodge any loose fitting dentures. It's truly bone-shattering stuff. And every muscle-mincing collision is greeted with cheers if the home player is the hitter and jeers if the local man is the victim. It's pure pantomime.

As it goes, it seems that this is a particularly physical match even by ice hockey standards. Players are getting clobbered at regular intervals and the odd punch-up helps sustain the steady stream of stick men into the sin bin. Billingham go behind early in the first session only for Gibbon to equalise for The Bombers with two minutes of the first remaining. Oh, sorry, I forgot to mention that this game is played out in three fifteen minute sessions – I'm sure there's a reason for it but for me it means there are the equivalent of two half times to get a drink and have a walk about. Each of the goals is greeted by the long, slow boom of a kind of fog horn sound that reverberates deep in your gut. On the first Billingham goal hitting the net I thought the Queen Mary was sailing into town. I was wrong. The ship's hooter is followed by a heavy blast of 'rockin' music to get us out of our seats. I don't know how old the bloke with the records is (and I use the word record advisedly) but everything has a definite seventies and eighties feel to it. I recognise Cum on Feel The Noize (the Quiet Riot version) and Garry Glitter's Rock'n' Roll Part II amongst others. I almost expect to see 'Diddy' David Hamilton emerge from behind a pair of turntables and at the moment Bachman Turner Overdrive belts out I swear I can see 'Smashie and Nicey' nodding to the rhythm in the corner. Whatever – they're all good stompers and I even find myself leaping from my chair at one point to celebrate the Bombers' second equaliser in the second session while all around me home supporters are clattering the wooden 'foldy' seats in noisy appreciation.

The sound of an ice hockey match is something quite different to any other team game. Shut your eyes and you can still get a sense of what is happening and where on the rink. There's the clatter of sticks as they clash and 'fence' for the puck. There's the clicking of the skates as the players half run and half skate to get up a good head of steam and that scrape and swish sound that is familiar to skiers, when the player swings to a halt or changes direction using the edges of his blades. It's a sound so fresh and clean you could use it to sell shower gel. There's the 'slap-crack' of the stick on the puck as a long pass or shot on goal is propelled bullet-like along the ice. Then there is the blood curdling crash as two bodies hit one another and simultaneously smash into the barriers. Unlike any other game, almost every move, every action has it's own distinctive sound. For anyone with sensory deprivation in the eye department, this is a game you can still enjoy. And you get the added bonus of Bachman Turner Overdrive. As they say, 'You Ain't Seen Nothin' Yet'.

The action is still coming thick and fast on the ice and a minute before the first break we are treated to the 'hit of the match' when Billingham's Scott Ward puts one of his opponents over the boards and out of play. The two players come together in the corner with Ward steaming into the hapless Spartan in a crouched position low enough to get under his centre of gravity. The Sheffield man leaves the rink like an apple being tossed out of a car window. The crowd goes wild. They love it. I take a moment and suspect that we're not a million miles from 'rollerball'. There's a degree of blood lust in everyone. Did I see someone throw a piece of raw meat onto the ice for Ward to chew on? Did I see Caesar raise his fist and give a 'thumbs down' sign, to the delight of the crowd? Did I see the victoious Bomber stand triumphantly over the vanquished Spartan before running a hockey stick through his heart? Perhaps it was just my imagination.

The second 'half time' break arrives and I decide to go walk about and grab a coffee. Two teenage girls are swooning over the 'hunky' players while chewing furiously on gum with that casual sneer so beloved of adolescents. A further look confirms my suspicions. It is Catherine Tate.

'Oi, you've dropped your scarf."

Stony look - "Am I bovvered?

"Yeh but you've dropped..."

"Does my face look bovvered?"

She dashes a murderous glance at her companion then picks up the scarf and wraps it round her neck defiantly.

"Like scarfs do you?"

"Yeh..."

"You cold then?"

"No..."

"Why do you like scarfs then? Is it cos you're a student?"

I look away in case she chews some gum in my direction and get into the queue for my refreshment. Trouble is the bloke in front of me can't have eaten for a

Watching Sport Without TV 99

month judging by the order he's placed. And it's all for him – greedy bugger. I want to tell him that the reason he's about twenty stone is because he eats like a condemned man, that if he could cut down to just three massive sausages per game he'd probably be doing the next Levi advert on TV. But what the hell. He looks happy. Ten minutes later I get my coffee and drift back to my seat in readiness for the final third – or the third half as I like to call it.

It turns out to be a rip-snorter. Goals are hitting the back of the net with increasing frequency and Bombers are hitting Spartans with increasing gusto. There are six goals in fifteen minutes. Such are the celebratory noises from the sound man, I feel like I'm in Southampton docks listening to a seventies revival show. The Queen Mary is blasting away triumphantly and joyously while a succession of good time rock bands has me reaching for my loons and stack heels. All I need now is a three day week and a black out and the return to my uncluttered and carefree teenage mind will be complete.

Just before the final hooter, local hero, Paul Windridge buries the puck deep and emphatically in the Sheffield net to seal a 7-4 victory that means The Bombers are level at the top of the league with Blackburn. There is a happy glow around the Billingham Forum Ice Arena as the home team celebrates and their supporters acclaim another step in the revival of the club. As the players head back to the dressing room, the huge ice re-surfacing machine makes a final appearance to plod up and down the rink scraping off the surface and throwing down thin films of warm water to build up the ice again.

The two blokes with replica shirts and beanie hats are particularly satisfied customers, tripping out of the arena just like any victorious football fans would from their home stadium. The only difference is that the two of them don't constitute a throng or a public menace. Catherine Tate and her pal swagger away much as they have strutted and swaggered all night. No doubt when they're behind closed doors and no longer have to act cool they'll be wrapped up in winciette jimjams, supping a cup of cocoa and cuddling up to a big teddy before being kissed goodnight by their mothers. The normal people, amongst whom I count myself, are content that this was five pounds well spent for some good, honest, exciting sport. We all head out into the cold night air, already in our top coats because we never took them off. And there rests the final plus point from an evening at the ice hockey – you don't feel the cold outside because you've been sitting in a room full of ice all night.

The best thing about the visit:
Two half times - an absolute revelation to us footie fans who only get one chance

at the bovril – and all that good rockin' music.

The worst thing about the visit:
Fat bloke with too many sausages.

The best thing about Billingham Forum:
Apart from having so many things under one roof, you have to admire the retro chic.

The worst thing about Billingham Forum:
If you don't believe in retro chic - it's old, knackered and ready for the Trinnie and Suzanna of the architectural world to give it the once over.

What happened next?
The Bombers did, indeed, win the English National Hockey League North. Their last home game of the season was a sell-out. It seems the revival continues. Suddenly some of their players are even getting international recognition. The Winter Olympics from Turin is on telly and helps to raise further the profile of ice sports. We win a silver medal for the 'lady on a tin tray sliding quickly down a mountain' event but sadly our only representative in the ice hockey is a referee. I give serious thought to buying a Bombers beanie hat. But, as my personal advisor tells me – "You're just not a hat person." So I don't.

15. Millfield, Crook

SATURDAY 4TH MARCH 2006,
CROOK TOWN AFC V BURY TOWN, FA VASE SIXTH ROUND PROPER.

Sometimes sporting excitement can be found in the most unexpected places. An arctic-like, sparsely populated Sedgefield racecourse, for instance, where picking the first four winners suddenly makes the weather seem tropical. An ageing, municipal ice rink like Billingham Forum, for instance, where you re-discover the raw, physical confrontation of ice hockey, a game that doesn't normally register on the radar of most sports fans. A warm and sleepy afternoon at a cricket ground like Durham's Riverside, for instance, where you suddenly get caught up in a 'slow burner' that could finally confirm your team as promotion certainties. Or in this case, at Crook, an ex mining town in County Durham where a proud amateur football team once won trophy after trophy and were regular visitors to Wembley but since scaling those peaks have been in the foothills for over forty years. But something's stirring in Crook – and I feel drawn. I've also had a call from someone up in those parts telling me to, 'Get my arse there because it's going to be a great day'. How could I resist?

The club may be plugging away fruitlessly but manfully in the second division of the Northern League but they're also on a run of success in the FA Vase. It's got the old boys from the town out of their armchairs, digging out their mufflers and history books and heading for Millfield with memories of the sixties re-kindled. The team has reached the quarter final of this national Football Association competition for non-league clubs and the crowds are flooding back. It's as if a bored youth has poked a slowly dying bonfire with a stick and a gentle breeze has helped fan the embers back to flame. Throw on a few twigs and you've got a decent fire again and the heat suddenly catches your face, snapping you back alert and alive. Crook Town is alive again. Let's just hope today's opponents, Bury Town, haven't arrived with a big bucket of water and a fire blanket.

Crook is a strange old town. It's a town built on long-closed coal mines but only five minutes to the west and you're in Weardale, one of the wonderful northern dales. Metropolitans, city slickers and people from Ponteland might consider it a bit of a throwback, something of a backwater even. Certainly, they wouldn't plan a night out there and wouldn't expect to be able to get a skinny latte and a chargrilled chicken and sun dried tomato panini – a milky coffee and a chicken sarny maybe. However, anyone with an ounce of romance where football is concerned or anyone with any sense of nostalgia for the days of corner shops, proper pubs and terraced communities – anyone with a sense of history, of roots, of admiration for the ordinary and unpretentious – will get a feeling of warmth when in Crook.

I've followed the A689, a road that literally wends up hill, down dale and round the houses and, so long as you follow the signs, will take the traveller from Hartlepool on the north-east coast to Brampton in the north-west, just shy of the Scottish border. That is if indeed anyone from Hartlepool wishes to make such a journey or indeed any Bramptonian should have the urge to visit the land of the hanging monkey. Well, it's there if they want it. It's known in my house as the scenic route and it takes me directly to the market square in Crook town centre where I've decided to leave the motor. It's a short walk from here to Millfield but there's no mistaking the direction as a steady stream of locals is marching along the road in a manner that is unmistakably that of a sports crowd. Hands are stuffed in pockets, scarves and beanie hats abound and if any further evidence were required, a decent sprinkling of Crook Town's amber and black replica shirts are also in the stream. It could be a scene from a McKenzie Thorpe – but it's not. There are 'blokes', kids, families, giggly girls, lads, codgers, the whole works. They all have different reasons for going but they're all willing to part with cash to watch Crook Town.

It's been a long, cold winter. In October, the weather men said it would be a bad one. We all thought they meant snow but as it turned out, what we got was prolonged cold, slate grey skies and months without sunshine or the pleasure of snowball fights and sledging. There are no early spring flowers, no blossom and no lambs. It's been bloody miserable, frankly. Everyone has S. A.D, the seasonal misery disorder and talk of global warming is starting to look like a bit of a piss-take. There's been another sharp frost and I took the precaution of ringing the ground this morning to see if the match is still on. A pitch inspection at 1.00pm confirmed that all was well. But it's one of those days when, as a kid, you dreaded getting smacked on the thigh by a sturdy clearance as you were sure to come away with a ball sized red mark surrounded by the blue halo of a bruise that looked like a love bite from a hippopotamus. This was only slightly less painful than a shot in the knackers where the pain was delayed but all the more nauseating and eye popping for the time lapse. I just hope the two teams today have plenty of embrocation on those legs because black tights won't be tolerated in these parts.

As I approach Millfield I can see policemen. The sight of bobbies around a football ground signifies an occasion. Got to keep order you know. But these are smiling bobbies who are also happy to be part of the big day. They obviously know a lot of the locals as there's plenty of casual chat with the passers-by making their way expectantly to the ground. The Crookites are out in force. There's a tingle of excitement in the air. You can feel it. It's not the raw, meaty passion of, say a Newcastle – Sunderland derby match. It's a cross between going to the school sports day to see little Johnny running in the sack race, turning up to see Billie Piper turn on the Christmas lights and what I imagine it was like watching George Best play for Fulham. There's pride, curiosity and novelty rolled into one. Even I have a little flutter in my chest at the thought of witnessing a little bit of history.

There are queues to get in the turnstiles, for heaven's sake. So much so that they've opened the big double gates and stuck a bloke there with a table to hand out tickets and throw the money into a big mixing bowl. I make a move for the mixing bowl rather than the turnstiles. It's moving quicker.

"Over here lads. You can pay here if you divvn't have a ticket."

"How much?"

"A fiver son." I hand over a crisp one, which is deposited in the bowl and receive my little yellow ticket – number 893.

"Thanks lad."

"Have you got any programmes?"

"Aye," the bloke says scrabbling under the table. "Aw, shit. No. The lasses round the corner'll have some. Just inside the ground where they're doing the raffle."

"Thanks."

There are steep concrete steps leading up to the open terrace behind the goal and to my right a scrubby pathway round to the grass banking on the east side. This leads all the way round to the opposite goal at the north end then sweeps round the west side of the ground where there are two modest covered stands, one, freshly painted in amber and black with seats and one for watching the old fashioned way, upright. The 'girls' are selling raffle tickets from a rickety old table in the space between the turnstiles and the steps.

"Do you have a programme please?"

"Yes, I think so…. Oh, no I'm sorry love. They've all gone. You'll get one in the bar. Do you want a raffle ticket? "

Armed with the chance to win something I don't want, I retrace my steps back out of the ground and round to the clubhouse at the front where a very helpful barmaid relieves me of a quid for a glossy match day programme while several club house regulars are finishing their pints in readiness for the big picture. My keen eye tells me someone's had a buffet. Probably the dignitaries.

I'm back inside the ground in the corner of the south terrace just in time to see the two teams enter the arena to the accompaniment of a great cheer and hearty applause from the 1,946 fans. This is the biggest crowd at Millfield for forty years and hopes are high. Bury Town fans are mixed with Crook Town fans in a reminder of more innocent times but it's the home fans, everyone of them wrapped up like Ernest Shackleton, who are in loudest voice and largest number and they're a mixed bag, to put it mildly.

The regulars - "Should have a good chance today if Danny stays fit. Milroy's always a good shout for a goal."

The ones who used to come – "Eh, Jack, brings it all back. Haven't seen a crowd like this for years. I remember the day when….. "

The footie fans who are here just for this match – "Well, you know, I thought I should support the local lads. It's nice to see them doing well. Anyhow, I'm sick of watching Sunderland."

The curious – "I'm not really a fan but I thought I'd pop along. Why, you can't go wrong for a fiver, can you?"

Those who are just pleased it is Crook – "Eee, why I don't like football really but it's lovely to see Crook in the papers and I just live round the corner so it's no bother."

The ones who've been brought along 'for the occasion' – "So, how many minutes do they play Darren? …What, there's two halves? …Which ones are we shouting for? …" Darren looks at Sharon and wishes he hadn't bothered.

The game hurtles along at a frenetic pace, the ball being thumped about the pitch with passion, vigour and the occasional hint of precision. But it's bloody cold and the ground is hard and lumpy. The slick Wembley turf it is not and the players are finding the most basic skills difficult. Frankly it's like watching a ping pong ball bobble about on a bed of nails. The ball will suddenly rear up from a rock hard divot and clatter a hapless defender on the knee or it will hit the same divot at a different angle and shoot along the floor under the flailing boot of a midfielder who is preparing to take the ball on the bounce. The result is a lot of ball in the air. You can't hit a divot up there you know.

After twenty-five minutes, local hero, Danny Mellanby escapes his marker and latches onto one of the few forward passes that hasn't been sabotaged by the concrete grass or the Bury defence only this time he is unceremoniously decked by Bury's Scott Field. Although, the way he takes him out is more reminiscent of Highlander. It takes five minutes for the trainer and a gaggle of St. John's ambulance men to pick up the pieces, chuck them onto a stretcher and remove the body from the field. From my vantage point in the south-west corner, I can watch the ambulance reverse into the ground in readiness to accept the slain Mellanby. Well, as they say, that's football.

The loss is a blow to Crook and after thirty-eight minutes they fall behind to Tatham's stabbed effort against the run of play. Football fans get feelings about things. And they're usually right. I sense that it isn't to be Crook's day but I hope I'm wrong. There's no despair in the crowd though. Still a healthy optimism and a party atmosphere. An oxo party that is. You know the sort of thing, 2.30 for 3.00, bring a cube. I remove a glove, reach into my special, big pocket for keeping big things in and extract my flask, which is full of the brown stuff. On glancing around, I can see I'm amongst friends. I don't know how much of a beast goes into one cube but there must be a small herd in oxo form at Millfield today. It's half time and the queues for refreshments confirm that I was wise to pack my own.

The other thing on show in force today is the humble – and in some cases not so humble - beard. Perhaps it's the arctic air bringing out the explorer in so many folk. To my right is Rolf Harris. It's not the Rolf of Two little Boys days but the white haired Rolf of Animal Hospital fame. To my left is Bill Oddie. Not the Goodie Oddie but the oldie Oddie. He's even dressed like a twitcher. Then, right in front of me, disguised as a St. John's Ambulance man, is Chris Bonnington. He's shorter than I imagined but he's quite chatty. I appeal to his sense of the dramatic with my opener.

"How's the lad that was taken off? He looked in a bad way. "

"Aye. It looked a bad'un. Mind I've seen some in my time. Well, you do in my business. We were doing a pre-season friendly at Darlington a couple of years ago and they had this lad on loan from Middlesbrough...good player...can't remember his name. Well he broke his leg, didn't he. Proper break... exposed bone, flesh, that sort of thing. Their captain couldn't look at it – thought he was going to throw up – in fact he did. Took an age to get him off. One of those inflatable bags – you know? ...Oooh, nasty. Aye, I suppose that was the end of his career. Oh, aye, I've seen some good'uns. "

"You'd be in bother if that happened on one of your Everest trips. "

"Wouldn't feel it up there, it's so bloody cold. Ha, ha, ha, ha, ...Oops, here's Jack with me coffee. "

I take my leave of St. John of Bonnington and decide to go on a little walk around the ground to keep warm while we wait for the action to start after the break. Heading off round to the east grass banking, I pass a couple of likely lads who've just descended from half way up the pylons holding the floodlights aloft. They've been celebrating Crook's big day by making a spectacle of themselves. Trouble is, it wasn't much of a spectacle. It was pretty obvious that nobody gave a damn. When they got down they looked a little deflated. A bit like the time when you told a funny story - you know, we've all done it - only nobody laughed and you felt a bit of an arse. While they slope away with their hands stuffed in their pockets, I carry on along the banking, which reaches the north-east corner where the ground backs onto the gardens of the bungalows and a few hardy old folk lean over the fence to catch the action. I pass a few happy Bury fans on the way around to the stands on the west side then descend down to pitch level where I cross in front of the players' entrance and dugouts. About twenty kids have invaded the pitch with footballs and started impromptu games and 'shotty in' around the goal. It could be the park. But it's not and there's serious business to conclude as the kids are ushered from the field of play in readiness for the return of the two teams. I tuck myself in at the front of the terrace in the west stand close to the action as Crook attack the south end. The sun, so far unhindered by clouds or tall structures, is now slipping round the back of the stand behind me casting sharp shadows across the pitch and accentuating the cold in the shade. It's a beautiful late afternoon and I'm reflecting on the virtues of being alive when a piercing scream from a woman beside me shatters my contemplative state.

"Come on ref! He can't do that. Come on ref! " she screeches like a seagull, then punctuates her heartfelt opinion with a more thoughtful and muted, "bloody useless."

To my surprise, amusement and, upon further consideration, admiration it turns out to be the government Chief Whip Hilary Armstrong, the local MP. No. I mean the real one. This was not one of my celebrity look-a-likes. Aha, probably the reason for the buffet. She's recently been slaughtered in parliament for getting her numbers wrong and allowing the Prime Minister to slip away from The House without voting on a crucial issue. The government subsequently lost by one vote and the opposition had her for breakfast. But when you see her in action at a footy match you realise she's made of stern stuff and probably couldn't have given a shit about a few Tories giving her the bird.

While Mrs Whippy continues being generally rumbustious I focus on the game, which despite valiant efforts is, alas, drifting away from the home team. I slowly inch my way back to my original position in the south west corner and note a gradual acceptance of inevitable defeat amongst the crowd. As I've said, football fans can sense these things. There's mumbling on the terraces. Groups of lads get the fags out and start to talk of other things, mainly beer and women, in preparation for saturday night. The Sharrons are tugging at the Darrens' sleeves in an effort to persuade them to leave early. Some of the Darrens duly give in. As Crook throw players forward in one last brave and defiant charge the final whistle brings to an end an almost glorious cup run. The crowd is generous with the players and the players with the crowd but ultimately it's disappointment.

By now I've positioned myself for a quick escape down the steps and out of the ground. As I make my way back through Crook to the market place, ahead of the crowd, which is by now oozing out of the big gate, I pass the front doors of one of Crook's many old terraces and there's an old boy framed in one of the doorways. He's about eighty years old and dressed just like my grandad did when he went to the pit. And believe me, I am not indulging in moist eyed sentimentality. That is the way he is dressed. He's even got the cap on. He sticks out a hand to catch my attention.

"Have you been to the match lad?"

"Aye, it's just finished."

"How did they get on? " He's genuinely excited and there's anticipation in his eyes. It's the face of an old man that only occasionally lights up these days. But now is one of those moments.

"Lost one nil but they played well. Gave it a go. Didn't you fancy going then? "

"Oh, no lad. Not any more. Never mind though. They gave it a go, you say? "

"Yep. Didn't let anyone down. "

"Ah, good, good. Never mind eh. See you lad. "

He knows it's perhaps his last chance to witness a return of the good old days. He smiles, nods, steps inside and closes the door.

Best thing about the visit:
Being part of Crook's big day and seeing so many excellent beards.

Worst thing about the visit:
They lost and there was real anti-climax.

Best thing about Millfield:
A real friendly ground, easy to find and a good bar.

Worst thing about Millfield:
Better grass on the banks than on the pitch. Maybe I caught them on an off-day.

What happened next?
Crook limped on to the end of the season. Hilary Armstrong hung on to her job as government Chief Whip – for a while - and Bill Oddie's Spring Watch was a hit yet again. The club continue to prepare for a potential move to a new purpose built stadium with leisure facilities and I had a devil of a job getting the smell of oxo out of the top of my flask. It's one of those you press a button in the lid to pour – if you're interested.

16. David Lloyd Health & Raquets Club, Stockton on Tees

SUNDAY, 26TH MARCH 2006
HALLAMSHIRE V NEXT GENERATION BRISTOL, NATIONAL PREMIER INDOOR TENNIS LEAGUE GRAND FINAL

Here's a little party game for you. Name a current British tennis player. The only rule is that it can't be Tim Henman, Greg Rusedski or Andy Murray..... Struggling? I thought as much. Therein lies the problem with tennis. Despite all the history, all the media coverage and the international appeal of Wimbledon, other than for the duration of the famous fortnight, nobody seems to give a damn about, what we in Britain still call lawn tennis. Or at least the game is ruled, with a racquet of iron, by the Lawn Tennis Association (LTA). How many grass (oh, sorry, lawn) tennis courts have you actually seen? Have you ever seen a top class tennis match, live, in the flesh? No, I thought not. As one famous but anonymous quote put it, "Tennis is not a popular sport in this country. Wimbledon is."

Well, popular or not, I'm off to see a tennis match or rather the conclusion of a tennis tournament. It's the National Premier Indoor Tennis League grand final at David Lloyds in Stockton on Tees. Yes, that's Stockton on Tees not Richmond on Thames. That's the north not the south. That's urban industrial Teesside not leafy suburban home counties. This is not your stereotypical location for the game of deuces, loves, advantages courts and "Oooh, I say!". But times are a changing. Teesside is trying hard to shake off a grimy image based on a heavy industrial past and tennis is trying – but not hard enough – to shake off a plummy image based on an unashamedly stiff arsed, class ridden past. The embarrassing lack of international success in any depth, considering the wealth of the LTA, has forced the blazers out of the club house to widen the net for talent. So Teesside reaches up and tennis reaches out and Hey Presto! we have top class competition in Stockton.

Now David Lloyd, there's a bloke. A perfectly decent player in the seventies. A Davis Cup Captain and many times Wimbledon competitor in fact. Brother of John Lloyd but actually a damn site more famous for becoming rich through opening a chain of health and raquets clubs. Consequently, I'm here in one of the healthy, raquety places named after the squat little Lloyd with the bandy legs to watch the conclusion of what is the biggest and most important doubles tournament outside of Queens and Wimbledon. Oh yes, this is no knock around in the park. Teams from all over the country have taken part in qualifying games with the aim of reaching Stockton on Tees and pretty much everyone apart from the aforementioned 'big three' have taken part at some point.

The final is between Hallamshire and New Generation Bristol and there will be four players competing for each team. Now, in these two teams, the two that have succeeded in reaching the final of this prestigious tournament, I can tell you that I will be witnessing the assorted talents of Aisam Quereshi, David Sherwood (remember mum and dad, Shiela and John from the 1968 Olympics?), Mark Hilton, Jonny Marray Jean Francois Bachelot, Ian Flanagan, Richard Bloomfield and Tom Spinks.... I can almost see the look on your face as you collectively shrug your shoulders, raise your eye brows and ask, "Who? " Well, we've got the British numbers seven, twelve, thirteen, seventeen and twenty-one, the current French number six, the former British number four and the number two ranked British doubles player. But this is a sport that seems condemned to be associated with anyone but the masses. Mats Wilander, the Swedish former world number one and multi-grand slam winner seemed to understand the limited appeal of tennis when, in 1983 he said to The Sunday Times,

"I rank only number five in the world. You aren't going to sell any more papers talking with me. "

Well maybe Mats was right and maybe the current British number twenty-one is not going to increase dramatically the circulation of the red tops and probably only gets birthday cards from his mum and the woman round the corner who used to baby sit him. But I've a hunch he's a pretty good turn with a tennis racquet.

One of my personal methods of gauging the quality of sport being played out in front of me is to remember what I was like at it in my prime and to remember how good were the people at the level of that sport that proved to be my personal apotheosis. For example, I once achieved the giddy heights of an eleven handicap at golf. I think of all the club players who were up to eleven shots better than me. I think of those that win club championships and lovely cut glass trophies. I think of those who played representative golf and feature on team photos hanging in club houses. I think of all the successful amateurs. I think of the club professionals and the teaching pros with those lovely languid swings and neatly pressed slacks. I think of the tournament players who struggle to get on the satellite tours, then the main PGA tour. I think of the ones who battle to keep their tour card, sometimes carrying their own bag and those who strive week after week to make the halfway cut. I think of those who occasionally feature on a leader board or nearly win a tournament then I think of those who earn a successful living from the tour. At this stage I probably haven't thought of anyone who most people would have heard of. I haven't yet mentioned the winners, the major champions and the household names. Then I think how much better all these people are than me and can only wonder at how much better are the best. I also think of how completely inadequate are most people who castigate sports performers without fully appreciating just how good they have to be to get onto their TV screens. Using this process of comparison, I have come to admire anyone who plays professional sport. So, perhaps you can understand why I am greatly looking forward to this tennis match between eight men who may not have registered on your personal radar but are probably better at this game than around sixty million others in Britain alone. Go on, try the test next time you're watching professional sport. I bet you find yourself being a little less critical…a little less smart arse.

My own experience of tennis is not vast, although it's a game I enjoy playing. The summer of '76 is when I twanged the cat gut more than at any other time. Like a true scholar, I spent my 'O' level revision time flogging a ball around the courts in an endless summer of doubles. I entered the autumn with an excellent tan, a return from my exams, which roughly equated to the amount of effort I had put in and an amusing Adam's apple injury from my time on court. Tarmac courts have a habit of going a bit gravelly causing certain patches to resemble a bed of ball bearings. I ambitiously over stretched for a drop volley, slid on the bobbles, missed the ball, caught the ground with the end of my racquet causing it to jab to a halt rather than slide. Following through, I fell forward and landed throat first on the end of the handle, which was by now perpendicular to the floor. The shock of the blow sent me reeling into the net where I flopped over like a rag doll making a sound like an old man hoiking out his throat to spit on the fire. The hoiking went on for several minutes till I regained my composure and was reassured that my larynx hadn't been shoved up my nose. Bloody dangerous game this. Extreme tennis.

The venue for today's spectator experience is rather more refined than my old stomping ground. David Lloyds is one of those places modeled on the American country club theme that seems designed for the middle classes to enjoy their leisure time without being bothered by the great unwashed. If you've got a thing about bored housewives, this is the place to be. How many light lunches can a lady have? From any one visit you could probably pick out about fifty people who, if they could act, could have starred in Cold Feet. It's all comfy sofas, healthy snacks, juice bars and glowing skin. You can get your hair done, relax in the outdoor pool, throw your kids in the creche and buy your expensive tennis shoes from the exclusive shop. If you like your leisure time with a hint of camomile, this is the place for you. I'm not knocking it, you understand, just faithfully describing what I have observed. That clever Mr. Lloyd certainly had an eye for the main chance. He spotted this one coming before anyone else and made a mint.

The centre piece of the venue is the huge shed-like structure that houses the indoor tennis courts, which are basically a big green carpet, surrounded by some long green curtains covered by a curved tin roof high enough to accommodate a decent running, topspin, forehand lob or a flipped-up backhand recovery from behind the baseline. Today, the hall is laid out with two courts flanked by two banks of temporary seating forming an arena containing both courts so the lucky spectator can watch two games at once. I check out the arena before retiring upstairs to one of the function rooms where I'm indulging in a bite to eat and participation in the 'charity auction'. The organisers have decided to raise money for Motor Neurone Disease as a mark of respect and solidarity with Willie Maddren, the ex-Middlesbrough footballer who was taken by this pig of a disease but remains a great hero in these parts. A 'celebrity line up' has been assembled to help attract the cash and to play a celeb tennis match before the main event. Ex Man Utd, Boro and England man Gary Pallister, Boro ex, Robbie Mustoe, Man Utd old boy Lee Sharpe and the BBC Look North sports reporter, 'little' Jeff Brown were the famous four. Though poor old Lee Sharpe is now probably better known to the general population for being the bloke on Celebrity Love Island who copped off with Abi Titmus. Mind you, there are worse things to be remembered for. For my part, after finishing my chilli and a couple of glasses of red, I foolishly get involved in the auction. Fearing no-one would want the signed 'Blackburn Rovers ball with certificate of authentication' and hoping to do my bit to support an excellent charity, I start the bidding at twenty quid. A bloke in the corner flicks out a finger to take the biding to thirty. I raise my hand to go to forty confidently expecting the room to catch the mood...Silence. I rise to my feet,

"Come on you lot, " I shout, "I don't want a bloody Blackburn Rovers ball. "

Silly move. Everyone laughs, sits on their hands and it's mine for forty pounds. A bargain. I should've just given forty quid to charity then at least I wouldn't have to find somewhere to keep my treasured Rovers ball replete with signatures of Robbie Savage and the likes – or 'Sav8' as he prefers to sign himself...Quite. Still, after all is said and done, I get my picture taken with two of my United heroes. Mind he's a big bloke that Gary Pallister. A lot bigger then 'little' Jeff Brown.

I slip off to the car to hide the ball then drift back into the centre to watch the 'celeb' game before the main event. I pass through the main loungey-bar area and witness more light lunches being taken, more skin glowing and seven ragged street urchins with muddied faces, tousled hair, blackened teeth and bare feet pawing at the window pleading pathetically for scraps of food or old tennis racquets. A street kid can live off a slice of bread and a discarded tennis racquet for a week. The cast of Cold Feet raise a sympathetic eyebrow, tut about the state of the country since Maggie was booted out of office, put their change in the charity box then turn back to the skinny latte and talk of quality time with the kids. I shake my head, open my eyes and the urchins have gone. Dreaming again.

Once in the arena, I take my seat just as the MC is introducing our star charity performers. There's a pretty decent crowd of knowing tennis aficionados, Lee Sharpe watchers and invited corporate guests who are not too sure if they like tennis but they are willing to give it a try for a free lunch. Well, wouldn't you? The game is actually quite entertaining 'Sharpey' and 'Pally' do some matey aping around and get a few laughs while 'little' Jeff Brown and Robbie Mustoe look like they can play a bit and seem to be trying. The MC, who also 'acts up' to entertain the crowd, is dressed in one of those linen suits that make him look like a hapless English official in A Passage to India. It's clear to everyone that he's going to meet an untimely and grisly end while buckets of sweat form on his forehead and his eyes bulge out of his skull. He'll be found dead round the back of the big rock with his face frozen in the final moment of terror and a cryptic message pinned to his chest with an ornate tobacco knife. And he thought he was just here to introduce a celebrity tennis match. HA!

After the Consular Official's body is removed from the arena and a couple of elderly ladies faint at the sight of the blood and the grotesque, twisted death grimace, the main event is upon us. The eight gladiators are introduced one by one to the spectators and coyly wave to the crowd in recognition. As ever, where the professional sportsman is concerned, I am impressed by their obvious trim, sinewy fitness. There probably isn't one of them over twelve stone in weight and apart from the one who was the ex British number four, there doesn't seem to be an ounce of fat on show. The teams, each with sponsored, coloured shirts, warm up as the crowd settles. However, the expected full house doesn't materialise. It is supposedly a sell out but there are probably only about three hundred and fifty of the six hundred seats taken. The theory is that the tournament has been trumped by the Boro match on the box and the fact that it is Mother's Day. People who have bought tickets - or been given them by their corporate hosts - have not turned up because they had to get their mother a bunch of flowers or the allure of Middlesbrough versus Bolton Wanderers was too great to resist. Frankly it's unbelievable. No wonder tennis is struggling to make a break through if it can't beat a bunch of daffs and a crap footie game. But there we are, football and mother, the national game and the national treasure. There are some things it's not worth competing with.

However, Hallomshire and Next Generation do their very best to demonstrate that the neat way around the spectator problem would have been to bring mother to a tennis match as a rare treat. They serve up a feast of high quality play, athletic endeavour and a clear passion for the ten thousand pound first prize on offer. All the grunting effort, growling frustration and fist pumping pleasure that you see at Wimbledon is on show today. These boys hit the ball hard too. They hit with pinpoint accuracy and employ beautifully long and rhythmic actions when executing a shot. They cover the court like - well like athletes. That is what they are, supreme athletes. These blokes are fit. In fact, there was a butcher in the crowd who had brought his dog for a day out. After one exhausting rally I turned to hear the dog saying to his master,

"Blimey, I thought I was fit."

This is high quality sport played by people very close to the top of their profession on these isles. However, they still have to compete with the likes of the two women behind me who eventually give up hope of ever becoming interested when one of them confesses,

"You know, I don't really like tennis, me. I don't understand it at all. Anyway, I only came to see Lee Sharpe. He's lovely isn't he?"

Her friend concurs that Sharpey is, indeed, lovely and she also doesn't like tennis but is afraid to say so. She suggests retiring to the bar and the pair of them skulk off giggling. The crowd is gradually whittled down to those who have traveled to support the two teams, the real tennis nuts, the general sports fans, amongst whom I number myself, and those who feel they cannot leave. But those who stay are not disappointed and I'm glad to report that, even though I've been surrounded by celebrities all day, I have also spotted my look-alike. Fantastic news. It's David Yip, the Chinese Detective. For two hours he's been sitting right in front of me and I hadn't noticed. He's quiet, as he always was, studied and understated and clearly here, under cover, to work on the mysterious and gruesome murder of the Consular Official. Personally I have my suspicions about the umpire who looks decidedly shifty and is wearing a spectacularly unnecessary zip up jerkin in a hot tennis arena. The perfect place to conceal an ornate tobacco knife. Nevertheless, I deem it unwise to interfere with the work of the famous oriental bobby and keep my counsel as he goes quietly and discretely about his business. It's humbling to see a professional in action.

Back on court, Hallomshire are, frankly, giving New Generation a bit of a towsing. Each of the pairs plays the two opposing couples over two sets, with a tie break if necessary if it reaches one apiece. Consequently, there are four matches played, each victory scoring a point for the team in the overall match. The Sheffield based Hallomshire team charges to a four-nil victory in swift order. And you know what, they're pretty damned happy about it. The team picks up the big cheque, the big trophy and they smile for the big photo. The truth is, if you play sport, you can't beat that winning feeling.

Outside, in the loungey-bar place, there are almost as many people watching Boro struggling against Bolton on the big screen as there have been watching the main event. The two women who left early after confessing they didn't like tennis, are far more at home cradling a spritza and chattering away in that way that people on bar stools with spritzas do. The knowledgeable people leave the arena nodding sagely about the merits of the match whilst discussing the technical qualities of the players. I can hear one or two novices admitting that they actually enjoyed it. A little like someone finally accepting that they are an alcoholic.

"My name is Colin …. I um… I think I like tennis."

"Oh, well done Colin, well done. We're with you Colin. Remember you're not alone."

David Yip has clearly had a good time with his missus. The event was made all the more enjoyable for him by the unexpected murder of the Consular Official, which I assume he has already solved since, as I remember, it usually only took him an hour and a half in his hey-day. Now there's a point. Someone has obviously worked out that the great British public can just about take ninety minutes of anything before they need to see a denouement. Look at football, look at rugby, look at the Chinese Detective. I noticed much of the audience getting ants in their pants at around the hour and a half mark. Perhaps that's what they need to do with tennis. Limit it to the length of one episode of a decent cop series and they'll have the crowds flocking in. Are you listening LTA?

The best thing about the visit:
Getting my photo taken with two United legends. YES!

The worst thing about the visit:
The bloke who had traveled with the New Generation team and stood at the edge of the seating shouting, "C'mon Bristol. You've got 'em Bristol. Go on Richard. Great serve Spinksy." He would shout out just as everything had gone quiet and he would clap encouragement at the same time with two massive hands like a pair of catchers' mits. What a pillock.

The best thing about David Lloyds
  Honesty. All those things I said about bored housewives and middle class havens? – you might not like it but at least it doesn't pretend to be anything that it isn't.

The worst thing about David Lloyds:
The awful but ridiculous feeling that you've sold out by being there.

What happened next?
Not much really. The big three remain the big three, only in a different order, but not quite big enough to win a major. Come back Fred Perry – cracking shirts. Dapper Roger Draper took over at the LTA after doing a job on Sport England, promising to overturn the old, knackered and fruitless regime and replace it with something – well, new, fixed and fruity I presume. And I still get a throbbing in my Adam's apple at the thought of falling on my racquet.

17. Gateshead International Stadium

Sunday 11th June, 2006
Norwich Union British Grand Prix

Here's a question for you. Is athletics a sport or is it a combination, an amalgamation of sports? You see, if it's a single sport, it means that many athletes, who only compete in one or two events, are actually only good at part of their chosen sport. However, if athletics is an amalgamation of sports, it means that decathletes are good at ten different sports, probably making them the best sports people in the world. Good, eh?

The other thing about athletics is this. If you've got any modicum of sporting or athletic ability, there's probably something in athletics you can do. You can run – a long way, a short distance, a distance in between, over little fences, fast, medium or slow. You can choose to jump – long ways, up over, up over with a long stick or in little stages like Jonathan Edwards (who ever thought of hop, skip and jump?) Or perhaps you like to throw things. Pointy things, heavy things, flat, dinner plate shaped things or balls on chains. Like the holiday brochure says, 'there's something for everyone'. It's just a great big school sports day really but it's this variety that also makes athletics great fun to watch.

So it's with a spring in my step, a pole in my vault, a shot in my put and a big bottle of black current juice in my bag, that I head for Gateshead International Stadium for the British Athletics Grand Prix sponsored by those lovely yellow people from Norwich Union. Norwich, the home of insurance, Delia and Allan Partridge. Don't you just love it. I'll tell you what, British Athletics loves it. They've signed a fifty million pound sponsorship deal with them up to 2012. Now you know where your insurance premium is going. It's paying for all those long socks that Paula Radcliff wears.

Gateshead Stadium is not in your leafy suburbs. It's in what might be called a challenging area and in part, the challenge is why it was put there in the first place. There was a cinder running track and asphalt cycling track opened on the site in 1955. Marathon runner, Jim Peters cut the celebrity ribbon to unveil Gateshead Youth Stadium. But it wasn't until 1974 when the famous tartan track was laid to accompany recent upgrading of the grandstand and addition of floodlights that the venue began to take on a national, even international profile. Brendan Foster, working for Gateshead Council, was the catalyst. He was an Olympian and a world class runner and he begged the question, 'why shouldn't a council estate in Gateshead be home to world class athletics? ' The stadium continued to develop into the multi sport venue it is today but it also prefaced the regeneration of the whole area. Would The Baltic Contempoary Arts Centre, the Sage Music Centre, The Great North Run and the whole Quayside development have happened without it?

Today the stadium is bathed in the mighty yellow glow of Norwich Union and everyone is looking forward to seeing Asafa Powell, the fastest man in the world. Yes, Billy Wizz is in town and BBC telly and radio are there as well. Now this is the thing about athletics. It produces excellence, uncovers the very best, the absolute pinnacle of performance in some very basic, human physical activity. Champions at games - football, tennis, golf - are to be admired. But any game is by definition contrived, invented, shaped to produce conflict and spectacle. But to run the fastest, jump the highest, throw the longest is to be the best at something natural and instinctive. Just imagine – there are over six and a half billion people on this earth and if they were all running for the bus, Asafa Powell would get there first. How good must that make him feel? That is, of course, if he has the right change because he might be caught and overtaken as he fumbles for his money and with only about forty seats on the bus and six and a half billion people trying to get on, he could miss it all together. But you get the drift. Every one of those people, unless in some way immobilised, can run or would at some time have had the instinct to run. How many of those six and a half billion have the urge to sit in a four man bob and skid down the Cresta Run for laughs? It's just not natural is it?

Entering the Gateshead Stadium is an easy, comfortable experience, not unlike the entry to a cricket ground. No mad throng of fans like a football match. This is families, kids, rucksacks, baseball caps, shorts and sunglasses. There are stalls laid out on the hard paved area leading to the entrance where skinny, athletic types are selling all manner of specialist clothing and footwear to other skinny, athletic types. It's like a Moroccan market without the spices, fabrics and the atmosphere. Actually, it's more like Walford market without the cockney banter and the fruit and veg. Come to think of it, it's actually a bunch of trestle tables with tee-shirts and trainers. I find it easy to resist and head to the ticket office to buy my way in. I inquire about the main grandstand but I'm informed that it's full, mainly of corporates and guests. Never mind, I'll take a spot in the East stand opposite the finish line. I'm told it's a good choice and then relieved of twelve pounds before making my way around the south east corner of the stadium up a ramp to the back of the east stand and into the arena. I'm twice implored to 'have a nice day' and 'head that way sir' by young, enthusiastic and improbably polite staff. Hmm, suspicious.

Entering from the top of the open, east stand, where I have a position on the back row, is like walking into a gigantic kid's birthday cake. You know the sort you can get these days, dressed up in layers of coloured icing to form some image beloved of the child. The stadium is a riot of colour. The base is the vibrant green of the in field area, it's surrounded by red seats, yellow advertising for the main sponsor, flanked by flag poles with the colours of many nations and sponsors and all topped off by a glaring blue sky with a scorching sun. Add to that the assorted hues and shades sported by the spectators and athletes and you get a vision that might persuade you that someone had slipped something hallucinogenic into your tea. To the north end there is a huge screen showing the action as through the eyes of a BBC camera and in the distant north-west, high on the Newcastle city sky line, is St. James' Park. Newcastle, always contriving to look down on Gateshead.

It's a beautiful, hot summer's day and the crowd is suitably relaxed as athletes mill about stretching and preparing in that body-conscious way they do, while officials float around in their official's uniforms and John Ridgeon, once an athlete, now an on-field commentator strides around the field, followed by a camera explaining events to the crowd and the watching TV audience. All the while, in between Ridgeon's revelations, we are treated to music, music, music. 'Push The Button' and 'More, More, More'. Quite. Pop music now seems to accompany events of every kind. It's as if we can't function without having Radio One on in the background. Never mind. The kids love it and combined with Lieutenant Ridgeon, it keeps proceedings moving along nicely, eliminating the boring gaps and leading us into each new event with fanfare and flourish.

At 13.51 precisely, the irrepressible Ridgeon makes his way over the pole vault runway immediately in font of our east stand. He is trailed, as ever, by his Passepartout, the scuttling BBC camera man whilst explaining the most unnatural of events in the athletics meet, the 'heaving oneself over a high horizontal pole with a long vertical pole' attraction – don't try this at home. The competitors are introduced to the crowd and wave coyly into Passepartout's lens before doing some more of that warming up, focusing, keeping in the zone stuff that they do when there's, frankly, nothing else to do. The first man up is on the runway. He turns to the crowd, the end of the pole held over his head and his second hand miming an overhead clap that is immediately picked up by the spectators who keep up the rhythm until he has launches himself down the runway. The pole waggles in a forward and uppish direction until the moment of the 'plant' when it is thrust into a specially formed box under the bar. It's at this point that pole vaulting becomes unfathomable to ordinary people. The forward momentum of the athlete is now forcing against a stationary pole, which bends into a great arc as the gentleman in the lycra twists his body under the held end contriving to push himself upwards, upside down with his feet reaching for the high, horizontal bar. He pushes himself away from the pole as it straightens, offering him the assistance of a sling shot. He is now facing down to the ground, his body arching over the bar and pushing up and away from the pole in order to clear the obstacle. He does so with space to spare and falls away from the bar, some seventeen feet above the earth below, to land casually, spread eagled on his back on a huge crash mat. As he clears the bar there is a roar of appreciation from the crowd. This is the one event that has even some athletes scratching their heads.

The performance is repeated by each of the vaulters, some with more success than others, and the crowd laps it up. Following the failures two little men in blazers attempt to replace the bar, high above their heads, with what appear to be a pair of cleft sticks on long poles. Everything in the pole vault has to done with long poles. But such is the nature of an athletics meet that a number of events can take place at the same time. Four minutes after the start of the pole vault we are treated to an invitational men's paralympic wheelchair 400m and a further thirteen minutes later, the 400m for men. At thirteen minutes past two the long jump begins on the far side of the track in front of the main stand. By the way, this is the main stand where the corporates are supposed to be and I couldn't buy a ticket. It's half empty. Corporate tickets – the scourge of modern sport. It's like paying to keep empty seats. A bleedin' disgrace. But I digress. Chris Tomlinson, the local lad and British record holder is introduced to the crowd to a great, appreciative cheer. His long mop of wavy, blonde hair flops around on the big screen as Passepartout, by far the busiest man in town, films a close up that offers us a ten foot high Tomlinson head at the north end of the stadium. As Tomlinson's head talks to us the pole vault continues with groans and cheers in equal measure as the bar is clipped off or cleared. Electronic scoreboards, strategically placed around the in field flash the heights, lengths and times as they are achieved. The ladies hundred metres and men's shot put each start within the next ten minutes followed by the one hundred and ten metres hurdles for men and the three thousand for women. The music gets more frenetic as the events flash by. 'Stayin' Alive' and 'Mission Impossible' have replaced the SugaBabes and The Andrea True Connection but it's the same beat and it's the same mad Ridgeon dashing about from pit to track to pole like a kid showing everyone his birthday presents.

But you know, it's very hot. The type of hot that hurts as it burns your forehead. So I want an ice cream. Who wouldn't? I ease my way past a couple of uncomfortable looking women with large hats and larger bags and head off around the back of the stand where the assorted refreshments are on sale. It's a long queue but it's moving reasonably quickly and I have the chance to observe since queuing offers no other real alternative. And what do I see? Or should I say who do I see? It's Alma from Coronation Street. Alma. Yes, you thought she was dead. But she's not. She's alive and kicking on the doughnut stall at Gateshead Stadium. She must have faked her own death to get away from The Street when she received the offer of the doughnut concession. Perhaps she thought she had taken the role as far as she could. Who knows? But I'm heartened to see her in good health and she seems to be as happy as Larry away from the lime light. For that reason, I don't make any attempt to break her cover. You see, all that money from Underworld couldn't put a smile on her face but a dough-based sugary snack? Well, that's a different matter.

But shock of shocks. The Alma diversion has made me take my eye off the ball. As I approach the van, next but one to be served, I realise that, while I've been admiring Alma's doughnuts, I've actually been queuing behind the real, the unmistakable, the legendary, Peter Beardsley. He looks exactly how he always has done with that boyish hair style with the badly cut fringe. He's dressed in neat, tailored, belted shorts, a white tennis shirt and a pair of massive trainers with white socks. He's not going for the trendy vote but I can report he's going for two twisters and a ninety nine. Fantastic. The twisters are for the kids. He gets straight into the ninety nine and as he slowly wanders back to the east stand, he is politely approached by a series of star struck fans – of a certain age – who tell him how wonderful he is and ask for his autograph. For my part, I just like the fact that a football hero is sitting with his family in the normal stand, eating an ice cream and watching the athletics. Now, that's the way it should be – never mind empty corporate guest seats.

I'm feeling pretty chuffed as I take my seat again. The pole vault and long jump have concluded. American, Brad Walker won the vault with a stadium record. Our lad, Steve Lewis, came last. Chris Tomlinson and his massive feet could only manage third in the long jump but every body still loves him. The women's high jump and four hundred metres hurdles have also started – and in the case of the hurdles – finished. Little white camera pods have chased the athletes down the back straight to give the watching millions those close up, moving action shots. It's like watching a big false eye on model railway. An army of little helpers on foot and on go-faster milk carts have been ferrying hurdles and javelins and all manner of equipment around the stadium in order to ensure everything is in the right place at the right time for the pampered performers and to be sure that the great god that is TV is not angered. But, in fairness to them all, it also keeps us 'live' spectators engaged. The action is pretty relentless and events are coming thick and fast which, is how you might describe one of the next men to go on show. Dwain Chambers is making his big time come back after being proved a drug cheat and serving a two year ban. He knew he was cheating and he admitted it. European Champion, multiple relay medallist and stupid enough to take drugs to enhance his performance. Thick and fast. Now he's wiser and slower but at least he's contrite. However, he's not the main man today. That honour goes to the fastest man on earth, Asafa Powell of Jamaica, a man who runs from here to there in 9.77 seconds. The heats of the hundred metres are upon us and we are treated, as ever, to the Ridgeon overture, the cheesy music and the personal welcome to each of the athletes. Powell is, of course, cheered to the rafters but how will Chambers be received in his heat.

The start of the hundred metres is always a little piece of theatre. The preening, strutting, incorrigible, immodesty of the sprinters is hilarious. They parade around the start line, chests out, chins up, shoulders rippling and those figure-hugging one piece racing leotards that say only one thing to the onlooker – meat and two veg. I don't know about you but I think all that the trouser department display is a bit too much and it's even worse when they get moving. Like watching a small furry animal trying to escape from under a blanket. Still, it seems that the whole psychology of sprinters is 'look at what I've got. You can't beat that'. Fair enough. But a pair of shorts and a vest was good enough for those Chariots of Fire chaps so it should be good enough for this lot. But when you put all that nonsense to one side, the racing is electrifying. The sound of silence on the blocks. The only noise is the distant hum of the city, the traffic. I actually heard a pin drop. Then, Bang! and cue the release of the crowd - a huge roar. After we've seen Powell run the first fifty metres, sit down, open a picnic hamper, finish a light lunch washed down with a nice glass of Chablis, then still have time trot over the finish line in first place, we get to see Chambers in action. Will he be the pantomime villain to Powell's hero or will the great British public forgive him because, well, because he's British. What do you think? Chambers is cheered to the rafters also and comes in third to reach the final, which will be the day's finale at sixteen thirty eight. You will have noticed that athletics meets like these precise times.

Following the one hundred metres race for the most vain men on the planet, we are treated to the women's eight hundred. Our rising young starlet, Beccie Lyne is the home crowd hope and she puts in another great performance to come home second in a time only two seconds behind Kelly Holmes' British record. But the most surprising thing is what happens next. After an interval of about fifteen minutes, when she's presumably had a warm down, Beccie Lyne suddenly appears from the back of the east stand and climbs over the seats to plonk herself down in front of me. Turns out that the people in front, cheering her particularly loudly and proudly, are relatives. She kisses them all. They tell her how good she was and a young lad from behind me clambers over the seat backs to get her autograph. She phones home to mum on the mobile.

"Hi mum, Did you see me? "

It's quite touching really. Just an ordinary girl with an extraordinary talent. And you know what, there's not a picking on her. This is a seriously slight individual in a way that simply doesn't come across on the TV screen. I want to buy her a pie. Two pies. I hope the wind doesn't get up because I don't want her to blow away. I hope she doesn't drop that pencil on her leg, she could be badly injured. But this is a top class athlete. She's strong, fast, fit as hell and certainly doesn't need protective thoughts from a slightly 'podgy round the edges' middle aged has-been, never-was. How in God's name can she run so fast?

The athletics crowds are knowledgeable. You can hear the talk in the stands. You just know that many of than have 'done' athletics in the past. Maybe they still do. Some of them are quite obviously club athletes. No-one else would dress like that. But you can't beat a famous face for bringing out the uncommitted punter and there are plenty of bodies in the crowd that are there because there are names that not only 'ring a bell' but are world renown. And the biggest and most famous is our man in Jamaica. The women's long jump, men's fifteen hundred metres and women's two hundred all conclude. Kelly Southerton jumps long to finish second, Nick Willis of new Zealand runs fast to finish third with a bloke in a cap, who must be his dad, standing up two rows ahead of me to cheer him on by name every time he comes around our bend and Sanya Richards takes the two hundred to show that no-one beats the Americans at the women's sprinting business. But it's the one hundred metres final for men that we are all waiting for.

Chambers and Powell are the centre of attraction as we go through he pre race ritual again. Ridgeon, preen, announcement, strut, introduction, swagger, eyeball…small furry animal. Then it's silence. Real, undiluted, uninterrupted, two minutes for Princess Diana type of silence. Then Bang! Roar and run like hell. Only this time, Powell doesn't have a picnic half way. This time he runs, that huge stride, those pumping arms, head still, no breath. He runs for only 9.77 seconds and the crowd erupts. He's equalled the world record. His own world record. We've heard about him. We've seen him on TV but now we've seen him do it. This is a lap of honour which is truly honourable. After four hours the grand finale lasts for less than ten seconds. Less truly is more. Chambers is beaten into third place in 10.07 seconds. Bloody fast but not bloody fast enough.

How can that not be fast enough?

It's over. I leave in a rush to beat the traffic if I can. The buzz is still going round the stadium and everyone seems to walk that much faster leaving than arriving. Perhaps inspired by what they've seen or perhaps motivated by the reality that no matter how good it's been in there, you still have to get out of a car park with hundreds of cars and only one small exit. Why does the reality of modern life always come back to sitting in a bloody traffic jam?

Best thing about the visit:
A fantastic world record and Peter Beardsley's ninety nine.

Worst thing about the visit:
Realising how unfit I've become and wondering how an athlete two stone when ringing wet can be so strong, and fast and fit.

Best thing about Gateshead Stadium:
What it stands for and why it was there in the first place.

Worst thing about Gateshead Stadium:
Empty corporate seats. They should be given to people who will actually turn up and sit in them. Also, large temporary car parks with small entrances and exits. The attendants said they would get abuse and they did.

What happened next?
Asafa Powell became the proud owner of the world record on his own when Justin Gatlin, the co-record holder was found to be a drugs cheat, banned and stripped of his record. Beccie Lyne went from strength to strength and is now one of Britain's finest even though she's now fifteen stone after eating all the pies I sent her. Still, she's a great shot putter.

18. So What?

Right. So here's the question. Does anybody really care whether we watch live sport or not? Well, I think they do. For all the reasons I outlined in my introduction, live sport knocks TV sport into a cocked hat. But even those who would say it's of no consequence to them – they may not realise it but they are in fact in total agreement that live sport must prosper. You see, without a live audience even televised sport lacks atmosphere and can be a turn off. Would anyone really enjoy watching a Premiership match played behind close doors in an empty stadium but televised for the armchair fan? No.

However, there's another, far more important, reason to get out and watch live sport. I'm going to break it to you gently. You see, I'm not against TV sport, in fact my favourite annual sports event is the Open Golf Championship. I've never been to one in person but I watch every shot from every round on TV. The thing is, life is all about balance. Moderation in great doses is normally the key to happiness and longevity. For instance, if you were to live off a diet of only eggs, nothing else, you would become egg bound, produce copious amounts of sulphur gas and lose friends. In the end, the diet would kill you. If you like a little tipple and eventually end up drinking nothing but whiskey, your liver would shrivel, your body would become poisoned, you would end up a decrepit, friendless wreck. In the end the drink would kill you. If you were a runner and became so obsessed that you ran everywhere, never rested, never changed your routine and gave up your job to run more, neglecting all other aspects of your life, your friends would desert you and your body would crumble under the strain. The running would kill you. If you like a cigarette - a bit too much - and smoking becomes an all consuming habit and you end up on two hundred fags a day, eschewing all nourishment, you'll stink like a fag end, develop ashen grey skin, turn your lungs into pumice stone and drive away your friends. Your smoking will lead to your death.

If you're one of these people who talk incessantly, never letting anyone else get a word in. If you love the sound of your own voice so much that you never stop to take a breath or listen for a reply, then eventually people will tire of you. Your friends and family will desert you, bored rigid by your self obsession and you'll be sacked from work. Your partner will abandon you, driven out by the pounding persistence of your peroration. Refused service in shops, unable to fend for yourself, you will be forced to live wild off the fruits of the land. However, untrained in such matters, you will succumb to a debilitating intestinal condition that will lead to your demise. In short, your immoderate, continual chatter will kill you.

So there we have it. Incontrovertible proof that the failure to achieve balance and moderation leads to tragedy. Extrapolate my thesis to watching sport and it is clear that if you are a sports fan and you don't make the effort to watch some live sport you will eventually surrender to an unsociable medical condition, lose all your friends and die.

I will be submitting this evidence to the British Medical Journal and I advise you all to select a live event and go buy a ticket.

Other titles by Kipper Publications

"One Dead Ref and a Box of Kippers"

Traces the lives and careers of the seventy-two men from the Borough of Sedgefield who played in the Football League or Premier League between the war and the Millennium. It includes such luminaries as Gordon Cowans, Colin Cooper, Eric Gates, Charlie Wayman and Stan Cummins.

It's full of anecdotes, memories and improbable tales plus some of the author's original Mad Ramblings about, well..... anything loosely connected to football.

ISBN 0-9540518-5-8

"Can You Get Bobby Charlton?"

Is the incredible but uplifting story of how, in 1976, a small amateur team from the north east of England, Crook Town, came to tour India, playing six matches before around 400,000 fans including sell-out fixtures at the Eden Gardens test cricket ground.

They became the centre of a media, political and social whirlwind in northeast India and were greeted by the county's President.

The story of the India Tour proves that extraordinary things can happen to ordinary people.

ISBN 0-9540518-8-2

Order direct and get big discounts!

If you'd like to purchase either of these previous titles direct, just complete this form and send it to:

Kipper Publications, 30 Spring Lane, Sedgefield, Co.Durham, TS21 2DG.

One Dead Ref   (was £9.99)   now £4.99   No. of Copies

Bobby Charlton   (was £9.99)   now £4.99   No. of Copies

Name:

Address:

Please add £1.20 for postage and packaging for one book and a further 40p for any additional book.

Total amount enclosed: £   Signature:

Please make cheques payable to S. Chaytor.